# IDENTITIES REDISCOVERED

# IDENTITIES REDISCOVERED

## GUIDO PARISI

Copyright © 2017 Guido Parisi

The moral right of the author has been asserted.

Apart from any fair dealing for the purposes of research or private study, or criticism or review, as permitted under the Copyright, Designs and Patents Act 1988, this publication may only be reproduced, stored or transmitted, in any form or by any means, with the prior permission in writing of the publishers, or in the case of reprographic reproduction in accordance with the terms of licences issued by the Copyright Licensing Agency. Enquiries concerning reproduction outside those terms should be sent to the publishers.

Matador
9 Priory Business Park,
Wistow Road, Kibworth Beauchamp,
Leicestershire. LE8 0RX
Tel: 0116 279 2299
Email: books@troubador.co.uk
Web: www.troubador.co.uk/matador
Twitter: @matadorbooks

ISBN 978 1788033 121

British Library Cataloguing in Publication Data.
A catalogue record for this book is available from the British Library.

Printed and bound in the UK by TJ International, Padstow, Cornwall
Typeset in 11pt Aldine401 BT by Troubador Publishing Ltd, Leicester, UK

Matador is an imprint of Troubador Publishing Ltd

## ACKNOWLEDGEMENTS

Many thanks to Sarah Fletcher for her assistance as editor and proofreader of this, as well as my previous book, *"Emotions of a Book"* – Amazon. Her cooperation is irreplaceable as to linguistic competence and understanding.

I am also grateful to Gianna Scarabeo, the Artist for her many illustrations not only for my books but also for other authors.

*Guido Parisi*

## ABOUT THIS BOOK

I had a cousin with whom I was very close when we were young. We were the same age and used to spend a lot of time together outside school hours. He seemed to be gifted with an extra sense. I do not know if it was a sixth or seventh sense or something similar that made his communication with the animal and plant world very special. I think that this 'sense' also extended to other fields, but I would not swear to that. I can only talk about episodes which I myself witnessed. There was a small river where we often went swimming in summer. As soon as he put his feet in the water, the fish approached to welcome him and began to party jumping around while ignoring me. Once, we went in search of blackberries in the countryside when two big dogs were about to attack us. Just a few metres away, my cousin turned and stared at them. They froze as though obeying a decisive and unquestionable order. The same thing happened with two snakes on a hot summer morning while we were hunting lizards on a country path. From afar, the two snakes struck out at us with raised, threatening heads and once again the boy's powerful eyes froze them. When we went to the zoo, it was visible that he had a special rapport with all kinds of beasts, even the wild ones. They seemed to talk to each other in a language that only they knew. As for plants, he liked to go into the gardens of people that had learned of his special skills in treating flowers and trees. To less lush plants that he believed were suffering, he acted like a true therapist. He cuddled and talked to them, he touched, caressed and hugged them and above all he visited them several times a day so that they did not feel alone. The results were always surprising: the plants recovered and revived as though touched by a magic wand.

I do not know if this has anything to do with the paranormal. It is difficult to draw precise boundaries in the vast and mysterious extrasensory universe. The more I read about it, the more I am disoriented. I do not want to enmesh myself in a discussion on modern research about this subject; I would not be able to pull myself out, or to conclude 'I believe' or 'I don't believe'. In the end, I think that each individual, on the basis of his own experiences, comes to believe or not without taking into account the scientific research. The fact is that this topic fascinates many people regardless of age, intellect or social standing. As to literature, the *fantasy* genre – that includes a wide range of subgenres – seems to have a very strong grip on the contemporary reader. It is possible that this success is in part due to the desire to escape from reality, an essential need that helps us to survive in a world more and more suffocated by an exasperated materialism and absence of communication.

I started to dedicate part of my writings to this genre when I was a school teacher. The stories that I wrote, actually, were conceived mainly for teenagers. Perhaps it is because of my vocational education that I have always tried to consider two or three ingredients as essential for making up a story – in my point of view – worthy of being read. The first is pleasure. This is a very subjective concept both for the writer and for the reader. Pleasure is often a point of unexpected encounter between the aspirations of the writer and the needs of the reader. A rare and difficult thing. The educational and instructive purpose is something that I often suggest to the potential reader. The settings I choose for my stories are mostly historical; in fact, I am convinced that history is an endless source of information that, besides the cultural aspect, is a key to understanding the contemporary world. Finally, the message constitutes the aim that, as an invisible thread, weaves the occurrence of the events.

Taking for granted that what has just been said has been written countless other times, I am going to write a few lines about the three stories of this book.

*Enchantment* is the story of an English girl called Helen, born in Castleton and attending a college in Caerleon. These two small towns house very important remains from Roman times. It sometimes happens that Helen, when in direct contact with this ancient world, such as touching ruins or artefacts, is shaken by strange perceptions and vibrations. At college she meets a new student called Giulio who has just arrived from a small town in the south of Italy that was an important centre in the times of the Roman Empire. The attraction, mostly due to the curiosity triggered by the two different cultures, sparks off a sequence of events that takes place in different dimensions of time in which the present and the past, and reality and a dream, overlap in a tangle of unpredictable twists.

In *Matteo Revives,* the protagonist is a man in his forties, a successful manager of an important company in Milan. Since he was a little boy, it happened that smelling burned body parts, such as hair, nails, or burnt skin caused him to lose consciousness for a few moments catapulting him into another reality far in time and culture. With the help of a friend who is a psychologist, under the effect of hypnosis, he finds out that he lived two hundred years before in West Bengal under another identity. Incredulous and shocked by the result of the hypnotic experiment, little by little, despite his scepticism, he convinces himself to get to the root of this mystery and he starts to investigate the life of an English captain who was a commander of a British garrison in Cossimbazar at the time Governor William Bentinck – first half of XIX century – was promoting important social reforms in India. Matteo's final trip to the places of his visions will allow him to exorcise the unbearable causes of his discomforts.

*Romeo and Juliet in Progress* tells the experience of a Canadian professor of drama while preparing the Shakespearean tragedy featuring an international group of students at his university. Through an exchange programme between foreign universities, the final performance will be acted out in Verona, the Italian town of the two unfortunate lovers, at the end of five months of rehearsals. A girl from Québec, Julie, playing the role of Juliet, confesses to her teacher that she is tormented by the presence in her life of a young Italian lady executed for adultery with her lover in 1391 in Mantua, one of the two cities where the story of Romeo and Juliet took place. The possessed student, more and more tied to the professor for his understanding, will dissipate, in a completely unexpected way, the mists of the mysterious possession, only after going to the spot where, on a cold morning in February 1391, Lady Agnese Gonzaga was beheaded.

*Guido Parisi*

"The ice was here, the ice was there,
the ice was all around:
it cracked and growled, and roared and howled,
like noises in a swound!

At length did cross an Albatross,
through the fog it came;
as if it had been a Christian soul,
we hailed it in God's name."

(The Rime of the Ancient Mariner. S.T. Coleridge)

# ENCHANTMENT

## A STRANGE ENCOUNTER

It happens to us all sometimes that we think of people we know. I mean, we think of them because we have not seen them for a long time and then, just afterwards, we see them. How strange!

Well, what would you think if this inexplicable phenomenon occurred several times a day, together with other strange events? It is difficult to explain these things because people cannot understand or rather, they do not want to understand. If you start talking of cases belonging to the supernatural world, they look at you as if you are crazy or insane. It is true. I myself have tried to tell such a story, but all that I received were mocking and insulting insinuations. I do not want this story to remain forgotten, so I am writing it down, hoping that someday someone might believe me.

At the time, I was beginning my first year at Caerleon College of Education in South Wales. Caerleon is a small town known mostly for its Roman ruins. I had never been there before my course began. I come from Castleton, a small town in Derbyshire, which, by a strange coincidence, has much in common with Caerleon. Castleton also has Roman ruins and is famous for its 'Blue John' stones, which were very well known to the Romans. Ever since I was a little girl, I have been strongly attracted to those Roman remains that unexpectedly plunged me into an ancient world known superficially through history classes at school or films. I remember spending hours and hours in the museum observing the ancient tools and jewellery handled by people so long ago. How long ago? How many centuries had passed? Seventeen? Eighteen? Nineteen centuries? It is frightening to think of all that time! I was looking at things made by people nearly two thousand years ago. I was trampling on the same ground, breathing the same air. Look! A patrol of soldiers, perhaps centurions... Look at their clothes: the helmet has to be very efficient to protect them from swords and spears. On the front of the helmet, above the rim, is a protrusion protecting the forehead. Also, the rear of the helmet has a guard that protects the neck. The body armour is made from overlapping iron strips fastened with hooks and laces at the front and hinged at the back. They wear a linen undershirt and a tunic made of wool, whilst *caligae*[1] protect their feet.

Shadows of the past.

All around me.

It was so easy and natural for me to immerse myself in that ancient world. I could slip effortlessly into an imaginary reality inhabited by people very different from us in dress, speech, and behaviour. The scenery in my other world was also different from today's: the countryside was greener, the air very clean, and the sky blue like the Mediterranean. Sometimes this juxtaposition of elements from Mediterranean landscapes confused me. At times I would seem to be wandering in the typical places of southern Europe: Greece, Italy, perhaps Spain – I did not know. The warm, sultry air, the fragrant aromas, and the vivid colours seemed to be characteristic of those countries. When I awoke from my reveries, I avoided talking to people. I would feel melancholy and somewhat uneasy after shaking those wonderful images from my mind. But I went on thinking about what I had experienced – of the other 'realities' I had visited. I cannot remember spending even one day without considering the world beyond myself for at least a few moments.

For a time I felt obsessed by these occurrences and tried to

---

[1] A heavy-soled Roman military shoe or sandal.

meet someone with the same problems. It was so difficult to explain and make myself understood. Once, I did meet an old woman from Egypt who influenced me deeply. I met her one day in Castleton, sitting in the park not far from my house. She was a tourist, tired after having walked all day. By chance, we began talking. I discovered she was an archaeologist, a very learned woman with a magnetic light in her eyes. Yes, I will never forget those eyes. Despite her age, her eyes were young and lively. It was refreshing to talk to her and to be heard – I had a terrible need to be heard. You know, I soon realised she was exactly the person I was looking for.

During our conversation, I told her of my vivid dreams which took me back many centuries to the south of Europe. What struck me most was that she was not at all surprised by what I was telling her. On the contrary, she often anticipated what I was going to say. As she spoke, I soon forgot myself and became completely absorbed in what she was saying. She revealed an immense knowledge of the ancient world. She spoke of the Pharaohs and other characters of the past as if she had known them personally, as if she had some way of conversing with them directly.

Energies.

This was the word she used. This was the word she often repeated. According to her, we all possess fields of energies which vary in intensity and power. For example, Hindu shamans are able to heal with their touch because they have strong energy fields. We call it 'charisma'. When someone with 'charisma' walks into a room or any other place, everyone seems to know immediately. How? It is difficult to give an exact explanation, but surely our powers, more or less hidden and unknown to ourselves, give us information on the reality that surrounds us. Along with energies, the basic element in the archaeologist's scheme is time. Time consists of past, present and future without any chronological succession. This means that among us are various fields of energies from the past and the future which can affect us, depending on our degree of receptivity. She added that our fields of energies are interrelated with the many other energies in the universe. Together they make a wide and immense network whose borders and limits are not yet defined and perhaps never will be. Among the myriad of factors which constitute the invisible web are the heavenly bodies (such as the stars and planets), spirits (such as angels), living beings (plants, trees, and animals)... and many other things.

Now, you might ask, how is this connected to my problem? According to her theory, my energies are strongly influenced by, and closely linked to magnetic fields of the past. This allows me to be acquainted with certain places, people, and events from the remote past. I asked her if all this had something to do with reincarnation or something similar. 'No,' she said, 'reincarnation does not exist. Our own bodies are manifestations of the power of the spirits, of materialised energy. So, it is only our spirit that never dies; in various forms, our spiritual energy has always existed, and always will exist in the universe.'

At the time I did not understand everything that the Egyptian woman meant. But later events, the story I am about to tell, made sense of those magnetic fields she spoke of. Looking back, now enriched by my studies and life experiences, I realise that she unwittingly expressed concepts that today studies in quantum theory try to explain scientifically. It says that what we perceive as our material world is not really physical or material at all. Well, it is not really the same, but certain aspects are similar. Another thing that I want to say regarding that strange meeting is that since then I have been wondering how much chance and/or other elements such as fate or the games of energies intervene or contribute to bring people together.

One morning in late October, I was sitting in the student common room at Caerleon College. As I sipped a hot cup of tea, I thought about the party at Sean's the night before. I had had a delightful time. In fact, it was the first time I had enjoyed myself at a Caerleon party. I liked Sean. I had met him a few times before the party, and I think he liked me too. Unfortunately, he already had a girlfriend. What we felt, and would have liked to tell each other, remained suffocated in a corner of our hearts for a long time.

Greg, a friend of Sean's, entered with another young man and they both sat in front of me.

- Hi, Helen! – Greg said.
- Hi, Greg.
- Beautiful as always!
- Hahahaha!... Stop it! You're making me blush.
- Come on, Helen, only shy girls blush.
- Like me, then.
- Like you?... Well, I admit; I can't tell who's shy and who's not.

He laughed.

- I can't tell when you're joking and when you're serious, – I remarked.
- Jokes always hide some truth.
- Only some?...Didn't you hear Mr Snow say that in Shakespearean theatre the role of fools was to express the truth through their jokes?
- Ah! I can see that you're very attentive in class.

While Greg and I were talking, his acquaintance smiled faintly without interrupting. Yet, his gaze stirred something inside me. I felt as if I had been struck by a strong jolt which reverberated from my head to my heart. I shuddered. For a moment I seemed to be living one of my dreams. This person was from overseas, almost certainly from Greece or Spain, but the expression in his eyes reminded me of the Egyptian woman. How strange! I was extremely curious. I would have liked to talk to him, but after glancing at the clock I realised my drama lesson was about to start. I finished my cup of tea and looked back at them both.

- I've got to go now... See you later! – And I rushed towards the door.

Nervous.

I remained nervous and troubled all day. I couldn't rid my thoughts of that exotic guy. I tried to remember if I had ever met him before. Perhaps years before. Or in another life... Kidding! Who was he then? Why this effect on me? The more I thought of him, the more I became convinced that he was connected with my visions. Who was he? Why did he have such a big impact on me? That evening I decided to go out with my friend Pauline to 'The Red Rose', a pub popular among students. Even if Pauline wasn't free to come with me, I wouldn't stay at home; I needed to see people and to be distracted in some way. Perhaps I would also drink a little more than usual. Although October, the weather was not yet bad and the multi-coloured leaves created fantastic sceneries all around. The melancholic crunching of dead leaves brought to my mind sad reflections on the meaning of life. But I liked autumn; I think this period of the year has always been my favourite. Every year my mother would tell me that the coppery colour of my hair and my green irises dotted with yellow were perfectly in tune with the autumn colours of nature.

- Where are you? – Pauline asked perhaps reading my expression.

- Oh, sorry, I had a strange day, I need to relax. I'm glad you're here.

- Let me know if I can do anything to help. It's important to help each other.

Pauline was a nice girl who came from the countryside, which made her simple and easy going, also naïve in some respects. I liked to be in her company; I felt good and I was sure that I could rely on her. She studied Welsh language and literature and it was thanks to her that, in spite of living in the same country, I had my first contacts with the Welsh world. One day we went to Cardiff and in the City Hall she stood for a long minute contemplating and meditating in front of a wonderful sculpture of a Welsh poet who lived in the 14th century: Dafydd ap Gwilym. I told her that, to be honest, I knew nothing of this poet. She didn't say anything but I'm sure she thought what many Welsh, Scottish and Irish people think of their not-so-loved English neighbours, that is that we are arrogant in every way. 'What is his most famous poem?' I asked her while eating a sandwich in a small park nearby. 'Yr Wylan,' she answered. '"The seagull...*A bydd, dywaid na byddaf, Fwynwas coeth, fyw onis caf...* And be, say that I shall not be, An elegant kind-servant, living unless I win her." He explained the meaning of this as: "Have the kindness in courteous wise to give her the message that I shall die unless she will be mine."[2]... Well, it's a bit difficult to understand the translation too.... Anyway, the poet addresses and praises a seagull flying over the waves, comparing it to, among other things, a gauntlet, a ship at anchor, a sea lily, and a nun. He asks it to find a girl whom he compares to *Eigr*[3] and who can be found on the ramparts of a castle, to intercede with her, and to tell her that the poet cannot live without her. He loves her for her beauty, and unless he wins kind words from her, he will die.'

This poem impressed me so much that in some way it influenced and affected many of my future events.

As we were entering the pub, I noticed the European-looking guy coming out with a student I knew. He didn't see me and I didn't say anything, but on leaving he turned as if called by

---

[2] Bell, H. Idris; Bell, David (1942). Fifty Poems. Y Cymmrodor, vol. 48. London: Honourable Society of Cymmrodorion. pp. 45–46.

[3] *Eiger*, the mother of King Arthur.

somebody. He looked straight at me, and for a few moments, our gaze locked. It seemed he was also trying to determine if he had met me before. He then waved shyly and turned away. The door closed. I didn't see him again that evening.

- Do you know him? – Pauline asked.
- Who?
- Do you know that guy?
- He was with Greg this morning, but I haven't spoken to him. He must be an exchange student.
- I think he is; I've seen him around lately.
- He looks as though he's...
- He looks French.
- Possibly... No, I'd say Spanish or Greek.
- Yes, you're right.

The pub was so crowded that it took a quarter of an hour to buy two pints of lager.

- What about your Spanish boyfriend? – I asked raising my voice because of the noise and confusion.

Pauline looked a bit pensive then she answered.

- It was a summer crush while I was in Spain. But it's all over now.
- You look a bit resentful.
- Maybe. I don't know. It was good while it lasted, but once I'd got to know him better, I realised that he wasn't the man for me... Inevitable cultural differences!
- Sure.
- Some southern Mediterranean customs and ways are so different from ours; I just couldn't go along with them.
- What do you mean?
- They're morbidly attached to their families. The mothers, in particular, have an obsessive and looming presence in their children's lives that lasts forever.

I laughed and laughed looking at my friend's facial expression which showed her loathing. The lager had already gone to my head so I preferred to switch to a lighter topic... For the rest of the night my mind seemed to be... free and relieved.

The following morning he was there, at the college, standing by the timetable in the hall. He was the first person I saw as I entered. Immediately my heart began to throb. I felt my whole being tremble. I had no doubt that seeing him was what caused this agitation. I don't know if words can describe this sensation, but I'll try. I felt as if an electric shock was pulsating in every small part of my body – of my whole being. I felt flushed, warm. I saw many colours before me, constantly changing as if I was looking at the world through a kaleidoscope.

- Good morning, – he greeted me cheerfully.

- Hi – I replied, a little embarrassed, uncertain of whether I should stop and chat.

No, I didn't stop, although I wanted to. During Mr Snow's lecture on George Bernard Shaw, I was completely oblivious. No matter how hard I tried, I couldn't concentrate on what he was saying. My mind was totally absorbed in this young man. What had caused that excitement if not his presence? I had never felt such an intense vibration. I wondered if he had felt the same sensations. I had met him three times and each time something I couldn't understand had collided with an aspect of that man. I wanted to know, I had to know who he was. I looked forward to seeing him again.

The moment class ended I rushed out to the common room hoping to meet him there. And there he still was. I saw him sitting alone where we had first seen each other the day before. He had a map of England unfolded on his knees and seemed to be trying to locate some specific place. This time he failed to notice me even when I stopped just a few steps away from him. My heart accelerated, my whole being was shaken by a new vibration. 'Gosh!' I thought. 'It's unmistakable; it is him who causes this.'

- I'm sorry to disturb you, – I half-whispered, slightly vexed by the fact that he hadn't seen me.

He slowly lifted his head and carefully observed me. In the morning light, made brighter by timid rays of sun, I could see clearly the features of his face and the shape and colour of his eyes. His skin was lightly olive-coloured and his eyes were the colour of walnuts or almonds.

- Hello! – He exclaimed a bit surprised. – You're not disturbing me... By a strange coincidence, I was thinking of you a few minutes ago.

He was thinking of me, then! At the same time as I was thinking of him! That was too much. Stunned, I sat down facing him.

- How come you were thinking of me? – I asked realising that my question sounded silly.

- Yesterday you reminded me of somebody... somebody I might have met before.

- You might have seen a person who looked like me in another place. It's not unlikely, not impossible.

- Yes, it's very possible.

- You know, it happens...that sometimes...

- What?

- That we meet people very similar to others we have known.

Although he was smiling, his eyes were extremely serious, as if his mind had been plunged into another reality. He spoke slowly, with an obvious foreign accent.

- Where do you come from? – I asked curiously.

- From Italy... From the south of the country. My city is called Naples... Originally *Neapolis*... 'New city' after the Greek who founded it.

- *Ne-a-po-lis*... – I repeated in syllables as a mysterious voice prompted from an abyss inside me.

- *Brava!*... *Neapolis*... Have you been there?

- No, I haven't...But...
- But what?
- Nothing, nothing at all.

I wanted to say that, just as he was mentioning the name of the city, I could see it clearly in my mind... A sudden fan of images unfolded in front of my eyes. Where did all those images come from? I was confused. What was happening to me?

- How long have you been here? What brings you here? What are you studying at this college?

Spurred on by my curiosity, I didn't give him time to answer my barrage of questions. I felt that I was being impolite.

- I'm sorry if I'm being cheeky. I'm just curious about you.
- Oh, thanks, I feel very honoured that I've attracted your interest. What exactly would you like to know about me?
- Please don't think I'm being nosy... British people aren't usually so indiscreet.
- Don't worry. I like the fact that you're interested in me. I'm a student of foreign languages at the University of Naples, I hope to graduate at the end of this academic year... I'm attending a course in English history and literature here. I'm fascinated by English literature... I'm twenty-three and, as is customary, I still live with my family: my parents and two older sisters.

Immediately Pauline's complaints about her Spanish boyfriend popped into my mind confirming the fact that this was one of the aspects that southern European people have in common. I was sure that if I told her what I had just heard this guy say, she would advise me to run as far away from him as possible.

- And what's your name? – I asked.
- My name is Gaio Giulio and Valerio is my surname.
- What do you find so fascinating about our literature? Are you interested in a specific period or aspect or authors?
- Oh, gosh!... That's such a big question!

- Sorry!

- No, please... I want to answer... Perhaps I will tell you little by little if you want to meet up again. Apart from the greatest authors such as Shakespeare, Marlow, Coleridge etcetera, I find that the issues and the way they are dealt with are different from the literature of other countries. From the eighteenth century your intellectuals – compared to those of other nations – anticipated social problems that would affect the whole of the modern and contemporary era. The first thing that comes to mind now is the effects of the industrial revolution, for better or for worse, and the enormous literary production generated by the social changes.

- That's very interesting. I admit I don't know much about the literature of other countries. I know more about theatre.

- Are you going to be a drama teacher one day, then?

- Yes, this is my plan... What about you? What will you do after getting your degree? Teach English literature in Italy?

Gaio Giulio appeared a bit lost. He looked at a specific point on the map resting on his knees then he pointed to the city of London with his pen.

- It depends on the *Procurator's* decision in *Londinium*. – He said making a circle around the name of the city.

What was he saying?... *Londinium* means London in Latin, everybody knows that... *Procurator*... *Procurator*.

This word reminded me of something; I couldn't quite remember what it was. He looked up at me and seemed to come back to reality.

- Excuse me, – he said looking around.

Yes. He seemed to have returned from wherever he had 'visited' and now tried to orient himself. I say this in hindsight, but at the time I didn't understand, or rather I had the perception without rationalising it.

- My life is a bit complicated, – he continued. – I'd like

to teach, yes. I imagine myself in front of a class of students explaining Joyce's *Ulysses* and *Finnegan's Wake* or reading poetry by Keats or Shelley or Coleridge.

- I would like to listen to you reading poems.
- *Acting* poems.
- Right... *Acting* poetry.

He was nicer than I expected. He impressed me. I felt at ease with him and didn't want the conversation to end. Also, the sound of his voice and his physical presence were becoming more and more familiar to me... Why? Whywhywhywhywhy?.....

- How long will you be staying here? – I persisted fearing that he wanted to leave for some reason.
- I'm going back for Christmas and I'll return the first week of January.
- Where are you staying?

I was irritated with myself for all the stupid and banal questions I was asking. I wouldn't have been surprised if he had found an excuse to escape from me.

- I'm staying at the secretary's house, Mrs Blythe. Do you know her?
- Sure, everyone knows her.
- She lives just down the road, in the house on the corner. She's very friendly and is a great cook. I didn't think people could cook well in this country. Her husband is a policeman and they have two children, Christopher and Heather.

He spoke slowly, paying careful attention to formulating his sentences correctly. I found it amusing the way he waved his hands about as if his whole body was involved in the conversation. As he spoke, I thought of the many Italians who worked in Derbyshire. Although there were some similarities, somehow he seemed different from them. Before speaking to him, I would never have guessed that he was Italian. Perhaps I had a distorted image of

Italians because those I knew belonged mainly to the working class. Despite looking a bit rough, the Italians here were generally good and generous and made the effort to integrate themselves into our country. There was something distinguished, however, in Gaio Giulio's appearance, in his manners, and in his way of speaking. His smile revealed a childlike innocence.

- But you haven't told me your name yet, – he remarked.
- Helen.
- Oh, yes! I think Greg told me yesterday. Your name is Elen.
- Helen. Not Elen. The 'h' must be pronounced in English...Forgive me for pointing this out.
- That's perfectly ok; I want you to correct me. I need to practise and improve my English as much as possible.
- My first name is Helen and my surname is Barry.
- Barry. Helen Barry... It sounds nice... Names are meaningful; they reveal the personality of the person.
- Do you really believe that? Actually, I've heard that before... Yes, it's possible. So, what does my name suggest to you?
- Let's see... Helen...
- This name is very famous; it's well-known all over the world.
- Are you referring to Helen of Troy?
- Yes.
- This name actually expresses a magical beauty...The power of seduction.

I laughed.

- The power of seduction, – I repeated amused.
- Yes, and you possess it...
- No, I don't! What are you saying? I haven't seduced my prince charming yet.
- Because you haven't met him yet. Hahaha!

I liked his good humour. And more and more he revealed a sharp mind.

- I have told you a lot about me, – he continued. – But you have only told me your name.

- You haven't asked anything else... Anyway, my life is not as interesting as yours.

- I don't believe you... Your beautiful eyes hide big secrets.

- Wow! I'm not aware that I'm hiding any secrets.

I winced, feeling exposed. I wondered if the power of his mind could penetrate mine and read my thoughts.

- Well, – I continued after a moment's hesitation. – I'm from Castleton, in Derbyshire. It's very much like Caerleon; we also have Roman ruins. My parents live in a cosy cottage just outside of town, but ever since I turned seventeen I've been living on my own in a flat.

- Did you like living by yourself at such a young age?

He sounded more surprised than curious. I knew that in southern Europe young people are not as independent as in the north.

- It's very common in this country to go off on your own after the age of sixteen. Until recently many parents encouraged their children to leave home because the government paid benefits to the unemployed.

- I see... But there must be more positive reasons for young people to live without their parents.

- If you like, you can come to Derbyshire with me one weekend, – I said, astonished by my boldness.

- Seriously! – he exclaimed, surprised. – I would really like to... Not this weekend, though. I'm going to London this evening and I won't be back until Monday morning.

- Ok, let me know when you're free to come.

- I've been told Derbyshire is very beautiful.

- You've been told the truth. Derbyshire is one of the most beautiful places in England. You will see.

- I sincerely hope so.
- And... and I'll show you many marvellous things...
- I'm sure you will. Thank you.

Our conversation continued until lunchtime. When I left, I felt a little uneasy thinking I wouldn't see him until Monday. I hardly knew him yet he already possessed me. Why was I so vulnerable? Was it possible that I wasn't in control of my emotions? I didn't like that.

When I arrived back at the flat, I knocked at Pauline's door, which was on the same floor as mine. She wasn't in. I hoped I would find her later because I needed to tell her my news and also because, like the previous night, I didn't want to stay at home alone. I preferred to go to a club to dance and drink. Actually, I didn't want to think of Giulio. Our short meeting had left me feeling unusually anxious and excited. In my room, I ate a light snack and listened to some music. Then I knocked at Pauline's door again. Nothing. As time passed, I felt increasingly agitated. I went downstairs and called five or six friends, including Sean and Greg. No one was free to go out with me; they were all busy. Ok. I would go by myself.

While getting dressed, I thought of Oliver, my ex-boyfriend. As I reflected on our time together, I felt a strong desire to talk to him and to be with him. I've heard that the past just hides in the depths of our being and resurges unexpectedly. Who knows if this is good or not? We had been together for over a year and we broke up just a few weeks before I came to Wales. So, it was still quite recent. Why did we break up? Perhaps it had been my fault. I hadn't yet worked out what exactly had gone wrong between us. Most likely, I hadn't understood him very well. In any case, looking back on that relationship, I have to confess that I didn't love him. Apart from the laughter and fun we usually had with friends, we had very little in common. As with Pauline and her Spanish boyfriend, I didn't see a future with Oliver. Why this longing for him now? Perhaps he was the one I needed for a relaxing evening. But he was miles away and I found myself terribly lonely. I had never felt this sensation so strongly before. This upset me immensely.

As I walked to 'The Red Rose', a piercing autumn wind whipped against my face. I found it invigorating and decided to change my plans. Passing the pub, I began to walk along roads I hadn't been down before. As I passed a row of bungalows, I slackened my pace, my eyes dwelling on the lighted rooms of the low houses. I imagined the families living there: parents and children playing chess or scrabble, chatting, or sitting together in front of the TV. I longed to be inside one of those houses and to be welcomed warmly by those people. I thought of my mum and dad. Now I looked forward to the coming weekend when I would stay with them for a couple of days. Yes, Giulio had been right to be surprised that I had left my parents at the age of seventeen. Perhaps I still needed them. I promised myself that when I became a mother, I wouldn't let my children leave the family so young. Until recently people didn't live like that; families stayed together and young people were better guided and protected. I think it was definitely better then. I could now begin to appreciate the views of my grandparents. Both mum and dad had been brought up in a happy, loving environment with brothers, sisters, and relatives. For the first time, I thought about my situation as an only child. Perhaps it would have been different if I had had somebody to talk to and to play with. Instead, I always had to invent a sister or brother. I used to spend hours in front of the mirror talking and gesticulating to myself or to invisible friends. What an odd creature I had been! Did other children do those things too? I mean, did others behave in this unusual way? Did they feel what I felt? Was it normal to live the bizarre episodes I had lived and was still living now?

I went to bed early that night. My last thoughts were of him, of Gaio Giulio. What a strange name! It was so difficult to pronounce correctly. While closing my eyes, I felt a little guilty hearing myself tell him that 'Helen' is not the same as 'Elen'... It was not fair. I shouldn't have been so pedantic. And I drifted off to sleep.

What did I dream? Of him all night, of course. And this long, weird, incredible dream must be told. But, was it a dream?... I seemed to have spent the whole night in another dimension, as though my dual personality had split exactly in two. One remained with my body, while the other flew like a seagull over the sea, following the sun to a Mediterranean setting. The strange thing is that I was aware I was dreaming. I felt so happy to be flying, to be detached from my body. It was a magical flight full of beautiful sensations and enchanting landscapes. Suddenly, through the same magical effect, I found myself by the sea in a city that I guessed was Naples. The city I saw, however, was not a modern city but looked more similar to *Pompeii*. I had never been there, but I had seen many pictures and had read a lot about it. The architecture of the buildings was completely different from contemporary architecture; there were several temples big and small, statues and colonnades all over; a lot of streets were narrow and crowded with people, merchants, stands. Also, the way of dressing and the clothes were more or less the same as those in films about the Romans. Actually, I was watching a wonderful film, or rather, I was living it.

I saw Giulio in the corner of a rather large square. He was wearing a garment made of reddish cloth which looked like a long scarf tied around his waist. Although I was close to him and wanted to speak, something held me back. I could neither talk to him nor touch him. I was unable to walk any closer. Why? This was the only unpleasant sensation I felt and it was frustrating. Giulio then went into a house with a well-decorated façade. Following him, I saw that inside it was beautiful, but here my vision became blurred. I could not clearly distinguish the objects inside. I could make out that the house was absolutely fantastic: marble everywhere and many statues of various sizes. I soon saw that it was a house of great wealth. Just past the entrance hall, a large courtyard attracted my attention. Paths led to roofless rooms. The courtyard contained a statue of an altar to the household gods. A long porch with a low wall and pillars had been built along the front of the house. I think that this was a system to keep the rooms cool in summer. I was really living in a film. Two girls with long black hair and white robes were lying on large cushions scattered on the floor. Another young woman, standing in front of the altar, seemed to be praying. I couldn't see her face but I remember my surprise when I noticed that her hair was a similar colour to mine. The atmosphere, however, was dark, as if something was obstructing the sunlight. I caught a glimpse of a great number of objects, but I can't describe the details because I couldn't distinguish them. One of the two girls got up and came towards me beckoning me to follow her. She looked sad. She took my hand and led me quietly to a beautiful garden. The atmosphere here was completely different. The sun shone with arrogance above the flowers, plants, and trees, which were being watered continuously. The girl looked at me and started to speak. I didn't understand her and told her that I spoke a different language. Then tears began to stream down her face and she turned and disappeared leaving me alone.

Just at that moment, I woke up. After a few seconds, the alarm began to scream. The girl's tears were still in my mind and at the same time, the perfumed smells of the garden pervaded my pillow. Illusion. And the seagull... Why the seagull? Pauline's poem... *Yr Wylan*... had left a strong impression on me. And now, this beautiful white bird was trapped in my subconscious...Trying to return to my real world, I looked about my flat. No more magical palaces ... my room was a total mess. Seeing the clutter of dirty socks, skirts and jeans on the bed, teacups and tins spread out on the rug, I realised I was back home. Outside the window, I saw the branches bent low under a torrential downpour. Terrible! It was better to take refuge in my dreams... What an incredible adventure I was living! Now I was absolutely convinced that a part of my being was firmly connected to certain places in the past. But what about Giulio? Who was he? Did he belong to the past or to the present? He was real; he couldn't belong to the past. Or could he? I had to solve this terrible mystery... I had to find out what linked us together.

## REVENANTS?

The week passed slowly. During the interminable hours of waiting, I remained in a state of continuous anxiety. The weekend at home, however, was rather pleasant; it was also an occasion to reflect on my life and on the world around me. It's healthy for the spirit and for our inner selves in general to stop from time to time and look at our whole person in the mirror. I had long chats with my parents, which was positive for all of us. It had been ages since we had last had a good conversation. I felt much closer to them and they were so happy to have me there. At home, I realised I would never be alone as long as they were alive. I felt comforted and protected. Yet, I felt unable to tell them about my connections with the mysterious world in which I sometimes found myself. Many times I had wanted to talk to them about this, but I could never find the chance or the strength. I think I was unconsciously afraid of their reaction. I feared they would think I was mad. I was not mad, was I?

That weekend, while tidying my room upstairs, I decided to go through my wardrobe and drawers. My mother had asked me to do this several times but since I didn't live there anymore, I had always put it off. Now, however, I was determined to accomplish my task and to separate the past from the present. It was not easy to get rid of things that had been important to me at certain times in my life. Micro mini skirts and sweaters with funny word games printed on them took me back to my adolescence prompting me to relive my feelings for boys I liked and the carefree days spent with my friends trying to learn more about the secrets of adult life. I was still in touch with a few of them, but the majority had already been lost in the tangles of life and along the different roads of the world. In one of the lower drawers of the desk, hidden under a photo album, there was a small bundle of letters written by boys who had meant something special to me. I tried to read some, but I was not able to finish even one. That was proof that when we are young, everything changes quickly and often vanishes like windswept fog. So, without any feelings of nostalgia or regret, I tore up the letters and threw them away. There were not many things to get rid of in my room after all. I would certainly never part with my talking doll. Lucy. This was her name. My dear Lucy. Still dressed in purple and white…How many talks and conversations we had had when I was a child, and not only then! My grandparents had given me Lucy as a Christmas present when I was only five. They had bought her during their holidays in Cornwall. I was fascinated by the fact that she could talk. Actually, she could only repeat the same few words every time she was switched on. I can understand that now but I couldn't at that age. We used to spend the whole day in my room talking and playing.

One wall was completely taken up by bookshelves filled with books because I have always been a great reader. I ran my hands over the covers of the books I'd read most often and thought back to the many hours spent among the characters of those novels. The Bronte sisters, Dickens, Jane Austen, Thackeray etcetera etcetera…. Giulio certainly knew a lot of them. I looked forward to showing him my treasures. Noticing that I had no books by James Joyce, I realised that I couldn't remember having read even one. Of course, I had heard a lot about him, but I hadn't yet read any of his works. Now I realised that this was a serious literary failing of mine and that my bookshelves, although full, appeared suddenly impoverished as such an important author was missing. I would feel bad thinking that Giulio wouldn't see Joyce among my collection.

-Mum! – I called nervously once downstairs. – Mum, have you or dad read anything by James Joyce?

- Yes, darling, we have, – answered my mother looking at me a bit worried. – Are you all right?

- Yes, I'm fine. It's just that I was convinced that I had some books by Joyce in my bookcase upstairs. I wanted to read 'Ulysses' because I haven't read it yet. Have you?

- Yes, and some of his other works too.

- Do you have any in your room?

- No, recently we've been borrowing books from the library as it's so close.

- It's a difficult book, isn't it?

- Yes, it's not easy to understand. Before reading it, take a look at the *stream of consciousness*[4] and at *Henry Bergson's intuitionism*...[5]

- Yes, yes, I will. Thank you, mum.

While drifting off to sleep, I thought that I had been behaving like an idiot. Why should I feel guilty for not having read Joyce yet? I was still a girl with strange complexes... Before closing my eyes, I glanced at Lucy leaning on the chair next to my bed. She looked happy that I had come back home. I was sure that she had a lot to tell me.

- Mum! Dad! – I started while having breakfast the following morning. – Why did Grandma and Grandpa go to Cornwall so often?

My father averted his eyes from the newspaper while my mother spread butter on the toast.

- Your grandfather had Cornish roots. – He was born here but his ancestors were from somewhere in Cornwall.

---

[4] The stream of consciousness is a literary technique which consists in producing the free flow of thoughts, feelings and sensations of the characters without comment by the author.

[5] Henri-Louis Bergson was a major French philosopher.

- I didn't know that.

- I've mentioned it on a few occasions in the past. Perhaps you don't remember... I'm sure I've already told you that my father traced his family tree back to more than three hundred years ago. To a woman. A strange old name, probably Celtic... Ailla... Yes, I remember... Two or three times he mentioned this name: Ailla.

During those two days, I never stopped thinking of Giulio; the dream and all the sensations kept recurring in my mind. On the train back to Caerleon, I was overwhelmed by a strong desire to see him as soon as possible but I also knew that I had to control my emotions. I was completely losing my rationality and I didn't know how to stop it from happening. 'I'm not a normal person,' I thought while my eyes chased the fleeting trees beyond the windows. 'Who can help me? I don't want to go to a psychologist; I don't think that my problems have anything to do with my mind. I'm convinced they relate to the inner part of me, to my depths. And to this guy from far away who has suddenly and unexpectedly appeared in my life, inexplicably familiar and unknown at the same time, a bit strange in some aspects and yet, with mysterious force, he has kidnapped my senses and perhaps my soul and my heart. But who and what is he? Should I fight against his will or abandon myself to him until I've figured out the meaning of this encounter and who or what decided it should take place?'

Once off the train, I rushed home with my backpack before heading to college. With him in my mind. My anxiety abated when I saw him as he was waiting for me. Again. Again struck by a powerful electric jolt. I feared that he could see me shaking... Contact with him was like a plug in a socket. But which one of us was the plug?

- Good morning, Helen! – He greeted me with his innocent smile.

He seemed pleased to see me. I was overjoyed. Thinking

of the past days without his presence, I had to admit to myself that I had missed him.

- Hello, Gaio Giulio, – I answered with some difficulty.

- Call me Giulio, just Giulio. Gaio is not necessary and it's hard for you to pronounce.

It was true. Generally, English people find it difficult to pronounce three consecutive vowel sounds correctly.

- Gaaiou, – I repeated smiling.

- Gaio. Simply Gaio.

- I've never heard this name before.

- It's not common nowadays, – he commented.

Watching him carefully, I noticed that he seemed a bit removed. He looked as if he was daydreaming.

- Did you enjoy London? – I asked

- Yes, I had a nice time and met some interesting people. We're working hard there.

He said, 'We're working'… What did he mean? What was he talking about?

- A new week is now beginning, – I said banally, changing the subject. – I imagine you're very busy.

- I have to work hard if I want to improve my language skills and knowledge of this culture.

- Your English is already quite good.

- Thanks, but 'quite good' is not good enough.

- In a few weeks you will be perfect, believe me. With all these students around, you will make great progress.

- And with a pretty teacher like you.

He laughed loudly.

- There are many girls prettier than me in this college, – I answered back sensing that he was trying to flirt with me.

He looked overly confident for the short time we had known each other. An English boy, in his place, would have been more cautious. But I was not displeased by the compliment and I decided to play the game.

- I'm sincere, Helen, – he persisted more seriously.

Groups of students were now arriving which meant we wouldn't be alone anymore.

- I must be going, – I said looking at my watch.

- Let's go for a drink this evening? – He asked and invited at the same time.

I had hoped he would, but I played it cool.

- Yes, why not!... – I said – I know where you live. I'll call for you at quarter to eight. Ok?

At that moment a couple of girls approached us loudly greeting only him, so I disappeared without waiting for his answer. During the lesson I was able to concentrate for the first ten minutes then my mind started to roam again. I was sure now that the attraction was mutual, I already imagined him at my side in different situations. I heard his last words over and over again, 'I'm sincere, Helen'... I had never before considered having a foreign boyfriend... Still too early to believe it could be possible and real. Yet, I could see some shadows. First of all, he came from far away. I didn't agree with Pauline, who was convinced that different cultures create conflicts in time. This was because of her own experience, so it could not be considered an absolute truth. I was more concerned by the fact that he was here only temporarily. The second shadow was in his mysterious attitudes; I mean his sudden absences from reality with references to a world long ago where they seemed to speak Latin. But why should I be so surprised? This was also my mystery; I too had those visions, I too was absent from reality from time to time... I wonder if Giulio and I are rare cases in this world. How many people, like us, live extraordinary experiences similar to ours and don't admit it? They fear being judged as 'crazy' because society has fixed the rules of so-called 'normality' according to which every individual should live with standard behaviours accepted by everybody.

I knocked at the Blythes' house at a quarter to eight. Mrs Blythe opened the door and invited me in. Since Giulio was ready I declined saying that I would have a cup of tea next time. It was a bit strange for me to see Mrs Blythe in a different context, different from her college office. People generally tend to stereotype others on the basis of appearance that often falsifies the truth. Seeing Mrs Blythe at the college in her daily robotic and monotonous work, I didn't expect she, like many other women, could also have a cosy home and dress in a way to appear feminine and attractive.

- You look fantastic! – Giulio started once we were alone.

My appearance had never been so much appreciated as by this boy. Having heard that Italian men are famous for their attention directed towards women, I deduced that these compliments are easily handed out regardless of the type of relationship they have with them.

- Thanks. I don't think of myself as… fantastic.

- If you don't mind, I will tell you again: you are fantastic!

We laughed. He injected a sense of lightness in his expressions which did not create tension or embarrassment in me, so I realised that he, and his way of showing that he liked me, were not to be judged with too much of a British eye.

- I know a nice, peaceful pub in the country, – I said wanting to avoid 'The Red Rose'. – It's half an hour from here. 'The Red Rose' is too loud. What do you think?

- I agree.

We headed off briskly. From time to time our hands touched which did not leave me indifferent. Once again, I found his company pleasant and I felt at ease with him. I thought that we were starting a sort of adventure together but I couldn't yet define how it would unfold.

- How were your classes today? – I asked breaking the silence.

- Not so interesting. Mr Heath is a little boring.

- Can you understand everything he says?

- Not everything...but most of the time I get the gist of what he says. Even Greg finds it difficult to understand him. Strange, isn't it?

- Not really... In Britain, we have so many different accents. Even I can't understand some of them. But teachers, of course, should speak perfect, pure English.

- Indeed they should! – he laughed.

- Giulio, – I said softly.

- Yes?

- Nothing... I just like to say your name. It's... It's... euphonic. Nice.

He caught my hand. His grasp, strong and delicate, teased the strings of my femininity confirming to me that my subconscious had already submitted to him. The yellow light of the street lamps gave our faces a pallor that slightly changed our physiognomy.

- I couldn't wait to see you this morning, – he said looking ahead.

- Me too...

A sparse mist, typical of that month of autumn, suddenly enveloped us but didn't succeed in distracting us.

- Who are we, Giulio, you and I? – I asked a bit worried and aware of his dominium over me.

- Two seagulls.

- Two seagulls?

- Each of us has an animal or... beast inside. Mine is the seagull. I see myself like a seagull.

- That's beautiful... Yes, what you're saying is beautiful. But I can't see an animal inside me.

- That's because you don't want to see it... Anyway, if you don't have one, with my magic wand I transform you into a seagull like me.

At that moment I remembered the seagull in my last strange

dream… Yes, it was a seagull, I remember it well. Giulio and I stopped and looked at each other happy and laughing.

- You're amazing, – I said without curbing my enthusiasm.
- Take it easy. I might disappoint you…
- I guess you must have a girl waiting for you at home.

His expression became sombre. He grasped my hand firmly then loosened his grip. I realised I had touched a nerve.

- She died some time ago, – he whispered with difficulty.

His words struck me like a whip and instinctively I released my hand from his.

- I'm so s-sorry, – I stammered.

He took my hand again and pulled me closer to him.

- She didn't surrender, – he said after some silence. – I couldn't have prevented it.

I looked at him inquisitively.

- I met her when I was eighteen, – he went on suddenly absorbed in his other world, the same as in the morning when he had been talking about his journey to London, which he had called *Londinium*. – It was a hot September day. Pompeo had invited me to his villa at the foot of Vesuvius for the vintage celebration. Pompeo was a dear friend. We had been educated by the same masters and we completed our Army training at the same place. We were both very good with the sword. Anyway, Pompeo had a sister named Claudia. Although I had known her since she was a little girl, I had never given her a second look before that day. On seeing her at the villa, I was thunderstruck. She was no longer a girl but had reached that wonderful stage of youth: she was like a flower beginning to bloom, yet still beautiful in her innocence and purity… You know when you meet the right person; flames suddenly ignite in your heart. Life takes on a new meaning and in your happiness, you see everything as wonderful, you believe in another dimension. For a time we were happy and in total harmony, but the following year something happened which changed our lives.

He paused staring at a light in the distance.

- There's a pub ahead, – he remarked.

- Yes, it's called 'The Three Merry Lads,' I confirmed noticing that he was present. – That's where we're going.

He quickened his pace.

- I'm telling you this story because I want to be honest with you, Helen. It's over. It happened in the third century after Christ. Almost two thousand years ago.

I didn't know what to think, but I was relieved to hear those words; I felt close to him again and felt guilty for my stupid reaction. How could I be jealous of a girl who had lived two thousand years ago!

'The Three Merry Lads' was a really old, quiet pub far from the usual haunts of students. It was frequented mainly by middle-aged locals, so Welsh was spoken more than English. Needless to say, English and Welsh are two very different languages, as are the people. Before moving from Castleton, I had very rarely heard Welsh spoken, but now I liked to hear people speak it and I wondered how two such different tongues could coexist in a small country like Britain with nothing in common linguistically. The Welsh language is rich in very long words with a sing-song pronunciation, whilst English words are generally short and the intonation is rhythmic. We bought half a lager for him and a shandy for me then we went to sit in a corner.

- Now it's your turn, – Giulio said sipping his beer. – Tell me about your romances… or anything else you want.

- Beer is not your favourite drink, is it? – I observed, intentionally diverting the topic of conversation.

- I like it but in my country we're not used to drinking as much as here.

- You drink more wine than beer, I imagine.

- Yes, and generally only with meals.

- It's good that people have different customs and

traditions... It's only feelings that are the same everywhere.

- Feelings yes, but the way of expressing them is different.

- I agree.

We were seated opposite each other separated by a little table, so we could look directly into each other's eyes. Now the hazel colour was darker, like his hair. He had said that flames suddenly ignited in his heart. I didn't think I had experienced these burning flames with my boyfriends, not even with Oliver, but I understood what he meant because a fire was starting to ignite inside me now.

- Tell me more about... Claudia, – I asked with curiosity.

- She was a Christian, – he began again. – She was converted by some adherents of that strange religion and became a devout follower.

His way of talking was really unusual and I found that to define Christianity as a strange religion was unfair and insulting. I didn't yet understand where his mind was; perhaps he lived in two dimensions at the same time, in the past and in the present. There was no other explanation. I wanted to know more. I also came to the conclusion that if I wanted to continue to see this guy, I shouldn't be surprised by what he said and did, but I should accept him for who he was. Only in this way would I truly know him.

- For a while she kept her faith a secret from her parents. – He continued – I, however, became aware of it. It was a terrible, dreadful time for me. And when my parents found out the truth about Claudia, they wanted me to stop seeing her and threatened to exile me to Sardinia. I then ran into a lot of trouble trying to prove my innocence, since some people suspected that I, too, was a Christian. Eventually, Claudia had to hide in the *catacombs*[6] with others of the same religion. I looked for her frantically, wanting to save her. I was desperate. No one would tell me where she was. Only after her death

---

6   Underground tunnels with recesses where bodies were buried.

- There's a pub ahead, – he remarked.
- Yes, it's called 'The Three Merry Lads,' I confirmed

did I learn what had happened. She had been caught and taken to the amphitheatre of Capua and there...there was torn to pieces by wild beasts.

I was stunned, incredulous and horrified. Did that really happen? Did I really hear words such as 'catacombs'... 'Christians' and... 'torn to pieces by wild beasts'? Did this man live in that kind of world or was he fantasising?

- Those Christians, – he went on, – were so dazzled by the principles on which their religion was based that they lost their reason. They were completely blinded. The worrying thing was that patricians and people of high rank also fell into the traps of their preachers... Rome had had a long tradition of tolerance towards other religions, but Christianity was becoming more and more of a threat to our society because they had an incredible ability to seduce anyone with their absurd theories on poverty, forgiveness, equality. They believed that after death our souls would be judged by God according to our behaviour in this life and that one day, after the end of the world, our bodies would be resurrected and would live forever... But they didn't say where we would live again. How could anyone believe that?... And they were so stubborn and so convinced that they had the truth. Their faith made them invulnerable to any kind of suffering and pain, they prayed all the time, they prayed even when they were being eaten by lions.

- You still love her, don't you? – I said trying to penetrate his gloom.

- I often...often wonder if I love her... I feel guilty.

- You couldn't have done anything to save her.

- I don't feel guilty about that... No, I couldn't have prevented it. I know. I feel guilty for not having understood what *love* meant for her... One of the last times I met her, we were on the road that led to the leper colony, a place a few miles from the city, avoided by most people because of the danger of this highly infectious disease... I told her not to go any farther ahead. She stopped and looked at me with a smile that disarmed my fears. Her eyes had a new light as if it was the emanation of an inner strength that constituted a shield against any kind of danger. 'God doesn't want only our prayers,' she said. 'He asks us to love Him through our love for our neighbour.' And I replied: 'What do you mean?' She answered, 'To love the people who do not love you, because we are all brothers and sisters. To forgive others for any wrong they have done to you, to hug them; Jesus came on this earth to open our eyes and to overturn the framework of our society made of selfishness and false myths such as power and wealth. The kingdom where we will live one day is not in this world, it will not be made of palaces and jewels but it will consist of an eternal happiness if we follow Him. To follow Him means not to despise the poor but to help them, to feed the hungry, to give drink to the thirsty and to help the sick, to defend and protect the weak, to fight for justice, not to judge others because nobody is without sin... I was blind and now I can see. Do the same, Gaio, don't be afraid of Him, your fears will take you nowhere, it's your courage that will save you, the courage to approach Him with the heart of a child and to devote yourself to good. You will understand that this life is just a flash compared to eternity. To get worked up amassing wealth and power is worthless; you won't take even one coin with you to the world beyond, but only your soul... Come to the leper colony with me now, take off your precious embroidered clothes and use them to bandage the sores of those poor, ill people. This will be holy water for the desert of your spirit... If you love me, put aside your ambitions, forget your past, take my hand in yours and let's walk towards the light.'... She turned without waiting for a response or reaction from me and walked with determination toward the leper colony. My eyes followed her until she disappeared around

# IDENTITIES REDISCOVERED

*She had been caught and taken to the ampitheatre of Capua and there… there she was torn to pieces*

the first bend in the road. I can't say what I felt and what was going through my mind. I can't say because I don't know how to express it. I didn't follow her. I had heard what she had said but I hadn't grasped the meaning of it... I would grasp it much later.

And what about me? What was I? I was born into the Christian religion and I was brought up abiding by the rules of the Church, but in recent years I had become sceptical of whether Christianity was the only true religion. I started to read and listen to what the principles of other beliefs were and found out that in each of them there are wonderful teachings. Sure, what Jesus says often has an unparalleled power to penetrate the consciousness of all who seek justice and meaning of life beyond this miserable life on earth. Another indisputable positive thing that I find in the life of Jesus is the position that He takes towards women in all aspects of social life, first of all, their equality with men. This is amazing considering the times and region in which Jesus lived.

- Did you see her again? – I asked after a long pause.

- I saw her briefly a few days later as she was entering a hidden cave where Christians were gathering. I think she had a premonition that we would never meet again. 'May God enlighten and bless you,' she said caressing my cheek. Then she left.

- That's a very moving story. Thanks for telling me all this about you.

- Thank you for listening to me. I needed to talk to somebody who would understand me. You are the right person.

Perhaps I was the right person because the historical setting where he had lived his past experience was familiar to me; it was the same as in my visions, my dreams. Otherwise, I wouldn't have been able to understand him.

- Can I ask you if you follow any kind of religion now? – I

persisted in questioning him. – Do you believe in God?... Did this story with Claudia affect your beliefs?

- We were pagans... Our gods were Jupiter, Saturn, Neptune, Mars and others... This experience with Claudia, her death, the strength of her faith depressed and tormented me, I didn't think this wound would ever heal. I tried as hard as I could to understand if she really had the truth. To be honest, I found a lot of wonderful things in what people reported about the life of Jesus, but I have never been able to believe that in His words there was the absolute truth... Now, at this time, I believe in a superior entity; I believe that this wonderful architecture of the universe must have had a creator, an inventor, a director... let's call him God ... I believe that it is not by chance that the magnificence of our existence, of our being, of our body – both material and immaterial elements – are what they are. I also accept that in all this, I mean in everything that surrounds us, there is meaning. There is meaning even in death. This is clear, understandable. What I do not comprehend, though, is the Creator's intention. The intention for which everything began.

Yes. This man had a sharp mind. I was not wrong. I liked what he was saying. I liked his reflections and his way of digging into the mystery of existence. But it was too complex a subject to be discussed in a pub...

There were very few people in 'The Three Merry lads' that evening. It was Monday. That's to be expected in the pubs outside the town centre. But it was good to be almost alone; it had been a good choice to go there. Time passed quickly, I was insatiable; I wanted to know everything about him. I don't know why I started to think of my parents and how they would react when I took Giulio home. Because I did want to take him home. 'Ulysses'. Oh yes... What was happening in my mind?

- What are you thinking? – Giulio asked noticing that I was distracted and that I was laughing at myself.

- Silly things... really silly.
- Tell me, come on, I could do with a laugh!
- Nothing... Well, if you want...
- Sure. Please...
- I have a confession to make.
- Oh!... Do you think I deserve your trust?
- I hope so.
- Well, what bad thing did you do?
- I... I have never read Ulysses. Nor any other book by James Joyce.

I became serious and observed his reaction. He looked a little confused.

- And what's the matter with that? – He asked surprised. – What's the problem?

I started laughing.

- My ridiculous complex, – I confessed. – When I went home for the weekend, I glanced at my books and I couldn't find 'Ulysses'... I imagined what you would think of me when you saw my bookcase without Joyce... In a panic I rushed to my mother to ask her if she had read 'Ulysses' and if the book was somewhere in the house, because I intended to put it on my bookshelf.

I couldn't stop laughing and he also looked very amused.

- Now it's me who's telling you that you're amazing, – he said sharing my high spirits.
- I haven't finished yet.
- There's more?... Ok, go on!
- Do you know what my mother recommended I read before 'Ulysses'?
- What?
- She said that before reading any of Joyce's books, I should learn about the *stream of consciousness* and *intuitionism*.
- Wise mother!
- Yes, but don't you find what I told you a bit childish?

# IDENTITIES REDISCOVERED

Giulio got up and came to sit next to me then he hugged me in a friendly way.

- You're adorable, – he said. – I found your story funny and I appreciate your honesty.

- Thanks... Thanks... Look, look how quickly the time has passed; we should go now.

The mist had become thicker. It was nice to walk with his arm around my shoulders as though he was protecting me and together to cut through the dense swirls of vapour with our joined bodies. Claudia was still in my head forcing me to imagine those horrible scenes I had watched in films about people being eaten by beasts in the amphitheatre. How can human wickedness be so merciless? And how is it possible that some people enjoy watching other people suffer and die in such a way just for pleasure? Only humans have these forms of perversions.

- We have known each other for only a week, – I said, – and this is the first time we have really talked.

- When we met in the student common room, I glanced at you a few times without really noticing you, but in the evening, as I was coming out of 'The Red Rose' – you remember? – well, when I saw you then, something lit up inside me. In London, I thought about you a lot and looked forward to seeing you again.

Now I understood better. Not everything, but I could see that several elements which connected Giulio and myself to the archaeologist's network were similar, very similar. Perhaps the energy fields were on the same axis producing similar actions, or were colliding like atoms causing us to meet and think the same things. Yes, but what about this guy who seemed to be a fusion of past and present? And what mystery gave me the sensation that I seemed to have been wandering for years in his past? My knowledge of all this was still very scant.

- I think we should try to find out what has brought us

together, – I said bravely, – two completely different people, from different countries, cultures, traditions. This cannot be due only to chance.

- Fate wants us together tonight.
- Fate.
- Fate. The power of fate is above everything. Even Jupiter submitted to it.
- And it wants us together only for tonight? Is your fate so stingy?
- Fate is not destiny. Today is today. Tomorrow is another day.
- Shakespeare wouldn't agree.
- With what?
- With what you said about fate.
- Would you?
- No... you and I know very well that between us there are other mysterious forces that want us together.
- What, for example?
- Have you ever heard about energies?
- No, I haven't.

He wouldn't understand. Behind his contemporary look wearing the latest fashion, the certainties of his remote past seemed to prevail. There had to be a line, a barrier or a switch separating or sharing past and present in his subconscious that, according to a mechanism still unknown to me, allowed or didn't allow him to live in both worlds. I decided not to continue the conversation on this topic, not that night. We walked in silence for a few minutes as far as a solitary lamp post then stopped in the ivory light that gave our faces a pale hue. He moved his arm away from my shoulders and stood in front of me.

- Although you might think that it's too soon for me to tell you this, – he said staring at me, – but, I feel that I love you.

Had I heard right? He loved me. How could he love me after one drink and a conversation? Perhaps it was only attraction. The same as for me. Physical and/or intellectual, or something else, I didn't know.

- I feel comfortable with you, – I confessed sustaining his gaze. – I feel reborn in a way, but I'm scared. You're from another country and you'll be leaving soon…

- Say no more.

He put his fingers to my lips. Then he kissed me.

What a mysterious and magical phenomenon the kiss is! Especially the first kiss between two individuals. There are many other clues in our body and spirit that communicate the messages which nature provides us with in order to recognise a possible itinerary where life might join together the paths of two individuals. No other clue, though, is more efficient and unequivocal than kissing in intercepting the possible combinations of mutual attraction. Unfortunately, the other essential element for a good path together, that of understanding, doesn't seem to belong to chemistry. But the problem of understanding occurs in the later stages of the encounter, which is, perhaps, the right choice of nature.

That first kiss was followed by a second and, by the time we reached my house, there had been many others. My head was completely full or empty; it depends on what is meant by these two adjectives. I could perhaps better express my state by saying that I was at the mercy of intoxicating sensations that did not allow me to think. Sometimes it's nice not to think.

- I've got to get up early tomorrow morning, – Giulio said, standing by the door of my flat.

- It's not midnight yet, – I remarked looking at my watch.

- That's good. If I'm out after midnight, I might clash with a witch. – He laughed.

- I'm sure you would clash with more than one witch in the night… So I feel obliged to protect you.

- How, my darling?

- By giving you a cup of tea first.

- Well,... I need to get up early because I have to make a quick trip to Bath tomorrow morning. I'll be back in the evening.

- Did you know that Bath is famous for its springs?...

- Yes. The Consul General is very interested in them. We're making plans there for the future.

- The Consul General!... Plans for the future!... What do you mean?

- I'll tell you next time.

- Ok, please don't forget...

- But a cup of tea... Why not? It's a good idea.

I was glad I had invited him into my flat. While I put the kettle on, Giulio sat down on the sofa looking at all the things around him.

- Sorry about the mess! – I apologised.

- Don't apologise. It's nice... I like this room; I like its simplicity and the warm colours. I feel good here.

It didn't feel like this man was a stranger in my flat, or an intruder into my privacy. His presence gave me a sense of complete contentment. After pouring the tea, I leant my head on his shoulder. I felt so snug and secure that I wished those moments would never end.

- My world is so different from yours! – Giulio exclaimed turning pensive.

- How so?

- The smells, the food, the sky, the people – the whole atmosphere... So, I'm surprised at myself... why do I feel so good here?... Is it because of you? ... Help me to understand, I feel so confused, it's like not having an identity... Even my name sometimes sounds strange to me. Who am I?... Excuse me, please, excuse my delirium, I don't want to scare you.

His unexpected torment grieved me and instinctively I felt

a sort of maternal care and concern. It was also the first time that I had detected a kind of weakness in him. As he realised, he was being manipulated and controlled by a power beyond himself which he simply had to obey. I started to understand his problem and his ordeal, but I didn't know what to think or do for now. I felt excited and tired at the same time. It was nice to be on the sofa, quiet, close, our bodies discreetly seeking each other, the smell of the hot, green tea in our nostrils, the soft light of an old *abat-jour* an accomplice to our glances that did not hide our desire.

- Recite a poem for me, – I said in a small voice abandoning myself to him.

- A poem… Yes. Why not! I like reciting poems… *'Bright star…*

> *Bright star, would I were stedfast as thou art--*
> *Not in lone splendour hung aloft the night*
> *And watching, with eternal lids apart,*
> *Like nature's patient, sleepless Eremite,*
> *The moving waters at their priestlike task*
> *Of pure ablution round earth's human shores,*
> *Or gazing on the new soft-fallen mask*
> *Of snow upon the mountains and the moors--*
> *No--yet still stedfast, still unchangeable,*
> *Pillow'd upon my fair love's ripening breast,*
> *To feel for ever its soft fall and swell,*
> *Awake for ever in a sweet unrest,*
> *Still, still to hear her tender-taken breath,*
> *And so live ever--or else swoon to death.'* [7]

Bright star… pillow'd upon my fair… my fair love's ripening breast…

I can't remember how or exactly when we both fell asleep.

---

[7] John Keats, Bright Star: Love letters and Poems to Fanny Brawne.

The fact is that once I closed my eyes the flight began. Giulio and I floated out of our bodies.

Two seagulls. High. Higher and higher.

Into the sky.

Into an ocean of azure blue.

Our faces caressed by the warm southern winds.

While our glances were stolen by the sun.

He was not jealous. He just wanted to remind us that he was the king of the universe.

The same countryside as in my previous dream. The same panorama. This time, I was not in a dream-like trance but was perfectly alert and aware of what was happening. I knew that I was entering Giulio's world completely. I didn't ask myself anything. I didn't possess the will to ask. I was at the mercy of stronger powers.

The rolling waves, a deserted beach, a beautiful sunset. All this was before me. With my feet submerged in the soft, golden sand and a warm sea-breeze blowing my hair, I stood enraptured, holding Giulio's hand. The first thing I noticed was that we were dressed in an unusual way. I had on an off-white, hempen overshirt while Giulio was bare-chested, wearing only a pair of shorts held up by a thick leather belt. As I observed us both, I was not surprised; it was as if I had always expected to play a certain role in another reality.

Looking back on my experience now – as I am writing this story – I must further explain how I felt during the dream. I was aware that I was living in another dimension. I had the use of all my senses, such as hearing, taste and so on, but my ability to feel emotions was not the same as usual; I felt numb as though a will upon which I depended prevented me from expressing my feelings so that I acted, I dare say, impersonally. From an external point, I saw myself acting as if I were simultaneously a spectator and an actor in my dream. Therefore, only as a spectator could I give a voice to my emotions.

# IDENTITIES REDISCOVERED

*Giulio and I floated out of our bodies. Two seagulls. High. Higher and higher. Into the sky.*

*The rolling waves, a deserted beach, a beautiful sunset…*

As we stood on the beach, the sun slowly disappeared behind the calm sea. I cannot forget that beautiful sight: the sun was a gigantic ball of fire immersed in an oceanic extension of indescribable colours. Although this spectacular array of colour left me in ecstasy, Giulio didn't seem to notice. Instead, he kissed me on the forehead. Then, without saying a word, he took my hand implying that I should follow him. As we walked ahead, the smile disappeared from his face, and he became serious and somewhat uneasy.

Walking up the beach I noticed we were very close to the town. As we approached it we met more and more people. Most of them were poorly dressed; most of the men had beards and the women long hair. The streets were paved with cobblestones, and many houses did not have doors. This aroused my curiosity. I scrutinised the buildings more carefully. Many of them had big, high portals at the main entrance. Inside I could see large courtyards surrounded by houses and stables. Just like in the past dream, I saw lots of animals, especially horses and dogs. The people we met, however, didn't take any notice of us. We continued on in silence, holding hands. We walked quickly, as if in a hurry. After half an hour, we arrived at the square where I had previously been in my dream. Giulio then stopped by a tall column of white marble. He looked tired, sad and worried. Instinctively, I looked up and saw that on the top of the column was the inscription: 'Neptunus Deus Maris'.[8] Opposite us, on the other side of the square, I recognised the beautiful house where Giulio had entered in my other dream. The façade had a majestic look and engraved above the portal were the words: 'DOMUS VALERII'.[9] The other houses in the square were also refined and well decorated, but none was as dazzling as Domus Valerii. I also noticed that the people walking about the square looked different from the ones

---

8   Neptune, God of the Sea.
9   Valerio's House.

we had seen on the street. Here they wore fine clothes and precious jewellery. Outside Domus Valerii there was a strange gathering of people that lacked the liveliness seen elsewhere; the men stood in a gloomy silence and the women seemed to be in mourning. Many people were going into the house, and those coming out joined the others standing outside.

Suddenly, Giulio let go of my hand. Without looking at me he began to walk towards Domus Valerii. I tried to figure out what was going on, but I didn't know why he had left me alone. Feeling lost and bewildered, I watched Giulio enter the house. Mechanically, I began to follow him. I halted before the entrance and tried to listen to what the people gathered there were saying. I didn't understand them; they spoke a kind of Latin, or perhaps a strange dialect.

I entered the house and started climbing the marble stairs. Outside it was nearly dark, but torches mounted on the staircase spread a warm, dancing light. I eventually entered a large room, unlike the one I remembered. This time, I was able to see everything clearly: a fine mosaic in the floor displayed elaborate designs recalling scenes from Greek mythology; reddish frescoes on the walls portrayed landscapes symbolising happiness and abundance; and dozens of small statues, amphorae, and strangely shaped objects gave the room a simple harmony. In the centre of the room, I saw many people surrounding a bed mounted on four small pillars. Moving closer, I realised it was a catafalque on which rested the body of a young man. The two girls I had seen the week before were there weeping silently over the body. Their heads were covered with black scarves which partly hid their faces. An elegant lady and a man wearing a majestic red toga stood at the foot of the body, both enveloped in a deep, dignified sorrow. Sitting in a semicircle around the catafalque, twelve women dressed identically were moaning loudly and bewailing the dead man. In a corner, a group of young people, also wearing identical

# IDENTITIES REDISCOVERED

*Instinctively, I looked up and saw that on top of the column was the inscription:*
*'Neptunus Deus Maris.'*

clothes, were standing with flutes in their hands. Suddenly, I felt a certain dread. Not knowing why, I moved closer feeling as though a magnetic force was pulling me towards the body.

It was him, Giulio. His face. His body. Dead. At this point, I realised that I was part of the scene, not a spectator.

Dazed and confused, I saw a blue plaque above his head on which were written the words: 'CAIUS IULIUS VALERIUS DUX LEGIONIS BRITANNIAE'.[10]

Giiiiiiuuuuliiiiiiooooo!!!!!

From the depths of my soul.

A howl. A scream.

Frantic and frightened I looked everywhere for Giulio. My efforts were in vain. I could see only one Giulio. He was there, lifeless, ready to be buried with all the honours of his high rank.

I wanted to cry, to scream, but I lacked the strength. Gradually, everything around me became blurred and confused. I was unable to see or do anything else.

---

10  Caius Iulius Valerius, Commander of the Britannia legions.

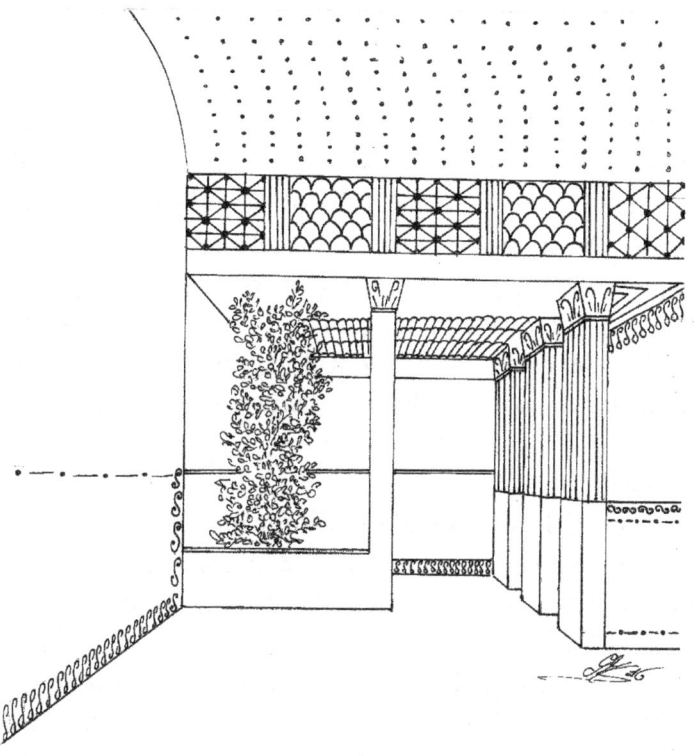

*The façade had a majestic look and engraved above the portal were the words:*
*'DOMUS VALERII'.*

## THE TRUTH

Half past seven! Oh no! My watch was the first thing I saw when I opened my eyes. I was lying on the sofa still dressed. And Giulio? Where was he? I frantically jumped up looking for him. On the table I found a note: 'It's six o'clock. You are sleeping so soundly, I don't want to wake you. Thank you for the wonderful evening. Love, Giulio.'

I was disappointed that he had left, but he had told me that he had to take an early train. Okay, I would see him that evening.

The dream.

What had happened? What fantastic power had permitted me to live that unforgettable night? With the dream still fresh in my mind, I examined every detail trying to discover its meaning. For the second time, I had experienced the same type of dream. Incredible! Flying like a seagull, visiting the same places with Giulio... What was the mysterious link that connected us? Why us? I no longer had any doubt that in the distant past something had tied us together. The magnificent house in the square belonged to him, to his family. But, supposing that all this was not the product of my imagination, how could he live a second time? And supposing he was living a second time, why my presence in his life and his in mine? Was I myself a revenant?

I thought of all this while taking a shower and getting dressed. I was baffled and confused. I felt as if lost in a labyrinth with no hope of finding my way out. I needed to talk to someone. But to whom? The Egyptian woman would understand, but she was far away and I didn't know how to reach her. Yet, despite all my uncertainty and fears, I was extremely happy. What I felt for Giulio was not a simple crush destined to soon vanish. No, this was more serious. He had ignited a fire in my heart; I felt reborn and renewed, everything seemed wonderful. Perhaps I loved him.

Absorbed in my thoughts, I walked to college through a thick mist. I felt exhilarated – full of anticipation. The day would go quickly and in the late afternoon I would see my love again.

- Hello, Helen! – I heard on entering the main building.

It was Mrs Blythe.

- Good morning, Mrs Blythe, – I replied, trying to maintain my composure.

- I was somewhat concerned about Giulio last night…

- I'm sorry… It's my fault. We were just having a cup of tea in my flat when we both fell asleep without realising.

- I see, – she said smiling.

I couldn't interpret her amused expression as approval or disapproval.

- And when I woke up this morning, – I went on, – he had already left for Bath.

- Yes, that's why I was worried. I knew he had to leave early this morning.

- He'll be back this evening. I'll ring him at tea time.

- You can have your tea with us if you like.

- Oh, thank you. I would like that. I had hoped she would invite me, so I didn't hesitate to accept.

- We'll expect you at six then, – Mrs Blythe confirmed. – Have a nice day.

The hours dragged on endlessly. Inwardly I had to struggle with contradictory emotions. On the one hand, I was overjoyed because now my life had new meaning. Yet, I remained uneasy; the images of Giulio in the casket and his talk of *catacombs* hammered persistently against my brain. Thinking of myself,

I realised that the shadows shrouding my life had not vanished but seemed even more obscure and gloomy. Looking to the future, I could perceive only a barrier beyond which I could not discern anything. I was unable to make plans. Everything I was doing – my studies, my daily life – made no sense at all.

The day passed with exasperating slowness. The lessons were boring as usual and at lunchtime I sat alone without speaking to anyone. I did meet Greg while clearing my tray and he seemed to want to tell me something. But at that moment some of his friends called him away so we just said 'hello!' In the past week, I had spoken very little to the people I knew there. I hadn't seen Sean, and I'd hardly even spoken to Pauline, who lived next door. I promised myself to tell her all about Giulio as soon as possible. She was a good friend and had confided many of her secrets to me, which I appreciated. In any case, I suspected that she knew something was going on between Giulio and me.

At six o'clock sharp I knocked at the Blythes' door. A young girl of about twelve came to answer. I already knew her name; she was Heather, and her brother was Christopher. Giulio had told me this. All of our conversations were imprinted on my memory.

- Hi, Heather! – I said cheerfully.

- Hello, Helen. Please, come in. Mum wants to talk to you urgently.

At that moment Mrs Blythe appeared in the hall. She looked worried and I understood immediately that something was wrong.

- I have some bad news, Helen. – She said meeting me on the doorstep. – Come in. Please, come in.

- What's wrong? – I asked apprehensively.

- Giulio had to fly to Italy today. I didn't see him but Heather did. He was leaving when she arrived home from school.

- Yes, – the girl interrupted. – I found him packing and after a few minutes a taxi came for him. Before leaving he told me that he had to go back home. He said that he would call my mother tomorrow to explain everything. He also gave me this letter for you.

She pulled the letter out of her pocket and handed it to me. Trembling, I opened it with voracious curiosity. 'My love,' Giulio wrote, 'in Bath, I met the *Praetor* (Roman Official) who had an urgent dispatch for me. I have to go back to my country. I'll be replaced by a new general. I love you. C. Iulius Valerius.'

Dreadful.

Three incomprehensible lines.

I was beside myself. I felt as if I would faint.

- Let me sit down for a moment, please, – I murmured, gasping for air.

- You are pale, very pale, – observed Mrs Blythe helping me to an armchair. – I hope it's nothing serious. Without speaking, I handed her the letter.

- I can't understand, – she said after reading it. – I can't understand what all this means... Praetor...a new general... C. *Iulius Valerius*... Very odd, isn't it?

I should have expected something like this. I had been anxious all day. Many times I had asked myself if last night had been real or a dream. Perhaps the whole past week had been a dream. But if I was dreaming, Mrs Blythe was not. And the letter was very real.

- I'm sure he will ring tomorrow, – she said trying to pacify me. – We'll find out what all this means.

I am not able to describe what was running through my blood, my flesh, my bones, my spirit...every part of me...I couldn't wait until tomorrow, I needed to see him now, I needed to hear him, to touch him. I needed to know the truth, to know what to believe and what not to believe. I also needed to know who I was.

- He must have a phone where he lives, – I said almost crying. – Do you have his number?

Somewhat perplexed, Mrs Blythe thought for a moment, then went upstairs and returned a couple of minutes later with a card in her hand.

- No, there is no telephone number... Only this address... I think it's an address.

On the card, I read: '*C. Iulius Valerius – Macellum (Forum) – Contiguus – Puteoli*'.

I immediately felt a new sense of resolve surge up from within. I was determined to find a clear and definitive answer to all my questions. I would get to the bottom of this mystery once and for all. There was only one way. I had to go to Italy. I had to find him.

- I'd better go now, – I told myself aloud as I stood up.
- Have your tea first. It will be ready in a few minutes.
- I'm sorry. I really must leave now.

Seeing how worried I was, she did not persist.

I left their house abruptly and hurried home. My mind was working full-tilt on the problems that lay ahead. I thought about how I could get to Italy: plane, train, boat. I had been abroad before but I couldn't speak any other language except a little French. Italian?... *Pizza, ciao... arrivederci...amore...* That's all... I would need to pack some clothes. I would need to get hold of some money to buy a ticket, and find somewhere to stay for a few days. Where? In Naples? I didn't know anybody there. But I had to go. Once there, I would find a way to survive and to accomplish my task.

Finding Pauline's door ajar, I entered without knocking. Fortunately, she was in. She was my only hope.

- What's happened? You look simply awful! – She exclaimed when she saw me.

It's true; I must have looked terrible. I told her roughly what had happened since we last talked. I left out the dreams because I knew that even Pauline would have laughed at me.

- I knew that something was going on between you and this... Giulio... – Pauline said when I'd finished speaking. – But I didn't expect you to fall for him so quickly.

- I don't know what it is...

- I don't blame you... Don't worry... I know enough about these things to understand.

- That's why I'm here. I know that you're the only person I can talk to... But... But I want to go to Naples. I need to go.

- So?

- I need to ask you a big favour, – I said coming straight to the point and looking her straight in the eye – I need some money. Not for long. I'll be able to give it you back shortly.

- Yes, – she agreed without hesitation. – Yes, sure... if it's a reasonable amount.

- To buy a ticket for the flight and...

- You will need a place to stay...

- Yes.

- Ok, it's no big deal...I'll transfer some money into your account.

- You're a real friend, Pauline, – I said, greatly moved.

Once again she proved to be very kind and generous. I knew I could count on her. I remembered the dialogue between Claudia and Giulio about loving our neighbour. Now, at that moment, I was Pauline's neighbour; I was the one who was hungry and thirsty and my friend hadn't turned away from me.

- I need to leave immediately, – I continued.

- What?... You can't leave now. Wait until tomorrow. You need to at least book a flight first.

- I can't wait until tomorrow... I just can't. I have to go now.

Pauline put her arm around me and tried to calm me down.

- Sit down and let's see how we can solve this problem, –

Pauline said in a soothing voice. – It's seven p.m. and the only way to get to the airport is by coach. I went to Italy a couple of years ago but to Rome, not Naples. I think I flew from Gatwick... Yes, it was Gatwick. There must be charter flights from there... I'll call the airport to get some information. Wait just a few seconds.

Pauline was very considerate. I'll never forget what she did for me that night. She is the kind of person who is available for everyone. She inspires confidence in others through her marked practical sense and extraordinary courage. I hadn't seen this side of her before. I promised myself that one day I would reciprocate. We have remained very close friends but I haven't had the opportunity to help her. Perhaps she will never need it. There are people destined only to give... Pauline is one of them.

There were two flights leaving for Naples the following day, the first was at eight a.m. It was too late to make a reservation; I simply had to go to the airport hoping to find a vacant seat. Pauline gave me a lift to Newport where I took the midnight coach. Before leaving, she gave me a little English-Italian dictionary and a healthy dose of advice.

– Let me know any news as soon as you can, – she said while I was getting on the coach. – And watch out! You are very pretty... You will be honey for all those dark-eyed guys.

I showed her a broad smile for her concern.

– I will dress like a nun! – I joked. – See you soon, Pauline. And thanks for everything.

Luckily, there weren't many people on the coach. I closed my eyes and tried to sleep; I must have slept for half an hour, certainly no more. I was excited, but it was no longer a nervous excitement. I thought of many things at once without being able to concentrate on anything specific. Alternating my gaze between the sleeping passengers and the window, I counted the minutes on my watch. From time to time I recalled Pauline's advice. I felt a little lost, but not worried.

Every stage of my journey seemed to be guided by an invisible presence. Everything went smoothly. There had even been just one seat left on the plane. Was it all by chance? – After take-off I soon found myself immersed in the boundless heavens, the blueness of which reminded me of my dream of flying like a seagull. I had almost slipped into another dream when the little girl next to me scrambled over my legs to look out of the window. Her mother scolded her, but the girl persisted in wanting my seat. Reluctantly I changed places. I was somewhat annoyed, but it all worked out for the best. The mother's name was Tina. She was from Bedford, born to Italian immigrant workers. Her parents, after working for twenty years at London Bricks, had returned to Naples where they opened a coffee bar. Tina, however, considered herself a British subject and remained in Bedford with her English husband. From time to time she went to Naples to visit her parents and younger brothers. But not only to visit family. She said that the islands in the Gulf and the resorts on the coast were beautiful places to spend a holiday at any time of the year; therefore, she tried to combine visiting her parents with a holiday.

Tina was surprised to hear that I didn't have a place to stay in Naples. With some difficulty I started to tell her my story inventing some parts and leaving out the details that she would not understand. In short, she saw me as a girl in love going in search of her boyfriend in order to clarify their relationship.

I think she felt a great deal of compassion for me. Recognising my naivety, she advised me to be very cautious. We continued to talk during the rest of the flight and while landing she said she would ask her parents if I could stay with them for a few days.

Tina's generosity made me think of Pauline again. Before then I had never experienced the goodness of fellow human beings. I had always felt that people were distant and selfish.

To tell the truth, I had never been in real need. But now I was. I needed help and here were two honest, good-hearted people who had come to my aid. Since then, both Pauline and Tina have had an enormous impact on how I view the world.

After getting off the plane, I found the climate very pleasant considering the season. The sky was blue and sunny, and the temperature warm. I was not surprised; there was something in the air that seemed familiar to me. Tina's parents were waiting for her and while they greeted and hugged each other warmly, I stood aside so as not to disturb them. But not for long. Tina hadn't forgotten me and invited me to join them. She explained my situation to her parents who welcomed me warmly saying that having me to stay with them would be a good opportunity to refresh their English. In fact, despite the twenty years spent in Britain, their Italian accent had remained strong.

In the car on the way to their home, I realised that what people say about Naples is not mere fancy. The chaos on the roads and the behaviour of motorists has no equal anywhere in the world. Drivers have no sense of respect: they pay no attention to speed signs or traffic lights; they overtake on the wrong side and heaven forbid if a pedestrian wishes to cross the road. The people, on the other hand, seem to live in perfect harmony with all this. Now that I know the city better, I can say that it is really unique, a carousel of contradictions. Where else can you find such a combination of wealth and poverty, of ancient and modern, of concern and neglect, of sagacity and contempt? You might say that all large cities are like that. Perhaps, but Naples possesses something more which is difficult to explain; the lights and shadows are wider – I'd say amplified – which causes an excess of good and evil. One more thing: Neapolitans like to sing. It is a talent, a vocation, a need, a desire – I do not know how to describe it – something innate in them that comes out naturally in any situation and at

# IDENTITIES REDISCOVERED

any time of the day or night. They sing while cooking, when washing up, when they are in the bathroom, when walking, when working, and especially when doing manual labour. They sing alone and in company, when they are happy and when they are sad. And they like whistling too; they whistle for any reason, from opera to contemporary songs, even when they are in bed. Funny! This is a wonderful aspect of those people that still today, after many years, enchants and intrigues me.

Tina's parents lived in a part of the old city called *Quartiere di Chiaia*.[11] To reach their street we had to climb steep, arduous stairs where numerous children were playing. The street was characteristic of the old city: narrow, cramped, and confined on both sides by high, musty buildings. From there the sky appeared to be an endless series of rectangular handkerchiefs, extended above a continuous line of balconies with hanging baskets and clothes. The apartment where Tina's parents lived was on the third floor, directly above the coffee bar. Inside, the unmistakable aroma of *'espresso'* was constantly in the air. I found it amusing to drink a small cup of coffee, or any other drink, standing up. Actually, the coffee bars in Italy are just like shops.

By now I was quite exhausted. After a marvellous dinner of *spaghetti con le vongole*[12] and white wine, I fell into a deep sleep. The next morning I awoke to the sounds of street workers below my balcony. Since it was only seven a.m., I didn't feel like getting up, but the noise from the street and the racket of the people in the apartment above made any further sleep impossible. I went downstairs to the coffee bar where my host family worked every day. I spent a very pleasant time with them meeting their friends and relatives. Very warm people, but their persistent questions about my private life irritated

---

11  Chiaia neighbourhood.
12  Spaghetti with clams

me somewhat. Although overwhelmed by this new context, I never stopped thinking of Giulio. Late that evening I had a chat with Giacomo, Tina's younger brother. I asked him if he knew about the *Forum of Puteoli*. He laughed at seeing the two words written down.

- What's wrong with it! – I exclaimed.
- Did you study Latin? – he asked me.
- No, I didn't.
- Puteoli is a town in the suburbs of Naples. It's now called Pozzuoli, and *Forum* stands for the modern square... I'm studying Latin at school... Why are you interested in all this?
- It's a long story... I need to go there tomorrow. How can I get there?
- There are good bus connections, but I can take you there if you like.
- Thanks. Thank you so much, but your family is already doing a lot for me... and you have to go to school.
- In this country, schools are closed the first two days of November. We celebrate the Saints and the Dead.
- The Saints and the Dead?! That's strange.
- This is a Catholic country. You will see crowds of people bringing flowers and candles to the cemeteries.

Until three years ago Giacomo had attended school in Bedford and his English was still very good. He was seventeen but looked more mature. After closing the coffee house, he took me for a ride on his motorbike. It was fantastic. Naples by night, particularly when seen from Posillipo Hill, assumes an enchanted appearance. The night's shadows hide the dirt and neglect. Even the narrow lanes in the worst reputed places have something magical and mysterious. Zigzagging dangerously in the disarray of cars parked even on pavements, I was shocked to see so many people of all ages riding motorbikes and scooters without helmets.

# IDENTITIES REDISCOVERED

*The street was characteristic of the old city: narrow, cramped, and confined on both sides by high, musty buildings*

- I don't understand why people do not respect the rules in this city, – I wondered aloud when our ride finished.

- We are... anarchists! – Giacomo ironised smiling at me.

- Anarchists? What do you mean?

- It's difficult to explain... I myself don't know exactly why. What I can tell you is that Italians, in general, have no sense of community, no sense of nation, of state. There is an innate instinct to disobey here, and in Naples these characteristics are much more accentuated and visible than in the rest of the country.

- There must be a reason.

- There must be, but...

- But what?

- If you fall in love with this city, you'll never want to go back to Britain again.

I laughed and asked:

- Why?

- Because Naples can be loved or hated.

- Hahahahaha!!!... My heart is hard.

- Hahahahaha! – He mimicked my laughter sarcastically. – You've been warned. I won't tell you again.

- Don't worry. A few days is too short to love or hate somebody or something.

The next day Giacomo and I took the bus to Pozzuoli. What he said about people bringing flowers to the cemetery was true; I could see many people with a specific kind of flower: the chrysanthemum. Chrysanthemums everywhere. The morning was glorious, nothing like the gloomy autumn in Britain. As the bus drove along the coast, I could see that the sea was incredibly still. I tried to associate what I saw with the recurrent images of my dreams. The houses, the people, and the roads did not remind me of anything in particular, but there was something in the countryside, in the atmosphere, which was not completely unfamiliar. As I got off the bus, the strong odour of fish temporarily made me nauseous. At last, I was in Pozzuoli. What should I do now? I felt embarrassed and lost.

- Here we are, – Giacomo said. – The only square I know is over there. But there are others in town. This one is not far from the sea. Follow me.

In the square, I looked all around. Lots of people were chatting or reading newspapers on the café terraces. I examined everything carefully, but there was nothing I could link with my night visions. From time to time Giacomo looked at me inquisitively, as if expecting some questions. After a while, I had the feeling that he was becoming a little annoyed. I couldn't blame him. In his place I wouldn't have been so patient, wasting time with a foreigner in search... in search of what?... Of nothing!

- I want to look for this name, for a young man called Caius Iulius Valerius, – I said at last, – It's Latin for Gaio Giulio Valerio.

- I know that, but we can't go around asking for Caius Iulius Valerius... Everyone would laugh. It would sound ridiculous.

- Ridiculous?

- Yes, ridiculous. It's somebody who lived perhaps two thousand years ago and you're talking about him as if you know him.

It was too difficult to make myself understood. I felt awkward and frustrated.

- I'm sorry, – the boy's apology came after a few minutes of a heavy and embarrassing silence. – I don't want to upset you. I'll do my best.

This made me feel better. Giacomo went to ask various people in the square for information. I didn't understand everything that they said, but I was able to catch the gist. Nobody was able to tell him anything definite, but a policeman and a barman said that the name reminded them of someone, and a lady selling newspapers added that the surname Valerio was common in that area. Finally, we met the right person – a retired headmaster very well acquainted with Roman history. He looked wise, his white hair gave him a distinguished air and he spoke slowly enunciating his words with clarity and precision. He also spoke some English, with an American accent, which pleased me.

- There is a story about this name, – he said, referring to 'Caius Iulius Valerius'. – I can show you something that proves he lived in the third century after Christ. It's not far from here.

We started walking towards the sea. My heart began beating faster, stronger. I felt near, very near the truth.

- This town was founded in 527 BC, – he continued, – by colonisers from Samos (a Greek island in the eastern Aegean Sea). Two centuries later, the Romans conquered it and named it Puteoli. Soon it became an important Roman port. The history of this town is very interesting... Not only of this town... I mean the whole region has more or less the same roots and a lot to tell... Regarding our subject, however, we don't yet know how much is legend and how much is fact. What we do know for certain is that Caius Iulius Valerius became a general at a very young age and was sent to Britain. He belonged to an upper-class family: his father was a senator and his mother's family belonged to the Greek aristocracy. After returning from 'Britannia', Caius Iulius suffered a long illness and is believed to have died at the age of 25 or 26.

Yes, all this was true. As I listened, I couldn't believe what I was hearing. He was speaking of Giulio, the young man who had kissed me so tenderly – who had slept with me on my sofa just a few nights ago. Now this stranger, this old headmaster was telling me that my Giulio with the innocent smile, who attended Caerleon College in South Wales, had lived in the third century AD. Was all this part of a dream? A dream within a dream? No, I was not dreaming now. This was real.

- What about the legend? – I asked anxiously.

- It concerns a love story between Iulius and a girl who became a Christian. The girl was persecuted and sentenced to death.

That was enough. I had no further doubts.

- Why is this love story considered a legend? – I persisted.

- There is nothing written about it... No official evidence. Perhaps only fragments. One hundred years later, when the empire was coming to an end, a poet wrote something about this love story without mentioning the names, but references to the context, the family and other indications were clear: it was about Caius and Claudia.

- Was that the name of the girl? – I asked.

- Yes, Claudia. She was also of high social status. This is one of the reasons that their story didn't go unnoticed and became a legend.

Meanwhile, we had arrived at the sea. I saw some Roman columns half submerged in the water. Walking up to them, I noticed something that shocked me – some writing on a long bar of marble. Although some of the letters were illegible, I could make out the inscription: 'CAIUS IULIUS VALERIUS DUX LEGIONIS BRITANNIAE'.[13] I immediately recalled what I had seen in my dream above Giulio's catafalque. I was looking at the same inscription, right in front of me. Suddenly my head began to pound. An intense tremor reverberated throughout my body.

- Are you all right? – asked Giacomo, catching my arm.

- I feel weak. My head's spinning.

- You look as if you've seen a ghost, – he continued. – Helen, what's wrong? Are you ok?

These were the last words I heard. When I came round,

---

13  Caius Iulius Valerius Commander of the Britannia legions.

I found myself lying on a sofa in an unfamiliar room, which turned out to be in the headmaster's house. The headmaster, his wife, Giacomo and a young doctor were standing around the sofa observing me attentively. At first, I was unable to speak. I was scared, but at the same time, I felt protected as I looked at these kind people around me. Giacomo was pale, looking clearly worried about me. The doctor spoke to them for a few minutes, then grasped my hand in a comforting manner and left.

- Don't worry, – said the boy. – The doctor recommended that you rest. Then he turned to the headmaster.

- The problem is that I have to go home...

- She can stay here, – the old man interrupted, – No problem... My wife and I will be only too pleased to look after her.

- Thanks, I'll come back this evening to pick her up then.

Giacomo quickly left. I felt sorry for him and for the trouble I had caused him. I hoped wholeheartedly to have the chance one day to repay his kindness. And how could I forget the headmaster and his wife? After Giacomo left, they prepared a hearty meal which made me feel much better. I regained my strength and after a while, the fainting was just an embarrassing incident to put behind me. The conversation during the meal was also pleasant. My host showed that he was highly educated. It was marvellous to listen to him. He had a way of explaining everything, which fascinated me. But all the time, my mind was occupied by Giulio; I couldn't erase him or the inscription on the marble pillar. My discovery that day had been painful and terrible. This additional evidence of my connection with the past was in some way frightening. I feared that the episode with Giulio might repeat itself in the future with somebody else... Oh, no!.....For goodness sake, no! And Giulio? Where was he? What remained of our encounter? What about my love, my passion that was just beginning to blossom? The sweet flower of dawning happiness was being supplanted by a sour bitterness. An aborted love – what an awful, agonising sensation!... But... in spite of this... I didn't want the day to end.

- I have not yet introduced myself and my wife, – the man said leaving the dinner table, – My name is Antonio and my wife's name is Antonietta. It comes from Antonia which is the feminine form of Antonio.

- Oh, that's nice! So, you have the same name.

- Yes, that's not unusual here... I see that the colour has returned to your cheeks, – he observed. – I want to show you something. Please, come with me.

I followed him into a room that must have been his office. Big bookcases full of books, maps, paintings. A writing desk made of thick dark wood covered with notebooks, sheets of paper, pens, pipes, cigars, lighters and other miscellaneous objects.

- I guess you spend a lot of time here, – I said looking at the many things around.

- Right. It's my favourite corner.

- I'm sorry about what happened. I didn't know I was so sensitive and weak.

- It seems that something gave you a nasty shock... perhaps something to do with the inscription we saw.

I didn't know what to say. I had a sudden urge to tell him my story. Instinctively I trusted him, but I had just met him and I wanted to be cautious. He approached a bookcase housing several maps, took one, which he unfolded on a small, low, rectangular table, and invited me to sit next to him and take a look at it.

- Part of this Roman town is now under water owing to a phenomenon called bradyseism... It's the gradual uplift or descent of part of the Earth's surface by the filling or emptying of an underground magma chamber. That's why the statue we saw is almost covered by the sea. The part where we are now was built later but the old remains are still visible. Here is the Flavian amphitheatre, one of two in ancient Puteoli. It already existed at the time Gaio lived, yet, the legend says that Claudia was taken to the amphitheatre of Capua, that is thirty miles away. And here, in the upper right-hand corner, there is a little map of the old city. It's incomplete because there's still a lot to discover at the bottom of the sea.

- All this must be so interesting and fascinating.

Antonio explored the map very carefully as though looking for specific places or details. The expression on his face revealed that he was absorbed in something most likely connected with the ancient world.

- When you fainted this morning, – he said dreamily, – I had something like a vision that brought me back to my research.

- What do you mean?

- I've done my own research into Caius Iulius; I like to dig into the mysteries of the past... The keys to understanding much of our present lie in the past.

Needless to say, the Egyptian woman immediately popped into my mind making me think that she had a lot in common with this man.

- May I show you something? – I asked wanting him to see the paper that Mrs Blythe had given me with Giulio's words on.

- Sure, let me see.

I took the paper out of one of my pockets and showed him.

- Who gave this to you? – he questioned after reading it.

- A student from Naples who is attending my college... it's too complicated to tell you...

- Don't worry, don't worry, you don't have to... This is his name... and... this word *Macellum* was the market square in the ancient town. If you come here again in the next few days,

I'll show you...and *contiguous* means 'next'... like in English 'next door'. *Forum* is square. In this case, *Macellum* and *forum* refer to the same place. He wanted to point out to somebody that perhaps he lived near the square.

- Now I understand. I thought that they were two different places.

- No. I will tell you the history of *Macellum* when we go there, so you won't forget it... This student must be passionate about archaeology... I can see that his handwriting is very clear.

The headmaster got up and approached the bookshelves again. He opened a folder and took out a photo. Then he came and sat next to me to show me. I could see a nun walking along an ancient road paved with large cobbles. I stared attentively at her face but it was not clear because her head was covered with the typical black headdress that nuns wear.

- You must be wondering who she is, – he said.

- Yes, who is she?

- Perhaps a ghost.

He laughed. I did not know what to say or how to react. In his laughter, I perceived something youthful.

- I wouldn't have thought that you believed in ghosts! – I exclaimed laughing too.

- I haven't seen any, – but many people swear to have seen them and even talked to them.

- I haven't seen any either. In Britain, there are many haunted houses and places. Ghost stories are very popular in my country. I don't know what to think... But why are you showing me this photo?

- As I said before, I have done my own research into Caius Iulius and I believe I have found out something that you won't find in any history book. This road paved with cobbles was important in Roman times, it's one of the so-called consular roads in the region; it connected *Puteoli* to the city of Capua.

I'm sure that you are familiar with the name *Spartacus*. Right? A lot of films have been made about him... Not far from this point where that nun is walking, there was a leper colony in those times.

Antonio took a pencil and with it pointed to a place on the map. A leper colony. Giulio had mentioned this to me when talking about his relationship with Claudia. At that moment we looked out of the window and saw, not very high in the sky, a few seagulls whose shrill cries were echoing human laments.

- It's rare that seagulls move very far from the sea, – the man said scrutinising the sky.

And I saw myself in the dreams.

And after a few seconds, one seagull, perhaps one of those that had just passed by, flew slowly and so close to the window that I could see his eyes.

- He must be a messenger, – Antonio observed getting up again to go to open the window. – Come here, Helen, come here.

I can't say what kind of emotions or emotion possessed me. I rushed towards the window and we both leaned out. No seagulls.

- The messenger has gone, – I observed disappointedly.

The window looked onto a beautiful garden full of orange, lemon and tangerine trees. They were still unripe, but the air was full of the distinctive aromas of citrus fruit. I inhaled filling my lungs.

- In a few weeks, the fruit will be ripe and the garden will be decorated with wonderful colours, – he said.

- Yes, I can imagine... orange, yellow...

- Red.

- Red?

- Yes. Red oranges. They are the best.

- You're very lucky in this country.

- For this, yes... but not in many other ways.

He laughed again. I liked how he laughed. He treated me in a sort of confidential manner that created in me an agreeable easiness confirming my first instinct towards him. It's surprising sometimes to notice how differences in culture and age can fade into insignificance in the presence of all those physical and spiritual components that make the so-called connection between individuals prevail over many other factors.

Energies. That's what the Egyptian woman would have said or would say. On reflection, I could see that everything led back to her words and theories.

- What are these 'many other ways' that you are not lucky here, if you don't mind me asking? Name at least one.

- Well, let me think... we don't have snow. We miss it.

This time it was me who laughed.

- If you had snow, I don't think you would have this garden full of citrus fruits, - I pointed out.

- You're right... Clever girl. Better oranges than snow... We can't have both... Let's close the window, it's getting cold.

- He had no message for us, then, - I said referring to the bird.

- Who knows!... It's getting dark. He might come back tomorrow.

- Perhaps he thought he would find you alone and when he saw me, he changed his mind or he got scared and flew away.

- What kind of message can he bring to an old man like me close to death?... No... no. He was looking for you.

- Recently I seem to have been seeing seagulls everywhere, especially in my dreams.

- It's a positive symbol... It means freedom, independence... But let's go back to our Iulius. I know that this young man from the past is important to you. I don't know why, but whatever the reason, I will tell you everything I know.

- Yes, he is important to me. I need to know.

Once again we went to sit at the table with the map.

- Now, as I approach the end of my life, – he said, – and on the basis of many strange episodes I have experienced, I have to say that telepathy plays an important role in many situations that apparently seem to happen by chance.

- What you are saying doesn't surprise me; I agree with you... Please, tell me more.

- When you felt bad this morning near the statue, I had a sudden flash in my mind, in my subconscious, somewhere in my being... You know, when Iulius returned from Britannia he was not alone. He had a Celtic wife whose name was Ailla. I found out that this name was probably Cornish... Ailla means 'most beautiful'. And... in this fleeting vision, I saw that this person looked just like .... you!

- My God!

My God! My God!... Ailla! Did I hear that right? My grandfather's Celtic ancestor, and therefore...my ancestor!

- Do you think that Ailla, my grandfather's ancestor, and Ailla, Iulius' wife, could be blood relatives?

- I can't answer that. They could be, but not necessarily so... What I saw in my vision was incredible... I really didn't know whether to tell you this, it's difficult for me, believe me, I wouldn't have dared tell anyone else.

- I don't know what to say, but I believe you... you are a scholar, an educated person, why shouldn't I take what you're saying seriously? But you do realise that the revelations suggested by your research are shocking!

- I can prove everything to you, with documents and evidence, except the fact that you and Ailla are the same person...of course... obviously, this is my surmise; let's call it extrasensory perception if you like. But I don't believe I'm wrong...

- So, I am the reincarnation of Iulius' wife?

- I'm sceptical... reincarnation... No, no.

- What then?

- Our energies continue to exist even after our bodies are dead.

- Energies... This is what I need to hear. Thanks, thanks, Antonio... But you said that Ailla and I are the same person...

- Yes, in a way, but I wouldn't say she was reincarnated as you. The fact is that the energies of this person who lived more or less 1750 years ago live in you.

- What?

- Actually, Ailla was Iulius' slave at the beginning and she became his wife here. They loved each other but Iulius was ill. Ailla was honest and faithful; in spite of her beauty, she refused the courtship of other men, and devoted herself to taking care of her husband until the end. After a few months, the widow asked Iulius' family for permission to leave and to go back to Britannia.

All the pieces of the puzzle were falling into place and everything was starting to make sense. I thought of my dreams and I understood that in the first one the young woman in front of the altar was me; in the second dream my identification with Ailla was stronger and clearer and I saw myself at the foot of the catafalque.

With his pencil, the headmaster traced a quarter of the way along the consular road on the map and stopped at a point where that road intersected a path.

- Now this path is almost covered in weeds, – he went on, – but at that time it led to the leper colony. It's at the corner, here, where the path and the road cross that some people swear to have seen the nun. She carries a sack full of gauzes and bandages. It's reported that not very long ago, an unsuspecting tourist offered to help her. She kindly declined. It was summer and at that time of the day, it was hot. 'Would you please give me a few drops of water?' she asked seeing that he had a plastic bottle of water with him.

'Sure,' the tourist replied giving her the bottle. After

drinking, the nun gave the bottle back to him, but he wanted her to keep it. 'Where are you taking all these bandages?' He questioned. 'I can't see a hospital nearby.' And she revealed: 'Many years ago there was a leper colony not so far away. Now there is a hospital for sinners and their wounds need more care.' The tourist looked at her trying to hide a look of compassion as he suddenly realised that the nun was insane. 'I understand,' he said pretending to agree. And smiling ironically: 'With all my sins I think I'm incurable!' 'You're a good man,' she retorted. 'I asked you for a few drops of water and you gave me the whole bottle. In the name of God, I forgive your sins.' She lifted her sack and turned to go down the path, but the man called after her in a loud voice: 'At least tell me your name, dear nun!' She slowed down for a moment and replied: 'Claudia'.... This is not the only sighting of Claudia, there are many others.

Antonio stopped talking. He looked pleased that he'd told me everything he knew about Caius Iulius. It was very likely that, in spite of his reputation as a historian, he found it difficult to tell others this story as he knew they would not believe him.

- So, what are we, then? – I asked pensively. – Revenants or something else? If so, is this the fortune of all humans?

- I don't know how to answer that. Only after death will the mist be wiped away that makes the mysteries of our life impenetrable. One day we will know...

- But today, you and I, what are we doing here? How did it happen that we met?

- Not by chance, if that's what you mean. I don't believe it was by chance.

- Everything is part of the game.

- Not everything, but a lot is. Definitely.

- Perhaps the energies we mentioned do not wander in the universe for those people who die in peace with the world and with themselves. They have accomplished their task...

But Giulio, Claudia and I, we didn't accomplish our mission, we still had a lot to say and do and that's why our energies continued to live after our bodies died, waiting and looking for the next opportunity to fulfil our role.

- Yes, Helen, you're perfectly right and I agree with you. But, *rebus sic stantibus*,[14] as the Romans used to say in those times, the game is not over yet.

- No... It's not over yet.

Giacomo came with his father at six p.m. On leaving, I told the old couple that I would like to see them again. I also gave them my address hoping that one day they might visit. Later that evening, Giacomo took me for another ride on his motorbike. He liked showing off with no helmet on his 'horse' and I guessed he wanted to prove how good he was. His daredevil driving both excited and frightened me. I held on to him tightly with my arms hugging his chest. This close embrace and the high velocity perhaps gave him a sense of power. Afterwards, we went with a few of his friends to have a drink in a bar. His friends were all well-mannered, but very interested in the 'English girl'. In my mind, I compared them with English teenagers. It seemed that young people in the south were more extrovert and warmer in their social contacts. When talking, boys made a lot of sexual innuendos and I noticed that it is much easier to talk about sex than in Britain or other countries. Also, it seems that, especially for girls, puberty starts much earlier there than in the north of Europe.

- Don't be pissed off if boys here start chatting you up almost immediately, – Giacomo tried to appease and reassure me seeing his friends besiege me after an initial brief shyness. – It's just what they do when they see a foreign girl for the first time.

---

14 Things thus standing.

- It's really difficult to know how to handle them. They're nice but too aggressive. I guess that many girls just walk away...

- Not all, – he interrupted with more than a hint of irony. – Ok, I don't want all these wolves to chew you up... Let's go for a pizza.

His friends reluctantly let us go and a few of them wanted to kiss me on the cheek. It's incredible how much physical contact Italians have with each other. Even people of the same gender hug and touch or hold onto each other. They do not do it with any sexual or bad intention; it's just their way of showing their emotions and feelings, not only love but also friendship, admiration or a strong sense of respect. In Britain, it would be unthinkable. Too weird for us. But that's the way it is. Although difficult for us to accept, I think that they are freer and less hung up than we are.

- Which is the best pizza? – I asked while sitting in a small pizzeria tucked away in a narrow lane in the old city.

- *Pizza Margherita,* the simplest.

- The simplest! What do you mean and why it is called Margherita?

- Margherita was the name of the queen at the end of the nineteenth century. It is said that this kind of pizza was cooked in her honour just with the basic ingredients: dough, tomato sauce, olive oil, basil and mozzarella. The three colours of the Italian flag: red, white and green.

- I see. That's nice to know... There's such a lot to learn about this city.

- You're right, there is a lot; the history of Naples is very rich and complex... For a few centuries, it was also one of the most important capitals in Europe, I think until 1860, the year of the political unification of the country.

- What would you say tourists need to know in particular about Naples?

- If I were a tourist guide, I would tell visitors the many legends and stories of this city and do you know what in particular?
- What?
- Some aspects of our culture... such as traditions, our mentality, and superstitions... Superstition here is not only an important aspect of our daily life but it is also a kind of 'philosophy' of living. We believe in the magic powers of amulets...We believe that all the unusual things that happen during the day are there to give warnings or specific messages, like accidents for example. And dreams... dreams are powerful and unmistakable messengers...
- Oh, I see, – I interrupted him pointing at a red horn hanging from the top of the front door...
- Yes, you're right; this is perhaps the most popular amulet in the city and in the whole region. It wards off bad luck and all forms of bad energy. Many people wear it as a pendant.
- Yes, I saw a couple of your friends wearing one.
- Right. Others keep a little horn in their pockets.
- Hahahahahaha!
- The horn is really popular, but we have others too.
- What about dreams? I find this subject really interesting because in the night I'm often haunted by terrible dreams.
- Dreams are said to be prophetic; they are full of symbols that need to be interpreted. We take them so seriously that there are specific places, such as kiosks or little shops, where you can go and tell an expert your dream. Through symbols such as water, fire, certain animals, objects or dead people they can tell you what is going to happen around you...There is a book here called '*Smorfia*' (Grimace) where these symbols are associated with numbers and then people bet those numbers on the lottery. Most Neapolitans know at least a few *Smorfia* numbers. For example, if you dream of God or Italy, then play number one; an insane person is number twenty-two; if you are frightened by a dream, bet number ninety.

- Gosh! That's really interesting... If I lived here, I would go to the kiosk every morning.

The atmosphere was relaxed and light-hearted. We laughed a lot. And our fellow diners also looked happy and carefree, talking loudly and having fun.

- Tell me, Giacomo, do you miss England? – I asked after tasting a hot piece of pizza, – Have you ever thought of going back?

- The first year was very hard here, but now it's ok... Do I miss England? Well, sometimes I do. I'm still in touch with a few friends in Bedford... I'll see what happens when I finish school, whether I'll stay here or not.

The conversation continued about his friends from Bedford then we mounted the motorbike again for a quick ride and eventually arrived home. I was worn out but when I finally got into bed and turned off the light, I couldn't sleep. All that had happened during the day passed before my eyes in an endless sequence of images. I felt empty and sad. The aim of my journey had been to discover the real identity of Caius Iulius Valerius, and today in just a few hours, I had touched on the truth. This young man had lived in the third century and what was known about him matched exactly what Giulio had told me. What the headmaster had said obviously impressed and touched me deeply, especially his certainty regarding my identification with Caius' slave or wife. I had to think more about that... Was I the same woman? Although it was not easy to believe or to accept, all reasoning led me to dispel my doubts: Ailla and I were the same person. If we were not the same person, then there most likely wouldn't have been such a strong connection between me and Giulio. Everything that was happening now was related to our common and shared past. The other 'character' that puzzled me was Claudia. For a person like me whose relationship with God and the church had always been tepid, the personality of this woman escaped my understanding. The last images that filled my mind before I fell asleep were those of Naples, this strange city that can be either 'loved or hated', as Giacomo had said. An enormous conglomerate that synthesises all the aspects of living and of life produced by its history whose roots pierce time immemorial. The incomparable chaos, the exasperated individualism, the cohabitation of the most extreme human conditions and contradictions move and live in an asymmetrical paradoxical order that can be understood only when one is integrated into that system.

Giulio.

Where are you…my love?

Not just a vanishing apparition. Not simply a shadow. I had touched him. I had kissed him. Many people had known him. Anyway, if he was a real person – if he really loved me – he would know where I was. The only thing I could do now was to book my return flight. Eventually, my fatigue triumphed and I slept wonderfully well.

- Tina, can I ask you one last favour? – I said at breakfast the following morning. – There's no reason for me to stay any longer. I'd like to book my return flight as soon as possible.

- Giacomo said you found something interesting in Pozzuoli… You can stay here as long as you want.

- Thanks. You and your family are so kind and hospitable… but one thing is very clear to me now: this relationship between me and Giulio has no future.

- Why do you say that?

I smiled bitterly. I didn't want to explain too many things that she would not be able to understand. I just wanted to go home now.

- Giulio is not interested in me anymore, – I tried to hastily bring the subject to an end in order to avoid further questions. – If he wants me, he knows where I am.

- Yes, you're right. I'd think the same in your place. Men are untrustworthy in love, especially when they're young.

The first charter flight to Gatwick would leave on Saturday. As it was Thursday, this meant that I would have to wait two days, otherwise I could leave by train at midday. In truth, I would have preferred to leave immediately but Tina and her parents insisted that I stayed with them. I agreed thinking that I would enjoy two more days in Naples. The weather was fine, the temperature very mild, and I really wanted to take a long walk by the sea.

As I walked towards the sea later that morning, I was surprised at how relaxed and calm I felt. Giulio had not left my mind but his image seemed to be slowly vanishing. I became convinced that what I had experienced during the past few days was perhaps a mysterious joke of life. With these melancholy thoughts, I arrived at *Mergellina*[15] where there is a long wharf stretching out to the sea. Here many fishermen spend hours casting their lines from big lava rocks. When the sun shines, young couples stroll up and down the wharf. Leaning against a mooring mast, I observed the young lovers enjoying the sea breeze. The sight of them filled me with tenderness as they walked by hand in hand, kissing each other and whispering words of love. Yes, I felt envious and alone. I thought back to last Monday night when Giulio and I had been walking in the same way. He had disappeared for reasons unknown to me... that wasn't honest. It wasn't right. But Giulio had been sincere about his feelings for me – of this I was certain. On my left, I could see an old castle whose walls were soaked by the lashing waves of the sea. It had a strange shape. I would have liked to know its history. The headmaster certainly knew all about it.

– It's called *Castel dell'Ovo,* – said a fisherman a few steps from me raising his fishing rod to check the hook. – *Castel dell'Ovo* means 'Egg Castle'.

I still do not know if it's the same all over Italy, but one more thing that I noticed in Naples was the ease with which

---

15  A district of Naples by the sea.

people communicate; even strangers talk comfortably and freely to each other. This happens in the bars, in the shops, in the lift, in the street. And they talk about their private life as if they've been friends for years. I was astonished by this. The fisherman addressed me certain that I spoke English and that I was from another country. Furthermore, he spoke in such a way that he seemed sure I would listen to him. He was evidently accustomed to the many foreigners who perched on those rocks to take in the view of the castle in the bay. The wrinkled skin on his face had been consumed by the sun like all those used to spending many hours a day fishing. Although he spoke in broken English, I could easily understand him.

- There are smart fish and stupid fish, – he went on, examining the hook. – This one was smart…too smart. It ate the bait without me realising.

- Perhaps it was more intelligent than smart, and others are more naïve than stupid, – I retorted while he attached more bait to the hook.

Absorbed in his task, he seemed to ignore me. Then, after casting his line in the water and smiling, he addressed me.

- You might be right, – he said as if reflecting on what he was going to say. – Sometimes, while observing their behaviour, I also think that they are intelligent or naïve.

I made a sign of approval without speaking then returned my gaze to the castle.

- This castle has a long history, – the fisherman informed me sensing my curiosity.

I didn't know why this man wanted to continue the conversation. I felt reluctant to remain there and let him go on, not out of embarrassment but just because my cultural background had taught me to be cautious. I had learned quickly, though, that here I had to take my foot off the brakes and let go of my inhibitions. After all, he wasn't doing anything wrong and I liked his observations on the fish.

- I know very little about this city, – I said after being silent for a few minutes.

The man's attention was drawn to the strong and sudden vibration of the floating cork on the fishing rod. False alarm. The vibration stopped.

- Which do you think that was? – he asked without looking at me. – Intelligent or smart?
- Intelligent. Very intelligent, – I responded right away.
- Do you know why?
- No, I don't.
- Many people fish here every day... The fish have learned our intentions and behaviours, so they laugh at us and play games with us.
- Why do you waste your time then?
- I don't waste my time. It's a challenge. I play with them. It's like a game of chess.

This time, he made me laugh.

- You haven't told me yet why it's called Egg Castle, – I said trying to change the subject.
- Oh, yes... You're right... There's a lot I could tell you about it. This city is very rich in legends mixed with historical facts... This is the oldest castle in Naples. Its first construction dates back to Roman times, long before Christ. It's built on a peninsula, but originally it was a small island called *Megaride*. It was the famous Roman poet, Virgil, and the legend of his magical and mythical egg that gave the Castle its name. Legend has it that Virgil placed an egg into a glass jar, the jar into a metal cage then hid it beneath the castle. As long as the egg remained safe and intact, so would the city.
- I see.
- And this city originated from the island called *Megaride*...

Just then, the floating cork disappeared under the water and the rod was pulled downwards by the strong, taut line. The man stood up reeling in the fish he had hooked. In an instant, the poor fish flopped into a bucket very close to me flapping about struggling to breathe and to survive.

- Poor creature! – I exclaimed disgusted, – I wonder what it did wrong to deserve this end.

The fisherman seemed touched by my reaction. He swiftly seized the fish with both hands and threw it back into the sea. I did not know what to think. I felt relieved but sorry for him at the same time.

- Perhaps I've deprived your children of their food today, – I said by way of an apology.

- They will eat something else... Anyway, a good chess player knows how to lose.

- You didn't lose. You won.

- With the fish yes. But not with you...You checkmated the king!

Wonderful. We both laughed. I found this unexpected conversation interesting and exciting. His appearance was that of a scruffy guy who you would avoid in the street. After looking at his watch a couple of times, he decided to pack up his rod and put everything away ready for going home.

- I'll not leave without telling you about the origin of Naples, – he assured me as if this piece of history or legend had great importance.

- Please do; I'd like to know.

- Naples was first called *Partenope*. This was the name of one of the three beautiful and dangerous sirens; creatures that were half woman and half fish, or half bird, that lived on an island to the north of Sorrento. They lured nearby sailors to shipwreck on the rocky coasts of their island with their enchanting music and voices. It happened that Ulysses, while travelling with his sailors in that part of the sea, wanted to listen to the singing of these cursed sirens. He was a daredevil and had been warned of the danger by the sorceress *Circe,* so he took precautions: he ordered his men to wear wax earplugs so they would not be able to hear. He, however, had himself tied to the mast of the ship and forbade his men to untie him even if he told them to. Bold, yes... But he was no fool!! His plan worked. The sirens were so hurt and disappointed that they committed suicide by smashing themselves onto the rocks. They were goddesses, but not immortal. The body of *Partenope* was carried by the currents between the rocks of *Megaride,* where you now see Egg Castle. There it was found by fishermen who venerated her as a goddess. And thus she became the protector of the place and that small village, as it was then, was named after her.

He picked up all his belongings.

- Thank you, – I responded in awe. – Thank you very much.

- Goodbye, beautiful stranger, and good luck.

- Thank you, good sir, I won't forget this extraordinary meeting.

I saw him move away and quickly disappear among the people. I looked at the castle again then my eyes seemed to get lost in the immensity of the sea. Ulysses... Ulysses... 'It happened that Ulysses, travelling with his sailors in the sea...'
... Castleton. My bookshelves. Joyce's 'Ulysses' was not there... Giulio.

Suddenly I was seized by a strong desire to see the inscription on the marble column once more. After all, I was still curious. I needed to go to Pozzuoli on my own. I needed to return alone to the same place: to watch, to carefully observe all the details and to breathe the air I had breathed in my dreams. Most of all I needed to bid Giulio 'goodbye forever'. Mechanically I set off towards the bus-stop from where Giacomo and I had left the day before. It was not far. Within half an hour I was on the bus.

The bus was packed. I couldn't find an empty seat. A young boy got up and motioned for me to sit in his place. I felt a little embarrassed. While I was sitting there, I thought of Pauline, of her warnings about the people and the city. In truth, all the people I had met had been friendly and kind to me. I had no reason to complain. 'There are good and bad people everywhere, you should know that, Pauline.' I remembered that I was supposed to ring her. I would ring her that day, without fail!

I thought of the fisherman. After our conversation we had left without even telling each other our names.

Weird.

In Pozzuoli square, nothing had changed from the day before: the same people, the same bustle, the same noises, and smells. At the coffee bar across the square, I saw Antonio caught up in a heated discussion. I was tempted to rush over to him, but I hesitated; a secret voice ordered me to remain alone. I was hungry so I bought a *calzone*[16] on my way to the sea. The sun warmed my face, and the thought of returning to England a little tanned pleased me. After a few minutes, I was again observing the marble inscription. This time I looked at it without agitation, without any shocks vibrating down my spine. In fact, I felt no emotion at all. Strange. I sat down on a smooth rock and finished my tasty *calzone*. I looked about with my gaze alternating between the pillars and my surroundings. The sea was as smooth as glass. The seagulls dived among the fishing boats in search of food. As I fixed my eyes on the pillars, I thought it would be lovely to return here in summer. Why not? To return with a friend, with Pauline, for instance. I was sure she would enjoy it. I would have to talk to her nicely and persuade her. Well, my trip to Naples had come to an end. I could already smell the English mist. Mist does not have the same smell everywhere. I can distinguish the mist of my country from many others. I was already sipping my shandy at 'The Red Rose' and chatting with friends. I could already

---

16  A kind of pizza stuffed with cheese and salami or with vegetables.

see myself in Mr Snow's lesson on Monday morning trying to regain my concentration. Perhaps I would miss Naples and all the people I had met. Not perhaps. I would definitely miss them. Difficult to say if we would meet again. But this is life. Events and happenings have a beginning and an end. And it is good that it is this way. This reflects the plan of creation. Is that correct, or am I wrong? I do not know. There's probably only one thing that has a beginning and no end: love. But not all people are lucky enough to find or meet it. I do not know what it depends on. And what about me? I sensed that although still young, I would not experience the good fortune of eternal love. I would not be lucky like my parents, who had met at the age of nineteen and had never been away from each other. My father, the only man for my mother, and she the only woman for him. Was theirs an exceptional case?

Love.

I read in a newspaper that 'love' is one of the most frequently spoken words. I do not know if it is true. I have my doubts. I think that this word is more thought than said aloud. In fact, it is not an easy word to say for many reasons. It is a big word; I would never tell somebody that I loved him if this word was not generated by strong inner feelings.

No. I don't agree with this newspaper.

A seagull, coming from an indistinct point in the sky with its wings spread majestically, landed firmly on top of the column and stared at me with human eyes. It reminded me of the eyes of the seagull that had approached the window at the headmaster's house the day before. Was it the same bird? For a few moments I felt uneasy and fearful, then I decided to sustain its gaze remembering Giulio's words: '... with my magic wand I transform you into a seagull like me!'

- It's you, isn't it?

These words came out of my mouth without my realising it. The bird opened its wings and flapped them as though expressing an emotion that I understood as happiness. Then it flew away. I followed it until it disappeared far, very far away. 'You always vanish into thin air,' I thought.

The inscription was there. Still clear and legible after almost two thousand years. I was looking at those letters carved in the marble perhaps for the last time, then I would turn the page and try to forget this episode of my life once and for all.

- *Forse questo Caio era un mio antenato.* (Perhaps this Caius was one of my ancestors.)

The voice came from behind me.

A voice that I knew. He spoke in Italian.

I instantly jumped up and turned around.

It was him! Giulio!... It was not a hallucination. I had not gone mad, yet. I was perfectly aware and conscious. There he stood: the same haircut, the same expression, the same smile. But he was looking at me as if he had no clue who I was.

- I don't understand Italian... Sorry! – I said still shocked.
- Oh!... You speak English.

Very funny! My heart was bursting. I needed to sit down but I did not want to appear surprised. Now I needed to be strong and clear-headed.

- Yes, I speak English.

I stared at him examining his features to make sure he really was the guy I was looking for.

He looked a bit disoriented. Then he asked:

- Which country do you come from?

Was he joking? No, he was not joking. He was serious.

- I'm from England.

I felt like an actor playing a role on the stage. Was all this a comedy? I decided to test him.

- Now you're going to ask my name, – I went on with my eyes fixed on his. – Then you will ask me if I'd like to have a chat with you, after which you will invite me for a walk. Then you will want to know if I have a boyfriend and little by little you'll try to get me into bed. And finally, you will vanish!

I was being very rude, very uncouth. I had never behaved like this in my life. Was the repressed anger inside me so noxious? The young man shook his head as if to determine if what he had heard was real. His expression became serious. I realised immediately that I was wrong.

- I don't understand, – he exclaimed in a trembling voice.

I was now gripped by a feeling of tenderness and regretted my irrational reaction.

- I'm very sorry, – he continued visibly upset, – if I did or said something wrong. I ask you to forgive me.

A wave of colour flushed my cheeks. What a shame! I felt like a horrible person.

- I-I apologise... – I stammered avoiding his eyes, – a misunderstanding... You said something in Italian...I misunderstood the meaning...

A hint of a smile reappeared on his lips. I no longer knew what to think, what to say, what to do. I no longer knew who I was or if all this was real or another dream.

- Ok, ok... come on, cheer up! – He comforted me, – Everything is clear now. It's my fault... I was simply saying that this Caius was probably one of my ancestors...

- Really? Why do you think so?

- Hahaha!... I'm not an exception... All the locals are convinced they still have a few drops of Roman blood in their veins... May I ask you what you are doing here? Are you a tourist? An archaeologist?

I was just thinking the same thing: what was I doing there? I was neither a tourist nor an archaeologist. I was just... what? A disappointed sweetheart... just a dreamer or a stupid girl. I definitely felt part of a theatre. The theatre of the absurd. In the whirlpool of images that streamed crazily in this mysterious meander of my – (what?) mind? Consciousness?

Subconscious?... – Is it the same for everybody? I was reminded of Samuel Beckett with his two bedraggled companions waiting for an unspecified person called Godot... who would never arrive! Who or what, then, was my Godot? Giulio or simply an emotion or gift of life called 'love'?

In the silence that preceded my answer, I averted my eyes from the *ghost* and looked around me. The sky suddenly darkened due to the huge clouds hiding the sun. And the smooth surface of the sea suddenly lost its serenity and rough waves rolled up. There was no one else around. Just two characters on the stage. No. Three. Me, Giulio, and the marble column. I tried to imagine what this place had been like almost two thousand years earlier. The sea did not come in as far, and in its place there were streets, buildings, people. The scenery and the people that had haunted my dreams. Had I really been here before? If so, which of the two was the real Helen? And the same applied to *him*. Which of the two was the real Giulio?

- I don't know who I am, – I answered with my eyes turned to the column.

I was a bit daydreamy. The merry-go-round in my head was having a strange effect on me. For a few moments, I feared I would faint again as I had the previous day. I needed to be strong and control myself.

- My name is Helen. – I continued as though talking to myself.

- Elen!

- Helen.

- Ah! Sorry... Helen.

- Helen Barry.

There was a rock near me where I had sat the day before when I had felt light-headed. I approached it slowly and sat down bringing my hands to my face. Then I propped my elbows on my knees and, supporting my chin on my clenched fists, I looked at him again.

- Does my name remind you of anything? – I asked curious about his answer.

I noticed that the young man was not looking at me as he had in the first instance. Now he was somewhat distant and certainly cautious following my rude reaction.

- Nothing at all.

His words were clear, leaving no room for doubt. Putting myself in his shoes, I might have had the same attitude. What could he think of this strange girl standing alone in front of the sea staring at an old eroded marble column?

- And what about me? – He went on after a few seconds. – Do I remind you of anybody or of anything?

- Yes, – I replied firmly.

Giulio laughed letting go of his cautiousness and once again adopted a friendly and relaxed tone. I felt better.

- People say that each of us has seven doubles.

- I've heard that too.

- And what or whom do I remind you of, if you don't mind me asking?

- I met an Italian boy at the college I'm attending in Wales who reminds me of you.

- Of me? In Wales!... I have never been there... I have never been to the UK. But I'm going there very soon...

- I'm almost sure you're studying English literature at university.

He shook his head as if incredulous at what he had just heard.

- Are you a clairvoyant? You must have magic powers.

His expression changed again. I understood that my self-confidence intimidated him. I was sorry but I wanted to continue the game until I understood what was going on. He stepped towards me until he was almost touching me. I did not move until he asked:

- May I sit next to you?... If you don't mind.

My heart was an earthquake, my face flushed again. There was very little room on the rock but I moved as far to my right as I could to let him sit down. Our bodies touched, I inhaled his familiar scent. This is what the beast inside me wanted. Him. Without a doubt. Since last Monday, I had been savouring our intimacy on the couch, so it was all I could do to curb a burst of excitement. I was wrong: he did not look intimidated at all. It was he who had the upper hand on me.

- I want to get a better look at your eyes, – he said staring at me and examining my pupils. – Your irises will tell me who you are.

I didn't know how serious he was in what he was saying or if he was just joking.

- Watch out, Mr Imprudence! – I tried to tackle him. – I might be a dangerous witch brought here by the cold wind of the North.

He laughed and put his arm around my shoulders. Just as he had done last Monday. My first instinct was to break free… but I didn't.

- How can you be so bold as to hug a girl you don't know? – I asked rather strictly. – Do you do the same with all the girls you meet?… Especially strangers?

- Not exactly, beautiful witch!… But you've just said that you have met me before, at your college…so you know a lot about me… But how can you know this? That means that there must have been something special between us.

He continued to stare at me with his penetrating eyes, our faces almost touching. We breathed each other. It all came back to me.

- Are you going to college to improve your English? – I asked.

- No.

- No?

- No... You see, you lied. A true witch would know what I'm going to do in Britain.

He released me and got up nervously, changing his mood again.

- Actually, I don't know, – he said stepping back pensively. Then he stood up in front of me. – I really don't know.... There's something I want to tell you. It's an incredible story. I haven't told anyone.

- What?

- People wouldn't believe me. Even my closest friends would say that I'm mad; they would take me to a psychiatrist!

It was me who laughed this time.

- Me too, I have an incredible story to tell, – I said continuing my laughter. – But, please, tell me yours first, then I will tell you mine...and afterwards... We will go to a mental hospital together... Hahahahaha!!!

He showed me an innocent smile. I was glad that the atmosphere between us had become more relaxed. I felt that little by little, we were becoming reacquainted.

- I'm persecuted by a doll, – he started.

- What!?... By a doll? What do you mean?

- As you know... as you proved that you know... I study English literature and last month I had to sit a difficult test on James Joyce... I'm sure you're familiar with him.

I was bewildered. Instantly, my whole body erupted into goosebumps. I nodded.

- I dreamt of a doll dressed in purple and white... – he continued – an English doll holding the book 'Ulysses' in her hands. That was the first time. Two nights later, she came into my dream again telling me that this book was too difficult for her, so she would remove it from her bookcase. I said that I would read it and explain it to her one day but not then because I was very busy. She seemed to understand and for a few nights I didn't dream of her. Then she reappeared; almost every night she was with me. She didn't behave like a doll... Well, I mean, she always appeared like a doll but she behaved like a normal woman, as if she was my wife.

He stopped talking and looked at me checking that I could understand him. Of course, I was thinking of Lucy. Now I was more curious than astonished. The incredible events that had occurred in the last couple of weeks had happened so quickly one after the other that nothing could shock me further.

- Go ahead, – I encouraged him. – I believe everything you're telling me.

- Thanks... I feel relieved now. There's not much more to say... For a few weeks she became an obsession, I saw her during the day too. I loved her so much that it hurt. A strange kind of suffering caused by undistinguished feelings and sensations. I loved her soul and I felt like she was my wife, but at the same time, I wondered how I could love a doll and consider her real enough, and take her seriously enough, to do all the things with her that a man does with a woman. I was angry at myself and at the same time, this anger was mixed with compassion and a deep concern that I could love a doll. She understood my worries and my sorrow, so one night she told me that she wouldn't visit me in my sleep anymore until she could be transformed into a real woman. Before disappearing, she gave me her name and address. Now I have decided to go and see her.

I could hardly catch my breath! So overwhelming were my emotions.

- What's her name? – I asked anxious to know. – Lucy?
- No.

He took his wallet and pulled out a small piece of paper and showed me what was on it. Ailla, 40 Pindale Road, Castleton, Derbyshire.

Ailla... Everything was clear now. Lucy... Ailla...Helen... One person: me!... Ailla wanted her energies to live in me to be a messenger, a connecting cable between me – Helen/Ailla – and Giulio... Was this guy's name Giulio? He had not told me yet.

- Are we friends now? – He wanted to know
- Definitely.
- What do you think of this absurd story?... Am I insane?... This is the proof, this little piece of paper that I found on my bed when the doll came into my dream the last time.
- Relax now; I will help you to find her... if you want.
- Really? Thanks. I would really appreciate that.
- I'm from Castleton and I know this address very well.

He looked dumbstruck and dazed; perhaps he thought that I was lying or joking, so incredible was the coincidence.

- Truly, reality often goes beyond fancy. – He asserted.

It was time to reveal who I was.

- Two weeks ago I met you at my college, – I said. – We started talking and I asked you your name, you told me at once. After some time I told you mine. Today we are doing the same.

- Ah! You seem absolutely convinced that I attended your college... My name is popular in this town; it's linked with a legend... You were looking at him...

- Caius Iulius!...

Giulio stepped towards the sea.

- My name is known by everybody here, – he said enthusiastically. – It is written everywhere. People here have been saying this name for hundreds and hundreds of years... Ask, ask anyone. Ask the things around you. Ask the wind, the waves, the seagulls... The seagulls know; ask them.

He walked up to me, took my hand and gently pulled me towards the water.

- Seeeeeeeaaaaaguuuuullllls! – he shouted in frantic excitement. – What's my name?.... Whaaaaaatttsssmyyyynaaaame?

A solitary seagull alighted on the top of a fishing boat not far away.

- Say my name, say my name. Come on, old friend, you know everything about me.

Inspired, he continued speaking to the bird with a resounding voice:

- 'The ice was here, the ice was there, the ice was all around: it cracked and growled, and roared and howled, like noises in a swound! At length did cross an Albatross, through the fog it came; as it had been a Christian soul, we hailed it in God's name.'

He went on enraptured by something in Italian that I could not understand.

- Yes, Giu-lio Va-le-rio, – he declared keeping his eyes fixed on the seagull. – Giulio Valerio.

- Giulio Valerio, – I repeated watching his dreamy look.

This was the final confirmation. Giulio Valerio. At last, like the sea after a storm, I finally felt at peace. There was nothing else I wanted to know. Here was Giulio. My hand was still in his, like last Monday night when we were walking to the pub, like in the dream, in front of the same sea. The seagull took off from the mast and began riding the wind. Soon a second seagull joined him as if they had a *rendezvous*. Swooping down towards us they performed a fast pirouette and circled us a couple of times. Then they turned upwards, soaring ever higher over the sea until they merged with the sky.

- It's taken almost two thousand years to meet you again!

It was the headmaster who spoke. He had walked up to us without our noticing him. His white wind-ruffled hair gave him the look of a prophet.

- As the fourth character on the stage of your story, I couldn't miss the last scene where the end and the beginning are one. My long investigation is finished and here, in the name of truth and love, I hand over the keys to happiness.

Antonio fell silent, turned and slowly walked towards the square.

It started raining. We did not mind. I had not realised that big tears were streaming down my face. I still do not know if I was laughing or crying. I felt only happiness – an unrestrained, irrepressible bliss. I was unable to speak. Giulio touched my cheeks with his fingertips and began to gently caress them. Perhaps he wanted to say something but, placing my hand on his lips, I stopped him. In an irrepressible outburst of enthusiasm, I kissed him and hugged him tightly.

At last, I had found my love.

*"Yada bhuta-prthag-bhavam
eka-stham anupasyati
tata eva ca vistaram
brahma sampadyate tada"*

*"When a sensible man ceases to see different identities, which are due to different material bodies, he attains to the Brahman conception. Thus he sees that beings are expanded everywhere."*

*(Bhagavad Gita – Chapter 31: Nature, the Enjoyer, and Consciousness)*

# MATTEO REVIVES

## MILAN (ITALY)

- Help!!!... My hair's on fire! Mum, Dad, help me! I'm burning!
- Francesco!... What happened? Try not to panic! – Marina shouted as she grabbed a towel and raced over to him. She covered her son's head in the towel and led him into the bathroom to run cold water over the burn.

And turning to her husband:
- I've told you dozens of times not to let Francesco get too close to the fireplace when there are sparks from the coal... Matteo, are you listening to me?

*Pluuuuffff!*

Scorched hair. Sour smell. Colourful eyes. A tiger's colourful eyes. Smoke.

In the air. In the nostrils. Inside.

Deeper and deeper.

Maaaaaattttttteeeeeoooooo!!!!

Maaaaaattttttteeeeeoooooo!!!!

From within.

Someone had called him from the darkest and innermost part of his soul. From inside, from where the smell had penetrated. The smell of scorched hair. Minute nauseating particles of unmistakable disgust. On the tongue, in the throat, in the stomach, in the gut. Sensations mingled with images: smoke, fire, olive-coloured skin, snakes, a big, beautiful, gold house...red flowers... red flowers everywhere... and the silhouette of a tiger. A blurred outline.

It was not the first time that Matteo had felt like that. It had happened at least three times before. Each time, he fell into a kind of trance. A mysterious voice from within would call him, and he would feel himself descending into another world far removed in time and space. Although it seemed to Matteo that it had gone on for hours, the whole experience lasted only a few seconds.

- Matteo! - Marina exclaimed, carefully observing her husband. – You're as white as a ghost... Are you worried about Francesco?

- No, – he answered, slowly coming to his senses. – Sometimes something strange happens to me. I feel as though something takes me far away and I lose consciousness.

The woman approached her husband looking very concerned.

- Look how pale you are. You need a doctor. You don't look well at all.

- Nonsense.

- No, it isn't nonsense. Look at yourself in the mirror. Even your lips have turned white.

- It's nothing, trust me. If I say that it's nothing, I mean it. It's happened to me before.

- Why didn't you ever say anything?

- It didn't seem important.

- Well, what's the matter with you? There must be a reason for this.

- What I can't understand is the way this phenomenon occurs. It seems somehow related to burning smells, such as scorched skin, nails, or hair. Yet, it never happens when I smell burning wood or paper. Then I feel myself plunged into another reality as if I'm returning to a familiar environment... to a life I've already lived.

- Darling, don't tell me you believe in these idiocies! You're a modern man. You manage an important firm. Your position is envied by everybody. How can you think such things?!

- Try to understand me, please. I'm not telling you I've

lived before, because I don't believe that. But I feel there is something mysterious going on and I want to find out what it is.

- You could discuss it with doctor Lanzoni.

- Don't talk to me about doctors, please, not now. You know what I think of them.

- It wouldn't be the end of the world if you asked him for some advice... You know, you have been working too hard lately. Have a rest and you'll see that all will be well.

Matteo's life was very stressful indeed. His many obligations and responsibilities gave him little time for himself and his family. He had not been on holiday for years. Lately he had been feeling the type of fatigue that comes from nervous exhaustion. Furthermore, he had become highly-strung. He became easily irritable with friends, intractable with customers, and unbearable to his employees. He realised that Marina was right. He needed a rest. He wouldn't worry about these strange episodes connected with fire.

His past experiences, however, kept recurring in his mind. The first time, when he was a boy, one of his friends had scorched his hands on a pan of boiling water. Then, ten years ago, he witnessed a cottage fire where a woman had been burnt to a cinder. A few months after that, a child had singed his leg on the exhaust of Matteo's motorbike. Each time, the smell of the burnt flesh had produced the same reactions.

The call.

Maaaaattttteeeooooo!

Maaaaattttteeeooooo!

A voice from afar, but clear, distinct.

And the images.

*Pluuuuufffff...*

Flames. Dark faces. A mansion in the style of eastern architecture with large, wonderful halls...

*Pluuuuuufffff!*

Colourscolourscolours....Colours everywhere... A woman is dipping her feet in a strange red liquid... A woman... Young. Just a flash. He can't see her face. But one night he had a dream where he was swimming in a river made of this red liquid. It was not blood. It was thick, like glue... Swiiiimswiiiimswiiiimswiiiim...

'I must make sense of this,' he said to himself one day, while relaxing for a moment in his office. 'But how? I should confide in somebody, but in whom? If I tell doctor Lanzoni, he will fill me with medicines and suggest I take a rest... Wait! Jacopo! Yes, Jacopo. Whatever happened to that crazy guy?'

Jacopo had been one of his schoolfellows; an extraordinary boy interested in the occult and paranormal phenomena. In their younger years they had been the best of friends. At university, however, they studied different subjects and had slowly drifted apart. Perhaps Jacopo was the right person to tell his problem to. He could give him a reasonable explanation. Matteo quickly consulted the telephone directory... Here he is: Dr Levi. That's him. He dialled without delay.

- Hello! – came the immediate reply.

- Hello, Jacopo, it's me, Matteo. I bet you don't remember me, do you?

- Matteo... Matteo Moscardi, of course! – The other exclaimed after hesitating briefly. – How could I forget you? I've heard that you are rich and famous now.

- Ah, less of that, things are not what they seem... I'd like to talk to you as soon as possible. When can I see you?

- Today, if you like. Come to my office after five so we can have a long chat. Ok?

- Perfect. I really appreciate it. I'll see you about five then.

Matteo was sure his friend would be able to help him. He already felt calmer on hearing Jacopo's voice and for a while was able to set his mind to his most pressing tasks... Then memories from school time flooded into his mind. Many thoughts from that wonderful past came back to him. When he was seventeen, he met his first girlfriend, Maria. In the decades that followed he would sometimes recall his emotions and special moments of that innocent love, and would confirm to himself the truth of the saying: 'you never forget your first love'. She attended the same school but was in the year below. Glances had already started a year before, then a few words while passing each other in the corridors or in the playground before lessons began. The turning point came at the end-of-year school party. They had their first slow dance during which he realised how much he liked her. Immediately afterwards, however, she was invited to dance by another boy and Matteo became jealous. The other boy asked her for a second dance without letting go of her hand, while a mix of aggression and pain in the stomach of his rival almost caused a sort of explosion. He was able to calm down only when, at the end of the second dance, he swooped in while the boy was distracted by one of his friends. Throughout the evening he did not leave her side. This was the start of the first and strongest relationship of his youth.

Jacopo's office was situated in the centre of town, on the third floor of an old building. While waiting for the lift, Matteo felt unusually anxious. He didn't know whether this was due to the anticipation of seeing his old friend again, or to the fear of discovering something about himself as yet unforeseen and unpleasant.

- You haven't changed at all! – Matteo exclaimed on seeing Jacopo, – you still look like a man of twenty.

This was not an empty compliment. Jacopo was in excellent shape. He had a boyish look, a full head of hair, a lean physique, and large, penetrating eyes.

- Thank you, – Jacopo replied. – I can't say the same about you; you look heavier and older. Your hair's almost grey.

- The effect of stress, you know… A long time has passed since we were at school. Do you remember?

*Lie on the bed, try to sustain my gaze as long as possible.*

- I remember everything, my old friend, and sometimes I long for the past very much. I miss those carefree times. Above all I miss the friends of my youth... Life speeds on, and we lose enthusiasm for the genuine and simple things.

- Time has brought us money, but what good is that?

- Tell me now, what brings you here?

Matteo sat down in a small armchair facing the doctor. He immediately began his story. At first he talked with difficulty and reluctance, but gradually he gained confidence. Jacopo listened to him attentively, without interruption. When Matteo had finished, he observed:

- Your story makes me think that you have been reincarnated, but you don't want to accept this possibility, do you?

- I haven't had the time to think about it. It's not easy talking about these things to others... And the very idea frightens me, terrifies me... No, I don't believe in it.

- So, how do you explain it?

- That's why I'm here. You tell me! You're the doctor.

- Then, trust me. You have known me for a long time.

- I do trust you.

Jacopo stared at him with a forceful intensity making Matteo feel uneasy then concluded:

- I'm telling you, you have lived before in another body.

Matteo felt Jacopo's words pierce his flesh like deadly arrows certain of their target.

- Jacopo, what are you saying? You're a well-respected professional, a physician, a man of science. I can't understand, – Matteo stammered. – I can't understand how you're convinced that... that I've been reincarnated.

- My friend, to be a man of science does not mean you must deny the spirit... and your spirit has lived before in another body.

Matteo nervously ran his hands through his hair and looked around as if seized by a sudden fear.

- Don't be afraid, – Jacopo went on. There's nothing to worry about. One person in ten has lived before, and you are one of them.

- It's absurd... It's crazy. If anyone found out, they'd think I was ridiculous. I'm a well-respected man, the same as you, everybody knows me and...

- Do you want to know the truth or not? – Jacopo sharply interrupted. – I can help you if you like. You'll feel much better afterwards.

Matteo calmed down. He could no longer run from the truth. He had to know who and what was hidden in his inner self. Yet, he hoped wholeheartedly that he would prove Jacopo wrong.

- Yes, I want to know, – he said at last.

- Good!... I realise this topic... I mean even talking about reincarnation is a taboo in our country, but the possibility exists, believe me. Now trust me and don't worry.

The doctor got up and went into another room. After a while he came back with a guinea pig. He took a syringe and injected a few drops of liquid into the poor little animal. It gasped for a few seconds then collapsed heavily with its legs apart, lifeless.

- What are you doing? – Matteo asked disgusted at such cruelty.

- I'm preparing an experiment.

- What kind of experiment?

- From this moment you must only answer my questions. Lie on the bed, try to sustain my gaze as long as possible. While I'm staring at you, try to concentrate intensely on the experience you just described to me.

Jacopo drew the curtains and placed a lamp with a reddish light close to Matteo's face. He turned the recorder on then went over and stood in front of him and started to stare in between his eyes, just at the top of his nose. The smell of the

# IDENTITIES REDISCOVERED

*- Are you a man or a woman?*
*- A woman.*

small, burning animal filled the air. The patient succumbed to the doctor's stare and to the smell. His mind became blurred and his eyelids closed like a falling curtain on the stage of his present life. At the same moment another curtain rose beyond which a strange world far in distance and time kidnapped him... Palms, flames, smells of burning flesh...

Here it is; it's coming.

Acrid smoke. In the stomach. Inside. Deeper and deeper. In the soul.

A loss. A precipice.

The absorption of consciousness. No longer himself.

His inner self in another being.

Maaaaaaatttttteeeeeeoooooooo!!!!!

Maaaaaaatttttteeeeeeoooooooo!!!!!

The white house. Heat. A huge heap of branches from rubber trees. Dark skinned people.

The lamp with the reddish light in his past. The guinea pig in the fire. Where? When? The present and the past at times merged or overlapped disorienting him in a dimension-free space and chronology. Jacopo realised that he was using a different procedure from his usual cases. He wondered if it had been necessary and correct to hypnotise this man who was now in a trance. Perhaps he had been too hasty. He placed his hand between the lamp and Matteo's eyes then asked:

- What's your name?
- My name is Subhadra Gosvami.

The tone of Matteo's voice had changed. It was now warm and clear.

- Are you a man or a woman?
- A woman.
- Where are you?
- In Cossimbazar, in West Bengal.[17]

---

17  To better understand this story it is necessary to give some information on the historical and social context of the time in which it takes place. Following the Battle of Plassey on 23 June 1757, the last Nawab

- What is the date and what are you doing?

Matteo shook his head violently and spoke incoherently, as if he was delirious.

- Again, what's the day and what are you doing? – Jacopo insisted in a strong tone.

His friend hesitated for a few moments then answered clearly:

- It's five o'clock in the morning, the fourth of January 1835. I'm in a wonderful room, sitting at the side of a golden bed made of silk. White veils are above the corpse of my husband, Ram Chund Pundit, who was from one of the many clans of the Mahratta caste.

- How old are you both?

- Chund is twenty-five years old... I'm nineteen.

Matteo paused, looking confused. He was sweating slightly.

- I know what my destiny is, – he continued after a few minutes. – Brahmin Ādiśūra is standing at the other side of the bed. He is meditating and praying... His presence in my life is very important... A child is crying somewhere. Not in the room where I am... Perhaps next door... I mean, a large room called Kali's[18] room. Instinctively I want to go to him but something impedes me from moving. I don't know what. He must be my child. Yes, he's my son... The goddess Kali

---

of Bengal was defeated by the British. The end of his reign marked the start of the rule of the British East India Company in Bengal. Although the traditions and religions were generally respected by the British, some were not tolerated. It was Governor William Bentinck who banned sati by law in 1829, supported by reformer Raja Ram Mohan Roy. Sati or suttee was the act or custom of a Hindu widow burning herself on the funeral pyre of her husband. The abolition of this old practice was not welcomed by a part of the aristocracy. Krishna Kanta Nandy, called Cantoo, (1720-1794), was a successful rich merchant at Cossimbazar (or Kasim Bazar) when he became banyan to Warren Hastings serving him until his departure for England. When Cantoo died, he was succeeded by his son Lokenath, who was also the first 'Maharajah'. The town of Cossimbazar is on the river of Bhagirathi, a tributary of the Ganges river.

18  Kali is a Hindu goddess.

will protect him... Her eyes are set in a column; they watch and see everything. Ram Chund's most trustworthy servant, Iswar, approaches the corpse and gently pulls the ring off his finger. The ring set with a delicate pink diamond is mainly a symbol of this clan, but not only. It is handed down from the father to the firstborn son when he gets married. It is said to have extraordinary powers besides the fact that it unites the body and the mind. For those who believe in these things, the value of these stones cannot be quantified. Regarding this specific one, the convincement and beliefs are that it has the power to curse or to bring good fortune to the bearer, but nobody has been able to ascertain what the choice made by the stone, considered more as a living being than an object, depends on. It is said that the energies of evil gave this stone its power... I don't know... Ram's father and grandfather, who were *zamindars*[19] had been lucky. The family had grown in power and wealth. It turned out to be a curse for Ram. After the ring is taken off, it emits such an intense fluorescence that it looks like a star. The servant should hide it in a secret place that only he, myself and my husband know about. Tradition dictates that the husband share this secret with his wife, and, if he chooses, with one or more persons selected by him. Devesh will not find it. The Brahmin diverts his attention from his meditation and looks at me as if expecting something. I know what it is. I declare that I am ready to be burned alive.

Silence again.

- Why do you want to die? - Jacopo asked - Who is Devesh? Why do you want to burn?

- Our religion obliges us to... I am a *sati* and the wife of an important man. A *sati* must sacrifice herself on the pyre to accompany her husband into the next life... Amir... Benjamin... Benjamin.

---

19  In Mogul India he was a collector of farm revenue who paid a fixed sum on the district assigned to him. In British India he was a landlord required to pay a land tax to the government.

New interruption.

- Who are these people? – Jacopo pressed.
- Who?
- Amir and Benjamin. Who are they?
- Amir is my baby. He's only three months old. What will happen to him?... My only hope is Ben.
- Ben is short for Benjamin? Tell me everything. Go on!
- I'll try. I want to... It's difficult, it's not very clear... wait... now the people and events are becoming more vivid. Benjamin is a British officer who's very close to Governor William Bentinck. He is the commander of a small garrison of British soldiers commissioned by the Governor. There are other garrisons depending on the British East India Company[20]... Ben's is different, all the soldiers are British... I thought he would come in time. My hope is almost completely vanished...
- What do you mean? Your hope of what is almost vanished?
- That he would save me from the pyre since this practice is illegal... I was sure he would come to save me. Something must have prevented him from coming... There have been many tensions between the Governor and Mahratta clans – and not only with them – because of the abolition of *sati*. This practice dates back to remote times, so aristocrats consider the ban blasphemy, an inconceivable violation of their traditions and religion... Don't cry. Amir, don't cry. I will protect you from above. Believe me, my son... I am preparing myself for the pyre. First I must pray with the Brahmins and then purify

---

20  The British East India Company was a privately owned company which was established to create profitable trade with countries in the region of Asia called the "East Indies". Granted a Royal Charter by Queen Elizabeth in 1600, it became one of the most powerful mercantile organisations in the world by maintaining a monopoly on the importation of exotic goods (notably cotton, tea, and silk) from India into Britain. It also maintained a standing military, which was used in many cases to consolidate and enforce local authority in Indian territories. Official Company rule of India, or raj, began in 1757, and was in full swing during the Romantic period, only coming to a close in 1858 following a bloody uprising and revolution. (web.utk.edu)

my spirit in the Ganges river. After bathing, I will spend some time with my female relatives... I will ask my relatives and Brahmins for permission to meditate for the last time before the flames devour my body. Permission is granted to me and I step aside to be alone... I can't concentrate. I don't have the strength to pray. Only my memories, sometimes they are all mixed together, other times they follow in quick succession or intermittently. I didn't know Ram Chund before marrying him. In our country marriages are arranged by our families when we are still children and very often the bride and groom do not know each other. I felt relieved when I met Ram the first time. He was not old, he was not ugly, he was always elegantly dressed and above all, he was kind. I had been lucky compared to the awful men that other girls are obliged to marry. The wedding party was splendid, it lasted almost one week and hundreds and hundreds of guests attended... *Plufff!* ... Before... before crossing the threshold of the new house where I will live with my husband, I have to stop to dip my feet in a mixture of milk and *alta*[21] in order to leave red footsteps behind me. I don't know if the feeling that invades me can be called happiness, perhaps it can, I am happy... Flowersflowersflowers... the bed.... Red, red flowers, yellow. And silk embroidered with gold. The many guests have disappeared, the many lights turned off, the voices fall silent and the music quietens to respect the complicity of the silence that surrounds the couple. The time of expectations is over; the prenuptial imagination gives way to allow reality to take its course. The stars, like brilliant diamonds set in the endless dark cloak of the sky, discreetly pierce the mysteries of the night. The erotic echoes of our panting bodies crash like cymbals shattering the windows, breaking through the walls and all barriers, invading the jungle and all that is part of it. Everybody and everything will know and must know that this

---

21  Rose Bengal, a red dye which women in India apply on their feet during their wedding ceremony.

is the young married couple's first night of love. The sensitive ear of the jungle listens and understands and finally responds in a single voice. At first it seems like a gasp then it gains strength and power expressing his proud dominion over everything that surrounds him in an unmistakeable roar: the Bengal tiger, the honour of expressing the jungle's blessing belongs to him.

Matteo gulped a couple of times interrupting his narration. Jacopo took a glass of water, then soaked a wad of cotton wool in the water and gently squeezed it on the lips of the patient quenching his thirst with single drops. While doing so, he looked at the hypnotised man carefully examining the colour of his face immersed in an apparent quietness. Only his pupils, under closed eyelids, moved imperceptibly as though following different directions or objects. Matteo's content and way of narrating had astonished Jacopo, though used to listening to stories told under hypnosis. It was clear that he had belonged to the world of Hinduism, a religion that unequivocally makes reincarnation the mandatory path towards purification. He had never had a similar case so he considered this one a good opportunity to refresh his knowledge of Hinduism... He had followed interesting courses in ethnology and the history of religions at university, which had equipped him with a bounty of knowledge and this had influenced his future choices. Continuing his studies and research after graduating, he had come to the conclusion that the greatest religions have many things in common especially regarding the concept of good and evil. The meaning of existence is where differences appear. Although brought up in a Christian background, now as a scholar and scientist, he didn't like to be labelled with a specific religion.

- You're slowly finding yourself and your identity, – Jacopo said. – Please, go on, you were describing your happiness during the first night of your marriage. You were in a bed of flowers...

- Yes... The tiger is beautiful... The tiger is the most beautiful creature of nature after Man. If I had the possibility to choose where and how to be born a second or third time, I'd be reincarnated as a tiger... We lived in a mansion outside the town on the edge of the evergreen forest. As often happens, this happiness was unexpectedly short-lived. Ram became ill. A relentless muscular disease took possession of his body devastating him. At first I didn't realise the seriousness of his illness. I was young and inexperienced besides the fact that his entire family was trying to hide the truth. I became aware of it little by little; I felt terrible, words cannot express what I went through... Ram was an intelligent and sensitive person... He was on top of me... One night, some time ago... not long after our wedding, he lay on top of me wrestling between the desire to possess me and the disease that did not allow him to express his power. Surrendering to his weakness he fell into the grip of despair and depression. 'I'm pregnant,' I told him one day. 'I'm carrying your baby.' Nothing. He decided to renounce me forever, closing and retreating into a gloomy silence and hiding from the world. Very few people were allowed to see him. Among them, his most faithful servant and his *guru*.[22] I heard that the *guru* was the only person capable of relieving his suffering and of giving him the strength to survive. As for me, I entrusted myself to the Brahmin Ādiśūra, who helped me to fight my loneliness. My family was far away. Even if they had been closer, nothing would have changed. When a daughter gets married in India, she becomes estranged from her parents, and for some reasons that I have never really understood, Ram's family kept aloof from me despite the Brahmin having reproached them for their behaviour. Ram's mother, Huddar, was a close relative of the Maharajah who died in 1794 and this kinship injected an arrogance in her even towards her husband and the Brahmin. A very unusual

---

22  Reverential figure, teacher and spiritual guide.

attitude considered to be very bad in Indian society where the superiority of the man is indisputable. The fact is that I was not allowed to see my husband anymore and I was relegated to a wing of the mansion with my servants. In the meantime, the presence of one of Ram's cousins became more and more cumbersome. His name was Devesh... Devesh.

Matteo stopped. In many cases the hypnotised person needs to be prompted with questions when he stops speaking for a long period. This favours the continuity of memories. And I didn't want him to get off track. His story had started to intrigue me. But it had been thirty minutes. The session could last only a few more minutes; the usual allotted time was already over.

- Why has Devesh become a cumbersome presence? – Jacopo asked interested in the fact that his friend had used such a strong word.

- The structure of the family in India is traditionally patriarchal, – Matteo said apparently ignoring the doctor's question. – The family generally consists of three or four generations living together in the same household... The mansion was huge but we didn't live in a very traditional way because, unlike most other families, Ram's parents had few brothers and sisters; they also used to spend entire months with their other son, Ajar, who lived on the north side of Cossimbazar with his wife's family... Brahmins are the highest rank in Indian society...They are priests, teachers and judges. They generally do not have contact with lower castes so as not to be contaminated.

The man's way of talking had now changed. He seemed to be aware that he was talking to somebody unfamiliar with the cultural background of where he had lived before and wanted to give information about the characteristics of that society. 'He is conscious that he has an interlocutor,' Jacopo thought. 'Yes, he is living simultaneously in two different realities; he is trying to help me understand the socio-cultural context of his past life. But what is his identity while speaking?... "...before crossing the threshold of the new house where I will live with my husband...", "... he was on top of me wrestling between the desire to possess me...". A woman, undoubtedly a woman. His emotions were those of a female. While speaking, he had abandoned his male gender. But, is his narration the result of the hypnosis or of the effect of the trance caused by the burned guinea pig?' He went back to his university studies and remembered that not all professors agreed to follow a strict procedure in this profession. The psychological understanding and intuition of the patient is essential in order to achieve good results... Stages of hypnotherapy: preparation, induction, deepening, utilisation, termination...

- I asked you about Devesh. Why was his presence cumbersome? – Jacopo repeated.

- He is a bad man, unfaithful to his wife... His father and Ram's father are at loggerheads because of disputes over property.

- Did he treat you badly?

- Yes; he wanted me to be his lover... He wanted my body and Ram's ring... Wait!... The preparation of the sacrificial pyre is beginning. I see a bower made of bamboo, dry branches and leaves, and now I see my husband's body placed on the pyre. The Brahmins begin the sacred reading from the *Bhagavad Gita*[23] and ask me questions. I place a leaf on the fire and circle it three times. I enter into a trance. Now I am ready and walk towards my destiny. I make a last bow to my relatives, and the Brahmins give me a final blessing. I now enter the pyre. I kneel and honour the body of my husband. I then sit down, totally absorbed in the words of *Bhagavad Gita*. The fire! In a second, my dress, my hair – my whole body – is engulfed in flames. I shriek, yell, screeaamm. Unbearable pain. Suddenly I don't

---

23  Ancient sacred Indian text.

feel anything. My soul is leaving my body. I can see and smell my body burning, but I am free! I fly higher and higher where I can see fantastic colours, indescribable colours. A choir of thousands of voices singing the verses of the *Bhagavad Gita*... and then... and then...

- Go on, go on. What do you see? Carry on.

- I don't know, I can't see anything else, everything is confused... I perceive somebody from afar, he seems to be coming towards me, but I'm not sure...

- Go on, try to understand. What can you see and hear?

- I hear singing, like a choir. It's incredible... The voices of angels. No words can describe it. Now I'm entering a giant cloud. There is only mist. I can't see anything else.

Matteo wasn't able to continue.

- Wake up! Wake up now. – The doctor ordered, then he switched off the lamp and went to open the window.

The patient opened his eyes and slowly and cautiously looked around.

- So, can you remember anything? – Jacopo asked, after the other had come round.

The man, still confused, rose from the bed and ran his fingers through his hair. In front of him, in an iron waste basket, was the poor guinea pig completely carbonised. He began to recall a few incidents from his dream...

- Yes, it seems that I have been dreaming, – he answered, trying to interpret Jacopo's serious expression.

- Now I can help you.

Jacopo repeated a few of Matteo's words. Then he took out the micro cassette from the recorder and handed it to him.

- You can listen to it at home. Your story is really fantastic and full of mysteries... In my opinion, you need at least one more session. But you can decide after reflecting on what you hear on the tape... Your origin comes from this place.

He pointed to Bengal on the globe next to him.... –

Cossimbazar... Look. I had never heard of this place before.

Matteo focused his attention on the town indicated.

- It's impossible. It was just a dream... a nightmare. A woman!... Me?!... Unbelievable. Please, keep this to yourself. If it gets out, then I'll become a laughing stock!

- It wasn't a nightmare. Your subconscious took you back to the past.

- How can you believe that?

- Sooner or later you, too, will be convinced that it's true.

- Why and how?

- Because now, what we did here, has enabled a connection between your conscious and your unconscious. After hearing the recording several times and after the next session, you will be able to dig into your past without being hypnotised. Your memories will become clearer and clearer and your past will reveal to you everything that you want to know.

- Perhaps you're right. In a way I feel better, as if I've rid myself of a heavy burden... Yet, in the scenery of my 'past life', as you say, there are some elements that could prove your theory wrong. There are symbols that each of us has in our subconscious... such as the ring, the stone... that come from legends... from I don't know where.

Jacopo roared with laughter.

- The ring, the diamond, – he said sarcastically, – typical symbols of legends and fairy tales that are buried in the foundations of our subconscious and that *it*, – the subconscious – enjoys reminding us of during our nightly dreams...

The doctor went over to his bookcase and took down a book. From where he was standing, Matteo was able to read the title: 'Man and his Symbols, Carl G. Jung'. Jacopo began to read studiously then asked his patient:

- How long have we known each other? You remember that since we shared the same desk at school, I have always been interested in, and enjoyed, psychology. What do you think I have been doing all these years? .... This! – He opened the book. – I've been studying and doing research.

– I believe you. I don't doubt you at all.

– Listen! – He leafed through the book, then lingered on a page and read: – '... As a matter of history, it was the study of dreams that first enabled psychologists to investigate the unconscious aspect of conscious psychic events. It is on such evidence that psychologists assume the existence of an unconscious psyche – though many scientists and philosophers deny its existence. They argue naively that such an assumption implies the existence of two "subjects" or two personalities within the same individual. But this is exactly what it does imply, quite correctly.... ....Whoever denies the existence of the unconscious is in fact assuming that our present knowledge of the psyche is total. And this belief is clearly just as false as the assumption that we know all there is to be known about the natural universe. Our psyche is part of nature, and its enigma is as limitless. Thus we cannot define either the psyche or nature...'[24]

– So, from what I understand, you want to study the psyche of the unconscious.

– This is one of the theories which still remains credible in my opinion... You know, in recent decades there have been many studies carried out on the self, psyche and soul making the interdependence between psychology and philosophy stronger, I would even say essential. The very strange – but also amazing – thing is the fact that the ancient peoples, especially the Greeks, were already aware of the inner being, and had understood everything about it...

– For example, you are referring to scholars like Jacques Lacan, Michel Foucault... I sometimes read about philosophy

---

[24] Von Franz Luise Marie Jung Gustav Carl 'Man and His Symbols', 1988.pdf, page

and psychology but don't question any of it... I have no time.

- Not only them.

- So, how is all this connected with reincarnation?

- It is and it isn't. My opinions and theories about it are my own... My way of interpreting reincarnation doesn't correspond with that advocated by some religions. Mine is a possibility of the power of the unconscious.

- A possibility...

- But why discard it?... My conclusion, dear friend, is that you have lived before. This is the only truth.

- I want proof. I need to touch everything I've seen with my own hands.

- That's easy. Go and find your roots, then.

- First of all I need to know if what I have seen in my visions is actually about real people and real events.

- I understand, but I don't think it will be difficult. It's possible to trace the existence of the mansion and the family who lived there... You talked of events and people... William Bentinck really was a governor in India and what he did to abolish *sati* is reported by all historians.

- Yes, you're right.

- It depends on what you decide to do now. Good luck, Matteo!

## THE QUEEN OF THE JUNGLE: ZARA THE TIGER.

Returning to his office, Matteo thought of nothing else but this past life experience. Neither the lights of the city nor the noise of the traffic distracted him. The images from his trance continually whirled before his eyes: the white mansion, the corpse of Ram Chund Pundit, the ring. 'Ah, the ring,' he thought, 'set with the splendid pink diamond... Kali... The goddess. Her eyes... Subhadra... – strange name! – How could I have lived as Subhadra?!... Me... a woman, nonsense! Only Subhadra, the servant and Ram knew about the existence of the secret place where the ring was hidden.' To find it would offer indisputable proof of his past life. To find it, however, after almost two hundred years, would be a very difficult task. He could try... How? With all the work he had to do, how could he quickly prepare for a journey to India? And then, once there, how would he be able to find the mansion? Did it still exist? This would all require some time. He would need to think it over.

While returning home for dinner, his stressed mind stumbled into another snag: what would he tell Marina? How would she react? He already imagined her cynical laughter at him for believing in such an absurdity. It was ridiculous and grotesque. Tell her that he had been a woman? No way!... He couldn't. Better not say anything. She would not understand.

- How do you feel today? – Marina asked kissing him on one cheek as she greeted him at the door.

- Fine, thanks... The usual stress, – he answered avoiding her eyes. – You know, the market is more and more demanding today...

- I meant about what happened to you a few nights ago...
- Fine, everything's fine.
- Ok, but you must find the time for a check-up. You'll be fifty this year and I've read that this is a difficult age... You never know. You never get your blood pressure checked for instance and you never get your heart checked. I hear that a lot of men in their fifties have sudden heart attacks...
- For goodness sake!... Please, my love... I will find the time for a check-up, I promise. Let me solve a few problems I have at work with the Americans then I'll talk to doctor Lanzoni. Ok?

Matteo tried to behave as normally as he could throughout the evening, but Marina noticed that he was absent minded and not very talkative even with Francesco. 'He's really stressed,' she thought. 'What's the good of having money but not being able to relax or have any peace? We need to change something!'... Also in bed the woman sensed something strange, a distance not only of their bodies but also of their souls. When the light was off, she gently stroked his ear because she knew that he liked it, but he did not react. 'So it begins,' a divorced friend told her one day, 'When your husband starts acting differently, when he's absorbed in something that doesn't involve you, when he neglects you, when he doesn't talk, that means that it's finished... He must have another woman.'... 'No. Matteo would never betray me.' She thought. She had never had any reason to doubt his loyalty and faithfulness; their marriage followed an engagement during which they had got to know each other very well. He was simply stressed.

The next few days passed quickly. Despite the images produced by the effect of the hypnosis being constantly in his mind, Matteo couldn't decide whether to go to Jacopo again or not. He hoped that they would all suddenly vanish as often happens after having a nightmare. He had in mind to do some research on Cossimbazar and on the names of the people in his 'past life'; perhaps he would go to the Indian Embassy to get more information. Intentions. Only intentions. In fact, he didn't do any of it. He seemed, however, to have regained the closeness with his wife, but accounts with the past never close. Whether he liked it or not, the experiment in Jacopo's office had opened a door of his life that had never been locked and, as the doctor had said, the connection between past and present had been uncovered. Fragments of memories wavered and fluctuated intermittently like the glow of a lighthouse on foggy nights. Not so much when he was busy with work; they occurred more frequently when he was alone or before closing his eyes while trying to sleep. Yes, those images brought him back to his identity as a woman.

It happened that a few weeks after being hypnotised, Marina and Francesco went to spend the weekend at her parents' place in the countryside. Matteo couldn't go owing to an important meeting on Saturday. After an endless lunch with two American businessmen, he decided to have a walk along the *Naviglio* canal to help him digest all the food he had eaten. As it was Saturday afternoon, there were not many people or cars around. He had always enjoyed the city when it was like this; he liked to observe the houses and buildings with closed windows, and to notice things he had never seen before despite having lived there all his life. Sometimes just an unusual decoration above the doors or windows made him curious, so he would stop to examine all the details. Milan, like every city and town in Italy, is full of art and history. Walking around, it is very easy to be attracted by all that remains of, and is witness to a long and interesting history. This made him very proud of his nationality especially when he went abroad. He found it astonishing that in some countries, houses and buildings dating back a few hundred years were considered archaeological pieces. What makes Milan even more special, in addition to its long and complex history, is the fact that it is the capital of industry and technology in Italy, which creates a co-existence of old and new that do not disturb each other.

He was very pleased with the contract signed by the two Americans. 'Very good job,' he thought congratulating himself. Lunch had been super. He decided that he would go home and relax all evening watching cartoons and playing on the PlayStation. 'You're the same age as your child,' Marina used to tell him when she saw her husband enjoying cartoons. As he entered his empty apartment, he told himself that he couldn't live alone all the time. His wife and child were part of him. But to live alone for a couple of days wasn't so bad. He was pleased to see that the place was tidy. Francesco was a very messy boy so sometimes it was difficult to walk around without stumbling over his things. After a long shower, he took a can of beer from the fridge and finally sat comfortably on the sofa in front of the TV. As he was so tired, he felt he wouldn't be able to move for hours, not even to put a cartoon DVD in the DVD player. He would watch the cartoon channels instead. He started flicking through the channels lingering for a few minutes on the news. No good news. Only bad news. Wars, terrorism, murders, robbery, corruption... He wondered if the world had always been the same or if only nowadays evil, in its many different forms, seemed to be so ubiquitous. He remembered that his grandparents used to tell him that in their day people helped each other, they left the doors of their home unlocked; in other words there was more goodness. Was it believable? If so, what had changed in people's hearts?... On another channel which he changed quite quickly, for a fraction of a second he was able to capture the image of a tiger. It was enough to make his heart jolt. Quickly he turned back to that channel, but the tiger had disappeared. He could now see a camera operator searching for the tiger in a mangrove forest and commenting on its possible movements. He called her *Zara* as if he already knew the beast. A female tiger, then.

*Zara*. Beautiful name. It reminded him of something but he was not sure of what. Maybe it did, maybe it didn't. He had always liked tigers. He felt that he and tigers had a mutual understanding. When he had taken Francesco to the zoo recently, he had engaged in a long and silent dialogue with one of the two tigers on the other side of the fence.... At last she appears, as majestic as a queen expecting the due respect of the jungle. Cautiously, the operator shot a close-up of her eyes... The golden brown colour of the irises glowed irradiating its powerful magnetism all around, so that the leaves, plants and trees, birds and snakes, everything quivered as if suddenly awoken from a boring immobility and gently bowed to the queen. The eyes occupied the entire screen of the TV and the mass of golden light spread all around, filling the room and wrapping everything in its majestic brightness. Stunned and helpless, Matteo was a passive spectator of all that was happening to him. A colourless and indistinct form seemed to float out of his body, soaring effortlessly then diving into the coloured light that welcomed *it* as if this were *its* natural environment. The man remained motionless observing this strange creature maintaining his rationality but unable to formulate any thought. At the same time, however, his inner self moved into this new ethereal presence uniting with it and assuming its identity. He understood: it was his own spirit or soul that had detached itself from his body. And from above, his soul was looking down at his body frozen on the sofa. A scene that he associated with such experiences reported by people in comas and those who claim to have seen their bodies and everything around from somewhere above. In his case, though, his body maintained its rational autonomy for at least ten minutes before falling into a sort of paralysing numbness. The golden brown colour rarefied and beneath a gigantic *banyan* tree the Brahmin Ādiśūra and Subhadra were sitting facing each other in the meditation posture. The Brahmin realised that this spiritual daughter needed special attention, special prayers. A curse had deliberately drawn every path along which she had to walk, planting evil traps. Therefore, the religious man didn't slacken his grip on her as she faced each snare. He knew and saw that this beloved soul possessed 'antibodies' against evil but needed his supporting energies.

- Fate is against me, – Subhadra had said one day when Ram, gripped by despair and sadness, explained to her that he could no longer live a normal life.

She had tried to comfort him assuring him of her love for him, that she was still his wife and that she had promised to be at his side in the good and the bad times. But there was no way of convincing him; the offence of nature was so strong that, despite the help of his family and his *guru,* nothing could be done to relieve his depression and pain. He was deaf and blind to the world. After consulting with their son a few times, Ram's parents decreed that after the birth of her baby, Subhadra would have to leave.

- You must not say this word! – Ādiśūra sternly warned referring to the word 'fate'. – The contamination of western culture is unfortunately already visible here. *Karma*[25] is the law that governs our life and spirit, not fate. God endowed us with the power to act with free will. The physical and spiritual pains that torment your life and that of Ram's are the remains of bad behaviour in your past lives.

- So, it's not the power of the diamond?... It's not the diamond's curse on Ram?

- Not at all. This is one of the worst superstitions that blur and confuse the minds of our people.

- What shall we do if we wish to reach the blissful state of union with God? What puts an end to pain, suffering and sorrow?

---

25 Karma means action, work or deed. It also refers to the spiritual principle of cause and effect where intent and actions of an individual cause or influence the future of that individual (Wikipedia.org).

- We must live according to the natural laws that Hinduism proclaims. The goal is to halt the process of dying and being reborn. This goal can only be achieved with positive *karma*.

- I must confess that sometimes... perhaps often... I don't know where or what the border is between bad and good. I feel weak and confused. Sometimes... Sometimes evil is disguised as good.

- These are the traps of evil.

The young woman closed her eyes and inhaled deeply searching for something in her mind on which to concentrate.

*Pluffpluffpluff...*

*...Pluuuuufffffff!...*

Devesh was Ram's senior by a few years but looked much older. They were cousins, the sons of two brothers. Devesh lived with his family some distance from Cossimbazar, but they had frequent occasions to meet. There were tensions between the families over the rights of a few properties that Devesh claimed for himself. Ram didn't like him, likewise many other people who didn't want to be subjugated to his arrogance. He belonged to the kind of people who are labelled or categorised by their own nature from early childhood. And he was labelled 'bad'. Capricious, stubborn, spiteful, quarrelsome, one who bossed about and bullied especially the weak. Ram was not weak, but being younger and with a gentle heart, often chose not to stand up to him. The tension between the two increased when Ram, during his wedding celebration, put the diamond ring on his finger for the first time. For different reasons, partly invented by himself, Devesh claimed to be the rightful heir of the ring, the same scenario as with the properties, and seeing it on his cousin's finger enraged him. Apart from the value of the stone, the ring, as previously said, had a great symbolic meaning for the clan. Skirmishes between the two cousins had begun long ago and continued until Ram became ill. When word spread that Subhadra's husband had confined himself to solitude and was in a serious physical condition, the older cousin's frequent visits to the mansion became disturbing. Devesh hated the British and didn't hide his anger. He was not the only one to feel this way; the resentment of their policy in Bengal and in the rest of India was shared by large numbers of people, especially aristocrats, religious castes and landowners. The climax of this anger would come a few years later, in 1857.[26] The exhibitor of taxes was the British East India Company whose power was increasing. If Devesh had been honest, he would have had many sympathisers and followers, but his greed had turned him into a double-dealer, available to offer his service to all European adventurers, including the British, who came to Bengal with bad intent. This made him unpopular and detestable. It was he who arranged the connections between English and Dutch smugglers of salt, opium and tea and gangs in the region.

- Beware! - Devesh warned one day while Subhadra and her servant Abha were hanging out some silk clothes under a palm tree. - A couple of European bastards ventured into the jungle and almost got eaten by a tiger. In the village nearby they say that it's *Zara*.

*Zara*, a female tiger, was well-known as a terrible beast, not so much for her aggression as for her craftiness. But she

---

[26] In 1857 an untameable Indian rebellion took place. It had diverse political, economic, military, religious and social causes. This was the consequence of a series of events which occurred much earlier. The Bengal Army (1756-1895) - that belonged to the East India Company - was mainly formed by native soldiers (sepoys). The sepoys had their own list of grievances against the British East Indian Company administration, caused mainly by the ethnic gulf between the European officers and their Indian troops. Also some Indians were upset by what they saw as the draconian rule of the Company which had embarked on a project of territorial expansion and westernisation that was imposed without any regard for historical subtleties in Indian society. Furthermore, legal changes introduced by the British were accompanied by prohibitions on Indian religious customs and were seen as steps towards forced conversion to Christianity. Finally many Indians felt that the Company was asking for heavy tax from the locals. This included an increase in the taxation of land (https://en.wikipedia.org/wiki/Causes_of_the_Indian_Rebellion_of_1857).

was also nicknamed 'the queen' for her unique beauty. For this reason she had attracted the attention of foreign hunters.

- I had hoped she would tear them to pieces, – the man continued while Abha, summoned by somebody in the mansion, was walking away. – But I don't know which devil saved them... In the village they say that she is around, hungry and angry. And this is not the safest place.

It was true. The mansion was a bit isolated and to reach it, it was mandatory to go through the road that runs along a mangrove scrub, the ideal habitat for tigers. Several had been seen by people in the village nearby, but as far as they could remember only once had a man been attacked and eaten... Subhadra didn't like it when Devesh talked to her, so she usually tried to ignore what he said. This time she couldn't avoid him; she felt weak after hanging out the clothes, more than likely due to her pregnancy, so she sat on a square stone and put her hands in her lap as if to protect her baby.

- You need a man, – he went on.

She didn't look at him in order to avoid his lust-filled eyes, and continued to look down at her belly.

- I'm married, – she said at last after a long hesitation. – And you are also married.

He laughed scornfully.

- You're married to a dead man. You're young and beautiful. You need a real man.

At that moment a man suddenly appeared among the palm trees near the entry gates. Somebody that Devesh knew, called Gagan. The man bowed in front of Ram's cousin ignoring the presence of the woman and began to speak nervously:

- The police suspect that the two Europeans who escaped from the tiger last night are criminals involved in smuggling and that you are their contact...

- Nonsense! – The other interrupted clearly pissed off. –

Idiots!... What about the information that I asked you for?

- It's only a small garrison, perhaps sixty including officers and soldiers. They are all British. I heard that their presence here was requested by the Governor.

- I heard that too and I know the reason. The British officers of the East India Company suspect that the *sepoys*[27] are no longer loyal. Not all of them, of course.

- Yes, this is the reason.

- And the commander?

- A captain whose name is Benjamin Attwood. As I understand, he has special powers.

- That means that the British are worried... They are destroying our traditions and offending our religions.

- Yes, that's true.

- Sooner or later we will teach these western bastards an unforgettable lesson.

- But you must stay alert, *sahib!*[28] They're patrolling this whole area at all times, with horses and elephants, even without the support of our police... In the last few days, they've been combing this place, as far as the village, no one knows why.

- I know. I have already seen them a couple of times at night... What else do you know about this officer?

- They have their own guides and interpreters... But the captain speaks our language, a bit.

- Our language?... You say that he speaks our language?

- Yes, it's no surprise... In Calcutta I heard some British people speaking Bengali.

- Ok, what else?

- He likes riding, as do all British officers here, but he rides alone also in dangerous places. I don't understand if he is very brave or very irresponsible... Perhaps he's still childish, a

---

27  Indian soldiers serving in the army under British command in India. Sepoys were mostly high caste Hindu. They were organised in numbered regiments and drilled British style.
28  Sir.

spoiled fop of the British upper class.

- I already know that, too. He was seen alone looking for something or somebody just a few hundred yards from here... I'm sure that he was on the trail of those two European individuals...

- Or on yours...

- Hahahahaha! Damn fool, that's all you are, you jinx!

Devesh turned towards the road beyond the exit gate. Three men in uniform were outside, two on horseback and one on foot.

- Here they are... Look! – He exclaimed.

Something had happened to the horse. The other two dismounted and also went to examine the horse's leg.

- They might need some help, – Devish said nervously. – Or it might be a trick to spy on us... I'm leaving; I don't want to be seen here. It is better if you go and see if they need help. It might be a chance to get more information.

In no time at all he had disappeared behind the rhododendrons while a soldier signalled to Gagan and Subhadra for help.

Gagan immediately rushed towards the soldiers, while Subhadra hesitated. She was not allowed to meet or to speak to strangers, therefore she decided to stop. But Gagan, after checking the horse, shouted to her to approach them. The horse had been bitten by a snake.

- I think it's a krait bite, – the Indian said to Subhadra.

In the meantime, the horse had collapsed. The horseman was visibly shocked to see his beloved companion contorting on the ground. One of the other soldiers took a syringe out of the first aid box and injected it into the horse's upper leg. Three people arrived in quick succession: Abha, Iswar and another man in uniform on his horse. It was the captain. Resolute in his authoritarian bearing, he dismounted and drew near the animal. He touched it with both hands.

- He needs water. He has a high fever, – he said to his subordinate.

- Yes, sir, he needs a lot of fluids.

Iswar ordered Abha and Gagan to go to the well and bring back water. At that moment, the poor horse's entire body shuddered then he lifted his head and neighed hysterically as if seized by violent pain. Instinctively Subhadra stepped towards the horse and caressed his forehead, touching him delicately as if he were a child. Very soon afterwards the horse calmed down. The young lady looked up and caught the captain's eye, who was still bending over the horse. Her eyes were dark green, an unusual colour for an Indian woman. As he had bent down, he had taken off his military beret and she was surprised to see that he had dark hair. Most of the British that she had seen were fair or had red hair... The water was brought to them. The subordinate soaked a cloth, passed it over the horse's lips then helped him to drink from the bowl. Quenching his thirst, the animal seemed to revive and tried to get up.

- The drug has worked quickly, – the soldier said relieved.

- Yes, – the officer answered, and looking fleetingly at Subhadra, added, – But not only the drug.

The other didn't seem to understand but the woman caught the meaning of his words and felt pervaded by an unusual emotion.

- The horse won't be able to return to the barracks, – he went on coldly speaking in acceptable Bengali. – From whom can I get permission to let him rest here overnight?

- We will take care of him, – Iswar said promptly in bad English so as to let the officer know that he understood and spoke his language.

With Ram ill and the in-laws not around, Iswar took care of everything.

-Thank you, thank you very much, – said the captain in

English this time. – Tomorrow we will come to pick him up.

Then he mounted his horse.

– *Sahib!* – Iswar called to attract the captain's attention seeing that he was ready to leave. – I would suggest that you ride well away from the edge of the forest. There's a dangerous tiger around.

The military man looked at him perplexed wondering the reason for that advice then told himself that there are good people everywhere, after all. He appreciated it.

– I've heard, – he answered. – Thank you for your help. And looking at Subhadra again: – I won't forget.

She knew only a few words of English but grasped the meaning. Embarrassment burned her delicate cheeks so she averted her eyes while listening to the knight's horse canter away.

Immediately Iswar ordered the two women to keep away from those strangers and to return inside. Ram's wife had never spoken to any foreigners before; she had only seen them in town. As for the English language, girls were not allowed to study in India in that epoch, only a few had this privilege depending on the wishes of their families. She had learnt to read and write English by listening to her brother since he needed this language to work with the British who had now taken over ownership of almost everything.

– He likes you, – Abha said while Subhadra was tidying up the room.

She would have preferred not to hear those words. Her heart jumped.

– Europeans living here, especially the British, look for women... – she continued. – My sister, also, lives with an Englishman in Calcutta... I'm unattractive otherwise I would have been somebody's *bibi*.[29]

Subhadra stopped and looked at her. It was the first time

---

29 Mistress.

that her servant had spoken to her in that way, as if she no longer considered her as her superior. She noted bitterly that in that house she had lost all her dignity.

- I'm married, – she said, – and I'll be giving birth to my husband's child in a few weeks.

Abha took her hand in a friendly way.

- Listen to what I want to tell you, – the servant said inviting her to sit on a bench. – You were born and brought up in a good family... You know nothing about life, especially life in this country, except from hearsay. Your husband has repudiated you; within a few weeks you will have to leave the house without your child. You cannot go back to your family... where will you go?... What will you do? I have seen many such cases ...

- What are you trying to say?

- You're a distinguished and pretty young lady...

- I will never be a... *bibi* to anyone.

- Try to use your beauty to survive, milady. There is only one alternative: hell.

Subhadra felt a deep despair, she put her hands to her face and the tears flowed copiously.

- This country is very bad for women... – Abha asserted bitterly. – We're nothing. And pray to God that your child is a male. Otherwise I'm not sure that Ram's parents will let a female baby survive... *Sahib* Ram Chund Pundit will die soon; I heard Iswar telling somebody that he's as good as dead. When he dies, you know what your destiny will be, don't you?... *Sati!*...You will be burned alive.

- I've heard that it's illegal now...

- But this law is not respected; traditionalists still want *sati* and this family is one of them.

Subhadra tried to dry the tears falling onto her neck and thought that she had never before been through such a sad and desperate time.

- Why are you saying all these things to me? – she asked staring at her servant.

- Why?... For people like you, who have grown up amongst wealth, it's difficult to believe that anyone can live according to the commandments of our religion. I want to help you; I'm doing this for your good and for the child's good; I'm doing this because my heart says that I have to do it; I'm doing this for my *karma* and for my *dharma*.[30]

Instinctively the two women walked toward each other and embraced strongly.

- I didn't expect that. I'm sorry, – Subhadra said, her voice choked by tears. – You're right, you're right... For rich people, this religion is quite uncomfortable. I just want to save my child. I don't care about myself. I'm not afraid of burning on the pyre, but the child...

- You have to go away from here. Soon. As soon as possible...

- How? Where?... The only person that might help me is perhaps a cousin who lives in Cossimbazar. We were very close when we were children... She is married to a good man; I met him at my wedding. She is my only hope...

- Don't be so sure, but at least you can try.

- How can I escape from this prison?

- We will think about that... Now, calm down, rest; your baby needs serenity.

Abha left the room to finish her jobs. Subhadra was exhausted, but the disclosure of Abha's goodness was a balm for her pain. Her last thoughts before falling asleep were of the Brahmin and of her soon-to-be-born baby. The next morning, the first thing that came to her mind was to work out whether the idea of escape was realistic or just a dream. In her condition she wouldn't be able to travel to the town and to the place

---

[30] Individual behaviour in conformity with the law that orders the universe.

where her cousin lived. There were risks and obstacles. Her departure wouldn't remain unnoticed for long unless she went under cover of darkness. But in the darkness there were other dangers: men and beasts. Frankly she feared men more than the wild animals. From a little terrace she saw two soldiers coming to pick up the horse that now seemed to be in perfect health. They gave something to Iswar, perhaps a little gift for the owner of the mansion and after a few minutes they left. Not much later Devesh appeared under a palm tree silently and cautiously looking around. Subhadra wanted to escape his searching eyes but was unsuccessful and he approached her.

- When Ram dies, you will come to live with me, – the man said sure of himself.

The woman was deep in thought and avoided his eyes.

- I'm the only person who can save you from the pyre, – he continued.

Subhadra persisted in her stubborn silence.

- I could whip you for your behaviour! – he threatened losing his patience.

He paced up and down three or four times looking pensive.

- Who else, apart from you, knows the secret place where the diamond ring will be hidden after Ram's death? – he finally blurted out.

'This is what he's getting at!' Subhadra thought. 'This is his objective.'

- Who else? – he insisted.

This time she decided to answer but with a lie:

- I don't know. I have no idea.

- The stone is mine. Remember that!

He turned and with his usual nervous countenance, fortunately, took his leave.

Enough was enough. Subhadra was gripped by panic realising that time was running out. She needed to find a way to save her child. The moment had quickly turned dramatic.

She looked around bewildered and instinctively tried to locate the things that were most necessary for a possible escape. When Abha joined her upstairs, she told her about Devesh. The servant had been sensing the situation between the two since the man started to frequent the mansion without any apparent reason.

- That's another reason why you must go away from here, – she urged, – he has raped many girls and you will be next... This evening we will leave...

- No, you won't, you mustn't. Don't take any risks for me.

- I will and I must... You cannot go alone since you're pregnant; you won't make it. I'll accompany you to your cousin's house and then come back. At night they won't notice my absence. We'll take the path behind the rhododendrons one hour before sunset so that we can cut through the forest before it gets dark. I know a *mahout*[31] who lives along the way; he will let us stay for a few hours; we'll be safe there.

- I hope Devesh won't be around; he hounds me all the time.

- I think his mind is occupied by other things. I heard him talking with Iswar this morning. He says that the soldiers of the garrison are around all day and all night. With all his dirty business, he must feel he's in danger... Anyway, in a few hours we'll be gone. Boil some rice and don't forget to take water too. I'll try to scrape together some other food.

Subhadra was excited, worried and happy at the same time. Her panic had vanished, and Abha's help encouraged her greatly. While boiling the rice, she was thinking of Ram, of how much she had loved him and how much she still kept him in her heart. For months she had tried to understand the underlying reasons for his behaviour, for his rejection of her. She was not able to understand. But her heart still belonged to him despite everything. She imagined a possible scenario after

---

31 Elephant trainer.

Ram's death: she would burn on the pyre together with Ram's corpse unless the new law on *sati* was respected; if the child was male, the grandparents would provide for it, but if it was female, it was difficult to foresee what her destiny would be. The decision once again was in the hands of Ram's parents. If she survived after the getaway, in one way or another her child would be with her.

When the sun had already disappeared, the two women left the mansion, cautious but determined. Subhadra was inexperienced. If she were alone, she most likely wouldn't know which direction to take, but Abha knew her way around, so she decided to take the path used by the elephants that linked the villages to the city. At that time there should be fewer risks. Night time in the jungle is not the same as in other places. No other place. In fact, wakefulness and sleep are synonyms with life and death there, and in no other place are the senses of its fauna and flora more acute than when helping each other or betraying each other. It would be more or less like the world of human beings but for a significant difference that characterises the two realities: the absence of evil in one of the two. In the jungle the relationship between predator and prey is governed solely by the law of physical survival, therefore, without the trigger of self-defence or hunger, the aggressive instinct is mute. Do beasts suffer less physical pain than humans? Perhaps awareness of their own weakness makes the prey almost immune to pain while dying, accepting it as subservience to the will of nature. Even the lion, despite his superiority, when condemned to death by the more powerful animal, submits meekly to his fate as the roar of arrogance falls silent… It is believed that when we were more animal than human, the perceptions of our senses worked in a different way. As for physical pain, suffering was less acute. Evolution of the species has made this perception more sensitive, perhaps because the instinct to survive has become stronger in relation to the arrogance of the ego. In a way not seen by everybody, but only by those few who understand its language, the plant world makes itself an accomplice to the strong and/or to the weak obeying the law of creation. In fact, it can hide or reveal, imprison or liberate, orient or deceive. A lot, good or bad, depends on the harmony of communication and energy between the plant and animal worlds both acting on the stage of life and whose background, consisting of the immense sky full of stars and games, plays an essential role.

Captain Benjamin Attwood was reflecting deeply on the life of the jungle while riding along its edge and keeping in mind Iswar's warning. He had given orders to six soldiers to patrol the area south west of Cossimbazar. They arranged themselves at a certain distance from each other so as to be visible to one another. The officer occasionally broke away from the group to do inspections alone where his instinct or intuition led him. In recent times the presence of foreigners coming especially from Europe had alerted the Governor and the British troops in the territory. They were not all smugglers. The intelligence had ascertained that some unshakeable French conquerors had not yet resigned themselves to their defeat in the battle of Plassey[32] and fomented the discontent of the *sepoys* and other anti-British local groups. Benjamin had been born in Manchester but had spent three years of his adolescence in Calcutta, as his father was a British officer, and two more years there before being posted to Cossimbazar. This is why he spoke some Bengali. When he returned to England, he chose to follow his father's profession believing it the best way to fulfil his ambitions. As a matter of fact, rather than it being just a military vocation, he thought that by being in the army he would better express his patriotic feeling. This was what he thought as a boy. Now he had another view of life and of the world and saw other horizons

---

[32] The Battle of Plassey was a decisive victory of the East British India Company over the Nawab of Bengal and his French allies on 23 June 1757.

in his future beyond his military career. He wanted to become a politician because he had a growing conviction that only in politics and through politics can a man have any influence over the directions that a nation takes.

While Ben was contemplating his future and riding slowly in the fading colours of the sunset, the horse suddenly stopped. He didn't neigh but was caught by an unexpected nervousness. Knowing him as well as he did, Ben felt he shouldn't spur him on to get him moving. He understood that something inside the forest had scared and agitated him. Slowly he dismounted his horse, and with his finger on the trigger of the musket, he approached the first *arjuna* tree straining to see and hear anything. He had learnt that smugglers had hideouts in the forests organised with the complicity of the locals, for which the leaders received substantial sums of money. Taking cover behind a huge tree trunk, he peeked out whenever he felt it was safe. Everything seemed normal in the usual immobility of the vegetation including the presence of a tiger that he saw out of the corner of his eye at a distance of a few metres from him. A female tiger, well camouflaged amongst the colourful variety of branches and leaves by her coat of gold and black stripes on her back, and black and white on her belly. The feline was observing him carefully, wondering who the strange intruder was who, in her opinion, was clearly not her friend. That beret and instrument pointing directly at her certainly did not inspire any confidence in her. The officer sensed that the big cat was poised to attack him. All her concentration was shown in her eyes, as if to make them impenetrable to the interpretation of her intentions. She hesitated for a moment perhaps to consider the unusual strangeness of the prey. He wondered whether he should shoot her or not. If he failed, it would be the end for him. If he fired, it was imperative that he hit between the eyes to kill her, because if he only wounded her, she would become more aggressive. The time for thinking had run out.

- Don't move and don't talk.

The woman who whispered these words was standing behind him. Silently she stepped forward and he recognised that she was person who had calmed his soldier's horse. He perceived a slow movement of the tiger's eyes as if her attention was diverted by the new visitor. 'It's *Zara!*' Subhadra thought. The two females stared at each other, curious and suspicious. The human touched her own belly gently to show she was carrying a baby inside. They continued to examine each other for at least three or four long minutes, a lapse of time in which the communication of the two 'animals' became the natural understanding of two mothers. Very likely *Zara* herself was pregnant which imposed on her the sentiment of solidarity. *Zara* must have been thinking that the law of the jungle, although ruthless, required certain ethics to be respected. Yet, she wondered if a human being would have had the same sense of respect in a situation where she was the prey... The wild animal moved her tail as a sign of peace then her eyes softened and changed colour losing their aggression. She shook her head as if to shake away all thoughts of attack then took one last look at the woman and swiftly disappeared into the vegetation.

Benjamin could not believe what had just happened and what he had just witnessed. He was stunned and confused. That woman had almost certainly saved his life.

- *Sahib,* – said Abha who had remained impassive a few steps behind, – put your rifle down. The danger has passed...

- Captain!... Sir! – called Burton, one of the soldiers of the patrol who had noticed the captain's horse standing alone.

- I'm here, Burton! – Benjamin answered loudly making himself visible.

At that moment, turning to the women, he saw that Subhadra was fainting while the other was trying to hold her up.

- What's the matter? – he asked worried.

- She might be about to give birth! – the woman exclaimed guessing that the stress had caused her to go into premature labour.

- Oh, my God!... Burton!

- Yes, sir!

- Rally everyone here, immediately.

- Yes, sir!

Subhadra had not completely lost consciousness but her cheeks were deathly pale. Benjamin thought how gentle the features of her face were, giving her a sweet, feminine appearance.

- She cannot remain here, – Abha said hoping the officer would help.

- We will take her to the mansion, we will find a way to take her there... She saved my life... It's unbelievable.

- It's believable, not unbelievable.

- Why?

- Only a mother can understand a mother.

- What do you mean? Do you mean that the tiger didn't maul me because your friend is pregnant?

Abha showed him a cynical smile.

- *Sahib,* Subhadra is my Lady, not my friend... *Sahib...* mothers are mothers!

This time Benjamin seemed to understand the meaning of those words much better, but he was also convinced that Subhadra possessed special energies. If she didn't have these energies, she wouldn't have been able to tackle such a situation with so much control.

- *Sahib,* – Abha continued without hiding her concern this time. – We cannot go back home. I will tell you the reasons on the way. There's no time now.

- We'll take her to the Mission; she will be safe there.

The soldiers knew their young commander was an

unemotional and cold man; therefore, they were surprised to see him so earnest and willing to give help to those two indigenous women. They didn't dare discuss their orders but did their best to deliver the two Indian women to the Mission. After preparing an emergency stretcher, they were ready to depart for their destination. Certainly Abha would never have expected in all her life that a number of British soldiers and their commander would escort her, a poor insignificant woman. She was used to seeing the British sitting comfortably in handheld rickshaws carried by thin and unkempt young men trying to earn a few rupees. On the way, the captain asked her to tell him about her Lady, and remained shocked to hear her tragic story. He assured her that he would help and protect Subhadra and would never forget what she had done for him. As for Abha, when he heard that she would go back to the mansion after delivering Subhadra to the Mission, he asked her to remain with the woman in labour. She would need her help.

So it was that Amir was born at dawn on the new day in the Christian Mission located in the outskirts of Cossimbazar. A beautiful baby boy that would certainly have made his father proud, but for now, everything had to be kept secret as Benjamin Attwood had suggested, even the identity of Subhadra. For a few days, he couldn't dispel the images of what he had experienced in the jungle and wondered from time to time if it had been real or just a dream. At the same time his mind captured the very short instances when his eyes had met hers. In some way he felt a sort of unfamiliar vulnerability that gave him a mixture of irritation and pleasure. However, the most important point was once again the fact that she had almost certainly saved his life. As a British officer and as a man of honour, he would not ignore Subhadra's bravery and generosity. He felt a strong obligation towards her. So, the first thing he did was to order his orderly, George, to provide suitable accommodation and arrange for her safety. This was vital. In fact, at the mansion when it became clear that the two women had disappeared, it was Devesh who showed the most concern since he considered Subhadra the main custodian of Ram's secrets. He imagined that it would not be difficult to find her. First of all, she was not a woman to go unnoticed because both her pregnancy and her social status were difficult to hide. He promised himself that he would find her.

- I don't deserve all this, – Subhadra said one day while feeding her baby.

She meant that the captain had been very generous to her and this caused her to feel deeply embarrassed so she hoped that as soon as the baby was a little stronger, she would be able to contact her cousin.

- Once, I told you that he liked you, – Abha reminded her. – Now I want to tell you that, actually, he loves you.

Perhaps owing to the circumstances or to another mysterious mechanism of life, the two poor wretches had become very close. On the other hand, living in such a situation forced them together in this way. In spite of this closeness, Abha was always respectful and aware of her social inferiority. But nature had equipped her with a good brain and sharp eyes and many times her Lady had to admit that what she said or thought was right, therefore Subhadra did not know how to react to her further revelation about the captain. She certainly did not remain indifferent; her heart beat suddenly accelerated as inside herself she felt that Abha had told the truth. A couple of times Benjamin came to ensure that everything had been carried out according to his orders. Two quick visits without many words but full of 'electricity' and energies that sprang from their bodies and spirits clashing in a mutual, but still unconscious, search for each other. After he had left the lodging she continued to imagine him around inventing dialogues about inexistent matters, and for hours inhaled more deeply the air under the illusion that she could taste the particles left by the particular smell of his uniform.

- You love him, – the servant insisted reading her silence.

Subhadra continued to breastfeed her baby without looking up. These sensations were new to her. She could not remember having felt such an emotion for Ram. Perhaps she had been too young when she had met her husband, or perhaps it had all been expected and obvious. She did not want to reason in her mind over these unimportant things.

- You must stay here, – Abha continued sounding very worried. – Devesh and Iswar are definitely looking for you… or for us, but I'm not concerned about myself. I'm worried only for you.

The mother did not move, did not look at her. Nothing. She felt suspended in space. She sensed the presence of Devesh somewhere not far from her like a bloodhound guided not so much by the smell of the prey as by that kind of instinct generated by an obsessive greed. She thought about what traces she and her servant might have left behind since they were taken from the jungle directly to the Mission. This was the only place that they had been seen by people from Cossimbazar who were working there, but it could be enough to create a tam-tam of rumours. Devesh, thanks to his devilish business dealings, had a huge network of contacts and he knew exactly what to do in order to get information on whatever or whoever he was interested in. He also knew that it was very unlikely that Subhadra had returned to her parents, as they would not accept her.

Only one week later an unexpected turning point occurred (or rather, it was expected but not so soon). One morning the captain arrived visibly gloomy at the lodgings of the two unfortunate women. Abha was not in, the baby was sleeping and Subhadra was in the meditation posture near the window. After knocking lightly, he slowly pushed the door without waiting for the invitation to enter. The woman looked absorbed in her world apparently ignoring the reality around. He had never seen her with her hair down as it was now. Her eyes disclosed a fake serenity while the shadow of her profile on the wall formed an icon that reminded him of a Christian Madonna. He curbed his impulse to speak and his eyes lingered on her face. The pleasant sensation that enveloped his being made him realise that Subhadra meant something special to him and this twanged his emotional chords. He had now been living in Cossimbazar for almost five months, but he had never been interested in meeting a woman, especially a native. The last time his heart had throbbed uncontrollably was for an English girl he had met at a Gala at the Army and Navy Club in London. They had liked each other at first sight and met up a few times after that evening. Unfortunately, he was about to leave on a military mission so did not want to get involved in a serious relationship. He was very well acquainted with the kind of life of military personnel and therefore convinced himself that an emotional tie, especially in the early stages, was unlikely to bring anything good when the couple is parted for such a long time. They exchanged letters for some time but did not meet again. He had hoped that once he left the Army, he would choose a suitable woman of his social rank with whom he could start a family.

Subhadra opened her eyes and showed a faint expression of surprise to see the man in uniform near the front door. She quickly regained her normal composure and stood up in front of him.

- I came to give you some bad news, – he said staring into her beautiful eyes.

Her eyelids moved perceptibly but she did not say anything.

- A patrol from the garrison, – he continued, – was in the

vicinity of your family home early in the morning when they noticed strange comings and goings in the mansion, so they decided to investigate. They learnt that your husband, Ram Chund Pundit, had died.

An immediate pain like that of being stabbed in a non-specific point in her body and in the deepest part of her soul caused her to sway so much that Benjamin feared she would lose her balance.

- I am very sorry, – he said rushing to support her. – Sit here and tell me what I can do for you.

He helped her to sit on a bench made of bamboo canes then sat down next to her continuing to hold her arm. His grasp was firm; Subhadra felt in its strength a great sense of protection that encouraged her. Surprisingly she did not feel embarrassed to be touched by that stranger and the closeness of his body was not disturbing at all. Yet, she was confused and did not know what to say.

- I'm leaving on a military mission today, but I shouldn't be gone for long, – Benjamin went on softly wanting to reassure her further.

In truth, this was a way to convey how much he would miss her, because that strange and unexpected seed that often pleasantly tortures the human heart had started to pierce his vulnerability since his first encounter with her. Despite the mystery that causes two people to be attracted to each other in different ways, he was also fascinated by a kind of magic power that he felt this woman had.

- Why are you doing all this for me? – Subhadra asked at last overcoming her shyness.

The question floored him and he answered after a long hesitation. Indeed, why was he doing all that for her?

- You mean a lot to me, – he found the courage to declare.

She heard well. Yes, once again Abha had been right: this guy loved her. She was suddenly pervaded by a deep tenderness for this soldier, who was strict only in his appearance.

- It's a difficult time for you, – he observed slackening his grip on the woman's arm, – but I wanted you to know my feelings before my departure... Don't say anything... I know that my words are inopportune in your moment of mourning. I apologise.

Subhadra imagined Ram's corpse on the bier and the room decorated with flowers, which brought back memories of their first night of love. With these images in her mind she was almost in the arms of another man. She felt an instinctive sense of shame for herself and stiffened while simultaneously a shiver of anxiety criss-crossed along her spine. At the same time she had to confess that she was not indifferent to the captain's charms.

The front door opened. It was Abha carrying small bags of rice, pearl millet and spices. She laid everything on a wooden board and bowed reverently in front of the couple. On her face there was no look of surprise to see the two so close.

- Your husband is dead, – she announced nervously looking at Subhadra. – One of Devesh's henchmen saw me and blocked my path. I couldn't avoid him. He gave me the news and said that the family wants *sati* at the funeral. He asked me a lot of questions about you. I told him that I didn't know where you were but he didn't believe me.

- *Sati* is illegal now, – Benjamin said standing up.

- Ram Chund Pundit's family is a powerful and traditional family.

- However powerful they are, they must respect the law. Even the highest religious authorities argue that this practice has no Vedic standing and only God can take a life that He has given. I will send a sergeant to the mansion to find out what is happening. As soon as I come back from the mission, I will go there myself. Do you know when the funeral will take place?

- Three days from today.
- I'll try to get there in time… Watch out and take care!

His last glance was at Subhadra who had lowered her eyes. As soon as he left, Abha approached her lady and hugged her.

- Ram knows the truth now, – the lady said in a firm voice. – Ram is waiting for me. I loved him. I have to go.

Abha had sensed that she would make this decision but her reason for doing so was not clear. She tried to put herself in Subhadra's shoes to understand what had pushed her to decide so quickly. She had escaped because she wanted to save her child, but now she had changed her mind completely.

- I will be a *sati*, – she went on, reading her servant's mind. – The child is male. He will be safe. I can't disobey the teachings of our ancient religion and tradition. I know that this rite is not accepted by many people in this country, even by Brahmins, but Ram's family wants to keep this tradition and I'm sure that Ram will be proud of my choice. There's nothing else to say. Let's go.

Abha understood that the decision would not be revoked, therefore, passively and with silent obedience, she would accompany Subhadra to the pyre.

## ON THE ROAD TO TRUTH.

At 6 a.m. in many churches in Milan, the Sunday morning church bells rang *ding dong* louder than on other days. Matteo woke up on the sofa in the same position as when he had fallen asleep, still dressed and with the remote control in one hand. The TV was still on with 'no signal' flashing on the channel that he had been watching the programme on the jungle. The images of his dream, or of whatever that phenomenon had been, made his perception of the reality around him seem alien to him. He needed a couple of minutes to become fully aware that his name was Matteo, that he was a man, and that he had never lived in India.

*Ding dong, ding dong, ding dong...*

The call for believers and devotees was unmistakeable. He wondered if the habits of church goers had changed since he was a child. Old people used to go to the early services, the children at 10 a.m., and everyone else after 11 a.m. Recently, he had read that there was a major crisis in vocations in the Catholic Church. A lot of seminaries were almost empty for a few different reasons. Before economic growth many poor families encouraged their children to enter seminaries as a means of relieving their financial burden. Italy has never had a welfare system providing sufficient benefits to poor families. In the sixties the economic boom brought about changes in many things and seminaries were no longer seen as the only option for providing food and education to underprivileged children. Among the other causes of this crisis was also the fact that the Catholic Church does not allow priests to marry. So, only those who have a true and honest vocation – who are able to renounce having a family and a normal sex life – can choose a religious life.

It is really difficult to understand if this restriction is right or not.

The tiger. The jungle... Ram Chund Pundit...The pyre...

'Hell! Fucking hell!' he thought getting up and stepping slowly to the toilet. 'How is it possible that this dream relates to my life? ...to my past life I mean. Was I really a woman? In the dream – was it a dream? – I lived my life like a real... female... Unbelievable!.. The diamond ring. I didn't know that these precious stones can also be pink. It's a wonderful colour... Marina would love it, she likes gems; she's made me spend a fortune... Who knows if this diamond still exists?... Only three people knew the secret place: Subhadra... I mean me... Yes, yes... Ram and Iswar... The hiding place was located in the adjoining bedroom. Only Iswar remained alive out of the three of them. What did he do with his secret? And Devesh? Did he ever find out that Iswar knew where the ring was hidden? Difficult to answer all these questions... Amir!... Poor child. What happened to him? What happened after I was burnt alive?... Horrible, I can't think of it... how could it be possible that I didn't feel anything, any pain, any sensation... Perhaps I can't remember. Flames and more flames... Yet... when my soul detached and left my body, the sensation was pleasant, I still feel it... Where was I going? High, in an ocean of fantastic colours... Amir... poor child, what was his destiny?'

Haunted by a carousel of images and visions from his night journey as his other self, Matteo moved through the house like a robot more and more convinced that he needed to find out the truth. After breakfast he decided to send a message to Jacopo telling him about his dream. The doctor replied saying that they could meet and talk over an *espresso* in *Piazza della Scala*. Matteo felt relieved. He needed to talk to him; the dream had been extraordinary, never before had he experienced such a thing. Only Jacopo could tell him something that would satisfy his curiosity.

The appointment was fixed for 11 a.m., so he decided to go out thirty minutes earlier and walk up to the square. As it was Sunday morning, the streets were not busy, which made walking pleasant. There are two points that appeal both to the eye and to one's interest as soon as one enters this famous square, two points that excite the imagination and whet the appetite for knowledge. One is the theatre *La Scala,* one of the principal Opera Houses in the world, and the other is the monument of Leonardo da Vinci. Matteo was very proud to be a compatriot of one of the greatest geniuses that ever lived on this planet. Who knows what Leonardo thought of the world beyond death!

- Glorious day! – exclaimed Jacopo while Matteo was looking at the top of the statue of Leonardo. – He maintained that 'the soul wants to stay with the body, because, without the organic instruments of that body, it can neither act, nor feel anything.'

- There is interdependence between the body and the soul, then!

- Between the body and soul, yes. But the body and spirit, no.

- What do you mean?

- The soul that Leonardo was talking about is not the spirit. Often there is confusion between the two entities. Many think that one is a synonym of the other. In reality they are not the same thing. If they were, they would not have names with such different endings and roots.

- I really don't know anything about this subject; please, help me to understand it better.

- Strictly speaking, the soul is the psyche. In this sense yes, there is interdependence with the body. The psyche is the sphere of reality that includes the mind and the feelings which, of course, without the support of the body cannot act or perceive anything and consequently will not hear.

- And the spirit?
- The spirit is unknowable in its essence.
- Slow down, please, this is all too complicated for me.
- Let me explain... The only thing that can give you an idea of the nature of the spirit is Universal Intelligence.
- I'll have to think about that. But not here in the middle of the square... No. I won't think about it. It's not important to know what the soul and spirit are... Each religion or philosophy gives different explanations. Which is right?

Jacopo looked at his friend like a teacher looks at his pupil after reaching the conclusion that his brain is somewhat slow...

- Which is right? – the doctor repeated absent-mindedly.
- This is the problem... What do you say to a coffee at *Bar Duomo*?
- Great idea!

They walked to *Piazza del Duomo*, only a few minutes away. This square is another wonderful sight and masterpiece of Italian architecture. It marks the centre of the city. Although it includes fabulous sites, the main attraction is the Gothic Cathedral (*Duomo*), which is one of the biggest in the world.

*Bar Duomo*, located in *Piazza Duomo*, is an excellent coffee-bar where *cappuccino* and *espresso* have a special flavour that seduces nostrils from a distance. When accompanied by one of the many kinds of *cornetto*[33] or *sfogliata*[34] it constitutes a typical and superb Italian breakfast. Sitting in two comfortable wicker chairs the two friends immersed themselves in the Milanese atmosphere made agreeable by the elegance of the Italian fashion and by the joyful light-heartedness of the people around.

---

33  Sweet bun.
34  Puff pastry.

- We are a people of indomitable aesthetes, – Jacopo observed looking at a woman elegantly dressed but in a way that showed off her sensuality. – This is one of the few good things we have inherited from the Greeks and Romans.

- I know; our history teacher never missed an opportunity to tell us these things.

- Yes... Romans were pragmatic and rational; we are theoretical, talkative, superficial and disorganised.

- I think this is a false stereotype... We are a people full of contradictions... It could not be any other way because of our long and complex history... Sometimes it is as you say, in a very general sense. I'd say that we are a people where deep darkness coexists with bright lights. This is a land of saints and devils, of great minds and absolute mediocrity.

- Lights and shadows, the same as everywhere... But you're right; they are more extreme in this country.

Matteo started to tell him about his strange night leaving out no detail. Jacopo looked away from the lovely ladies in the room and listened carefully without interrupting. He found this case interesting not least because Matteo's subconscious had returned him to his past without him being hypnotised a second time.

- What do you think? – Matteo asked shaking his friend out of his pensive look.

- I'm trying to analyse a number of elements in your story. And once more I find it very true what many scientists maintain: they have defined our consciousness as a form of energy which, in obedience to the first principle of thermodynamics, is not destroyed but is transformed into a new and different form of energy suited to continuing a different form of existence or on a different plane of existence.

- What do you mean?

- Matteo, you are the protagonist of a fantastic story, you can't imagine how lucky you are... The tiger, you, and

Subhadra... The diamond... The pink diamond.

- I can understand Subhadra and myself but what is the connection with the tiger?

- When we were at school, you used to tell me that tigers had a special significance for you, a sort of presence that you couldn't explain... This is not a coincidence. Particles of tigers' energies are in you... I repeat: energy is not destroyed but it is transformed into a new and different form of energy suited to continuing a different form of existence or on a different plane of existence... That means that part of us can live in plants, animals and other beings... *Zara,* the tiger, and Subhadra (you), facing each other in the jungle... a fantastic scene of solidarity and compassion that apparently escapes our superficial understanding... The strange power of this pink diamond...

- As far as I know, because Marina is a great expert in this field, pink is a very rare colour for diamonds...

- And you are the only person who knows where it is, aren't you?

- Yes... this was the first thing I thought when I woke up this morning... But... I'm confused... What would I do if I found it? I wouldn't like to possess this stone... What I would like, though, is to know the fate of the child after his mother died.

- You do need to know the truth. If you don't, you will never be free.

- Yes, you're right. How and where should I start?

- I would start with Benjamin Attwood... It's not difficult; you can easily find his name... Consult the National Archives or The British Library... As for India, I have a close colleague in Calcutta. I could ask him to help you.

- Ok... Thanks. Yes, that would be helpful... But it's not going to be easy knowing what to do after tracing the captain's descendants... What shall I tell them, that I'm the reincarnation of an Indian woman who their ancestor called Benjamin Attwood fell in love with almost two hundred years ago?... It sounds ridiculous, don't you think?

- Your case deserves the utmost scientific attention, believe me... You have to carefully plan your steps, as you said. You must find a way to resolve this situation... I'll help in any way I can, ok?

Jacopo was right. Matteo would start by finding out about the officer, but would also investigate Ram Chund Pundit's family and the existence of the mansion where Subhadra had lived. With all these images and thoughts and after a long chat with his friend, Matteo headed home. He was a bit hungry. He was tempted to enter one of the characteristic *trattoria*[35] to have a homemade lunch, but he felt he wouldn't relax and enjoy it with all that was occupying his mind, so he decided to go home and cook something himself. He enjoyed cooking sometimes, especially for friends. This time he would cook *spaghetti, aglio, olio e peperoncino*[36], a very popular and quick meal that was both tasty and filling, and... a great aphrodisiac!... He filled a pan with water and boiled it, dropped in a little salt and a handful of spaghetti. Then he took another pan and put in two spoons of olive oil, a clove of garlic and a little chili pepper. He turned the stove on and waited until the garlic turned golden brown then he added some parsley. For the final step, after boiling the spaghetti for five minutes, he drained it in the colander and then put it into the pan with the other ingredients, mixed it together and... there it was! Tasty *spaghetti al dente*. A good glass of red Chianti was obligatory, of course!

Marina and Francesco returned home a bit late. The woman's first question was how her husband had spent the weekend. His answer was laconic and without many details. It was the first time that Matteo had faced the problem of

---

35 Small restaurant.
36 Spaghetti, garlic, olive oil and red chili pepper.

lying to his wife out of necessity, something that bothered him very much. Lying was not one of his skills. But would she understand if he told her the truth? No. He knew her very well. She would not understand. One day in the future, when everything was clear, he would tell her the whole story hoping that she would at last understand and forgive him. Now he needed to concentrate on the tasks at hand.

Worried and agitated he couldn't sleep that night. Doubts about the decisions to be taken tormented him. He was not convinced that starting with Benjamin Attwood was the right choice. Once he had traced his descendants, how would he introduce himself? What would he say? What would he ask? Instead, it seemed more logical to find out what had happened in Cossimbazar after Subhadra's death. But similarly in this case, how would, and could, he proceed?

Imprisoned in a tangle of questions and decisions, Matteo left home early in the morning leaving his wife still in bed between wakefulness and sleep. He had a slight headache having slept little and badly. He felt nervous but determined to make a breakthrough in resolving this story. Apart from the security guards in the lobby of the building where he worked, none of his employees was at work yet. After giving a fleeting look at the documents and diary on his desk, he started to surf the web looking for information on Captain Benjamin Attwood. It was not difficult to find. It showed that he had been a British officer in India but gave nothing except his date of birth: Manchester 1810. Yet, another Attwood, whose name was Harold, also an officer from Manchester attracted Matteo's attention. He was certainly Benjamin's father. Information about him was more abundant and detailed. He had held important roles both in Calcutta and in England and it reported the address of his house in Manchester: Oldham Street. No number unfortunately. Yet the details were valuable for a possible contact. But who could he contact? Did this house still exist? If so, the descendants probably still lived there. He opened Google Maps to check that the name of the street was the same. Mechanically he switched his research from Manchester to Cossimbazar and Bengal. Here the investigation seemed more difficult; it was not easy to navigate the thicket of information about the name Pundit and the places of that vast region. He realised that he needed some help; perhaps he would ask Jacopo since he had said that he had acquaintances in India. He was about to dial his number but changed his mind when hearing his secretary, Nadia, knocking at his door. He had remembered that she had some connections in England and more precisely in the Manchester area, as he had heard her say a couple of times. Nadia had been working for him for at least five years now and he knew a lot about her. She was a loyal and trustworthy person and Matteo hoped she would never leave this job. Yes, she said she had an uncle in Manchester who had left Italy many years before. He had married an English woman and had a grown-up son and daughter, who were married themselves. Without going into detail he explained what he needed.

– My cousin works in the police, – Nadia said taking notes, – I'm sure that he can find out what you want.

Matteo felt pleased and relieved. He found the fact that Nadia had relatives in Manchester a strange and wonderful coincidence. He felt optimistic. He decided not to continue his own search for information about Cossimbazar for the time being. He would wait for some results from England. Reassured by this fortunate occurrence he plunged himself into his work even though the images of his 'past life' continued to flow incessantly in his mind. More than anything, he repeatedly saw Subhadra burning in the pyre. What had happened to Amir? Thinking of this poor baby and again hearing him cry, something in the depths of his being reproached him and he felt a sharp pain as if pincers wanted to extract from the darkness of the abyss a reality never definitively buried. This pain disoriented him; in fact, for a few long seconds his identification with Subhadra was complete and absolute forcing him to experience the perceptions that only a woman forced to abandon her child can feel.

When one works, especially when doing a demanding job such as the manager of a major company, time flies. You often look at time just to meet deadlines and appointments but you never stop to think that the clock on the wall or the watch on your wrist ruthlessly mark the fast passing of our existence. One of the few things that compel us to reflect is when we are in front of the mirror. It is this strange object that only humans use to help us notice the changes in our skin, our hair, our body in general. 'Are you still Matteo Moscardi?' he asked himself in the toilet of his office observing the first wrinkles on his face and his hair streaked with grey, although only in his forties. 'It's you but it is not you!' a voice answered from inside. *Panta rhei*[37] the philosophy teacher at school used to say. Yes…yes. It's true. Tomorrow we will not be what we are today… God, why did you make everything so complicated?

That Monday night Matteo got home around midnight. He opened the front door trying not to make a noise to avoid waking Francesco. He was hungry because he had eaten only a sandwich around seven p.m. He did not like to eat late at night so he decided to drink a glass of milk just to quieten the rumblings in his stomach. A yawn. Two yawns. It was time to go to bed. The bedroom door was ajar while the dim light of the little lamp on Marina's bedside table spread a pale pink glow all around. She was sleeping, or pretending to sleep, curled up in the same position he had left her in the morning. In a way he was pleased that she was asleep so he would not have to face her curious eyes and unpredictable questions.

---

37 'Everything flows' is a famous saying of the Greek philosopher Heraclitus to mean that everything is constantly changing.

In another way he felt a sort of anguish triggered by his own guilt, a disturbing sensation caused not only by his behaviour following the embarrassing situation he was living, but also by the fact that his work impeded him from being present in the family as much as he would like. His contact with Francesco was rare and communication with Marina had become almost non-existent. Very few were the occasions when they sat all together to have dinner or to go to a restaurant, and as for weekends he couldn't even remember when they had last spent one together. Bad. Very bad... He undressed slowly and approached Marina's bedside table to switch off the light. Her eyes were closed, her breath slow and shallow. He understood that she was not asleep. In the darkness he crept round to the other side of the bed and silently slipped under the covers. Though in the same bed, his wife was miles away and their bodies frozen in this 'cage' of incommunicability.

- Good morning, Mr Moscardi! – Nadia welcomed Matteo the next morning in the office. – I told you that my cousin would find the information you requested. He has just sent me an email... Here it is.

- Great! May I have a look?

- Sure, have a read and if there's anything else I can help you with, please let me know.

He took the printed sheet and sat at his desk while Nadia returned to her office.

He read:

*The estate at 11 Oldham Street in Manchester was built in 1799 by one Edward Attwood, a rich merchant from Lancashire. One of his sons, Harold, was a British officer as was Harold's son Benjamin. The four storey house has always been occupied by the Attwoods whose names have been handed down from generation to generation with few variants. Except for the ground floor that is now occupied by a fashion company, the rest of the property has been left as it was, in particular the external façade on Oldham Street, which is virtually intact. Now the house is inhabited by Benjamin Attwood, a man in his seventies.*

Good news! Now he was sure that the Benjamin Attwood who he had met in his 'past life' really had existed. Determined not to waste any time, Matteo took a headed sheet of paper with his telephone number on, and with his best ink pen and neatest handwriting wrote:

*Dear Sir*
*This brief letter will seem a bit odd. Indeed it is. My name is Matteo Moscardi and I am from Milan. As a result of strange incidents that have occurred in my life, about which I am unable to speak or describe just now, I am doing research on Captain Benjamin Attwood, born in Manchester in 1810. This has led me to the address of your home. If this name is no stranger to you, I would be most grateful if you would contact me as soon as possible as this will be in the interests of us both. I look forward to hearing from you.*
*Yours faithfully*
*Matteo Moscardi.*

As he slipped the paper into the envelope, Matteo tried to step into the shoes of the person who would receive it. How would he react? It was not easy to imagine, but he thought that this was the best way to make initial contact. He called Nadia and requested that she send the letter by express mail for it to arrive as quickly as possible. A little later that morning, he received a call from Jacopo who was very curious and anxious to know what decisions he had taken since their last meeting.

- I think you should plan a long trip to England and India,

– Jacopo advised after hearing the latest piece of information from Matteo.

- I think so too... A lot depends on the answer I receive from Manchester... I'll keep you updated.

After the short conversation with Jacopo, Matteo realised that in the event that he should leave on a long trip, he would need to provide a replacement at work. His deputy director would certainly be able to stand in for him, but the problem was not so much work as... Marina... He thought... What would he tell her? Sure, it often happened that he had to go away for several days but he was used to telling her where he was going. He had never lied to her nor would he. He had already been to Britain and to a few Far Eastern countries, so she should not find it strange to hear where he would be going on this trip... But it was not a business trip! He had always considered that telling a lie was absolutely contrary to his nature, but recently the possibility of him actually lying to his wife was becoming an obsession. Pushed by a strong need to create a reassuring atmosphere, Matteo called his wife to tell her that he would be home early that evening, a good opportunity to have dinner at their favourite restaurant. However, pleased as she was by her husband's proposal, she said she would prefer to cook dinner at home. He thought that deep down he also liked to sit at the table at home with his family while the fireplace gave off a cosy warmth. At least for this evening he would be a good father and a 'normal' husband. It is incredible how the smallest transgression of so-called normality leads our minds to create the conditions for the theatre of our behaviour. A theatricalism that springs from a need of duplicity, of falsehood and hypocrisy conceived with that perverse mechanism of intelligence that evil makes extremely creative. We are not as creative and fruitful in building good as in building evil. Why?

The evening was unexpectedly calm and pleasant. Marina

had cooked *cappelletti in broth* as the starter and *melanzane alla parmigiana*[38] as the main course. Delicious. And, of course, the meal could not be served without a bottle of wine: *Cirò rosé* from Calabria. Matteo congratulated her and told her that he appreciated the fact that she had cooked. Marina appeared cheerful, happy. She was talkative and it seemed that his neglect of her in recent weeks had not tarnished their relationship in any way. Matteo did not know what to think; perhaps it was he who had created non-existent problems. He was about to tell her his story and his plans for the coming days, but something prevented him: a feeling that she would not understand and perhaps would not accept what he was doing and what he was going to do. He knew her well... but not very well. It was better not to risk ruining the evening.

- I have something to do abroad in the coming days, – he said later helping his wife to clear the table. – I don't know exactly when... and I could be away for several days.

- Well, it's not the first time... – she replied without hesitation as if everything was normal. – Work is work. But be careful, take care of yourself... I feel that you're overdoing it... I've already told you that you work too hard, you have too much stress. And when you're under stress those strange things happen... I mean... those weird things like last time... Your visions... Hallucinations... Paranoia... Stress can easily cause paranoia.

Matteo found Marina's way of expressing her thoughts disarming. He could not understand if she was just being ironic or if she wanted at all costs to remove from her mind those nagging worries and fears that perhaps he really was ill. He did not know how to react, what to say. No, he did not know her. Not yet, despite them having been together for twelve years.

- Go and relax, Matteo! – she continued from the kitchen.

---

38  Eggplant with parmesan.

– I'll bring you your coffee in a minute. The cleaner's coming in the morning and she'll tidy all this up.

Puzzled and a little confused, the man did what his wife said and went to sit on the couch with Francesco, who was leafing through a book of fairy tales.

- What are you reading, Francesco? – his father asked.
- Little Red Riding Hood… It's the third time I've read it.
- Ah! You like it that much!?
- Dad, I don't like fairy tales anymore… I'm not a child.
- Hahahaha! You're not a child, right. But you're not an adult yet either.
- I'm a boy, then!
- Yes, you're a little boy.

The aroma of coffee served on a silver tray permeated the air around.

- Thanks, Marina, that's lovely – complimented Matteo as she sat by his side.
- At last we're all together in our home, like a normal family.

Marina said these words while looking at the flames in the hearth and with one hand resting on his arm. Matteo could not remember how long it had been since he had felt the touch of her body. He felt relaxed in this warm family scenario, sitting between his wife and his child, sipping the last coffee of the day. What is more, the images that had persecuted him over the last two days seemed to have given him a momentary respite. Their conversations were few and brief but the silence in between was not awkward. They went rather early to bed as the wine had made them slightly drowsy. The atmosphere of the evening had drawn them closer. In bed they lay facing each other looking into each other's eyes.

- Who or what is between us? – asked Marina quietly.

She didn't expect an answer.

In fact, no answer was offered. And she closed her eyes.

Two days after that unusual evening, at 11.00 a.m., Matteo received a call on his mobile from an unknown English number.

- Hello! – he answered guessing that the caller was Benjamin Attwood.

- Good morning, sir! – Am I talking to Mr... Matteo Moscardi, from Milan?

- Yes, that's correct... I sent you a short letter that I imagine you must have found rather unusual.

Matteo's English was not perfect, but he was able to make himself understood and to understand well enough. He had studied English grammar very seriously when he was a student and he was obliged to use this language frequently at work with his many foreign contacts.

- I wonder what kind of interest you could have in my ancestor? – the English man said with a posh accent that revealed his high social class.

- If you give me the opportunity to meet you, I will explain everything, sir... Now... on the phone it's rather difficult.

- Very well, when would you be able to come?...

- I could come tomorrow... I would be very grateful.

- Perfect, give me a ring when you arrive in Manchester tomorrow.

- Thank you very much. I'll see you tomorrow then!

Finally things were going in the right direction, Matteo thought with satisfaction. The first thing he did was to find a flight leaving the next day. No problem. There were a few from different airports. He booked a flight leaving at nine in the morning and also made a reservation at a hotel in Manchester where he intended to spend the night. He would come back the following day. He was suddenly gripped by a feeling of excitement consisting of curiosity and impatience, as though this trip to Manchester would give answers to his many questions. He was also looking forward to breathing a different air at least for one day. He had been in Manchester a few times before but only on business. Apart from the city centre, he did not know very much of that big city, but he seemed to remember Oldham Street. Not well but he was sure he would remember once there. When he was a student, he used to attend English courses a few weeks every summer in London, but he did not practise the language as well as he wanted because the other students were not as advanced as he was. However, he did get the opportunity to practise a lot one year when he went to work in a library in Richmond. He spent almost six months there, which proved very valuable in improving his English. He had fond memories of that experience and still kept in contact with a few people he met there.

The aircraft took off exactly at nine from Orio al Serio airport. It was not cold and the sky was blue and clear, but he could see on his smartphone that in Manchester it was cloudy. In fact, he remembered that every time he had been there it was raining. He tried to sleep a little during the flight. An old man looking through a photo album was sitting on his left while behind him he could hear the gossip of two Italian women going to visit the English daughter-in-law of one of the two. He closed his eyes without falling asleep. His mind was a whirlpool where everything was mixed together, but the frustration that followed the hypnosis and the dream in front of the TV had left him having to accept the fact that he would have to live with the ghosts of a life he had lived before.

It was not raining in Manchester when the aircraft landed but the sky was terribly grey and heavy. As he exited the airport he called Mr Attwood who answered immediately. In just a few words, he had invited Matteo to have lunch with him at his house at 1.30 p.m. He accepted the invitation with some hesitancy due more to the surprise than to the fact that it was already 11.30. He found it strange that this man had invited a stranger to his house for lunch. He hailed down a taxi and as he got in he asked the driver to take him to the hotel. Once seated inside, since he only had a small bag with him, he changed his mind and gave instructions to be taken directly to Oldham Street instead. Apart from the usual traffic, the journey was uneventful. From time to time he would stare out of the window but his mind was elsewhere. When he got out of the taxi, he began to get his bearings and to familiarise himself with the street. It was a main road. He thought that it would not be polite to arrive empty-handed. He wondered if Mr Attwood had a wife; maybe he would buy some flowers. Maybe not. A bottle of wine would be better, a bottle of good Italian wine, of course. It would be appreciated more. So, he rushed to Market Street where, after browsing the shelves, at last he found what he wanted. With a *Chianti* wrapped in beautiful silver paper, he was now ready to knock at the door of his mysterious past life. The upper façade of the building, as written in the policeman's email, looked intact in its original architecture and beauty, but the ground floor, occupied by the fashion company, and part of the first floor showed signs of restoration. Inside, the staircase leading to the upper floors was large with a handrail made of thick brown wood. At the top, there were two gigantic stained glass windows, one that looked onto Oldham Street and the other onto an inner courtyard. He wondered how many people had climbed those stairs in more than two hundred years. Looking up and all around he deduced that the house was much too big for just one family.

Mr Benjamin Attwood, although in his seventies, was youngish in his physical appearance and elegant in his bearing. 'He can't have done any heavy work in his life,' Matteo thought noticing that there were no wrinkles on his face. 'Perhaps he doesn't drink alcohol, or smoke, or eat fatty foods, or ever have any stress. Very unusual for a British man!' If Matteo had not known his age, he would have guessed he was at least ten years younger.

- Welcome to my house, Mr... Moscardi, right? – the man said inviting him to step into the hall.

- Call me Matteo or Matthew, it's easier for you.

- And I'm Ben!

At that moment a middle-aged woman appeared smiling at him, she helped him take off his coat then put his bag away. Matteo imagined that she must have been a governess, a maid or have had some such profession. They headed along a large corridor where the eye got lost amongst tapestries, antique console tables and large mirrors, then he was invited to sit in the dining room furnished with simple but antique furniture. On the walls there were several paintings depicting the four seasons while on the large hood of the fireplace large plates were attached and copper trays embossed with hunting scenes.

- This is for you, – Matteo said putting the bottle on the table that was already set for two people.

- Thanks, thanks, you are very kind... This wine is delicious. But it wasn't necessary for you to bring anything.

The woman returned wheeling a trolley and, after the two men had sat down at the table, started to serve hot mushroom soup.

- Thank you, Linda, – he said, and looking at his guest: – Linda is a fantastic cook... Actually she is fantastic at everything. I'd feel lost without her.

- I believe my short letter aroused your curiosity.

- In a way, yes. As far as I know none of my family has ever been the subject of particular attention or interest by outsiders... To receive such attention from an Italian... yes, I confess, it seemed a bit strange. Perhaps I wouldn't have been surprised if the target of interest of your research was Harold. He was a great man, mentioned by all historians for what he was and for what he did, not only in India but also in this part of the country.

- What I remember from school books is that it must have been a very busy town at that time.

- We were at the height of the industrial revolution that increased the size of this town tenfold or more ... This house was built by Edward Attwood at the end of the eighteenth century. Business was booming; Edward was involved in the cotton trade and other products. He became rich and bought many acres of good land in this county. But, he had other ambitions for his children that didn't have anything to do with trade. He wanted the Attwoods to climb the social ranks in society. He coerced his daughter, Rose, to marry an aristocrat twenty years older than herself and ensured that his son, Harold, was accepted at the military academy although not the son of a military man, as was the law at the time. But Edward had many contacts in the high ranks of British officers serving in India and he got what he wanted. Harold displayed excellent military qualities for which he was entrusted with important assignments. He took advantage of his experience once he returned to Manchester and devoted his life to politics. Benjamin also showed great potential, but a few years after returning from India he became ill and died at the young age of thirty-five... He had married an English girl with whom he had two sons: Edward and Christopher. Edward was my grandfather and remained in this house. Christopher went to live in London. He inherited part of the land and relinquished his claims on this house. My father, Harold, was anything but a military man, neither did he have anything to do with business or trade. He was an intellectual, a scholar, and became a professor at the University of Manchester. My sister Lauren also lives here, but on the top floor... In short, this is the history of the Attwoods.

Linda uncorked the bottle of *Chianti* in the kitchen and

came to pour the wine into our glasses. Benjamin looked at it, smelt it and breathed in its aroma.

- Cheers! – he toasted lifting the glass slightly.
- Cheers!
- Wonderful... Thanks again.

Linda took the empty bowls away then served a cod stew with boiled potatoes and carrots. Once again she disappeared into the kitchen.

- I had no idea Benjamin died so young, – Matteo said thinking of how to start to explain the reason for his visit. – What I'm going to tell you may sound ridiculous and hard to believe... My wife is cynical and sceptical when she hears these things too... Actually, even I have found it difficult to accept...

- I'm intrigued, Matteo. Go on, please. Whatever it is I'd be interested to know since it concerns a member of my family.

- Well, since I was a little boy, it has happened that...

So, Matteo, stumbling through the beginning of his story, was able to attract the attention of his interlocutor. In truth, while venturing further into the story, he could not discern from Benjamin's expression if he believed him or not. He knew that it would not be easy for anyone to believe him therefore he was rather brief, omitting many details and made no mention of the ring or the diamond. Matteo paused a few times to take mouthfuls of the delicious meal, but his listener never interrupted before he had completed his narrative. When mentioning Amir, it was apparent from the surprise shown in Mr Attwood's eyes that he was talking to someone who knew that what he was being told could not have been invented. Linda popped in only once while he was talking but did not seem to be interested in what he was saying, or perhaps she was displaying a courteous sense of discretion.

- This is the story, – Matteo concluded sipping the remnants of the wine in his glass. – Apart from my friend,

Jacopo, you are the only person I've told this to. I realise that it's very difficult to understand all this rationally.

- I have something to show you, – Ben said getting up and inviting him to follow.

They walked along another stretch of the corridor and entered an area that aroused the admiration of the Italian man. His eyes were delighted by the amber silk damask on the walls. The same fabric, in a darker colour, was also used in the upholstery and dividing curtains. A number of armchairs and sofas of different sizes with tables, also of different dimensions, gave the environment an inviting and aesthetically pleasing appeal. Two large windows tried to capture and convey inside the faint light of a non-existent sun. A series of large rugs, most likely Persian, lay on part of the floor while the remaining area was covered in parquet that did not hide its age with the obvious use it had endured. This reception room must have witnessed much entertaining and many parties. Hand-made cupboards and special tables displayed porcelains and silverware with famous names. Matteo tried to imagine what kind of people would have frequented this house over the two hundred years. Throughout the Victorian period, in accordance with the social ambitions of the patriarch Edward, a mix of aristocracy and bourgeoisie enriched by the neo-capitalism produced by manufacturers, traders and mine owners, must have been used to giving vent to the boredom of their affluence. On one of the walls, the portraits of the male Attwoods were arranged in succession starting with the oldest, Edward, while in full military uniform, Harold proudly showed off his glittering sword. Benjamin, too, was in full military uniform. Matteo's heart jolted... Did he recognise him? He approached the painting examining his face carefully straining to see and review the images of his visions.

- This is your Benjamin! – the host exclaimed.
- Yes, I'm trying to see his features in my mind... I'm sure

there is something familiar, especially about his hair and his eyes... His gaze... Yes. You said he died at thirty-five... He must have had this portrait made shortly before his death.

- You're right, he was born in 1810 and the date on the back of the picture is 1843. That means he was thirty-three... But there's something else that will have greater significance for you.

- What do you mean?

Matteo followed him into a room less ornate than those he had seen until now. A wonderful brown wooden desk stood in front of the tall bookcases propped against two walls, while on another wall there were other portraits of smaller dimensions than those in the reception room. Only two depicted women: one of Rose Attwood dressed in plain Victorian style; the other, Lauren, who was still alive, painted when she was probably in her twenties. A third picture showed a boy, perhaps 10 or 11 years old, with obvious Asian features. On a small brass plate riveted to the lower part of the frame was the inscription: Amir Chun Pundit, 1845. Matteo was magnetised by the appearance of this little boy. Suddenly bolts of lightning flashed in the darkness of his *other self* illuminating memories of Subhadra with her child sleeping in her arms and Benjamin sitting next to her holding them both. Immediately, as at all other times when reliving his past, an intense sharp pain penetrated the depths of his being while a dull and distant peal of an indistinctive voice echoed inside him: 'Maaaattteeeooooo! Maaaaattteeeeooooooo!'

- This must be him, – whispered Matteo pointing to Amir. – Amir!

- Yes, this is Amir. The portrait was made a couple of months before my ancestor's death... When he came back from India, he brought Amir with him, who was only two years old at the time.

Mr Attwood approached the lower part of one of the

bookcases. He took a leather-bound book and held it so that Matteo could see it. It was not really a book but a handwritten diary. On the cover, in gold letters, was written simply the name of the author: Benjamin Attwood.

- My father had once shown this to his students during a lecture and had told them that it was not a very interesting diary except for the chapters regarding his military experience in Bengal. He performed his service during a time of important reforms in India and he was the trusted officer of an important governor... William Bentinck. It was mainly thanks to him that the horrendous tradition of burning widows, called *sati*, was abolished. In one chapter he tells a story of a woman called Subhadra, the mother of this child, Amir, who was burned on the pyre at her husband's funeral. He also reveals his feelings for this woman. After her death he felt a moral obligation towards the child and on completion of his mission he returned to England bringing the child with him. Amir was brought up here, in this house, and when Benjamin died, his wife, Mary, continued to look after him in accordance with the will of her husband. Edward and Christopher always considered Amir their older brother.

Mr Attwood leafed through the diary a few times then selected the chapter about Amir and his mother.

- Matteo, I cannot give or lend you this diary, – he said handing me the book. – It's not a long chapter... You can sit here, feel free and take your time to read whatever you're interested in. Then, if you want, I'll make photocopies of the chapter. I'll leave you alone for a while with the characters of your past life, so you can read and meditate...and have a chat with them. Meanwhile I'll send Linda in with a nice cup of tea for you.

As Ben left, Matteo sat on an armchair and looked around, his eyes lingering on different objects: a small wooden elephant, a special tool with an ivory handle, a showcase full of military medals, an English manufactured musquet used in the first half of the nineteenth century, a precious letter opener next to a leather folder on the desk, a dark green crystal ashtray and cigar case, a pair of quills next to a bottle of ink, an old camera and various photos on a shelf, other trinkets, trinkets everywhere ... He was curious about the diary. In the first ten pages the officer recounted how it was that he came to be posted to Bengal, first to Calcutta and then to Cossimbazar, and the reasons his garrison was given a special task. He had some difficulty in reading the handwriting but in general it was legible and clear. Matteo thought that these pages constituted an important historical document, but he was not a historian, so he could not really judge. Linda knocked quietly at the door and came in again wheeling her trolley loaded with a Wedgwood tea set: a hot teapot and teacup, Sheffield-made silver cutlery, a sugar bowl, butter and marmalade, and an assortment of biscuits.

- Indian tea, – said Linda smiling. – I've read that in Italy you're not used to drinking tea as much as we are here.
- That's right, not as much as here... More coffee...
- You mean *espresso*... not our coffee!
- That's correct... A small amount served in little cups.
- And drunk very hot!
- Drunk?!... I wouldn't say drunk... It's not the right verb... Sipped... First inhaled for its aroma...and then sipped.
- Wonderful! I will have to try this *espresso* sooner or later.

The two laughed then Linda disappeared and Matteo started to read something that woke him up from a sudden drowsiness that the cocoon-like environment and the greyness of the weather made heavier.

'I met Subhadra by chance owing to an accident that had befallen one of my soldiers in the vicinity of the mansion where she lived.' he read. 'She was married to one of the sons of the Pundit family regarded as one of the most powerful and respectable families in the region, that is to say, respectable according to the standards of Bengalese culture. Even today. I can't say what kind of power she exercised over me from the very first instant that our eyes met. Apart from the highly seductive charm of her beautiful person, she was gifted with a penetrating energy to which the elements of nature were also not indifferent. One day, thanks to this special and innate strength, she saved me from being devoured by a tiger. Facing each other and staring into each other's eyes, there was a mutual recognition, they spoke with their eyes, and the beast, in obedience to a law that Nature commands be respected, wagged her tail as a sign of peace and disappeared into the vegetation. Subhadra was the innocent victim of the depression of an ill man who was not able to accept the impairment that the disease caused. His awareness of the certainty of his imminent death forced him to isolate himself from everyone, including his wife. Today, in hindsight, I am convinced that Ram's rejection of Subhadra was a great act of love. Added to this there was a litigious atmosphere between the families of the same clan because of old rights of ownership, and the unbearable presence of a cousin named Devesh, who besides claiming these rights, wanted Subhadra for himself. Devesh was also an instigator of the opposition to the politics of social reforms wanted by the British and at the same time he was the cunning weaver of the smuggling system between Europeans and Bengalese gangs. There were rumours that Ram was the owner of a pink diamond to which superstitions attributed strange powers, but only two or three people knew the place where it was hidden. When Ram died, his wife was condemned to death by burning on the pyre. She would have been able to avoid it because she was under my protection, but she did not want to betray the principles and traditions of her religion. *Sati* had been outlawed but the caste did not accept this, so the practice continued to be upheld in some areas. I was not in Cossimbazar when Subhadra was burned otherwise I would not have allowed it to happen. With the powers bestowed by law I had Ram's father arrested as the one responsible for Subhadra's death and for not complying with the law. The most conservative representatives of the caste protested and after only four weeks from his arrest, the man was released. The decision to release him came after a series of consultations between the Governor of the Presidency and the emissaries of Ram Moham Roy.[39] They agreed that in order not to exasperate the still powerful conservative caste, it was better for the time being to release Pundit to encourage a process of reform that required more time. Ram's father would die not much later after his release during a journey to Bengala Delta owing to an attack of malaria, a very common disease in that area. As for Amir, he was under the care of his grandparents when his mother died but with the death of his grandfather things took a turn for the worse. Abha, who had been a loyal servant to Subhadra, found the way, one day, to inform me of what was taking place in the mansion. While hiding, she had heard several quarrels between Devesh and Huddar, Ram's mother. Each time, Devesh would argue and raise doubt that Amir could really be Ram's son since he had been ill. It was obviously a despicable game whose aim was to deny the child's right of inheritance and thereby benefit himself. He ensured that this gossip spread. Furthermore, he accused Subhadra of being my *bibi,* the *bibi* of the captain of the garrison in return for his protection. Huddar took this allegation as a terrible insult but understood that without her husband she did not have the strength to oppose the will of that devil. It happened that Iswar also died after being squashed against the trunk of a tree by an elephant…'

---

[39] Ram Moham Roy (Bengali 22 May 1772-27 September 1833) was the founder of an influential socio-religious reform movement Brahmo Sabha. He is best known for his effort to establish the abolition of the practice of *sati.*

On seeing the name Iswar, Matteo interrupted his reading. Iswar. 'He was the only one left who knew the secret of the diamond ring,' he thought. 'He kept the secret to himself. Why? As a sign of unquestionable loyalty or for other purposes? So, unless the mansion has been destroyed the diamond is still there...'

'Iswar was soon replaced by Baldev.' Matteo continued to read, 'Huddar, in Abhar's opinion, sensed that Devesh was concocting a plan to get rid of the child. He was a ruthless man willing to do anything to get what he wanted; therefore, she devised a plan to move to the home of her other son. A difficult decision to take since she knew that to abandon the mansion would make it easier for Devesh to fulfil his evil plans. The man was also obsessed with the fact that there was a third person who knew the whereabouts of the diamond. He suspected it to be Iswar since he was one of the very few people to have direct contact with Ram during his illness. He tried questioning and threatening him but got nowhere. I asked Abha what she thought of Huddar's fears and she answered: "*Sahib,* I also think that Devesh will get rid of the child... You are the only person who can save him." These last words shook me deeply. I asked her what I could do. I had no rights to Amir. "*Sahib,*" she continued looking at me intensely, "Subhadra loved you... and you loved her." These indiscrete words uttered by a servant annoyed me somewhat, but I overlooked it and saw her in a different way. She was a woman whose appearance was miserable; she was poorly dressed and looked older than her age, frail and thin, living on the streets like many other people in India or whose only shelter sometimes is a house made of dry, hardened mud where children and adults are crammed in all together and with no hygiene. Yet, I had to admit that she was sensitive and intelligent. We, who represent the higher ranks of society, think that some feelings and some qualities of intellect belong only to us and we look at the poor and slaves like people whose brains and whose hearts are unable to think and to feel like ours. Will God one day uproot and overturn vanity and arrogance that make the human race so bad and unfair?... Utopia. Who knows! – Following on from this meeting with Abha, the protection of the child became a priority for me. I had never met Devesh but for sure he knew me and, furthermore, he hated me. I felt that sooner or later I would have to face him. I knew that the police were aware of the misdeeds of this individual especially concerning his contacts with smugglers, but he was one of those untouchables always present where there is corruption. One evening I was invited to the Officer's Club at the British East India Company and there the topic of conversation with one fellow officer turned unexpectedly to the subject of smuggling. I learnt on that occasion what kind of unscrupulous man that Devesh was. He was included in a list of people suspected not only of various criminal activities, but also of fomenting anti-British movements. At Headquarters they were planning to frame him and sentence him to a severe punishment. But fate, or the energies that govern our lives, wanted us to meet sooner than I thought. He and his henchmen had been studying my behaviour for months. My early morning ride, which I hardly ever missed, was pretty routine for me. I varied my routes but for those who spied on me it was not hard to work out where I was going. I was more or less in the same place where the incident with *Zara* happened. I do not know why from time to time I felt attracted and drawn to this stretch of thick forest. Perhaps, unconsciously, I needed to see her again to show my gratitude. It was definitely the frequency of my rides there that gave Devesh the opportunity to ambush me. Getting close to the clump of tall shrubs on the edge of the forest, a premonition, perhaps given by the spirit of Subhadra, ordered me to be cautious, so I ensured that my dagger and my Flintlock gun were in place. It was thanks to this sudden warning that, by the skin of my teeth, I escaped being captured by an ugly creep hiding in the leaves of a *peepal* tree who launched his lasso at me. But then from behind, someone succeeded in throwing his rope around me, but fortunately I already had my dagger in my hand and was able to cut through it. There were three men, one of whom must have been Devesh. He was proudly wearing his turban and at his side holding a beautiful *talwar* sword with a curved blade. He shouted something to the two henchmen who lunged towards me with daggers in hand. I dismounted my horse with a jump and as I did so managed to kick one of the two in the face while with my dagger, I slashed the other's arm. "You two, get out of here if you want to save your life," I shouted pulling out my gun. And addressing Devesh: "You scoundrel, you who shows your strength against the weak, take what is left of your dignity and face me in a duel!" While the two wounded men dragged themselves away into the forest, the criminal and I remained on the scene. He made a grimace of contempt and looked at me as if to assess my moves and then unsheathed his sword. I put my gun aside leaving me with only my dagger. Devesh was a man of medium height but well-built. He certainly had not suffered hunger like his skeleton-like minions. From the expression in his eyes, I could now better understand the fear he instilled in people and, thinking of Subhadra, my anger fuelled my aggression. I realised that having only a dagger, I was at a great disadvantage and I had to be very skilful at dodging the lashes of his sword, and attempt to disorient and tire him. Sure of his superiority, he lunged at me with all his strength. Out of the corner of my eye, I caught sight of a few sticks of different lengths propped against a tree trunk, which had probably been collected by a *mohout* to train elephants. The tip of his sword cut through the fabric of my shirt but did not even scratch my skin. Pretending to step back, I quickly bent down and plunged my dagger deep into his calf then rolled along the ground to reach the sticks. I grabbed one while my enemy was caught off-guard by the searing pain in his leg. Fast and unpredictable like a feline, despite his wound, Devesh sprang towards me swiping his sword at me. I managed to shield my face with the stick which easily broke in two upon impact with the blade. Seizing the opportunity, I grabbed his hand that held the sword and with all my strength I pulled him to the ground hurling punches at his head. He tried to fight back but I had the dagger pointed at his neck ready to thrust it into his jugular vein...

"*Sahib! Sahib!*"

It was Abha's voice; she had appeared like a ghost from nowhere followed by one of the henchmen that had likely rushed to the mansion to ask somebody to intervene to break up the fight. She pleaded with me not to kill him because that would further fuel the anti-British feelings of Devesh's clan. I hesitated. Although livid, I knew that I had never killed a man except in battle and with a musket. Bringing my anger under control, I told the defeated man that I would save his life, but I could not let him go. He had ambushed and attempted to kill a British officer, which constituted a serious crime. He risked being hanged. With his face to the ground, motionless and humiliated, Devesh remained silent while my soldiers, after having lost sight of me, had now arrived after searching the area. Witnessing the scene, they rushed to arrest the men. The blood from my enemy's wound had soaked and stained a large area on the trousers of my uniform. Abha said that she would wash them at the mansion but did not know how Huddar would react. I looked at her with pity appreciating the generosity of that woman whose heart was bigger than her. I told her to go back to the mansion and to report to Huddar that Devesh would no longer bother her or the child.

After that harrowing incident, I did not learn anything more about what took place at the mansion for at least eight months. As for Devesh, he had to stand trial. The charge was based primarily on the premeditation of the attack, but during the investigation important facts emerged about his illicit activities and his scheming against the British. There was no getting away from the fact that I was ready to forgive. However, he was sentenced to be hanged, while the other two wretches were sentenced to five years in prison... It was the end of May 1836. After three months my mission would be over and I would return to Britain. One day my batman, George, came to inform me that Abha, the servant at Pundit's mansion, wanted to see me. I told him to accompany her to my residence and wait for me. When I entered and she saw me, she bowed reverently, which made me feel uneasy. She did not hide her happiness to see me. I, too, was happy to see her but I did not show it in such an obvious way. Abha started to tell me that Amir was twenty months old now, that he walked well and had started to speak. For a short period she had left the mansion because Baldev, the man who had replaced Iswar, did not like her, so he had convinced Huddar to send her away. The truth was that, after having got to know a lot of information about her, especially about her past closeness to Subhadra, he considered her a dangerous person. Furthermore, he preferred much younger women around him. After leaving she remained in touch with one of these girls who reported back to her everything that happened at the mansion. After one month Huddar forced Baldev to accept Abha back at the mansion. There she learnt that there were still problems regarding Amir's right of ownership. Devesh's brothers, although not as bad as him, claimed the rights and persisted in maintaining that the child was not Ram's son. Abha sensed that Baldev supported Devesh's brothers and feared that Amir was in danger. Huddar thought the same but she was very ill and weak, so she decided that the only solution would be to send the child away from the mansion. "That's why I'm here," the poor woman concluded. "Huddar wanted me to contact you to ask for your help once more because she is dying and Amir will have no one to protect him." I felt agitated and angry after hearing these things. "Get Huddar to send me a written request of what she wants." I told her resolutely. "As soon as I receive it, I will send my batman with two soldiers to fetch the child." She thanked me bowing again and turned to leave. I noticed that she was barefoot. I asked her to wait a few seconds. On a small table there was a tray with English sweets. I put them in a small box and handed it to the woman, who looked embarrassed. Then I also took some rupees from my wallet and gave them to her, she hesitated before accepting, because, I think, she would never have imagined that such a thing could happen. She did not know what to say. I asked if she had a family, children, etcetera. She said that she had married when she was fourteen and had given birth to four children, three of whom had died. Only one girl remained alive. Luckily one of her sisters had taken the girl to Calcutta with her. "In this country, life is very short," she concluded before leaving. "Hunger and disease kill mainly the poor, who are the majority, and first of all the children." I knew, I knew. Especially in Calcutta I had seen corpses along the streets and starving people everywhere. But I had never attached any importance to that reality. Most people belonging to the upper social classes consider misery a plague to be avoided and a world deprived of God's protection. I am one of them, of that privileged race; therefore, I am blessed and protected by God, the God of everything and of everybody, the God who seemingly does not love everyone equally. In that situation where Abha was standing right in front of me, my heart suddenly softened, maybe not suddenly because, since meeting Subhadra, I had already begun to be more sensitive.

Huddar sent me a letter straight away via Abha explaining the child's situation and imploring me to take care of him.

I did not waste any time. I told the servant that she could come to live in the lodgings where she had stayed before with Subhadra. I trusted her and wanted her to look after Amir. Then I ordered George to provide everything they would need. Amir looked very much like his mother. I welcomed him warmly as if he were my own son. A strange feeling that even today I do not understand. After a few weeks I felt that I would not be able to leave him, therefore, in view of my return to Britain and aware of the responsibility that his grandmother had conferred on me, I decided to take him with me. In those three months Abha proved a worthy substitute mother. I could not imagine what she would do to endure the difficulties of life when I departed. "What can I do for you?" I asked her a few days before leaving. She did not answer but simply looked lost. "I am worried about you," I insisted. Finally she spoke: "*Sahib,* you have a gentle heart and I thank you for your concern, but you must not... You must not worry... You see us through your western eyes." "What do you mean?" "Our relationship with life and death, especially with death, is different from yours. Here death does not bring suffering, and our philosophy of life is not the same as yours... For a Hindu, the world, the body and the mind are illusions." I understood, and once more I felt a sense of guilt press heavily on my chest. "*Sahib!*" she continued. "Subhadra will follow you forever, she is looking at us now, she will be reincarnated in people and in other elements of nature; one day her soul will dwell within somebody from an unimaginable place in this world and her story will be revived in order for her to achieve purification according to the dictates of our religion." "And what should this person do, the one in whom her soul dwells?" After a long pause she concluded: "Good; they must do good."

Abha did not come to say goodbye either to me or to the child when we left. I think it was because the pain of separation would have been too much for her.

I left the army a few months after arriving in Britain and subsequently tried to follow in the footsteps of my father in politics. Unfortunately, our ideas put us on opposite sides (I will talk about this in the next chapter). Amir was at ease in his new reality and when I got married, my wife, Mary, accepted him, as did I, like a son.'

At the end of every chapter Benjamin had pencilled a little drawing. He must have been quite artistic. Here he had sketched a portrait of Subhadra. It was clear that this picture was the result not only of his skill, but of something more that could only have come from love. In those features I recognised the woman of my visions: it was me two hundred years earlier! Incredible! I had been completely absorbed in reading the diary. It was an extremely interesting story written in a clear and concise way and filled with facts about what India was like not so long ago.

- I'll briefly tell you the remaining pieces of Amir's story, – Mr Attwood said on entering the room with an unlit cigar between two fingers.

He sat on an armchair in front of me and asked if I minded him smoking. I answered that it did not disturb me although I was a non-smoker.

- I'd like to ask you, – I continued as he lit the cigar, – what were the different political positions that Benjamin and his father held?

- Ben was a dreamer, – he said inhaling just a little of the white smoke. – He was an idealist. When he came back from India, his idealism was stronger than when he had left. His contact with poverty had made him so sensitive towards this aspect of society that he tried to fight against its injustice for the short time he had left to live. As I have already mentioned, at the time, we were at the climax of the industrial revolution and the exploitation of workers and children created great social distress.

- Yes, yes... I read a lot when I was a student. I liked Charles

Dickens, Elizabeth Gaskell, Frank Forrest...

- Exactly, these and other authors wrote a lot about the exploitation of children. Ben was well aware that poverty and its problems affected not only India but also his own country. His adherence to a socialism that became more and more aggressive forced him away from his father who saw socialism like a cancer that could destroy progress... But Benjamin fell ill and this prevented him from playing an active role in his political party. A journalist at the time reported that his father, Harold, had not cried at his son's funeral... Ben's wife, Mary, continued to look after Amir and raised him in accordance with British customs. He was intelligent, respectful of others and at school he was among the best. Secure and confident due to the solid foundation of his British education, at the age of 23 he decided to return to his country of birth where he still had many outstanding accounts. He soon secured a prestigious social position in Bengal then worked to regain possession of his properties, the mansion included. The descendants of Amir and the Attwoods have never cut their tie. My father went to visit them and I myself had planned to go there, but for various reasons I was unable to go.

The man got up and walked over to a table. Picking up a bottle of Scotch, he poured some whisky into a glass and returned to his armchair.

- Amazing! – Matteo exclaimed. – Very touching... I feel moved. It's a novel, a great novel.
- Yes, you're right. It has all the ingredients of a great novel.
- But the ending has not yet been written.

Mr Attwood laughed.

- I can't imagine what it would be, – he said in an ironic tone. – I don't think that you will come across Subhadra in that mansion anymore.
- You said that Amir returned to Bengal because he had many outstanding accounts to settle there... Well, I want to go

there for the same reason. I want, and I need, to go inside that mansion for the last time to see and touch the very proof of my past.

- I won't ask you what that proof is... however, if you want to go there, I can call Ram, the last descendant of Amir and explain the situation to him before you contact him.

- I'd be very grateful to you, and I hope to return this great favour one day... So, Ram is the name of the last owner of the mansion and descendant of the Pundits?

- Yes, we had a conversation on the phone last Christmas. He doesn't live in his ancestor's mansion... I understand that he has health problems but I didn't ask what... Anyway, as he's a devout Hindu, I am very sure that he will treat you with kindness, listen to you and believe what you tell him.

It was almost 5 p.m. Dusk was yielding to darkness and the raindrops became glittering pearls in the yellow light of the street lamps.

- I sincerely thank you for your warm hospitality and for all your help, – Matteo said handing the diary back to Ben. – I'll go to my hotel now. I have a few phone calls to make.

- You're very welcome. I'll try to contact Ram and I'll call you as soon as I've spoken to him.

- My private number won't be busy, I'll be waiting anxiously.

Very rarely did Matteo use an umbrella. He liked hats. Different kinds of hats, depending on the occasion and on his mood. His sailor cap protected his head well enough from the English drizzle, which did not bother him at all. Those timid droplets that fell on his skin and his clothes without getting them too wet brought him sweet memories of his work experience at the library in Richmond. In his first few days there, Darlene, a red-haired girl with freckles and dark green eyes, had taught him how to register and catalogue the new books. It wasn't long before they were holding hands after work, meeting for a drink, and planning their weekends together. Then, reminded by the wet weather, he recalled that she liked to walk in the rain and get wet through. Once, in the countryside, she had even taken off her shoes while it was raining and paddled barefoot in the puddles. At the time he did not understand that 'crazy' girl, but now looking back although several years had passed, he saw her in a different way. How he longed to see her again at that moment!

The distance from Mr Attwood's house to the hotel was not far, but Matteo decided to take a walk through the city centre streets lit up by the many colours of the shops. It was nice to walk and think, to remember, to hear different voices and languages. Feeling slightly weary, he went back to the hotel; he needed to make some phone calls but gave up. He lay on the bed with his hands folded behind his head. He thought of the captain, of his personality, of his sensitivity, of how different he was from his father. It can't have been easy to have that kind of sensitivity among the people of his social rank at that time. And for that precise moment in the history of his country, he must have been seen as a loser. He had sensed that Mr Attwood can't have had a high opinion of his ancestor either. In truth, even though Mr Attwood had proved to be friendly and helpful, he had not aroused much sympathy in Matteo. He had felt him to be distant and cold, and did not believe that his story had touched him in any way whatsoever. Nevertheless, he appreciated his availability.

Ben called him at around 7.00 p.m. saying that he had managed to contact Ram and that they had had a long conversation. Ram had seemed a bit incredulous at the start then he had shown a deep curiosity, so he was willing to talk with the Italian manager whenever was convenient. Good, now he could take the final step! He would travel to Bengal from Milan. Now, though, he was tired; he needed to relax. He had half a mind to have dinner out, but he was not that hungry; a cup of tea and the few biscuits on the table in his room would be enough. After eating the last biscuit he dialled Marina's number to ask how everything was. Her voice was as vivid as ever; she was a woman who never showed moments of sadness or pessimism, so it was difficult to understand what she really thought. She told him that, as the next day was Friday, she and Francesco would go to stay with her parents again for the weekend.

- I'll try to meet you there on Saturday... I can't promise, but I'll try, – he said, his voice wavering.

He knew that he would not go and she knew it too. He thought it would have been better not to call her. At least he would not have told her a lie! In his mind, the echoing of Marina's last question before they had fallen asleep: 'Who or what is between us?'... He was so tired. The swirl of images and situations had been enriched with new characters, and with new initiatives to undertake. He would think about that the following day. Now he had an overwhelming need to go to bed and to sleep. Sleep for eternity. The strange thing was that as soon as he turned off the light, his mind cleared of everything and of everyone except Darlene. It is very true that everything we do is recorded somewhere inside ourselves and comes back, often unexpectedly, to torment or to encourage us. James Joyce, the famous Irish writer, dealt with this subject very well in a few of his books... Yes, in *Dubliners*... The English teacher at school dwelled on Joyce's epiphanies for at least one month. Well, now, from the abyss, once more Matteo saw, more alive than ever, images of the first time they had slept together, then he heard the words they had spoken and felt those emotions all over again. She liked joking and playing with words. He smiled thinking of those jokes while having breakfast the morning after that magical night. 'You have improved remarkably in the space of just a few hours,' she observed almost laughing. 'All credit goes to you... my wonderful teacher!' He answered playing along with her allusion. 'New and useful words... Taught using an infallible method...' And she: 'Provided that the student is clever!... And you are!'... What a wonderful thing to fall asleep with such memories and a smile on the lips!

The first thing that Matteo did when he arrived at his office in Milan was to thank his secretary Nadia for her invaluable help. As usual he looked through all the correspondence and notes on his desk then called his Deputy Director for a business meeting. Only around noon was he able to pause to make his phone call to Bengal without being disturbed. The phone was answered immediately as if the person on the other side had been waiting. It was Ram. He gave his first name and surname. After briefly introducing himself Matteo sketched out the main points of his story. The man on the other end of the line did not sound as enthusiastic as the manager had expected, perhaps he was sceptical or surprised, but then again some comments that he made gave Matteo the impression that he probably did believe him, so he expressed his desire to see the mansion. Ram said that it was possible but that in one week the property would be in the hands of a foreign company which intended to restore it. So, it had to be done soon! The two made arrangements to meet as soon as possible and Ram advised him on how to get to Cossimbazar or Kasim Bazar once in Calcutta. After surfing the web for around half an hour, he concluded that the quickest way was to fly from Milan to Calcutta with one stop in New Delhi. A car would take him to Cossimbazar where he booked a suite at the hotel *Cedar Inn*. He bought the ticket and confirmed to Nadia once again that he would be abroad for a few days. He rushed home to pack his bag with more suitable clothes for the Indian climate. Marina and Francesco must have left just a short time before he arrived back. He was uncertain whether to call his wife or not. He intended to do so. But he did not. Another reason to feel guilty. Another punch in the stomach.

At 6 a.m. he was already on board. His seat number was 22. It occurred to him that 22 and 11 were two numbers that he came across quite often but he had never wondered if there was any particular or special meaning to these occurrences. He was not superstitious. The flight would be a long one, almost twelve hours including transfer times in New Delhi. He hoped he would be able to have a long sleep on the plane. He sat between two people, a woman on his left and a man on his right by the window. Both looked Indian. He greeted them and decided that the trip would be more enjoyable with a bit of conversation. The lady was probably a member of the group of people sitting in the rows on the other side of the aisle. For now, though, he preferred to be quiet and close his eyes. In fact, he did not even realise when the plane took off and started ascending into the vast clear blue sky. At least one hour of deep dreamless sleep. He was woken up by the smell of coffee and by the voices of the hostesses serving breakfast. He slowly came round and politely asked the hostess to serve him. An hour of sleep, although short, had done him a lot of good; now he felt lucid and awake. The woman next to him was eating and talking with her friend or companion in the row on her left. He noticed that the man near the window did not have breakfast, only water, but was discreetly chewing, almost secretly, something that he had taken out of a pocket in his tunic. Matteo turned his gaze to the window; he really wanted to get a good look at the face of his neighbour who, in turn, looked at him and smiled. He was wearing round glasses. His dark Asian eyes emanated an intense light. It was difficult to estimate his age, perhaps he was seventy. His hair was completely white but his skin was smooth, almost without wrinkles. He picked up a small book from the table and opened it. Matteo peeked with discreet curiosity. He guessed that the book was written in Sanskrit. He would have liked to ask him something just to start a conversation, but he refrained so as not to disturb him. The opportunity to exchange a few words came when the man got up to go to the toilet, starting with 'Excuse me, sir'. Later, on his return, he repeated: 'Excuse me, again', and after sitting back down, he said in a soft voice:

- I'm very sorry. I hope you don't mind; old men need the toilet more frequently... I'd have been wiser to have chosen an aisle seat.

- That's quite all right, sir, I understand.

The Indian man smiled and started to read. Matteo noticed that after a few minutes he closed his eyes keeping the book open. He didn't seem to be asleep. Perhaps he was thinking or meditating. Strange man. Was he a religious person? Perhaps a Brahmin! A professor? Maybe. No... perhaps he was a scientist... The book slipped off his lap and onto the floor. He opened his eyes wide as if he had been disturbed by something unexpected.

- I'll pick it up, sir! – the manager said bending with difficulty.

- I appreciate your help, – the other replied expressing his thanks.

- You're most welcome.

- These apparently insignificant gestures express a person's charitable spirit.

The elderly man spoke as if saying these last words to himself. 'He must be a monk... a priest... a Brahmin!' – Matteo thought, and after a short pause he remarked:

- Only kindness.

The Indian man smiled, but did not say anything. He opened his book a second time and, after a while, his eyes closed again. He was certainly praying or meditating. It was clear that he was not interested in talking. Matteo had the still-unfolded newspaper in the pocket of the seat in front of him. When he travelled, he liked watching people or simply...

dreaming. The woman on his left continued to be engaged in a long conversation with other people, so he decided to concentrate on the aim of his trip and tried to imagine what the following day would bring. Nothing else happened until lunch time when the smell of different kinds of food pervaded the air. As before, the man on his right refused the meal and accepted only a cup of tea.

- It's a long journey, – the manager observed intrigued by the strange man sitting next to him. – Aren't you keen on airline food?

The other hesitated, perhaps a bit surprised by his audacious question.

- Food is irrelevant for physical survival, – he finally replied. – Apart from liquids.

'He must be crazy!' Matteo thought while taking a mouthful of the mashed potato. Then he said:

- You are right, sir. A friend of one of my friends was healed from cancer by fasting. It's difficult to believe, but apparently it's true.

- It is true.

- It would be impossible for me... I like my food too much!

- A true Italian! - The old man exclaimed laughing. Despite his age, this individual appeared naïve and somewhat childlike. He displayed a sort of disarming innocence.

- Excuse me, sir, – Matteo continued after the hostess had collected the tray when lunch was finished. – I'm very curious about you... If you don't mind, may I ask you what your occupation is?

- Indeed. I may look bizarre to others but sometimes I happen to meet somebody who is curious about me... My occupation... I take care of people.

- Ah! I guessed you were a religious leader...

- Religious?

- I mean a Brahmin... a Hindu priest...

- No, sir, not at all... My religion doesn't depend on one particular belief.

- I'm not sure I know what you mean.

- I mean that God is the same God for everybody... The only religion is love... God loves those who love others. It's that simple.

- It is so easy listening to you... Yet, people act in different ways, they have different religions and fight in the name of God and they kill in His name... So, you are not a Hindu, a Buddhist, a Christian, a Muslim or anything else?...

- Sir... Sir... God is the same God for everybody... Do you think that my house is open only to Hindus or to Christians or to Muslims? No, everybody is welcome.

- What kind of house do you mean?

- It is called *The Haven of Hope*.

- *The Haven of Hope?!*...

- Yes, it's a place of suffering and happiness.

- And what do you do there?

- We take care of the poor, of the unfortunate, of the unhappy... of the 'least' according to the laws of this world.

The Indian man inserted one hand in the inner pocket of his tunic and pulled out a small photo album.

- This is *The Haven of Hope* – he said handing the album to the man sitting next to him.

In the first photo *The Haven of Hope* stood in capital letters on top of a big gate outside a British colonial-style three-storey building in the city of Calcutta. The other photographs portrayed people in despair, sick and in desperate need. A few were clinging onto the arms of the helpers, while many starving, skeletal figures lay on the ground. Terrible scenes. Matteo was shocked by what he saw and while looking at these images, he had flashes of his past where one person more than any other emerged clearly: Abha. He remembered Benjamin's description of her in his diary and associated her with the poor people in the pictures.

- The helpers are volunteers, I guess, – Matteo half-whispered.

- All volunteers, all angels from all over the country.

- I feel very moved... I feel very lucky to have met you... I feel I am nothing compared to you.

- Sir, please... I don't deserve these words... I'm a man like many others. I'm just following my vocation trying to do what God wants me to do.

- You are a very privileged man.

- I am. But God sees inside everybody's heart, therefore you could also be privileged without knowing it. God reveals His will in so many different ways.

- I'm not religious, sir... My faith is weak. I go to church sometimes... You know, my life is so full and complicated.

- May I ask your name?

- Matteo, Matteo Moscardi.

- My name's Kabir... Call me Kabir...

- Thank you, Kabir.

- Matteo, let me tell you something... Although people may not know each other very well, as in our case, there are clues that immediately give us an idea of what the person we are with is really like. I sense that your heart is good and I'm sure that God wants something from you, too. Try to read the messages that life sends you. Sometimes they seem illegible... They only *seem* illegible... Do you understand?

- I'll bear that in mind... Yes, I understand.

He noticed that Kabir was sweating. He didn't look well. He got up to go to the toilet again but he had no strength to stand up and fell back onto the seat. Matteo realised that there was something seriously wrong so he turned to look for a hostess. The woman on his left also became concerned and rushed to get help. At last a hostess, a steward and a doctor came to see what was happening. The manager and the woman left their seats and, after checking the elderly man's blood pressure and heartbeat, the doctor gave him an injection in his arm. After ten minutes Kabir seemed to come round but the doctor wanted to remain near the patient, so he asked Matteo and the woman if they wouldn't mind moving temporarily to seats in first class. They agreed and were led by the hostess to two free seats. Two hours later the aircraft landed in New Delhi. Before leaving, Matteo went back to see Kabir. He looked fine now. He looked pleased to see the Italian, showed him his gratitude, and said that he would be taken for a quick check-up at the hospital in New Delhi, so they would not be flying together to Calcutta. He hastily picked up his photo album, pulled out the first picture showing the façade of *The Haven of Hope* and asked the manager to keep it and look at it from time to time.

On the flight to Calcutta Matteo lapsed again into the swirl of images of his past and present. This time the dominant presence was his most recent encounter with Kabir. Strange encounter. He was stressed and tired; his mind was able to see but not to think. The people sitting near him appeared distant and absent minded. His eyelids lowered like the curtains on a stage. Then darkness... When he disembarked from the aircraft, the characteristic hot, humid air of Calcutta suffocated him, and his mind immediately plunged back into the world where he had lived during the experiment in Jacopo's office. At the exit of the airport he spotted a man holding a board with his name on. It was late in the evening so he thought it would be more sensible to spend the night in a nearby hotel. The young driver was kind and obliging and took him to the nearest hotel. He would be waiting for him at seven a.m. The atmosphere, the air, the smells and the people joined forces to haul his inner self backwards. He slept badly; he was suffering from jetlag and the visions of his previous life were becoming more vivid. Subhadra, who had vanished in the last few days, had now returned as though wanting to take possession of his soul and of his identity. In fact, he felt the same stinging feeling at certain times during the night when re-experiencing her emotions at specific occasions and in certain situations; he felt shivers running right through him as he witnessed Subhadra crossing in front of Benjamin's eyes. Incredible! What kind of cruel game was nature playing with his being and inside his being? He got up at six and after a quick breakfast went out to the waiting car. The driver, called Amar, welcomed him with a loud 'good morning' then asked the visitor if he could pay for the service in dollars. Matteo only had euros and British pounds, which fortunately was acceptable. The trip to Cossimbazar would take just under three hours. The first thing he did once in the car was to call Ram to tell him that he was on his way. This time Ram seemed more enthusiastic about meeting the stranger. The car had to drive through many areas of the immense city before taking the main road to his destination. The contrasts between wealth and poverty were strident, but his eyes were drawn more to the evidence of decay and suffering. From his pocket Matteo took the photo of *The Haven of Hope* and showed it to the driver asking if he knew where it was or if he had heard of it.

- Yes, – he answered, – I know where it is… It is not the only charitable institution here. We need help, a lot of help. You see, there are too many of us in this country.

- There are also many rich people in this country.

- Many? I wouldn't say many compared to the population. But, yes, there are some very rich people.

At one point they drove past a big poster with a Bengal Tiger on it.

- Beautiful beast, – Amar remarked noticing that his passenger was looking at it enraptured. – There are not many left… When the last one dies, it will coincide with the end of the world.

As time went on Matteo was surprised to feel comfortable in

that unfamiliar land whose climate was considered intolerable by those who go there for the first time. Who was he at that moment? Matteo or Subhadra? He felt more *she* than *he* and constantly pondered on the mysteries of Nature and Creation, always coming back to the same question: God, why did You make everything so complicated? He tried to force himself to think of his family, of his work, of the people who filled his daily life, but he was not able to. Suddenly everything became very confused and distant, almost as though it was all being erased from his mind. How was that possible?

Amar was a talkative man; he liked to talk of his country, of both the good and bad things, and he showed great curiosity about the way of life in European countries. He found it amazing that in such a small continent like Europe, so many countries with different cultures and historical backgrounds could coexist. His passenger told him that it was not at all as easy as he believed. A few miles before arriving in Cossimbazar, Matteo suggested that they stop somewhere to eat. The driver was very happy with the invitation and stopped at the first restaurant they came to. It was not very clean inside and the menu was rather poor. Matteo was content with what he considered the least bad option but was glad to see that the young man ate with a voracious appetite. Once back in the car, the manager recognised a building in the distance that he had seen in his visions: it was the British East India Company factory. Still there, then! A lively heritage of the colonial past like in many other places, especially in Calcutta. He could not remember anything of the urban structure of Cossimbazar; progress had changed many things and the roads were jammed with cars and motor bikes. Poverty was less visible, but confusion and disorder were still present. The town had been small at the time, now it was much bigger but not as big as he had expected. Directed by the Sat Nav, Amar found the address in about ten minutes. The avenue was large and by the look of the houses on both sides, it was clear that it was a middle class area, according to Bengali standards. A man wearing a turban was standing near the gate of the house indicated in the address. Matteo told the driver to wait then he got out. The man greeted him as if he had been waiting for this visitor and invited him to enter since *sahib* was looking forward to seeing him. The smell inside the house, the many objects and the furniture inlaid with typical Indian floral decorations took his mind back to the bedroom of the mansion. A strong sensation of dismay overwhelmed him and he feared that he was about to faint. Ram, a man in his thirties, was sitting in a wheelchair, while standing next to him was a pretty, young lady and a little girl.

- I'm Ram, – the man said smiling and moving towards the stranger.

The two shook hands then he introduced the woman and the little girl:

- This is Gita, my wife, and Hamsa, our daughter.

- Welcome to our home, – his wife said, and taking her daughter's hand left the large room.

Matteo was surprised to see the man sitting in a wheelchair. He had not expected that.

- It must be a hereditary gene, – Ram specified sensing the curiosity of the other. – A disease that affects the muscles and bones. A sort of multiple sclerosis… but not exactly.

'Like his ancestor,' Matteo thought shivering. 'Yes, just the same…' – I'm so sorry, Ram, how can I help you? – And while he was expressing his compassion, he felt that Subhadra was melded with him and every movement, every thought was the action of both of them.

- Your ancestor, also called Ram like you, had the same problem, – he said with certainty.

- That doesn't surprise me. I've heard snippets of information about it, but not the whole story. You know, there are many legends in old families like ours... But you, sir, you must know everything, from what you and Benjamin Attwood have briefly told me.

- Yes, I know all about it.

- I believe you... You don't look like a braggart. I'm sure you have an honest motive... I mean, you must have a very good reason for travelling all this way to come here. Besides, my religion claims that reincarnation is true and the only way to obtain complete purification... But I must say, I didn't expect Ram's wife would ever be reincarnated as an Italian... It sounds a bit strange... Well, it shouldn't... Sorry... I hope you don't misunderstand me.

- Nevermind... In your place I'd feel the same.

- You said you wanted to go to the mansion... You came just in time. In a few days it will not belong to me anymore. This house is quite sufficient. Actually it was my father who, before his death, had already decided to sell it; he wanted us to move and grow up in the city... But you, sir, tell me, why do you want to go there? What connection do you still have with that place?

- In one of the rooms in the mansion there is real and concrete proof of my past life. It's important... It's important for me and for you.

- Let's go then, I'm curious. There's no reason to delay our visit.

- Just one second, please. I have a request before we go inside the mansion.

- Please, feel free. What is it?

- I'd like us to be alone, me and you, only me and you... It's difficult to explain everything now. You will understand once we're inside that room.

Ram assumed a serious and thoughtful expression.

- Well, – he said after a long pause, – your secret must be something extraordinary. One of the legends tells that a ring with a pink diamond is hidden somewhere in the mansion... This ring was one of the reasons for the conflicts in the clan... Is this a legend, then? Or does this story hide some truth?

- I will tell you everything when we get there.

Ram called the man with the turban and ordered him to drive them to the mansion. The rear of the car had been adapted for Ram's wheelchair, so Matteo had to sit in the front seat. Moving away from the town, he was seized by a strong agitation. He did not recognise the places because part of the vegetation had been destroyed but his heart seemed to beat erratically as soon as they approached the mansion. The building, although neglected, retained much of its importance and fascination. Now he could see everything clearly: the big bedroom windows, the balconies and terraces, the tall trees, the flowers, and the people; everything seemed more alive, more real. Anguish and pain gripped the visitor; he could not hide the deep sadness on his face. The servant helped Ram as far as the big front door, opened it with a huge key and, as soon as they entered, left the two men alone. Matteo looked around with bated breath and again his heartbeat accelerated. Many of the objects, apart from a few little statues, were not the same, but the layout had not changed. Ram realised that this stranger who had come from a faraway country was acquainted with the place, so his doubts regarding the reincarnation of Subhadra vanished completely.

- I feel very moved and hopeful watching you, sir, – Ram said. – Only the outward appearance is Matteo Moscardi. But I can see that it is true, that Subhadra, my ancestor, lives inside you... It's wonderful, I can't believe it. But it is true, it's real, and today you are giving me the great privilege to be the witness of this truth.

Matteo did not answer. He was enraptured by his world. He still did not know exactly who he was. *He* and *she* were the same person. They moved slowly into the old bedroom. It was

# IDENTITIES REDISCOVERED

*The building, although neglected, retained much of its importance and fascination*

empty but Ram's corpse was clearer than ever on the catafalque, while Amir's cry in the lounge still pierced his ears. *Her* ears. So, *he* and *she* stepped towards the large room. The column was still there. Intact. The eyes of the Goddess Kali stared at the visitors questioningly. It was difficult to understand what was going through her mind. Perhaps she was wondering why they were so late, or maybe she was warning them not to violate her sacredness. But *Subhadra* and *Matteo* did not, and could not, keep this secret for one more second. *They* approached the column and with *their* thumb pressed the Goddess's right eye. The cover opened without breaking. The ring was there. With two fingers *they* gently pulled it out. The shining rays of the precious pink stone radiated all around as if a star, fallen from the sky, had broken through the darkness of the house in order to wipe out all the evil that had accumulated over hundreds of years. *They* and Ram remained enchanted and astonished before that miracle of Nature, but now the last step had to be determined: ownership of this precious object. *They* held the ring in the palm of one hand admiring its beauty for many seconds. The lives of generations of people influenced and conditioned by the existence of this piece of jewellery seemed to be imprisoned in the lapse of those eternal seconds. *Their* eyes met Ram's, who was sitting in his wheelchair looking bewildered then *they* reached out and declared:

- There is no doubt, Ram, that you are the legitimate and sole owner of this diamond ring. *We* are here to consign it to you.

Ram sat there speechless then finding words said:

- This wonder seduces me for its extraordinary uniqueness, but not for its value. The legend says that the destinies of the Pundits have been influenced by its power. I reject this superstition, but supposing it does have power, it should be used only for good. As to the ownership, all of us, *you* and I are the legitimate owners for different reasons.

- Thank you, Ram, for your honesty and for the purity of your mind. *We* want to propose that you donate this jewel to *The Haven of Hope* in Calcutta to benefit many, many poor people.

- I have heard about this *House*. Yes, I agree.

At that moment, a very strange phenomenon took place: like that night when Matteo lost consciousness in front of the TV and saw the strange ethereal creature come out of his body, now, the same thing was happening again. A female figure, at first formless, stood between the two men. Little by little, it assumed the appearance of Subhadra. Yes, there was no question about it; it was Subhadra, as beautiful as ever. First she looked at Ram then she turned to the manager and, after emanating a sudden bright light, disappeared. Matteo did not feel her anymore; he was seized by a sense of lightness and his mind had regained its lucidity. He understood that Subhadra was no longer dwelling within him; she had left him forever. At that exact moment another miracle was in progress: Ram, seated in the wheelchair, was rubbing his arms then he touched his face and his legs. He was looking at the parts of his body in disbelief. What was happening?

- Help me, please! – Ram begged, – please, I can't believe it, please... help me!

Matteo did not understand what was happening. He put the ring down on an old table and approached the wheelchair. Ram gripped his hands as he struggled to stand up. He was standing! At first he seemed to lose his balance then, supported by his friend, he took a few uncertain steps. The Indian man started to cry. His strength had come back. He was recovering... He had recovered. He was completely healthy. Matteo, astonished, was moved to tears.

- We are free! – he exclaimed aloud.

- Yes, we are free, free, – Ram repeated moving forward

still supported by the Italian. – Nobody will believe it.

- It's not necessary to tell anyone. Let's keep the truth to ourselves. Nobody would understand.

- Yes, sir, you're right, but the ring, the diamond… Look!

- What?

Both men looked at the stone and noticed that it had lost all its shine and radiance. No rays. No light. Now the stone looked like just a simple stone, still pink but with no extraordinary effect. Matteo picked it up and they both examined it carefully.

- I don't think that this is a diamond, my friend, – the manager said.

- Neither do I.

- So, I don't think that it will be any good to *The Haven of Hope*.

- You're right. What shall we do, then?

- I know what we should do.

Matteo resolutely took the ring, approached the column and put the stone in its place setting the cover in its correct position.

- There we are! – he exclaimed exhausted. – Everything in its rightful place.

- Yes, here ends the story of my beautiful and unfortunate ancestor Subhadra who, through you, returned to her origin to free her ancestors from evil and to join her purified spirit with God.

Matteo had no wish to spend the night in Cossimbazar. It was not late and he was anxious to go back, so he cancelled his reservation at the *Cedar Inn* and asked his driver to take him back to Calcutta. Online he booked the first flight to Milan which happened to be the following morning. Finally he felt free. He felt himself again, Matteo. Simply Matteo. He wanted to scream, to run, to fly, to sing, to express his happiness in any way. There was one last thing he wanted to do: once in Calcutta he asked Amar to take him to *The Haven of Hope*. He would not feel right leaving without going to see Kabir. He hoped he would find him there. And in fact, he was there. He was very happy to see the man who had sat next to him on the plane and said that he had remained in New Delhi only a few hours. Kabir showed him around *The House*. Matteo would never forget what he saw and would never be able to describe in words the scenes of squalor and of suffering that he witnessed in those few minutes. But he also saw the angels who were trying to relieve the suffering. All that he could do at that moment was to offer money. As soon as he arrived back home, he would make a bank transfer.

Thanks to the time zone, when he arrived in Milan it was not late. Shops were still open. He thought of Marina and Francesco. He called his wife to tell her that in half of an hour he would be at home. She was very surprised because she thought that the business trip would have lasted much longer. She seemed happy and said that she was in the kitchen cooking for Francesco. So, now she would cook for the whole family. Matteo thanked her and went to the first florist he came across and bought some flowers. Roses. Only red roses. Then he walked home with his bunch of roses in one hand. It started raining. It was not the same rain as in Manchester. Not the same rain as in Richmond. It was the rain that had soaked him in his childhood, in his youth and in his adult life. It was the rain of Milan.

- Oh, what a wonderful surprise this evening! – Marina said when Matteo handed her the roses after kissing her. – You haven't brought me flowers in a long time.

- This is for a special occasion.

- It must be very special, my love! I guess you've closed a good deal!

- Hahahahaha!... much more... much more.

They laughed together. Marina noticed that her husband seemed different somehow. He was in high spirits... perhaps even happy. Also, his eyes were brighter...

- You seem like a different person today, – Marina said. – I'd love you to be like this every day.

The evening was pleasant. While Francesco was watching his cartoons, they went into the sitting room to leaf through the photos of the years before they got married. A cascade of memories. The day was over. Francesco fell asleep on the sofa. Matteo picked him up and carried him to bed. Shortly afterwards, the couple was also in bed with the light off and facing each other.

- You didn't answer me last time, – Marina whispered in the dim light that the full moon cast through the curtains.

- You're right. I didn't. I'll answer you now: nobody and nothing is between me and you.

He caressed her cheek and drew her close to him, both of them feeling the fire of a rekindled pleasure burning within.

*Tomorrow, and tomorrow, and tomorrow,*
*Creeps in this petty pace from day to day,*
*To the last syllable of recorded time;*
*And all our yesterdays have lighted fools*
*The way to dusty death. Out, out, brief candle!*
*Life's but a walking shadow, a poor player,*
*That struts and frets his hour upon the stage,*
*And then is heard no more. It is a tale*
*Told by an idiot, full of sound and fury,*
*Signifying nothing.*

From "Macbeth", by William Shakespeare

# ROMEO AND JULIET IN PROGRESS

When I worked in the School of Linguistics and Language Studies at the Universities of Ottawa and Carleton, I was asked to develop a project with the aim of improving the learning of foreign languages. In this case, the second language was English. Many foreign students coming to Canada with the intention of starting a new life there needed to learn English in the quickest and best possible way. Through my experience in teaching drama, I had concluded that acting is one of the best inductive methodologies for learning languages. Now I can also better appreciate how useful my studies of linguistics were. Psycholinguistics/sociolinguistics. Skinner. Chomsky. Widdowson. Spiro. Lakoff…Mental/physical schemata in poetic action…"the ongoing process of interaction between the reader's subjective background experience and formal organisation of a poetic text"…All still in my head after many years…Multiple, as well as individual voices – Textual control. *"Dimension of dramatic communication in poetry. The acting reader's appropriation of the sender/addresser's voices…Acting poetry as 'self' creation."*

Acting poetry as 'self' creation. Yesyesyes! It's amazing to see how much potential we possess without knowing it. I saw people – young and old – at first extremely shy and reticent on stage, and then, step by step, once having tasted the pleasure of acting, the potential artist-actor produces an unexpected and surprising metamorphosis of himself.

I was given six months, starting in September, to form a group of foreign students and complete my project. In April we would perform a show at the University of Carleton. And, in accordance with agreements we had with foreign universities, there was the possibility of acting the play abroad. This time we would go to Verona and Mantua, in Italy. We would be notified of the final decision after Christmas. I am proud to say that all my previous similar experiences had been successful. But one never knows! Every group of people, and every individual, is different. This time I wanted to be more ambitious. When I heard Verona and Mantua my mind immediately associated them with Shakespeare's Romeo and Juliet. Without a doubt, this was the play to perform. It would be very hard, I knew, but life is also made up of big challenges. And this challenge was really big!

Julie Marcotte was a twenty-year-old student who came from Québec City. She was brought up in a strictly traditional francophone family where it was forbidden to speak any word of English. Even the most widely used word *stop!* was replaced by the French *arrêtez!* It is incredible to realise how much the history of nations can influence and affect the attitudes and behaviours of people. Often, grudges take root in the souls of individuals and of the masses remaining for centuries and creating unshakable barriers. Of course, when Julie finished school she would have to face reality. Nowadays, reality requires the knowledge of English if one wants to secure a good job. After some hesitation due to a certain resistance from her parents, she was able to help them understand that the past is past and that she wanted to look to the future. On first seeing her, I knew that she would be my Juliet. I didn't tell her immediately, although there was not much time for all the preparations, as I wanted to get to know her a little better first. One day, more sure of my decision, I invited her to my office to inform her of my choice. Now, with her standing in front of me, my eyes could linger on her physical features: her elegant and feminine posture, the delicacy of her face on whose cheeks appeared two charming dimples when she smiled. But what convinced me was the sort of southern European look she had which I juxtaposed to my idea of Juliet. After expressing my decision I sensed that she had almost expected this proposition.

- There is something Italian about you, – I said. – Especially in your eyes.

- My ancestors came from France; it's possible that in the remote past there was a mingling of French and Italian blood.

- You don't seem surprised that I've chosen you for the role of Juliet.

- She smiled almost bemusing me with her appealing dimples.

- Telepathy. Energies.

We didn't talk further because there was a knock at the door. Only in the following weeks could I understand what she meant by the word 'telepathy'. It is difficult to be a teacher. At the beginning of my career I was not aware of the many difficulties there were to tackle. I would understand in time. It is difficult to be a teacher in the classroom and, sometimes, it is harder to continue this role outside. Going back to the past, to my adolescence spent in the classroom and to my earliest years as a student gives me a better understanding. I liked to enter into discussions with my teachers and professors. I needed a Socrates who could understand me, speak to me and who could answer my questions. I never forgot what a few of my teachers had meant to me and now, being one myself, I tried to better understand what students expect from their educators. A teacher is a teacher. He cannot be a friend, he cannot be a father. But he can possess elements of both. A teacher can be or become a solid reference point, with the power to influence the choices of the young. A teacher is not allowed to make mistakes. If a friend makes mistakes, you can forgive him. You can forgive your father. But if the teacher is wrong, he is not forgiven. I remember at school how readily pupils put teachers on pedestals and how quickly they dragged them off.

Alfredo was a young Italian student who came to Ottawa to study journalism. Manuel, a Spaniard, also attended the same faculty and, as far as I understood, intended to move to Boston the following year. I hesitated slightly in deciding which of the two to ask to play the role of Romeo. Manuel had more adolescent traits which seemed to be closer to the real age of Romeo. Finally, my choice fell on Alfredo for two reasons: the first was his Italian look and origin, the second was that he gave the impression of being an impulsive type which made him more suited to Romeo. I hoped that he would not disappoint me. Manuel would play Benvolio. Tybalt would be played by a German boy, Peter, and Mercutio by the Argentinian, Ramón.

Every character in this play deserves particular attention to be given to the choice of actor who will take on the part, but a few of them deserve more careful consideration. One such character is the nurse. She is a trusted family servant to Lord Capulet in Verona and she maintains an active voice in his family affairs. The Nurse has been with the Capulet family for nearly fourteen years, the entirety of Juliet's life. She had a daughter, Susan, born on the exact same day as Juliet. Susan died, and since her death the Nurse has taken care of Juliet and becomes more of a mother to her than Lady Capulet. This could further be explained by the fact that the Nurse was actually Juliet's wet nurse and, as has been proven, a bond between a baby and the one who feeds it is very strong. There is also another important point about this character. Even a tragedy needs some comic relief and who better than Juliet's bawdy, lower-class nurse? She is a lower-class woman, so that is already funny; and she is a nurse, which means all she can talk about is bodies – bodies having sex, bodies having babies, bodies nursing babies. Not to mention the fact that she has a real way with dirty jokes, like this one: *I must another way/ To fetch a ladder by the which your love/Must climb a bird's nest soon when it's dark...* Here, she's talking literally about fetching a ladder for Romeo to climb up so he can spend the night in Juliet's bedroom. But there is never just one level with the

Nurse – To "climb a bird's nest" is also slang for "to have sex".

Camila, a Portuguese student was the one I considered the most suitable to play the nurse. A full-figured girl whose face expressed a deep sense of maternal reassurance and kindness. She was the right person for this character, I was sure. When the whole group was ready to start, I recommended that they read as much of the play as possible in order to better understand the psychology of the characters and other aspects that I would expand on each time before rehearsals. To encourage them further, I reiterated that they were not professionals or aspiring actors; rather, they were good students participating in a one-off academic project to enrich their language beyond merely grammar. Above all, they would discover the aesthetic side of different forms of writing and discourse. As for myself, every time I started acting with a new group I wondered which technique or methodology I would use. I didn't have a fixed method. I was convinced that for a teacher the greatest authors can be very important reference points, but in the end he must create his own methods on the basis of a number of factors which give each individual, or group of individuals, their uniqueness. However, what I learnt from the history of theatre was all stored in the pillars of my cultural background, a precious source ready to help and prompt me. More and more I became convinced that the concept of a 'laboratory' where actors and director work together on the training and preparation of the performance is the most valid as a setting for research and experimentation. Names like Pirandello, Grotowski, Brook, Barba, Stanislavskij, Brecht, Becket and such like popped into my mind quite often like invisible prompters.

– Next Monday we will begin rehearsals, – I said during the lesson which preceded the practical part of the acting. – Now I'm going to give you a summary of what you will be performing and a few other details about the play. Shakespeare's plays, including "Romeo and Juliet", are written in five acts. In fair Verona, where the scene is set, there are two prominent families constantly at war with one another: the Capulets and the Montagues. The play opens with a fight erupting between members of each rival family in the middle of the city. The Prince (Escalus) arrives and breaks up the fray. He then proclaims that the next person to cause a civil disturbance will pay for it with their life. We now meet Romeo, a Montague who was not involved in the earlier incident. Romeo is sad because he has been unable to woo a woman named Rosaline. Meanwhile, we are introduced to Juliet, a Capulet. Having been informed that she is to be married to the County Paris – with whom she is not in love nor barely knows – she is preparing for a big party that her father is hosting that night. Back to Romeo… in order to cheer him up, his best friend, Mercutio, suggests that they crash the Capulet party (which we know is a bad idea because any Capulet would gladly kill the first Montague they see). Reluctantly, Romeo agrees to go to the party. There, Romeo and Juliet see each other for the first time and immediately fall in love. The problem is that they do not realise that they are from the two feuding families (because they have never met). Even when they are told that they each belong to their enemy's family, there is nothing that can be done to keep them apart. After the party ends, Romeo sneaks around the house to Juliet's balcony and calls to her. They share sweet words (during the famous "balcony scene") and plan to marry before long.

Although boring for non-professional actors, I must comment on some technical aspects. Some of what Shakespeare wrote is in verse. Some of the verse is in iambic pentameter. A pentameter is a line of poetry having five metrical feet ("Penta-" is the prefix meaning five, as in Pentagon). An iamb is a metrical foot having two syllables, the first one short, and the second long. So iambic pentameter feels like a heartbeat:

# IDENTITIES REDISCOVERED

Short, Long; Short, Long; Short, Long; Short, Long; Short, Long. An actor uses scansion to interpret the meter of a piece of verse. I understand that it's difficult to grasp the importance of what I'm saying, but, if you repeat it over and over again, read and re-read it, I'm sure that it will make more sense to you.

— Excuse me, — stepped in Ivan who played Friar Laurence. — Back to the story… Juliet is only thirteen… almost fourteen. Don't you think that, in the first part, the way she talks and behaves reveals a sort of feminine cunning that is beyond her years?

— The word you use…"cunning" is too strong. I'd say mature femininity. During the Middle Ages and the Renaissance, children, especially those belonging to the upper classes of society, were brought up knowing that they had been promised in marriage at a very early age. The girls, often, were to marry men much older than themselves, therefore their way of reasoning was not comparable to the girls of our time. To better answer your question, Juliet is pensive and practical. For example, when her mother insists that she consider Paris a potential mate, Juliet is clearly uninterested, but understands that to refuse will get her nowhere. Her act of apparent innocent submission will allow her to be devious later on, to her advantage. In Act 1, Juliet is already showing her powers of deception by asking her Nurse about two other men before asking after Romeo because she does not want to arouse her guardian's suspicions. This is the behaviour of someone older compared to girls of that age nowadays… Any more questions?

— I want to tell you that I'm so thrilled with my role! — said Alfredo, his voice betraying his shyness. We were on the thirteen floor of Dunton Tower. It was the end of September, the weather was beautiful and the view filled the eye and the spirit of the spectator with an endless ocean of innumerable and indescribable autumn colours. – Thank you for giving me this task and honour. I've seen this play twice in Italian and I never expected to play Romeo one day. When I was only ten years old, I performed in the Italian *Carnevale*. I was dressed as a clown. I hated it. I felt clumsy and ridiculous. I never wanted to act again.

- What persuaded you to participate now? – asked Camila visibly intrigued.

- Oh!… I can't really explain why. The challenge perhaps. The need to exorcise my first disappointing experience… Also, being the only Italian in our group, I thought I would enjoy a role in this play set in Italy…

- Italia Italia! – interrupted Julie excited and smiling. – May I ask you which part of Italy you come from? It must be a country of such diversity. I've never been there but Italy is in me.

I noticed that her French 'r' was so strong and wondered if she would ever be able to correct it. It seemed that Alfredo and Julie had a good rapport and while they were looking at each other, my imagination juxtaposed them with two students who had acted in a previous play I had directed a couple of years before. Luc, from Montreal, was a simple and open guy, a guitar lover and in tune with nature, a climber and explorer in his free time. Janet had been brought up in Ottawa but her parents were of British origin. Even after having lived many years in Canada, they still made a point of retaining their Middle England accent. Now, smiling to myself, I thought how annoyed they would be to see Juliet being acted in a Canadian English accent mixed with Québec French. Anyway, it happened that by playing the role of two lovers, they fell in love with each other, which is not so unusual in the environment of the theatre especially when the actors' emotions are involved and they can easily identify with the characters. The fact is that Janet was engaged to an upper class

Canadian who had a great career ahead of him. The wedding date was already fixed for the following summer. If I hadn't been involved in this story, I wouldn't say any more but what happened deserves a brief mention. When the rehearsals started, I don't think that Janet ever suspected that her love for Gordon was so fragile and would never have believed that an unconventional mannered boy could place in doubt her certainties regarding her future. I don't think it was a physical attraction that disrupted her certainty; rather it was the sharing time and emotions with a person who was in every way the complete opposite of her future husband. One day Janet came to my office. "I'm not sure why I'm here and I don't know exactly what pushed me to knock at your door," – she said. "All I know is that I'm confused and concerned. I'm worried about how my behaviour could affect those around me. My soul has felt distressed for many days now and at the same time pervaded by a sort of excitement that I've never felt before; it has torn me away from the person I have been until now. I need to talk to somebody, I thought of talking to a close friend, perhaps to a priest. Instead, I'm here, in my professor's office, sure that you are the only person that can at least listen to me. I want to apologise for burdening you with this but I know that you know; I know that your eyes search and examine Luc's heart and also mine. Discreetly. Silently. In good faith, with no ulterior motives. Thank you for your discretion, thank you for your understanding. I'm not here to ask you for your advice or help with any decisions or anything like that... I love him... That's all there is to it. How it happened belongs to the mysteries of life." What can I say? I was proud that she felt able to confide in me but I did not feel I should express any comment on her decision. I had met Gordon and her parents several times which now left me feeling very uneasy inside. A few days after Janet's confession, Luc also came to my office to talk about the same matter. I don't know if he came just to copy the girl and even now I don't know if she told him that she had talked to me. The fact is that he seemed more confused and distressed than she had. "I certainly had no intention of disturbing, or interfering with, Janet's love life," – he said visibly embarrassed. – "I respect women who are emotionally tied to other men and when I realised that our mutual pleasure in sharing time together was due to reasons beyond our academic task, turmoil started to possess our beings at all levels. I tried to keep my distance from her but I found out that she had decided to pull out of the play because of this. I too had decided the same thing and one day I was in the corridor, waiting outside your office for somebody to come out so that I could tell you of my decision...but, while waiting something made me change my mind, and I left the building."

Luc was honest and sincere. He felt very sorry for Gordon. For some time he had wanted to apologise and talk to him but held off doing so believing it would be inappropriate. Gordon understood that he was the loser; he fought, hoping that his fiancée was only going through a period of doubt and uncertainty then gave up and disappeared forever. The bitterness and disappointment was too difficult for Janet's parents to bear. There was no way they could convince their daughter to reconsider and I suspect that they never completely accepted this bohemian as part of their family.

Now, sensing a sort of special understanding between my new actors, my heart jumped imagining that a similar situation would be created.

- Italy is in you? – questioned Alfredo. – Tell us what you mean!...hahahahaha!...*Io vengo da Perugia*... I come from Perugia.

- Oh, nice, – I said. – I was there once ... *Io vengo da Perugia*... Sounds nice. When I was a student I had a close friend who spent one year in Perugia at the University for

Overseas Students. Wonderful town.

- Very old and very important, especially in the Middle Ages, – Alfredo remarked. – It's the capital city of the region called Umbria…Saint Francis was born in this region, in the small town of Assisi.

- We'll have more opportunities to talk further of Italy… – I assured. – And we'll look forward to you helping us get better acquainted with the country, ok?

- Sure.

- So, that's it for today, everyone. Have a good weekend! There are times when you think of a person and he or she rings you after a few seconds. There are times when you meet a person you know two, three, four times consecutively and in different places. Perhaps you haven't seen that person for ages and now, all at once, you see them everywhere you go. While walking in the park. At the post office. In a situation where you wouldn't want to be seen. Weird! There are times when everything goes in the right direction or in the wrong direction. In the latter case, when for days and days nothing goes right, my grandmother used to say that in these circumstances the best thing to do is to hide somewhere or to stay at home until the bad energies leave you. Is it true and possible that invisible and mysterious energies have the capability to condition our actions and behaviours or is everything that happens to us and around us simply due to fate? According to my grandmother's theory (her brothers accused her of living in the clouds), our navel (she meant not only physically, as in the central part of our body, but she also wanted to give a spiritual meaning to this mid-point) is linked and connected to a bigbigbigbig (she used to say) network that connects the entire universe, the whole of nature. The life of trees, of mountains, of animals, of flowers, of water and fire. "And God?" I asked her one evening sitting by the fire while she was knitting. I was nineteen and was studying hard in order to pass the entrance tests for university. "Does

God have anything to do with all this?" "God is the creator. Out of all creation He needed something special. He needed a being gifted with a specific power: reason. Intelligence. This being is called Man. Intelligence puts Man above everything in nature." "Why did He need this kind of being? Wasn't the whole of creation enough to prove His existence?" "He needed a being like Himself but not the same as Himself, an image of Himself with His own power; I mean the power to create. This being completed the sense of creation because 'it' was made of substance and spirit, for which 'it' represented the mediator and the point of unity between God and nature." "Grandma, in your opinion, did God make us free or not?"

My grandmother never answered this question. Our conversation was interrupted by the barking of our dog that gave advance warning of visitors.

Now, many years after the death of my grandmother, this topic regarding energies came to my attention because of a few coincidences that happened to arouse my curiosity during the preparation of the play. The first was Julie's telepathic power, as she said on different occasions, the second was that during that time it so happened that everywhere I went or whatever I did, I came across something connected with Italy: people, books, films, food, holidays, language and so on. The same procedure, as I said before, that everywhere you go, you meet a person that you haven't met for a long time. Is it due to energies? And how is it possible to ignore this topic while navigating through the world of Shakespeare where beings and energies live in a constant interchange taking us back to the dynamics of reason that we know as the place of so-called rationality and communication? Does the concept of fate in Shakespeare's plays have any connection with the game of forces which rule the universe? I think in some way they do, but the individual is not a completely passive victim of fate. His freedom gives him the opportunity to choose and his will is not a passive executor of fate... Well, let me tell you that surfing the web I found that the simplistic theory of an almost illiterate old woman had in some aspects an abundant amount of truth. It is written that the theory of quantum physics states that through our five senses we perceive an external reality which is not the complete and definitive reality. What we perceive through our five senses, at quantitative level, is only a very small part of reality. All matter is energy and at a level below energy there exists impalpable information. Every particle, every body, every aspect of existence is the expression of information that through the brain or mind we interpret as the physical world. All physical things, including Man, all the material universe: particles, stars, planets, rocks, living organisms...none of that is material. All these things that appear as matter are complex waves in the quantum vacuum...energies...energies.

My grandmother.

I want to tell you more about her. In her blood there were "a few drops, a little more than a few" as she used to say, of Iroquoian blood.

My great grandmother was called Kateri, which means pure.

My grandmother's name was Orenda. It means magic power.

\*

University of Carleton. Dunton Tower.

- The chorus introduces the play and establishes the plot that is to unfold. We don't have the chorus. We need at least three more students. Mark will introduce it. He will explain the reasons for the grudge between the two families in Verona – the Capulets and the Montagues – and how two lovers, one from each family, will commit suicide after becoming entangled in this conflict. These lovers are Romeo Montague and Juliet Capulet. Only after the suicides will the families be able to choke their hatred.

Ok. Let's start!
*Sampson:* Gregory, o' my word, we'll not carry coals.
*Gregory:* No, for then we should be colliers.
...
.....

*Capulet:* What noise is this? Give me my long sword, ho!
*Lady Capulet:* A crutch, a crutch! Why call you for a sword?
*Capulet:* My sword, I say! Old Montague is come! And flourishes his blade in spite of me.

Buata, who played Capulet, came from The Congo. Ling, who played Lady Capulet, was a sweet Chinese girl whose initial curiosity for the places where the tragedy was set increased day by day, becoming a springboard to deepen her interest in Italy, so much so that she started to attend an Italian language course. Coincidently, a few Italian courses took place on the same floor, the thirteenth in Dunton Tower. Looking at Buata and Ling and watching them act, I imagined how an Italian audience would react when seeing Juliet's parents being played by a black man and a Chinese woman. In no way am I racist. Being brought up in a multicultural country, I consider it completely natural and normal for people of different countries and of different races to work together in every context, but it is not a secret that in Europe racism is still felt in several areas. I wanted to talk to Alfredo about this fear but, cautiously, I resisted and preferred to discuss it first with Franco, the director of Italian Studies. I knew him quite well and we had had the chance to talk together a few times. He was born in Italy but moved to the States when he was twelve years old and later to Canada where he remained for the rest of his life. His ties with Italy had remained very strong. He used to go there twice a year for different reasons. He still had relatives in the town where he was born and every second semester gave lectures at a few Italian universities. We had a long and interesting conversation and I appreciated his advice. He said that there were two aspects to note about tolerance. Italy has a very long, complex history mainly because of its geographical position in the Mediterranean. It's like a bridge that links Europe with Africa and the Middle East. The unprotected miles and miles of coastline made it vulnerable to invasions by different peoples and countries through the ages. Many cultures mixed throughout the country, overlapped and influenced Italian society, therefore foreigners, whatever their backgrounds and religions, are well integrated and tolerated. Jews, Muslims and others have always lived in peace with Italians but the majority of the population is still jealous of their own traditions and race. Mixed race marriages or marriages between people of different religions are accepted albeit rather reluctantly.

- Don't worry about your show, – he concluded. – You will be welcomed with enthusiasm and friendship. I'm absolutely sure.

I felt very relieved.

I was a bit ashamed of myself. I felt guilty. Before then I couldn't remember that any thought regarding the inferiority of any race had ever crossed my mind. I wondered why I was attacked by the sudden and unexpected doubt that a black boy would be seen unsuitable for that role owing to the colour of his skin. "It's not your fault," said a feeble voice inside me. It was the *other* me who wanted to excuse and justify myself. "Your skin is guilty."

When the rehearsal was over I congratulated the actors and told them that when running these projects, as a rule, I organise social events from time to time in order for the students to gel as a group. Ivan almost preempted me. In fact, just after my announcement he said:

- I'd like to invite the whole group to my house in Rockliffe this Friday evening. My parents would like to meet you all.

— Oh, lovely! — I exclaimed. — What a nice surprise. Everybody was happy about the invitation. Before leaving the classroom, once again I recommended that they continue rehearsing on their own.

Rockliffe is a beautiful residential area of Ottawa where the majority of residents are rich and belong to the middle and upper classes. I knew a few people there and at least a couple of times a year I received invitations to visit them. Minto Place, the street where Ivan lived, was also very familiar to me because Alain, a friend of mine from university, had lived there since childhood. As I expected, Ivan's house was big and beautiful. I had passed by many times but had thought that somebody else lived there. Ivan's parents where Russian, his father had business connections with oil companies and, as I understood from our conversation, they had arrived in Canada two years earlier. Every corner of the house was a little piece of Russia. Even the smell reminded me of places I had visited in Saint Petersburg and inevitably my mind was flooded with pages of Russian literature. My drama teacher, in the year I spent at Caerleon College of Education in South Wales when I was only 21, taught a fascinating course on Anton Chechov, which I have never forgotten and which taught me many things about the beginning of modernism. I still remember pages of his most famous works such as "Three Sisters" and "Cherry Orchard". The atmosphere in Ivan's house was warm and exciting and the food excellent. I tasted Russian specialties that I hadn't tried before. None of us, the students or myself, could have expected such a generous welcome. Ivan — I found out that evening — had a great sense of humour. He was a wonderful entertainer telling jokes accompanied by a surprising combination of gestures and facial expressions. 'He would make a fantastic comedy actor,' I thought. What's more, he was a brilliant impersonator; he proved this by spontaneously imitating famous actors and politicians throughout the evening. But, for me, the most exciting and surprising moment of the evening was when Alfredo and Julie approached me, and, smiling and a little shyly, said that they had spent many hours preparing a 'present' for me. At that moment, everybody moved aside leaving the centre of the living room free. It was clear that what they were going to do had been planned and organised by the whole group. The light dimmed leaving only a spotlight illuminating the space occupied by Alfredo and Julie who positioned themselves in such a way that you could imagine that Juliet was on the balcony and Romeo below. Manuel announces:

*Act II*
*Scene II (Capulet's Orchard)*
*Enter Romeo*


ROMEO

*He jests at scars, that never felt a wound*
*[Juliet appears above at a window]*

*But, soft! what light through yonder window breaks?*
*It is the east, and Juliet is the sun.*

*Arise, fair sun, and kill the envious moon,*
*Who is already sick and pale with grief,*

*That thou her maid art far more fair than she:*
*Be not her maid, since she is envious;*
*Her vestal livery is but sick and green*
*And none but fools do wear it; cast it off.*
*It is my lady, O, it is my love!*

*O, that she knew she were!*
*She speaks yet she says nothing: what of that?*
*Her eye discourses; I will answer it.*
*I am too bold, 'tis not to me she speaks:*
*Two of the fairest stars in all the heaven,*
*Having some business, do entreat her eyes*
*To twinkle in their spheres till they return.*

*What if her eyes were there, they in her head?*
*The brightness of her cheek would shame those stars,*
*As daylight doth a lamp; her eyes in heaven*
*Would through the airy region stream so bright*
*That birds would sing and think it were not night.*
*See, how she leans her cheek upon her hand!*
*O, that I were a glove upon that hand,*
*That I might touch that cheek!*

JULIET

*Ay me!*

ROMEO

*She speaks:*
*O, speak again, bright angel! for thou art*
*As glorious to this night, being o'er my head*
*As is a winged messenger of heaven*
*Unto the white-upturned wondering eyes*
*Of mortals that fall back to gaze on him*
*When he bestrides the lazy-pacing clouds*
*And sails upon the bosom of the air.*

## JULIET

O Romeo, Romeo! wherefore art thou Romeo?
Deny thy father and refuse thy name;
Or, if thou wilt not, be but sworn my love,
And I'll no longer be a Capulet.

## ROMEO

*[Aside]* Shall I hear more, or shall I speak at this?

## JULIET

'Tis but thy name that is my enemy;
Thou art thyself, though not a Montague.
What's Montague? it is nor hand, nor foot,
Nor arm, nor face, nor any other part
Belonging to a man. O, be some other name!
What's in a name? that which we call a rose
By any other name would smell as sweet;
So Romeo would, were he not Romeo call'd,
Retain that dear perfection which he owes
Without that title. Romeo, doff thy name,
And for that name which is no part of thee

Take all myself.

## ROMEO

I take thee at thy word:
Call me but love, and I'll be new baptized;
Henceforth I never will be Romeo.

## JULIET

What man art thou that thus bescreen'd in night
So stumblest on my counsel?

## ROMEO

By a name
I know not how to tell thee who I am:
My name, dear saint, is hateful to myself,
Because it is an enemy to thee;
Had I it written, I would tear the word.

## JULIET

My ears have not yet drunk a hundred words
Of that tongue's utterance, yet I know the sound:
Art thou not Romeo and a Montague?

## ROMEO

Neither, fair saint, if either thee dislike.

## JULIET

How camest thou hither, tell me, and wherefore?
The orchard walls are high and hard to climb,
And the place death, considering who thou art,
If any of my kinsmen find thee here.

## ROMEO

With love's light wings did I o'er-perch these walls;
For stony limits cannot hold love out,

*And what love can do that dares love attempt;*
*Therefore thy kinsmen are no let to me.*

JULIET

*If they do see thee, they will murder thee.*

ROMEO

*Alack, there lies more peril in thine eye*

*Than twenty of their swords: look thou but sweet,*

*And I am proof against their enmity.*

JULIET

*I would not for the world they saw thee here.*

ROMEO

*I have night's cloak to hide me from their sight;*
*And but thou love me, let them find me here:*
*My life were better ended by their hate,*
*Than death prorogued, wanting of thy love.*

JULIET

*By whose direction found'st thou out this place?*

Alfredo and Julie stopped acting and, turning to me, apologised for not continuing. I understood that they had put a lot of hard work into this mini show. An interminable clapping moved the two students almost to tears as they hugged each other tightly.

I felt my heart swell with satisfaction. They had been a little embarrassed when they had started acting then had become more self-confident. The part of the play they chose to act was one of the most difficult; I understood this and appreciated their attempt. I was sure that their final performance would be excellent. All our hard work had begun to bear fruit. Something else that impressed me that evening was Julie. For the occasion, she and the other girls had changed out of their normal clothes of jeans and T-shirts dressing instead very elegantly. Julie was dressed in such a way as to look younger than her age and had put her hair up in two pigtails. It was clear that she wanted to appear a young teenager since Juliet was only almost fourteen. In fact, she had once asked me for suggestions on Juliet's appearance. Shakespeare doesn't say very much about her appearance, but we can surmise a few things about it especially on the basis of what Romeo says about her. He frequently says how brightly she shines. From this we can assume that she has a fair complexion and blond hair. But we must also remember that this play is set in Italy, and most Italians have a dark complexion therefore we can deduce that, even though she may have dark hair, she most likely has very fair skin. I suggested that everybody watched "Romeo and Juliet" by the renowned Italian Director, Franco Zeffirelli.

- We expected you to kiss passionately! – Camila blurted out while laughing and walking over to our corner.

We all laughed too. Camila was always in a good mood, her presence and company was always pleasant and well accepted.

- I wanted to give you all a ...sexy show... – Alfredo confessed.

- But I said no, – interrupted Julie looking serious. – He... he's jealous!

- He? – said Camila looking at me and Alfredo. – She must be joking... Come on, you said you don't have a boyfriend.

- My boyfriend lives in another time...

- Ahahahahaha! – mocked Camila. – You don't seem the type to have a ghost as a boyfriend...

A smile appeared again on Julie's face. Her dimples looked deeper than usual. I found her very charming and judging from how Alfredo was also looking at her, I guessed that I was not the only one to see her in this way. Ivan's mother, who until that moment had kept a low profile, approached us, apologised and for some reason asked Alfredo and Camila to follow her.

- I felt confused, – Julie admitted to me as Alfredo and Camila moved away with the Russian lady.

She slumped into an armchair that was next to her. Immediately her expression changed. Her cheeks became white and it seemed as though she was going to faint.

- What's the matter? – I asked worried, touching her trembling arm. – Is there anything wrong?

- *Rien. Rien de grave,*[40] – she said in French. – For a few moments while acting, I got lost. I became disoriented.

- How do you mean?

- I thought that this scene was in Mantua and not in Verona.

- The last scene will be in Mantua.

- I know. Now I know...I had a vision. A large cobbled square with a palace...It's in Mantua. I've never been there but I've seen this place on the internet.

- Don't worry. Everybody can get confused when they're stressed. – Perhaps you had a bit of stage fright...It's normal. But I want to congratulate you and Alfredo again. There are a few things to go over, but there's plenty of time.

- *Excusez-moi!*[41] I hope I won't let you down... Now I feel too weak to speak any more.

---

40 Nothing. Nothing serious.
41 Excuse me!

At that moment a few students approached asking me to participate in a game. I preferred not to. I thought that it would be better to leave and let them have fun without me there. They would be more relaxed. I noticed that, pulling herself together, Julie got up from the armchair.

- Come and see me one day, – I told her. – If you need to talk, don't hesitate to call me.

She nodded silently.

I left Ivan's house before the others. I hadn't driven there because I guessed I would drink a little original vodka. And, in fact, I did. Leaving the house, my blood felt 'boiling hot' and I was full of energy. I started walking in the direction of the city which was a few miles away. The air was fresh but not cold. The period at the end of September and into October is wonderful in Canada and it's the best time of the year for me. This had been my favourite time to explore nature when I was a boy. Most of the time I went with one or two friends but I also used to go alone. When I am very old, but still of sound mind, sitting by the fireplace, I want to write a book on the National Capital Greenbelt. I want to unveil secrets that nobody knows. My family lived in the countryside just a few miles from Nepean which is today considered a suburb of Ottawa. Mine had been a very healthy and happy life. A very simple life, I would add. Filled with pets, hens, turkeys and rabbits. My father was a passionate horse rider, which I never was, and when my father died my mother sold the horse with great sorrow and regret. We learnt that this horse died a few months later. We never found out the cause of its death but depression was the first thing that the rest of my family suspected. Our family was big but not as big as many others we knew. There were my parents, my grandparents (in those times it was not unusual to take in grandparents and live all together), one sister, one brother and me. The first to disappear was my grandfather. My grandmother died a few years later and my dad followed them when I was at university. My mother lived ten more years, but, contrary to how she had treated her parents, welcoming them into her home, none of her children did the same for her. My sister and my brother lived, and still live, far away, and I was always an inexorable 'gypsy' travelling around the world. Another memory from my adolescence was maple syrup including all the steps from A to Z of how to make it. My grandmother, who had Iroquoian blood, was an expert in following the whole process and when tasting her syrup, people used to say: "There's no other like it!!" My great grandmother, Kateri, was Iroquois. She met a British man who was a fur trader. When he met my Iroquois ancestor, he fell madly in love with her (like Romeo when seeing Juliet). Natives hated the colonisers. In those times it was not easy for the natives to rebel against the rules of their tribes, especially in the case of mixed marriages, but she was able to convince the elders of the tribe that she was making the right choice. A good thing was that this British man treated his Iroquois wife with respect and, in fact, proved to be very respectful of her culture. In short, my blood – I'm not an exception of course, being a Canadian – contains a mixture of different bloods. For years, before going to Europe, I had lived with the great desire to visit and possibly live there. Like many Canadians with European roots, I regarded Europe, especially Britain, like a sort of motherland. But I was to change my mind once there. Although I lived there for two years, I can't remember even one day when I wanted to settle permanently in a European country. The first thing I missed was the immensity of my country. There, everything was small and my eyes never had to look far to see the horizons. I often felt suffocated. Also, many aspects of the European mentality and way of thinking – not only the British – are too complicated for us. Over the years I understood, also from my own experiences, why the majority of Europeans who came, and still come to Canada, don't want to return to their original country and those who tried, and still try to go back, almost always regret it.

I arrived home around two o'clock. I went straight to bed but it took some time before I fell asleep. What happened at the party replayed in my head. A really exciting evening. But my main thoughts were of Julie. Reviewing the end of the evening, I deduced that there was something strange about that girl which reminded me of the first meeting I had had with her in my office. Her words echoed round the whirlpool in my head. She said she had had a vision, that she had felt disoriented. She was as white as a corpse in the armchair. Trembling. Why was she trembling? I was curious.

I slept incredibly well. The long walk had certainly been tiring but relaxing. I usually have a lot of dreams; I can start dreaming even if I sleep for only a few minutes in the most uncomfortable positions and places, but that night I didn't dream, or at least if I did, I don't remember. Excuse me if, once again, I mention my Iroquoian grandmother. She meant such a lot to me that it is impossible to erase any part of her from my conscious and subconscious. It's also incredible how many of her theories about dreams corresponded to Freud's and his followers. I'm sure that she had never heard words such as psychology or psychoanalysis. Her father belonged to a group of men considered special because the Great Spirit had bestowed spiritual powers upon him. These powers enabled him to interpret visions and dreams. The Iroquois did not consist of one single tribe but a set of tribes that constituted a league or confederation in a very large territory. Traditions and ways of living were generally the same and also the meanings and powers attributed to the Great Spirit were more or less shared. In the past, from time to time, I enjoyed visiting the wonderful and unique Museum of Civilization in Ottawa and delving into the history of North America. There, I could relive many of my grandmother's stories regarding her Indian background. Speaking of dreams, on many occasions my family and I, all but my mother that is, would tell my grandmother our dreams so that she could reveal the meanings or messages. "Because in these drops of Iroquoian blood in my veins," she said, "there must be at least one drop from my ancestor gifted with the special powers of the Great Spirit". My mother smiled listening to her and sometimes laughed openly at her. She was a rational and practical woman. All this talk of dreams, energies and such like amused her greatly.

*

Ottawa is a very depressing city in the late fall. The days are short, the sky almost always grey, and the air heavy. Heavy. Heavy. Friday, between five and six p.m, if you don't look at the time, you might say that it's ten or eleven o'clock at night. It's difficult to know. Perhaps all northern cities are the same at this time of year. I read that suicide rates increase dramatically during these months. Round Christmas time, with all the festive lights, one would expect people to be in high spirits. In North America electricity is cheap. Trees sparkle. Strings of fairylights illuminate gigantic shop windows. Buildings are hidden in oceans of neon lights. The 'civilised' folk of North America hate the darkness. In these late-afternoon hours everyone looks frantic. Work finishes a little earlier, people rush to their cars to get home, they dash to catch overcrowded buses, speed walk along the streets and to the shops and bump into each other firing the word 'sorry!' tons of times.

Saturday Night Fever, do you remember? Early Seventies, I think. Everything has moved back a day and now it's 'Friday Fever'. *Hardware* and *software* are two tiring and stressful words. We will hear them again on Monday. For today it's over. Except for the innumerable stores bustling with bodies pushing trolleys crammed with almost everything, many of the activities cease. The steel monsters at the construction sites and in industries that din, pollute, smash up, crush, grind and vomit waste, for a few hours sag like old exhausted skin, hiding from the eyes of the hateful man who looks forward to taking off his stinky coverall. The myriads of computers tortured by millions of schizophrenic fingers that will touch other surfaces this evening, now silenced in the dark sanctuaries of electronic communicability, eye each other up through tiny green, yellow, red lights that jealously safeguard their secrets. In a couple of hours the entertainment will start: dinners, parties, dances and balls, pub crawls, *hard core* and… *soft core*. Many web chatters meet for the first time and are surprised that they are living beings like everybody else, with a body that moves, equipped with legs, arms and eyes, perhaps also with a soul. Tonight several new relationships will begin and many others will end.

Ottawa, although the capital city of Canada, is not the largest city. It is not very big but experts say that in twenty or thirty years it will be as large as Toronto, Montreal or Vancouver. This is credible because, as one of the capitals of software, it attracts a lot of people from all over the world. Since it is the seat of government and of international diplomacy, people from all countries live there, therefore it is a babel of languages and a mosaic of races and skin colours, cultures and sub cultures. Faces. Faces. Faces that come and go, that appear and then vanish. A transit city for many. This is one of the reasons why contacts and relationships are rather cold. A Spanish guy, my colleague at the university, made me laugh once by saying that the 'journey' in a lift is an adventure in the meanderings of incommunicability. Those who live on the top floors of tall buildings, during peak hours must allow at least twenty minutes longer to reach their workplace, and prepare physically for absolute stillness in an assembly that pretends to be without eyes and that pretends to be plunged into the depths of serious and sombre thoughts. 'Good morning!' he dared to say in the lift at the beginning of his stay in Canada. Tongues chained. Furtive embarrassed glances. 'Hi!' some brave individual seldom answered. 'A far cry from our lifts!' my Spanish colleague told me. 'In our country, in the descent and ascent of five floors, the aspect of communicability can intertwine the destinies of the beings *on board*, animals included, in the most unthinkable ways. "Good morning! You live on the fifth floor, don't you, madam?... Oh yes! You are Marta's friend, my cousin's boyfriend...They often talk to me about you, you know! I've heard that you have just got divorced. I'm very sorry. Come for a coffee this evening..." and: "How cute this little dog is!...a little boy dog. So cool! What breed is it?... Ah...it's a Yorkshire Terrier. My sister has a little girl dog. It's really cool too! We could get them together! What do you think?"'

Wonderful guy this Spaniard.

Canada is not only Ontario or British Columbia. It is also Québec, an immense territory, in fact. It is the kingdom of Francophones, where you can breathe a vaguely Latin atmosphere. Francophones are very proud of their Latin kinship and any time is good to mention it. It is well known that Latin *DNA* equates with being noisy, warm and open in social relationships, of shaking hands when introducing each other (whereas English speakers do not always touch when greeting someone), also of exceeding speed limits by a few miles an hour, of having a different concept of life (possibly lighter). 'Lighter' is a synonym for an aesthetic side of living by which they want to perpetuate the memory of a classic Roman lifestyle where the enjoyment of pleasure is free from any kind of inhibition. All this is very true. I am an Anglophone because the origin of my father's family is

British, but bilingualism is compulsory in many sectors of society. Being the seat of government, Ottawa is the most bilingual of all Canadian towns. My French is not as good as my English, but I speak and write it fluently. I like Québec. I have a few friends and acquaintances especially in Québec City and Montréal. I feel comfortable there and these two cities are wonderful. I also find that the presence of Francophones in the universities makes the atmosphere livelier and raises the cultural level. Luckily, Québec is not far from where I live; just one mile from the bridge over the river. I live in a very popular street downtown called Laurier, on the fifth floor of Elizabeth Tower, a 32-storey building very sought after in the seventies when it was newly built. Approximately one thousand people live there. Needless to say, the synthesis of all races and peoples of the world live there. The condo rules are very strict. Rarely do I come across the same people, and the corridors are always as silent as churches. The only acoustic sign that makes you aware of the presence of other living beings is the gushing of bath water through the pipes. Something has just popped into my mind. It sounds like a joke, yet it really happened, something that my Italian estate agent told me when I bought my apartment. He has been living here for twenty years and is a kind of 'landmark' for many Italians who want to buy or rent houses. He told me that an Italian woman had lived in my apartment before me. It was Christmas time like now. She lived on her own so felt the need to talk to somebody. One evening, hearing an Italian song in the next flat, she felt relieved and a bit excited. With a smile on her face, she went to knock at her neighbour's door. She knocks. After a few seconds the song stops playing. She knocks again. Nothing. She hesitates, uncertain what to do, whether to go back home or to knock one last time. Finally, she decides to knock louder.

Police arrive a few seconds later!

*Le marché aux mots*[42] (so called by a few poets) is a local book fair that takes place from time to time in Rideau, the centre of the city – let's say the old part for what can be considered old or ancient from the North American perspective, – that is, from one hundred to two hundred years ago, a little further back is archaic. Usually this *marché* takes place in the daytime but at specific periods like this many poets and writers remain until evening. Alexis is an old poet of Greek origin. He has travelled a lot and lived most of his life in the States and Canada. He also teaches Aesthetics at the University of Hull. I have known him for many years. We don't see each other often but when we do, we like to talk for hours. His books are displayed disorderly on the stand. One with a red cover attracts my attention. *Curtain on the Sun* is the title and I start to leaf through it. On the page with the biographical notes there are a few lines on his Greek origin. On one side of the notes, there is a photo of him as a child holding the hand of his pregnant mother who is carrying another baby in her arms. Alexis – Alex to his friends – introduces me to a lot of people who come to this place to show and sell their books. I wanted to say that I too like to scribble stories sometimes, but I didn't because as I was about to say it, there was a stern voice inside me ordering me to 'Shut up!' Ok, I'll be quiet.

 - Words on words, words on words and paper and paper, – raves a poet in another stall. – Who buys these fuckin' dreams anyway?!

 - You know, – says Alex sipping a hot coffee, – in this city there are at least five thousand illiterate people. You wouldn't believe it. To buy a book. What is a book!...In some respects this is still a wild country. The soul of the whole of America is still wild.

---

42  The Words Market.

I had heard somebody say the same thing before.

- You are younger than me, – he continued, – and you are a Canadian born here.

- It's not a privilege anymore. You know that very well.

- But you don't know what it means to be an immigrant. I arrived in New York when I was eleven. My father was already fifty one. At his age he had to leave his country, uproot and with a wife and three children start a new life on a different continent where we were told we would stumble upon dollars while walking along the streets. We lived in New York for one year then my father was given a better opportunity in Canada.

- Yet, the sacrifices of your parents served to give you a better upbringing.

- Sure. Canada has given me a lot. In Greece, my parents more than likely wouldn't have been able to afford to pay for my studies.

- Perhaps you wouldn't have become a philosopher and a poet. A well-known poet.

- It's difficult to say.

- More and more people, especially young people, enjoy writing poetry. This is fantastic.

- It is…

- Is it so easy, then, to be a poet?

- You should know as well as I do. You like writing, you teach drama…

- I scribble… Nothing else. Just stories. No poetry.

- It depends on what you mean by poetry. Poetry can be expressed also through well written prose. The history of literature offers many examples.

- The history of literature also tells us that poetry, as an artistic expression, causes and provokes many debates, discussions, strong contrasts between poets and intellectuals. That's why I'd also like to hear your opinion.

- Thank you for the high regard that you have for me.

Alex started to pack his books into a cardboard box since the crowds had started to dwindle.

- In recent times, – he continued while piling up the books, – I have become more and more involved in conversations and academic debates relating to poetry as a universal expression of the soul. It affects each of us in some way because its expression is linked to the world of emotions. I think that almost everybody is tempted at least once in their life – spontaneously and unexpectedly – to express their feelings, sensations and impressions 'poetically'. So, it is natural to wonder if poetry – which certainly stems from a heightened sensitivity – can be an expression of the many rather than of the few. From time to time I am asked to sit on literary juries. Well, the avalanches of verses, by which I am overwhelmed, often confuse me and lead me to re-examine my thinking about my own 'poetry writing'. After a few moments of bewilderment I return to my beliefs. Having a poetic soul can actually be a virtue and a gift of many, but that does not make them poets. And even finding a novel way to describe the moon or the buds of the forest is not enough to be defined as, or to be, a poet. I remember a peasant in Greece from my area who was completely illiterate but who had acute powers of observation, of nature in particular, and with almost no effort could make verses rhyme as he contemplated flowers and trees. He was also very good at music although unable to read it. Today, looking back, I think that potentially he had great talent especially as a poet, but he was not educated. Poetry, true poetry, is a marriage of education and talent.

- Yes, I agree with you. In fact, throughout the history of literature I have never come across even one poet without a solid semiological background. There have often been attempts to make poetry 'approachable' to a vast audience, not necessarily a cultured and intellectual audience, but this has had only limited success.

- Like in early Romanticism. Wordsworth and Coleridge are an example. They were very close friends and shared their literary anti-classic aims and views. According to Wordsworth, a poet must adopt a simple language and a simple style, that's to say he must speak a language that is simply 'human'. Many didn't like this. The first to disagree was Coleridge although he had previously endorsed this principle. Then he understood that this obligatory 'simple language' was an intolerable diktat. There arose a disagreement that resulted in the breakdown of their understanding and friendship. For them, the bone of contention was the concept and nuances of language and speech.

I helped Alex to lift the heavy box onto a desk. He had trouble breathing and was visibly fatigued.

- Sit down and rest, Alex, don't worry, I'll help you put away the rest of the books.

- Thank you, dear friend, – he said sitting and watching me rearrange the remaining books in another box.

- Do you think that a misunderstanding, however serious, can break a good friendship? – I asked.

- Why not! Friendship is a form of love purer than that of a couple therefore it's more vulnerable.

- Really? I thought the opposite.

He seemed somewhat inattentive then resumed his thread:

- A few years after the disagreement between Wordsworth and Coleridge, Paul Valéry's lesson on 'pure poetry' masterfully clarified the concept of language and speech influencing the greatest western poets of the twentieth century. For him, the poetic word must be the unifying vehicle of human experience, not dry semantics, but tears or smiles which have their roots in the depths of existence. Therefore words must be the result of reflection and careful study.

- Speech and language!

- In poetry, then, what must be understood is not only the language but also the speech.

While Alexis was talking I looked at him sitting on that wobbly chair and I had the impression that he was daydreaming, imagining he was in the classroom giving a lesson to his students. An effect of age, perhaps? Do we all become like this?

- Speech and language... Do you understand what I mean?

I didn't think that he was addressing me, therefore I didn't answer leaving him to lecture in front of his imaginary audience.

- Two different aspects that need to be dealt with in the context of the set of problems connected with hermeneutics. It's hermeneutics that helps us to read, to decipher, to dig deeper and to go beyond the word. Because if language can be understood rationally, the same is not true for speech, which is often sensed and perceived by creeping patiently through the maze of semantics. The poet, then, is one who captivates the reader, capturing the attention through a varied game of images, sounds, impressions, feelings...

- Hello! Good evening!

The one who cut in on Alex's speech with a thunderous greeting was Alfredo who suddenly appeared in front of the stand. I looked at him a bit surprised and at the same time I breathed a sigh of relief considering him a *deus ex-machina* arriving just in time to save me from an embarrassing situation. In fact – not to be disrespectful towards Alex – I seized the moment. I thought that Alex needed to go straight home and rest after such an exhausting day. I asked him if he wanted me to take him home. He said that his car was parked very close and would drive back.

- Have a merry Christmas, Alex! – I wished him while helping him to get up from the chair. – You have a big family, I'm sure the atmosphere will be wonderful.

- Thanks, my friend, we'll continue our conversation on poetry when life allows us to meet again.

- We could also force the hand of fate sometime, – I laughed. – Call me any time, I learn more and more from you every time I see you.

- I will! I need special listeners.

All three laughed.

- Is everything ok? – asked my student when we were alone. – Perhaps I shouldn't have interrupted you.

- No, believe me, you came at the right time.

- I was here with a few friends taking a look at the stands.

- Well, if you still have time we can go for a drink and have a chat.

- Sure, thank you.

We didn't go far. There were a lot of pubs nearby and we entered the first one we came to. He started by updating me on the rehearsals. He admitted that two or three students had been a bit discouraged two weeks earlier, but now everybody seemed to be happy although there was a lot to memorise. He presumed any reluctance would be won over since the story was so captivating. They would resume rehearsals after the Christmas holidays. Most of the students had already left including Julie.

- And where will you spend Christmas? – I asked.

- Here, in Ottawa. My family have come to visit me and are staying for two weeks. Unfortunately, it's too cold for them. I would have preferred them to be here in a different season.

- I hope they won't experience any ice storms like we had a few years ago. It was devastating. But it's a rare occurrence. I'm sure they'll enjoy the Canadian Christmas. There are so many events on over these days! I think it would be a good idea to contact the Italian community here.

- I've already done it. My father has tracked down somebody from Perugia who has been living here for many years. I can see that Italians are well integrated here.

– Definitely. Very well integrated. They've contributed greatly to the development of this country... My friend Alex just told me that America is still wild... "The soul of the whole of America is still wild," he said.

– Do you agree? Do you think that Canada and the States are on the same level?

– I have my opinion on the matter. – I hastened to clarify: – I was born and brought up here and I'm very patriotic, yet this doesn't prevent me from being realistic and objective... Are they on the same level? Yes and no. It's a very long and complicated subject. The Francophones here represent a diversity within the diversity. It's a good thing that they are mitigating an Americanisation that is becoming overwhelming, but I fear that in the future – as far in the future as possible – their war will be lost. We are destined to become the umpteenth State of the USA and consequently Francophones will see their influence diminished. Our economy and finance are almost completely in the hands of the Americans...We have no alternatives. Basically, we are a small population concentrated in a few towns in an immense and rich territory. This is one of the reasons we will become Americans... Look around you, go a few miles out of the city and you won't meet a human for hundreds of miles apart from in Toronto and Montreal, and if you're not careful you risk ending up in the mouths of wolves or mauled by bears. Wilderness. Those who upped sticks and came here have had to deal with this world. Nothing has been easy... These were the territories of the Native Americans that we see at the cinema: Iroquois, Algonquins, Hurons and others...Here, there were the Outaouais from whom the name of the river and the city comes. In the beginning, it was a place for the trade of wood and furs. It still is. Explorers and pioneers in search of fortune and conquests, hunters, adventurers, mercenaries in the pay of the British and of the French, these were the kind of people passing through here. Violent, unscrupulous people, maybe with good feelings but hardened and made wild by circumstances. One or two hundred years were not enough to soften this hardness. It must be said, however, that the British have been able to impress the mould of their civilisation here so, much of the positivity that these people now show, is British heritage. The Canadian constitution is largely based on the ideas and principles that made Great Britain the symbol of democracy.

- I'm really astonished to hear that the economy and finances are completely in the hands of the Americans.

I smiled to myself seeing the horror on Alfredo's face at my statement. Maybe I exaggerated…But maybe not!

- I may have told a fib! – I laughed. – But not a big one.
- You're an Anglophone but you don't seem to like Americans very much…
- There are also a few drops of Iroquoian blood in my veins, you know?

Alfredo didn't hide his wonder.

- Really! That's fantastic. I want to know more about the world of the Native Americans. This is a promise that I've made to myself.
- Don't expect it to be like it is in the films … Anyway, next time I want you to tell me about Italy…You already promised. Do you remember?
- Yes, I do.

Alfredo was a really nice boy and I think also a bit naïve. I liked him a lot. I'm glad we had that chat.

I confess that I have never been enthusiastic about Christmas time, even when I was a boy. I have never understood why. I read somewhere that people with depression don't like festivities, but I don't think that's why since I've never suffered from depression. Also the mania of present buying irritates me. I have always preferred to give and to receive presents at times other than at specific celebrations. But I realise that I'm an exception, so I don't let people know.

'Am I weird?' I sometimes ask myself looking at my face in the mirror.

'A little!' A mysterious voice answers.

Yet, as long as you live in a particular social context certain conventions and formalities must be reasonably respected. If you do otherwise, there is always a price to pay, the price that every individual pays who moves to so-called diversity. 'Civilisation' has turned society into a big prison where rules are the guards. Rules depersonalise behaviours, cancel individualism and frustrate consciences turning the masses into colourless and soulless flocks. Teaching drama taught me a great deal, especially with regard to the observation of human behaviour. The discussion on the real identity of the individual, on what and/or who we are and on the masks that rules dictate we wear in order not to go beyond the limits of 'normality' has involved great playwrights, actors and intellectuals in particular in the twentieth century.

So, let's have a look at what presents to buy. Just a look. I'll be going shopping tomorrow because I'm not good at choosing gifts and it usually takes ages. My sister, Ruth, and my brother, Ryan, with their respective partners and children are coming to spend a few days in Nepean, in our old house. I think that another reason they want to come is to discuss the sale of the property as it's empty. Anyway, it's good to have a family get-together from time to time.

I usually turn on my computer and attend to my correspondence online every night. That night, among the many emails, I found one from Julie written in French.

*"Excusez-moi!"*[43] – *she wrote.* – *"Good manners require that students wish their professors a Merry Christmas in person, especially since we are all working so closely together. In fact, the atmosphere in our group has made the relations*

---

43  Excuse me!

*between us all more friendly than professional. This experience is benefitting us immensely and I want to thank you also on behalf of the whole group. Since the party at Ivan's house, I have been meaning to ask you for an appointment for a few reasons. The first is that my behaviour at the party, after acting, was embarrassing therefore I owe you an explanation. Which is not easy. It is not easy to talk about myself and about what makes me appear strange to others. Although I know you better now than a few months ago, I am not yet ready to reveal to you what is tormenting me. During these days that I have been away from Ottawa, I have realised that my decision to wait was wise, but my need to talk to you has been growing stronger and stronger every day. I hope you will allow me the opportunity to discuss all this on my return. Apart from being unsure about whether to come and see you the last few days, I have been absent from lessons because I have a few guests staying with me. I apologise for not greeting you in person.*

*Have a Merry Christmas!*
*Julie."*

I appreciated her letter. But I did not reply immediately. I wanted to ponder over what to say, so the next day I decided to text just a few lines thanking her for the kind gesture and assuring her that I looked forward to a long conversation with her.

Although empty, the house in Nepean remained perfectly functional. Ruth and Ryan liked to return there at least once a year and I too popped in once or twice per month. The garden was large and required constant maintenance. Despite the fact that essentially the affection we felt for the house was because it was a source of memories linked to our parents, grandparents and to a considerable part of our childhood and youth spent there, we came to the decision that it was time to sell it. This Christmas, very likely, would be the last one we spent there together. It really is true that things can also be, or are, living beings gifted with a soul and a heart, capable of breathing and of expressing feelings. Is this poppycock? Each of us can think what he wants. The fact is that now, having the certainty of the last farewell there, everything around seemed to express its sadness or to cry out its sorrow. I had this strong perception and feeling the day before the family arrived while tiding up the rooms and the garden. Never before had I felt so intensely overwhelmed ....

In the stable, the neighing of Nelson, my father's last horse, echoed in my ears and brought back to my mind the expression in his eyes when my father died. I am certain that human tears could not convey such searing pain. From that day on, he never neighed again. Dear Nelson, I'm sure that right now my father is riding you in the vast prairies of heaven where death has no power to uproot our loved ones from our lives. The two armchairs in front of the majestic fireplace saw two generations sitting and enjoying the warm flames that greedily devoured the crackling logs. When I was a child, the two wooden arms of those armchairs held a great fascination for me. Jacket and shirt sleeves of the people who used to sit there, over time, rubbed on them making them so shiny that I never tired of stroking those smooth brown surfaces. There my grandmother Orenda used to talk to me and to my sister and brother about the Iroquois and told us their tales and legends...

*Pluffpluffpluffpluff...*

> *At the beginning of time, on earth there was only an abyss of water, but above, in the Big Blue, there was a community called the "World of the Sky" where there was a woman who dreamed dreams. One night she dreamed that the tree was the*

*source of light. The dream inspired her so she went to ask the man in the World of the Sky to plant a tree. They dug around its roots to make room for even more light, but the tree fell through the hole and disappeared. Consequently, there was only darkness. Taken by surprise and not knowing what to do, they pushed the woman through the hole. She would have been lost in the abyss if a fish hawk had not come to her rescue by catching her on its back. The fish hawk could not keep supporting her all by itself, so it asked for help to create a solid ground on which the woman could stand. A bird dived to the bottom of the sea and brought back mud in its beak. It found a turtle, and smeared the clay on its shell, and plunged back into the water again and again. Even the ducks filled their beaks with the ocean floor and smeared it on the turtle's back. The beaver helped to build the land, making it much bigger. The birds and animals built continents until they had made the whole earth round, while the woman was sitting safely on top of the turtle. The turtle continues to hold the earth on its back. When it was all finished, one of the spirits from the World of the Sky came down and looked at the earth. After he had travelled around it, he concluded that it was wonderful, so he created people to live on it and gave them special abilities; each tribe of the Iroquois nation was endowed with special gifts to share with the rest of humanity.'*

The smells were always the same. In each room there was a different smell. Let me count approximately how many years the house was inhabited by our family. I think fifty five or sixty years. The house had been built by my grandfathers, so nobody else had lived there and in those times it was an isolated house in the countryside until the eighties when the irreverent aggression of urbanisation started. It is understandable, then, how all the items and objects that filled the house, including the walls, windows and doors had absorbed the energies of the living beings that, after years of absence, still emanated particles of their breath, of their voices, of their skin. How could I be insensitive to my recollections of my writing desks on which I had worn out the elbows of my shirt sleeves or to the memories of the drawers that had preserved my secrets for years? Yes, yes. The bottom drawer on the left is the only one that locks. As far as I remember, my secrets were mainly letters from girlfriends and a diary that I used to write in from time to time. I kept them locked away because I shared the room with my brother who was so nosy; he liked to peek at my things and then to tell my mother everything. I kept the letters for years; I don't remember how I decided in which order to destroy them, I mean whether it was according to how much the girl had meant to me or to the beauty of the letters. The first thing to tear up was the diary. When I became an adult, I found out that I didn't like to read things from my past; they made me feel uncomfortable. The thought that others could read what triggered my emotions bothered me. No. Finally, I concluded that keeping the diary was ridiculous. For me. I tore it up. I felt relieved after getting rid of it and I didn't regret it at all.

Everything can change in life. Fortunately!

Regarding the letters, to tell the truth, I kept only Della's for many years and, this is a confession, I didn't have the heart to destroy all of them. I still have two. Della was the biggest love of my life. I should really write a book about it ... perhaps I will in the future. What I want to tell you about now is how we continued with the preparation for the staging of Romeo and Juliet. Actually, ... before I do, just because I have written very little about myself, I want to mention briefly something about Della and me, starting from where we are now. Now we are friends. Very good friends and still see each other from time to time. She is married to a good man and they have two children. Several times I have heard people maintain that it is difficult or impossible to remain friends with an ex-partner or partners. It depends on each individual case. Some years ago, I too did not expect that it was possible but, as I said, everything in life can change, even feelings. I think that time or other factors that I do not understand have created for us a sort of comfortable dependence on each other. We do not meet so often but enough to tell each other things that we would not tell anyone else and to keep our connection strong. Yet, there is a shadow over our relationship: her husband. She tried to assure me that Richard, her husband, has nothing against the fact that we are friends and that we sometimes meet. In spite of his discretion, I am not totally convinced that this is true. He has never told me or asked me anything about my past with Della but the few times we have spent some time together, once at their home, and other times in town, I felt that he was not completely comfortable in my company. Seven years spent with his wife, even if the past is past, cannot be so easy to ignore. Though it is subjective, putting myself in his shoes, I can understand his mistrust and unwillingness to accept me as his wife's friend. To be honest, I don't think that I would be able to accept it either. One day I met Richard downtown. Ottawa has an extensive territory but the centre is like a village where it is not difficult to bump into people you know. It is easier to meet your next door neighbour at Rideau or in the most frequented markets than in the corridor of your building. It was the first time that Richard and I had had the chance to be together without his wife, which made me hope that the atmosphere between us would be more relaxed, especially on his side. I tried to be frank and open. Sitting outside a pub with a pint of lager to sip, I told him a few jokes about *Yankees*. One strange guy from New York asked me if we still live in igloos in Ottawa. And when I said that igloos are in the region of the Inuit he laughed. And I laughed because he laughed. Actually I laughed because I expected more of the usual American bullshit. In fact he said: "Hey! Do the Inuit live so far away? I thought they lived in the Bronx!" Richard seemed to appreciate my spirit but was not very talkative. Every time, before meeting Della, I wonder if it is right to do so or not. I do not hesitate to tell her that I always feel a hint of guilt.

- Ours is a special friendship, – Della said one day while having coffee in my apartment.
- Friendship is friendship. It's always a special connection.
- Right. This is the point.
- What do you mean?
- After splitting up, we didn't see each other for at least three years, right? We ignored each other. It was my intention to erase you from my life, then I met Richard. I was happy with him. I know that happiness is a very abstract word, but with the meaning that people generally give to it let's say that I was happy. I felt that he was the right man to start a family with. This was important for me…
- It's strange you saying that because we often used to talk about the possibility of us having children.

Della realised she had made a gaffe and lowered her eyes to avoid my gaze.

- Yes, – she confirmed. – We talked, we only talked, but every time I tried to broach the subject with you about us actually starting a family, you always avoided it. It took many years to understand you, but now I understand you better.
- What do you understand better?
- You can be a good lover or a good friend but you're not cut out for being part of a couple; you're not cut out for family life. You are what you are. You are a loner and you belong to everyone at the same time.

I think she had wanted to get that off her chest for a long time but had never found the right time. I smiled. I did not know what significance to attach to what she had said. Part of what she thought of me was true, but I found her way of speaking a bit harsh, almost revealing a hidden resentment.

- Thank you for your frankness, – I stuttered a bit clumsily. – What made you decide to contact me again, then?

- I needed you.

This time I did not notice the previous harshness and I looked at her a little bewildered, not knowing exactly what she meant. For a few moments, I detected a sensual vibration in that 'I needed you'. She was still in her forties and in spite of two pregnancies she seemed to have taken good care of her body appearing young-looking and attractive. She used to say that nowadays the secret of success is mostly due to the image that you portray of yourself.

- Not in a sexual sense, – she hastened to clarify wanting to escape my piercing gaze. – Over the years I thought a lot about our empathy, our talks, something indefinable and specific that belonged and still belongs just to me and you, to our world and that I couldn't find in my husband. I needed it. It took a while, but finally I made my decision.

- You've told Richard what you are telling me, haven't you?

- Yes. He's intelligent and wise. He understands my psychology…

- More than me?

- You want to provoke me, don't you?

She laughed.

- If he understands you, – I insisted, – in what other ways do I satisfy you?

- You're pretending not to understand. A partner is a partner. He is not a friend.

- And if I hadn't considered you just a friend, what would you have done?

- I would have been disappointed. If not a friend, what else could I have been for you?

- A lover!

- A lover? You must be joking. That kind of attraction is

over. When the glass is broken, it's impossible to put it back together.

We both remained silent for a long minute.

- There's something not quite right about this broken glass, – I said pensively.

- What?

- If the glass is our past love affair and if it broke, then nothing would have remained or could have been saved. Even the good wine inside, supposing there was any, is lost forever.

- Go on!

- Which of the two is physical attraction? The glass is in pieces and the wine has gone.

- Ah, my darling! You liked to study only languages and literature at school. If you had studied chemistry and physics better, you would know that nothing can be destroyed. It can, however, be transformed.

- You're right, I was hopeless at physics.

- All the little pieces can be gathered and reassembled in the way that we like or choose. We can create a sort of mosaic where every piece is a symbol of what is still alive from our past.

- It's not true that the past is past...

- A man of the theatre, as you are, knows very well...

- Sure! In many ways the past remains alive in the depths of our being...But we are two different people, which also means that shared experiences are lived with different emotions. The symbols that you want to assign to each piece does not necessarily correspond to my vision.

- I don't concede. I want to gather up all the pieces...

- You or we?

- We. We'll gather all the pieces and make a new glass. This glass is friendship. It's shinier.

- Wrong! ...Della...It's shinier than what?...

- Friendship is pure, it is free.

- You worry me.

- Do I?

- Is it not love that binds a couple together and makes them free? Is it not shiny? Isn't the glass called love as shiny as the glass of friendship?

- They shine in different ways and with different colours.

- So you need both.

- Yes, you do.

- You said you were or you are happy with your husband. Love is love. Love is everything. A person who loves doesn't need other emotions or excitements outside the world of the couple.

- My dear, this is not absolutely true. To be happy as a couple doesn't mean to keep the world around you out.

- Della...

- Yes.

- Tell me...Tell me one thing...

- When you stutter you are going to say something ... dangerous...I know you.

We both laughed.

- We know almost everything about each other; we know our bodies, our intimacies... Supposing that circumstances conspired to cause moments of unexpected temptation...

- Don't go any further. What you said is correct...'we know almost everything about each other'...But as for our bodies and intimacies, we do not know them now. We once knew them. Look! We are not young anymore...Your hair is almost grey and I dye mine...Despite working out at the gym, my butt is still big and your stomach is growing...We are two different people. What you imagine is an illusory revival of a season of life that doesn't exist anymore...Supposing that circumstances...to mention your words...our reason would prevail, we would not allow a momentary desire to destroy our tie. That desire would be false. And in the end, what you fantasise would be a disaster.

Della had been very honest and clear. Now I was convinced of how she really felt towards me.

- Don't blame me for my doubts, – I said.

- Blame you? Our conversation is great. This is what we both need. I feel better now...We give a lot to each other.

- Yes, we do. We're lucky...How many people are so lucky?

- Thank you for saying that. Yes, we are lucky.

- But...Forgive me if I insist...Your husband is still a shadow over our connection.

- He's a shadow over your basic instinct.

- What do you mean?

- You have not yet cut the cord of the physical possession rooted in your subconscious, the possession of me.

- I don't have the strength to cut it.

- For men it's more difficult.

- Which means that my feelings of friendship towards you will never be as pure and free as yours are for me.

- Never is a big word. I'll help you...Ok, my dear, now I have to leave. I see a script of Romeo and Juliet on the desk.

- Yes. A new adventure with the students.

- Adventure!

- Setting up a group for a performance is like conceiving a baby and being pregnant.

- Wonderful...But your last pregnancy was a bit difficult, as I remember...The case of that couple who split up.

- Yes. You have a good memory, it was when we had just got back in touch.

- Thank you for talking to me about your work. I appreciate it.

- It's good to talk about certain situations with people outside our work environment. They can be more objective.

- Good luck, then. Next time, update me on your 'pregnancy'!!

★

- I appreciated your performance at Ivan's house, – I told the students who had taken part in the second act. – But, as I said, there are a few points that we need to go over before you perform it again.

It was a very cold Friday in January. On the outside of the glass windows, ice had formed beautifully intricate flowers. For several days the thermometer had been permanently set at -22°C. From inside, seeing how the sun shone and how clear the sky was, one might have been tempted to go out without gloves or a hat. Very deceptive. People who come to Canada for the first time must know that the cold can be a cruel enemy here.

- The scene opens with a particular soliloquy of Romeo, – I continued, – who is talking to Juliet knowing that she can't hear him, and is interrupted by another soliloquy, that of Juliet who is speaking to herself believing that she cannot be heard. The two soliloquies in blank verse intertwine as if to form a dialogue, until Romeo decides to respond to Juliet so that poetic language (soliloquy in verse) is transformed into theatrical language (dialogue in prose). From the dialogue of the two lovers their respective characters emerge: Juliet as more mature and conscientious, who immediately sees the dangers of their love, and the more dreamy and hasty Romeo who lives almost detached from reality in a purely poetic dimension… When you acted this scene at Ivan's house, you were too far from each other, too cold. While the two soliloquies are in progress, people need to see and feel your growing emotion that reaches the climax in the dialogue… And now I have good news for you. Our performance is confirmed for April 26th in Verona, we will also go to Mantua but only for a visit, not to perform.

A roar of excitement broke the intense concentration and

distracted them all from my teaching. I understood that it was not possible to continue the rehearsal today while they were so hyped up, so we postponed it until the following Monday. What we did instead was to talk about the costumes that they would wear on stage; this took up the remainder of the two-hour lesson. It was important to deal with this as going to the homeland of the two lovers required greater attention from the aesthetic point of view. After announcing that we would go to Verona, I saw Julie's face light up, her eyes were wet and her cheeks flushed, she pretended to participate in the conversations of the classroom but I perceived that her mind was elsewhere. Our eyes met a few times. The moment for our talk had arrived. In fact, she came to my office a few minutes after the end of the lesson.

- Here you are at last, Julie! – I said showing her into the room in a friendly manner and inviting her to sit in front of me.

- How was Christmas in Québec City?

- *Comme d'habitude.*[44] My parents are Calvinists; our celebrations are much more sober than those of Protestants and Catholics.

Julie had started speaking in French then switched to English guessing, perhaps, that it would be better for me.

- Is it only your parents who are Calvinists? – I asked curiously.

- I was brought up with those principles and in that way, but for several years now I haven't wanted to follow my parents' religion or any other.

- You don't have any belief, then?

- I feel confused…There's no space for any god in my life. Not now.

- Julie, I know that you are trying to tell me something important about yourself, which is also related to our play.

---

44 As usual.

Several times in the past few months you have given me the impression that you needed to talk...It has taken a while for you to decide to come and see me. Now you're here. I'm very glad. Be free to tell me whatever you want. It's not the first time that I've been involved in aspects or episodes of my students' private lives. I myself was a student and, like you, I experienced circumstances when I needed somebody I could trust. I don't have anything else to do today. We have time.

When she had first entered my room, she was out of breath as though she had been running or exercising. Perhaps it was because she was anxious or nervous. I had some candied fruits on my desk. I took two: one for her and the other for me. While she was unwrapping it I noticed that she had calmed down and appeared more relaxed.

- I don't know how to start or from where, – she said looking at me and then avoiding my eyes. – There's a risk that what I'm about to tell you will make me appear ridiculous or even insane. The person sitting in front of you right now is not a normal person.

I laughed chewing the candy.

- Come on, Julie! – I encouraged her. – Do you know any normal person? Could you give me a definition of so-called normality?

- Do you believe in the paranormal?... I mean, in extrasensory dimensions.

I recalled her references to telepathy.

- I have never experienced anything extraordinary apart from strange dreams and weird coincidences...but I don't exclude the possibility of paranormal dimensions. Everything is possible.

- It's happening there, in Mantua. Antonio and I are to be sentenced to death.

Now, as I report the dialogue between me and Julie, I am certain that she started her story absorbed by a world that had nothing to do with the present and where my presence constituted an intermittent link with reality. In fact, when she kept silent or interrupted, she expected me to reply. It took me some time to fully understand this while the dialogue was in progress. Even now, after telling this case to a number of scientists, I do not have the full answers to what had taken possession of the mind, body and soul of that young woman.

- Perhaps you are mistaken, – I pretended naturally.
- The law of the world says it's not a mistake.
- For a few seconds, the silence was awkward but it was useful for me to understand what my role was to be.
- Who am I? – I asked.
- You are my professor.
- And where are you?
- I am here with you, my name is Julie Marcotte. Now, at the same time, I'm in Mantua and my name is Agnese... Agnese Visconti Gonzaga.[45]

Incredible! I didn't know what to think.

- If you don't believe me, – she continued, – and if you don't understand me, I won't be able to tell you any more.
- I'm trying to understand you, Julie, I believe you. But this is very unusual. Please, go on.
- It's February 6th, 1391.
- How old are you?
- Twenty-three.
- What's your name again?
- My name is Agnese Visconti Gonzaga. *Messer* (My lord) Francesco Gonzaga is my husband. Bernabò Visconti was my father.
- Carry on!
- We have a daughter, *Messer*[46] Francesco and I, called Alda. He wanted a boy but fate decided to give us a girl.

---

45 Author's note: The House of Gonzaga was a princely family that ruled Mantua, in Northern Italy, from 1328 to 1708.
46 Sir.

- Where are you now, exactly? Tell me everything you need to.

- I'm a prisoner in the palace. It's the *vespro*.[47] Tomorrow morning my sentence will be carried out. I will be beheaded. The judge says that only *Messer* Francesco has the power to save me from execution...Antonio, my handsome and generous Antonio, will also be executed; he will be hanged. His heart is a volcano of bravery and goodness and his love has no limits. He has tried to save my life shouldering all the blame for what people call adultery. If it were so, I ask God to condemn me a second time to a worse pain.

Julie put her hands on her face and rubbed her cheeks and forehead several times as though gripped by fear or doubt or discouragement. Then, with one hand, she pushed away something at her side, invisible to me, and sighed deeply.

- And now I am myself... now I'm Julie Marcotte... I feel that this will be too much for you, let's stop now, – she said almost in despair. – Please, excuse me, it's too difficult.

I got up and stepped towards the small fridge near the door of my office. I took out some blackberry juice and poured it into two glasses. I passed one to her and sat on a small more comfortable armchair close to her so that the writing desk was no longer between us.

- Her soul or spirit is inside you, right?

I asked this question without thinking. She suddenly looked relieved and her hands seized mine. She sighed again.

- Thank you...thank you. Yes, I can see that you understand... I'm so glad, I was right to trust you. I know that I can confide in you now... She possesses me. She has been invading my life since I was twelve years old. It started slowly, she appeared from time to time vaguely and for short periods, perhaps only for a few seconds every time. She was more or less my age and we became friends... Friends! I don't really know what we were.

---

47 Sunset.

- Did you tell your parents or anybody else?

Julie let go of my hand and took something from her little rucksack. It was a picture book of Mantua. Somewhat old and worn.

- I told my parents many times about this presence in my life, but they paid no attention to my stories. They used to tell me that children and even adolescents, as I was at the time, have imaginary friends who we treat as real.

- You've never been to Italy, I remember you told me once. How do you explain this Italian presence?

- I've thought about this many times. A few days before this phenomenon started, I met an Italian family, the parents and a boy a little older than me, in a little restaurant run by my uncle. My mother used to go and help her brother in the kitchens at weekends and I often went there too. These people were tourists from Mantua and had come to Québec City for a few days. They were staying in a hotel near the restaurant. They used to have dinner at my uncle's place and so we started to talk. The boy, called Giacomo, spoke only a few words of English that he'd learnt at school. His mother was a bit strange but friendly. She talked to me a lot about Mantua and before leaving she gave me this book as a present. They also wrote their address here, you see, but I have never contacted them. This is the only link that I've had with Italy. And now Alfredo. But, I confess, because of this presence, in recent years I've read a lot about Italy and learned a lot. Last summer I decided to go to Mantua, but my boyfriend at the time, who was from Québec and who I'd been going out with for a few years, didn't let me go. Fortunately, that relationship is over now.

- The presence of…what's her name?…Agnese, is that correct?… did not worry you, as I understand.

- No. Not until she met Antonio. Antonio da Scandiano.

- Who was he?

- He was a knight at the court of Francesco Gonzaga, lord

of Mantua, who entrusted him with the task of escorting his wife when she went out of town.

- And who became her lover, right?

Julie fixed her gaze on an indefinite point. She spoke after one minute:

- The trial for adultery ended with a guilty verdict. A number of slanderous accusations and testimonies left the judge with no other option. Antonio tried as best he could to defend Agnese but there was no way he could be considered credible. A number of judges and many people believed that Francesco would not sign the death sentence. However, he did after only a few hours… Throughout the following centuries, not all historians would agree with the verdict of the trial. Examining the events of the time, many were, and are, convinced that the trial was a farce orchestrated by the lord in order to eliminate his wife for political reasons. Yet, doubts, well-founded doubts about the adultery remain.[48]

- And you, what do you think?

- It was a great love, a great love story that Agnese, or a power above her, wanted to make me live in part in two different ways: one as a witness and the other in person.

- What do you mean exactly?

- I'll try to explain … Until a few years ago, Agnese broke into my life every now and then. In the beginning, she wanted me to follow her to the palace where she lived. I noticed more and more that she needed me mostly when she met her husband. After the birth of their daughter, Alda, these meetings were always dramatic, always explosive on both sides. Every time I asked her why she needed me in those specific moments, she never gave me a clear explanation, she

---

[48] Author's note: The names and the events reported in this chapter are real. Sources of research: "I Gonzaga di Mantova", Giancarlo Malacarne, II Bulino Publisher; Archivo di Stato di Mantova; "InStoria" Rivista online-Ginevra Bentivoglio Editoria. The dialogues are invented by the author.

merely begged me to be close to her, to sit in an armchair and not to move. But even if I had wanted to, I wouldn't have been able to do anything other than what she wanted. The more she needed me, the stranger I felt, in the sense that my identification with her became incredibly strong to the point that I could no longer distinguish who I was, whether myself or her. I felt her emotions, even actual physical sensations; her possession of me – during the time that they lasted – nullified my personality. Fortunately, these complete possessions did not occur often. I realised that they happened when she was emotionally and/or physically stressed by certain events. The possession left me when she calmed down, which always coincided with her losing consciousness for a few seconds.

- Now you are using the past tense, – I observed. – When you started, you expressed your action in the present tense.

- You're right. It happens when I identify with her because in those moments she possesses me completely and I'm transported to her historical context.

Absurd. Unbelievable. I thought that these kinds of stories only belonged to the creativity of writers such as Edgar Allan Poe and Robert Louis Stevenson. Yet, here, in the heart of Canada, in the twenty first century, I was living this fantastic adventure with a student possessed by somebody who had lived in the Middle Ages in a country thousands of miles away. How was it possible? – My grandmother would certainly have said that it was a matter…no…a game played by energies!

- Agnese, – the student added, – was the daughter of Bernabò Visconti, Lord of Milan and one of the most powerful men in Europe. He was a terrible and strange man. There are many anecdotes about him, true or untrue it doesn't matter, but almost all comment on his weirdness and cruelty. Like many powerful men of his time, including priests, he had a lot of children both legitimate and illegitimate. Historians say that ten of his daughters and five of his sons were legitimate and that an unknown number were illegitimate. Agnese was one of the legitimate girls. Amongst the aristocracy of the time – you mentioned these things when we started the play – especially for political reasons, marriages were agreed when the betrothed were still very young children.

Mantua was a small ancient town almost one hundred miles south of Milan with a rich history. Francesco, Agnese's husband, was the heir of a rich and powerful family but whose roots were neither aristocratic nor dated back to ancient times. The family was called Gonzaga and rose to power after overthrowing the previous lords of Mantua, the Bonocolsis. Gonzaga was growing remarkably quickly in power and influence, therefore Bernabò took the first step in agreeing to the marriage between the 12 year-old Agnese and the 14 year-old Francesco. As they were so young, they waited some time before consummating the marriage. They went on to have only one child, a daughter named Alda. When Francesco was 16, his father died and, in spite of his tender age, he had to assume power as Captain of Mantua. However, the events made the atmosphere in the family very tense because one of Agnese's cousins, Gian Galeazzo Visconti, planned to take over the lordship of Milan, therefore he imprisoned his uncle (Agnese's father) and after a few months – allegedly – had him poisoned. Francesco switched allegiance and became a friend of Gian Galeazzo against the will of his wife who would not bow to the wishes of her husband. After all, she had loved her father and in many ways she resembled him so, to her, the behaviour of her cousin was despicable and outrageous. He was not only her cousin but also her brother-in-law since he was married to her sister, Caterina. She would never forgive him and did not hide her contempt and hatred for him. This behaviour enraged Francesco, who feared that the new alliance with Gian Galeazzo would be compromised. Furthermore, he was disappointed because Agnese was not able to give him a son. In the meantime, he had illegitimate children by other women…

'I gave orders to your brothers Carlo and Ludovico to leave my palace no later than tomorrow.'

It was Francesco who spoke. He entered the room on the first floor where Agnese used to spend time alone or in the company of her ladies. Beyond the big windows, life went on as usual in Piazza San Pietro. Especially at that time of the day, it was always crowded with different people: merchants, pitchmen, coveys of gossiping women, well dressed sycophants of the court loitering near the entrance of the palace, numerous noisy children, clerics and priests coming from and going to the cathedral. The lord had entered visibly upset and stared at his wife in anger. It was the first time that Lady Agnese had taken me to this part of the palace and it was also the first time that she had possessed me completely. It happened while they were at the height of their quarrel. The palace was all so unusual; the architecture, the interior design, the home furnishings. Wonderful carpets and tapestries made of special fabric, and frescoes that seduced my eyes. Francesco appeared dressed in a red tunic under which he wore a large shirt and fustian brown trousers. From his thick leather belt, a dagger hung in its golden sheath. Agnese, too, wore a tunic, but of a different colour, a shade of purple, under which a tight black corset and long black skirt gave a slender shape to her body. The large belt, made of woven silk, accentuated her elegance.

'All you do,' – growled Agnese, – 'day after day, is insult the dignity of me and my daughter.'

'And you expect me to continue to put up with your family around me and the conspiracies that all of you, yourself included, plot against me…Ah!…Insolent woman! May God be with me!'

'God with you! You have betrayed the trust of my father… You, traitor, you accuse me of plotting against you when you ally yourself with the murderer of my father… That worm, whose blood, in part, unfortunately, also flows through my veins…God with you!… Is God also with you when you make poor and naïve girls pregnant who are powerless to defend and protect themselves from a bastard like you?'

The man moved closer to his wife seizing the sheath of the dagger. At that exact moment, Agnese's anger was also mine. I felt my heart race and the sphere of my emotions characterised by an expression that was different from my own…Yet it was still me!

He bawled:

'That's it! You've exhausted my patience… You show the same arrogance as your father. His cruelty was very well known, that's why he was hated by all his subjects, and that's why people looked forward to seeing the back of him…You saw how your cousin Gian Galeazzo was welcomed, how the people were happy to hear that he had taken power… You, miserable sterile woman, unable to give me a male heir, how dare you address me in such a manner!'

'Damn your ambition! Your blood will never be anywhere near as noble as mine…'

'Poisonous tongue!…that's what you have…'

'Who and what were your ancestors, man with a short memory? What was their emblem apart from the shit of a vulgar bloodline?'

'Haughty and ungrateful woman!'

'Ungrateful for what…You are ungrateful…You have increased your prestige by marrying me but what have I gained?'

'Keep in mind that I am the fourth Captain of Mantua and I will soon become Imperial Vicar.'

'Coward!…You sought an alliance with Gian Galeazzo just because you think that he can protect you from the ambitions of Antonio della Scala,[49] who wants to rule and take possession of Mantua.'

---

49  His family ruled Verona from 1262 to 1387.

'Keep silent, wicked woman!'

'You deceive yourself into believing that my cousin has no enemies…You will see what kind of trap you will fall into.'

'Not only do you think these things but you go round telling others.'

'I see that your spies are faster than the speed of light.'

'Your resentment and your feelings have already reached the ambassador of Gian Galeazzo…'

'Giorgio Lampugnani… Ambassador…Arse licker!'

'Idiot! Irresponsible woman…He reports everything to your cousin. Shouldn't I be worried?…Your behaviour is affecting my relationship with him.'

'So be it!'

One of his hands met my face with a strong violent slap … Actually, it was Agnese's face but, because during that time she was possessing me and identifying with me, I felt her pain. More painful than a lash.

'From tomorrow take off your mourning clothes!' – he ordered. – 'I have already told you many times and you do not respect my will.'

'My father deserves more respect than you and my cousin put together.'

'Keep your grief to yourself then and don't show it… Especially in the presence of the ambassador and of all those people close to Gian Galeazzo…I don't want to see you dressed in this colour tomorrow evening for the Carnival party…His Excellency Giorgio Lampugnani and other aristocrats from Milan will be here.'

'All arse lickers that shat themselves out of fear when they were in front of my father…I know them, each one of them. And I'm sure that when they see me, they'll continue to tremble because they'll see the spectre of my father in my eyes.'

'Fool! Keep in mind that your father is dead, he doesn't

exist anymore…In this world the strongest survive…This is the law of life.'

'He was strong.'

'Braggart!…Strong, yes, but not wise…not wise enough to realise that among his closest kin there was his worst enemy…' Francesco suddenly moved back and started to pace up and down the room. I calmed down and came out of Agnese now assuming my role as witness. The Captain opened one of the doors and ordered a servant to call Lady Beatrice di Ser Gori, one of his wife's two dressing assistants. Then he stopped and spoke more softly:

'I want to inform you that I'll be leaving on a mission soon… Valentina, the daughter of Gian Galeazzo, is going to France to marry Louis de Turenne. I have offered to accompany her. It will be a long journey. I have already instructed that during my absence Antonio da Scandiano, knight and gentleman, will escort you everywhere.'

Lady Beatrice arrived almost immediately. Francesco told her about the way in which he wanted her to dress his wife for the party recommending that she chose bright colours, then he left the room. I cannot say what happened afterwards because Agnese let me go. I was with her again only during the party. But I can imagine what poor Agnese had to go through in the twenty four hours following that conversation. She was obliged to receive a number of guests who were staying the night. She had to pretend to be happy to them all. In those times, the palaces where these high ranking families lived were crowded. The apartments strictly reserved for the family were mainly frequented by varlets and ladies and gentlemen of the court who were entrusted with a variety of tasks, while in the extensions, mainly on the ground floors, out of sight from the family apartments, servants, cooks, stablemen, millers, gardeners and many other people assigned to the maintenance of the mansion lived in close quarters. I'm describing very briefly the environment of a palace as the residence of an important family because living with so many people around, even though in the highest position in society, it was almost impossible to keep secrets and to protect one's privacy. Therefore everybody in Mantua was aware of the unpleasant atmosphere in the Gonzaga Family.

Things got worse during the party. At first, Agnese wanted me at her side, then, for one of the most dramatic moments she needed me inside her. I arrived almost at the end of the party. It is not necessary for me to describe the incredible elegance and originality of the costumes and masks. Let's not forget that Venice is not so far from Mantua and that its influence in terms of culture and other aspects of society was strong in the north of Italy. The Lady was sitting in a comfortable armchair surrounded by a number of ladies wearing masks or full costumes. She, however, wasn't wearing a mask or a costume but maintained her outstanding appearance in her elegant dress and Roman Empire hairstyle. The large hall was full of guests almost all of whom were wearing wonderful masks and enjoying the entertainment which included comedy and games. The atmosphere was very relaxed with the sound of laughter mixed with the music from the orchestra. I later learnt that the carnival I was witnessing in the palace did not correspond to the way of celebrating it in the streets of the town. The feast there, lasting one week, was a magical time when the relaxing of all the rules of society gave people the opportunity to satisfy needs and wishes suffocated or restrained throughout the whole year. Like in the Roman *Saturnalia*,[50] social roles were allowed to be overthrown so that the servant became the master and the master the servant. Shrove Tuesday represented the culmination of the festivities with masked processions, singing and dancing. Needless to

---

50   Saturnalia was the most popular holiday in the Roman year. During the holiday, restrictions were relaxed and the social orders inverted.

say, overeating was an excuse to cope with the fasting of the upcoming Lent.

Francesco, in the middle of the room, dressed in his exclusive and colourful clothes, was entertaining his most important guest, the ambassador Giorgio Lampugnani, who proudly showed off the Visconti emblem, consisting of a blue grass snake on a silver background, pinned to the lapel of his coat. The distance, intended or accidental, and the people in between impeded Agnese and the hated diplomat from catching each other's eye, but she could feel the envious and poisonous glances from the covered eyes of the disguised ladies of the Milanese court. At a certain point, the Captain gave an order to the musicians to fall silent and drew the attention of everybody, loudly announcing:

'I have the pleasure and honour this evening to express my gratitude to my ally and friend His Excellency Gian Galeazzo Visconti via his noble ambassador Giorgio Lampugnani. In tough times like these when the greed and ambitions of unpredictable enemies threaten our territories, our alliance with Gian Galeazzo reassures us and makes us proud.'

Francesco finished his announcement and moved towards his wife. He politely offered her his hands inviting her to stand and follow him. Surprised, she hesitated for a few moments then followed him without taking his hand. He proceeded to take three chalices from the nearest table and gave one to Agnese and another to the ambassador.

'And now,' he continued, 'on this wonderful occasion I, along with my wife and yourself, Excellency, propose a toast: may the Lord of Milan enjoy success and long life!'

While the waiters filled the chalices of the other invitees, Francesco and the ambassador raised their own as a sign of hope. Agnese remained motionless with the chalice in her hand staring haughtily at the ambassador who was trying to escape those eyes that he had known for a long time and that reminded him of her cruel and powerful father. I sensed that something was going to happen because I underwent a sudden identification with her; my soul entered her body. I felt my face blaze with a burning anger.

'I will never wish success and long life to a traitor!' I exploded in the silence that dominated in the hall.

I saw the look of disbelief on the suddenly darkened faces of the Captain and of Lampugnani. I turned around resolved and contemptuous, and, accompanied by the buzz of those present, I stormed out and rushed along the corridors to my rooms. I threw myself on the bed covering my eyes with my hands to make myself sleep, but after a few minutes the door was thrust open loudly, the Captain burst in moving furiously towards me. He seized my left arm forcing me to get up then pushed me violently against a wooden pillar and landed two hard slaps on my face:

'You want to destroy my life,' he snarled with fire in his eyes. 'You make me sick... I will not allow you and your brothers to accomplish your plans.'

'You poor dreamer! Poor you... I have known my cousin since childhood; you cannot even begin to imagine how cunning he is...'

'Shut up! You will pay for what you have done tonight.'

'You are blind... Your power overrules your wisdom. I will tell you once again, *Messer*, keep well away from Gian Galeazzo. His good-natured appearance hides a dangerous devil.'

Francesco said no more, turned and left, realising he needed to calm down and return to reassure the ambassador. My arm and face hurt. I touched my lips and saw that I was bleeding. In the mirror, by the light of two candles, I could see one side of my face swollen from the blows; I dipped a handkerchief in water and held it on my wounded lips. How I had changed from the first time I met Francesco! I was only twelve and he only fourteen. He was incredibly shy and introvert while my temperament made me sociable and self-confident. When we married, we were forbidden to live together for a while because we were considered too young to consummate the marriage. Despite my sisters frequently issuing me with instructions on how to "consummate" it and on the meaning of this strange word, not everything was clear to me until the first time my husband asked me to procreate, after a long embarrassing talk in the full darkness of my bedroom. The household proceeded quite well until the birth of Alda then he started to change and things continued to get worse and worse. Wait. What's happening to me now?

Agnese lost consciousness for a few seconds and let me go.

Julie stopped talking. Her voice had become a little hoarse. I poured more juice into her glass.

- Mike! – she exclaimed. – I appreciate your patience. You're a great help to me.

It was the first time that I had heard my name spoken by her. It touched me a little; she seemed to want to eliminate the professional barrier that, until then, had maintained a distance between us.

- You look tired. You are tired.

- Mike, – she repeated, – excuse me. I need to tell you all the details otherwise you won't be able to fully understand.

Although interesting, I didn't really know if I wanted to know all the details; it was too much for me, but I didn't want to displease her.

- You can tell me everything but you need a break now. Please!... I'm a bit hungry. You must be hungry, too. Let's go and have a snack somewhere.

She didn't refuse my invitation. Without thinking twice, we walked to the elevator then we walked along the avenue that leads to the parking lot and got into my car.

- I know a good Indian restaurant in Nepean, – I said. – What do you think?

She thought then looked at me:

- If it's ok with you, how about we go to my place?

It is very uncommon and risky in our universities for teachers and students to make and to accept such invitations with each other. I did not know what to think or how to answer.

- I have some left-overs from yesterday, – she pre-empted, – and other food that my parents brought me for the weekend.

I did not think there was a hidden agenda behind her proposal. Her aim was merely to tell me her whole story in a safe and quiet place.

- Ok! – I said. – Where do you live?
- King Edward Avenue.
- Good. It's not so far.

The temperature was still -22°C. The distance between the building and the parking lot was enough to freeze my feet. My mind took me back to the fireplace in the house in Nepean and once again I filled my lungs with the smells of my past.

- I understand your hesitation, Mike. – Julie said as we stopped at a traffic light. – No misunderstandings between us, please.

- If I take the risk, it means that it's worth taking.

- Don't you think that I'm shameless, then?

- There are many warnings in our universities against possible relationships especially between teachers and students.

- Yes, I've heard. I also heard that a professor at Ottawa University was transferred to a different one following an affair with a student.

- That happened last year.

- Do you think that warnings are enough to prevent this from happening?

- Definitely not. I've always had colleagues who have married their students. There are two or three at Dunton Tower.

- I read that this new puritanism only started a few years ago. In the seventies and eighties there was much more permissiveness...

- Yes, the long remnants of Woodstock...Now all's changed apparently.

- Apparently...Yes, you're right.

Her apartment was on the third floor of a newly-renovated building on a part of the road that I knew very well.

- Do you share this flat with anybody? – I asked when entering and seeing that it was too big for one person.

- No. I live on my own. My parents help me. Every now and then they like to visit me for a few days so they can stay here and there's no need for them to go to a hotel. It would be difficult for me to share this space with somebody else. Also I earn some money from a little job that helps pay for it.

There were a lot of paintings on the walls: landscapes, portraits, still life. The bookshelf near the TV was filled with books, many of which were novels by authors from different countries but all translated into French.

- Make yourself at home, please. I'll be there in a minute; I'll just prepare something for us to eat. I have mushroom omelette, *tourtière québecoise*[51] and *gateau aux amandes*[52]... all homemade by my mother.

- Wow!...You know the best way to seduce me!

- Ahahahahaha! – she laughed. – I don't think it would be so easy to seduce you.

- No?!...Watch out, my tender fawn! In front of you there is a dangerous wolf.

- Really?... And in front of you there is a scary witch... Kidding, just kidding!

We laughed a lot. I admit it was a nice atmosphere. Julie

---

51  French Canadian meat pie.
52  Almond cake.

showed a different side to herself that until a few minutes earlier I couldn't have imagined.

I noticed that she was very quick. In no time at all she had put the food in the microwave and set the table: two plates, knives and forks, red serviettes and two glasses.

- Can I help you with anything? – I asked.

- Help me with anything?... I've kidnapped you today so I can't be too demanding!

I liked her 'I've kidnapped you today.' She revealed a good sense of humour.

- I let you kidnap me because it's Friday, – I retorted playing her game.

- Ah...I understand...Because it's Friday you have the excuse to get rid of me...

- On the contrary, Friday is traditionally sacred for young people...I guess for you too.

- Two Fridays per month I work. Today I'm free; no commitments tonight unless someone calls and asks me to go out... Also, while living as I do with this other presence, sometimes I'm not completely in control of myself so I avoid seeing people.

- The nightmare will come to an end, I'm sure.

- Thank you for your optimism... You know, I've said it before but you really are a great help to me. I needed this day; I needed to tell you this story.

- Do you know what?

- What?

- If my grandmother were alive, I would take you to meet her right now.

- Great!... Did she have supernatural powers?

- She was descended from the Iroquois and she would have had a lot to say about energies and such like...

- Oh, that's amazing! But from what I've heard, the Iroquois were not such good people.

- Why do you say that?

- They treated their prisoners very badly, very cruelly, especially religious prisoners; they martyred a lot of Jesuits, Calvinists and others. Among Amerindian tribes they were perhaps the only ones to practise cannibalism... Oh! ...I don't want to offend or hurt you. I'm so sorry!

- Don't worry. You haven't offended me. Truth is truth. I like your sincerity.

Julie brought all the food to the table and invited me to sit there.

I talked of my grandmother during the whole of lunch, which was absolutely delicious. I knew that I would trigger the curiosity of my student; in fact she was impressed and asked me a lot of questions.

- Now we need a nice cup of coffee, – she said switching on the coffee machine. – Have a seat in the armchair, please, you'll be more comfortable.

- Thank you, Julie, the food was superb. My thanks to your mum, too... I hope to meet her one day.

- Sure. I've told my parents about you. When they come next time, they'll be glad to meet you.

We sipped the coffee in silence sitting in two armchairs facing each other. She was more relaxed compared to how she had been in the morning, her cheeks had some colour now and her hair was a little ruffled, which gave her a slightly sensual look. I thought of Della and wondered how I would tell her about this. Should I talk to her or not? I didn't know. I would have liked to, but how would I explain to her that I had spent a whole day with a 20-year-old girl? That I had been at her place eating and talking for hours? Her advice would be valuable but my sixth sense told me that it would be better not to say anything for now.

- Antonio was a handsome young man. I can't find all the right adjectives to describe him.

Julie had put aside her good mood assuming again the pensive and absorbed demeanour of the morning.

- He was clever, – she remarked. – He was generous, brave, kind and friendly to everybody. A perfect knight, an incomparable gentleman. I doubt that any woman could have resisted his charm; in fact he was wanted, wooed and desired by all the ladies in Mantua and in the surrounding area looking for a husband or an 'adventure'. His first contact with Agnese was marked by a cold formality. Despite her beauty and elegance, she had proved insusceptible to the charms of men. During the five years when things had been good in her marriage, she had been faithful and loyal. She had loved her husband. Nobody had had reason to gossip about her... The knight informed her of the instructions he had received from the Captain. She was annoyed to hear that there was no place either in the palace or outside where she could be certain of her privacy. It's difficult to say who first fell in love with the other. Antonio was used to being sought after and cherished by women, but the way Agnese looked at him and treated him caused any kind of desire he had for her to subside. She had a very peculiar nature: she was apparently sociable and extrovert but not with everybody and not all the time. When alerted by her instincts, she suddenly became standoffish and icy showing that haughty air that gave her the look of her father. A hideous and fearsome side for those who had dealings with her. Had she not seen him as a spy sent by her husband instead of a *bodyguard,* to use a modern term, the first contact would have been without suspicion. As for Antonio, he accepted this task without being completely aware of what exactly his lord wanted. Initially, he understood that his role mainly entailed escorting the Lady then he was asked to report back on everybody she came into contact with, especially those directly or indirectly related to her family in Milan. He had heard that two of her brothers were scheming against the lord of Mantua and that she was plotting her revenge by supporting them. To be a sort of spy was not the kind of game suited to a gentleman like him but he was a loyal knight of the court and his position did not allow any room for disobedience or discussion regarding the orders imposed by his lord. That his family had not been great fans and supporters of the Gonzagas is true, but he used his own reasoning and saw *Messer* Francesco differently from how his parents saw him.

The first time the relationship between Agnese and Antonio reached a turning point was one month after the Carnival. The Captain wanted his wife to go with him to *Canneto sull'Oglio,* an ancient borough north of Mantua. 'Oglio' is the name of the river which flows through Canneto. There was an important castle that Francesco intended to take over as soon as possible because of its strategic position. The people of the court considered it strange that he took Agnese with him. Many thought that he wanted to show her how much his power had increased, a way to impress her and to make her understand that his enemies would not find him undefended. He made his wife and her entourage stay there just one day and then ordered Antonio to take her back to Mantua the next day. As it was only thirty kilometres away, one day would suffice for the two coaches, one with Agnese and Lady Beatrice, and the other with the servants, to return to Mantua. Antonio escorted her on horseback. Yet, it happened that near the small town of Goito the mist was so thick that it was impossible to proceed. The whole of the Po Valley, in fact, which stretches for many kilometres is often covered in mist since it is a marshy area. The horses could not see the road, it was afternoon and Antonio did not want to risk them having an accident. He knew the area very well therefore he decided to send two of the servants to the town to make arrangements for them to stay there the night.

Julie interrupted and asked me if I wanted more coffee or anything else to drink.

- Just water, thanks, - I answered turning my eyes to the bookshelf. - I peeked at your shelves earlier and I saw a few books on Italy.

- Yes, as I told you this morning, I wanted to know more about this country. Here, in North America, we have another view of history, we have no idea what the Middle Ages was like in Europe or how people lived. Agnese is sometimes a cumbersome presence in my life, but I must admit that I have learnt a lot from her and I'm greedy for knowledge of European history and culture. I see France or Italy in my future; I might live there one day.

- At last you have the chance to go there in a few months.

- At last. Yes, you're right. I wanted to go last summer but my boyfriend at the time caused a lot of problems for me. He was so clingy and possessive, like a little child with its mother. I lost my freedom, my space, my privacy, everything. It was really difficult to get rid of him. But I'm free now. I hope I won't get involved with a man like him ever again!

- You won't...Now you know more about life.

- Much more.

- Your Italian story intrigues me. You're a great story-teller.

- Thanks. One day I'll write a book on Agnese and Antonio...And you can write the foreword.

She smiled. I smiled too.

- It will be my pleasure! - I said. - What happened next, that evening in the mist?

- Before that evening I had only been in the palace. I had no idea how normal people lived outside. The majority of people lived in houses consisting of one big room which was sectioned off by pieces of wood or other materials. The whole family lived in this room. Often the bed was large and four or five individuals slept together, all naked. In general, they took off their clothes once already in bed or, since it was completely dark, except in spring and summer, they could undress without being seen. In one corner of the room there was a hole for their physiological needs. These 'loos' were also positioned outside, at the rear of the house. In those times the sanitary conditions were very bad. People never used to wash much, perhaps just once a week. In bigger towns one could find public baths which were often promiscuous places and where sexual activity was the norm. Needless to say, mortality rates were very high especially among children and the average life span was perhaps 30-35 years. The house where their group was accommodated that night belonged to a rich family, but there were not many rooms. Lady Beatrice slept in the bed with the owners and two children, and the servants lay at the foot of the bed. The only one to sleep alone in her own room was the wife of the Captain, while Antonio and the two coachmen slept in the coaches. The knight was the last one to go to sleep. He wanted to ensure that everything was all right also in Agnese's bedroom. He went to knock on her door, lighting up the dark with his torch. She was still dressed but with her hair arranged for the night. She looked visibly tired and sad.

'Thank you for your help,' she said quietly, keeping the man in the doorway. 'We all feel safe with you.'

The flame of the torch lit up her face with a warm glow and reflected in her eyes making them appear big and bright. But beyond that momentary glare he sensed a bitter loneliness and wondered how true the rumours were about her. He was taken aback slightly and for a few seconds felt confused.

'My priority is the Lady of Mantua!'

He slowly withdrew then soon disappeared into the darkness. Agnese had also seen him in a different way. Until that evening she had looked smugly at him or with indifference and detachment. Now, in the bed of an unknown house suffocated in a gigantic cloud of mist, she closed her tired eyes but continued to see the image of the imposing figure of her sentinel with his gaze still penetrating her. She knew that this young man was very well known first of all for his participation in tourneys where he always emerged the victor, she knew that her husband thought highly of him as a knight, and she also knew other things such as his reputation for the strong attraction that women felt for him. So, why would her husband choose him to escort her? It would have been more logical to have given this task to one of his less flashy loyal soldiers.

The trip had been extremely stressful for Agnese whose health had deteriorated since giving birth. It must also be said that in those years the country had been hit by plague and a number of epidemic diseases that exterminated a portion of the population, so any discomfort or symptom could have been warning of a serious illness. As soon as she arrived back at the palace, Agnese ordered the babysitter, Elisabetta, to keep Alda away from her while one of the varlets summoned the court doctor. After examining her, the doctor ruled out anything serious; it was simply a cold. He recommended that she stayed in bed for a few days, so she immediately followed his orders as she felt so weak that she was unable to stand. In the following days, Antonio visited her at least twice a day but she was never alone. Yet, they both perceived that something between them had changed. Their eyes met more often, also in the presence of others, and each time their glances seemed to explore the labyrinth of an unknown dimension, a strange mixture of pleasant and jarring sounds vibrating within them. One day, when she was completely better, taking advantage of a series of sunny days, she wanted to go to the countryside with her daughter, so Antonio arranged a short excursion outside Mantua. Spring came early that year, so, in mid-March, the country was carpeted with the light green colour that announces the awakening of vegetation and here and there a spattering of colour from various plants, flowers and timid buds. Alda was very happy to run freely in the fields, but Elisabetta never took her eyes off her. When Agnese was her daughter's age, life was lived very much outdoors in Milan. She and her many siblings used to play and run almost every day in the gardens and parks of the palace; her childhood had indeed been very happy. But this little girl had no brothers or sisters. What's more, her father looked at her with detachment and did not hide his disappointment that she was not a boy. Now Alda was three years old and Agnese was sure that she would never have another child even though she was only 22. After the birth of Alda, Francesco had become increasingly cold towards her. At first she could not understand why he didn't repudiate her. The law allowed him this right, but he had chosen not to. So, why this torture? Why was he so cruel? Why treat her so badly? He wanted her and the people to believe that he was punishing her for having plotted against him! Maybe. But this was not the main reason. Little by little she understood, and Carlo, her brother, confirmed the same before leaving. Francesco was intelligent, educated, rational, cold. He had been brought up with a strong sense of the state and Mantua, for him, came above everything. To have a son was very important to continue the dynasty and for his pride. Furthermore, Agnese's resentment towards her cousin and her plotting with her brother Carlo to take back possession of Milan had created an untenable situation for him. It was possible that he had decided to get rid of his wife, which was not difficult in those times. But he had to consider his options very carefully first, not least because despite her father's death, her kin was related to all the powerful families in Europe. He did not want to be suspected of murder or any other crime. A suspicion of this kind would backfire on him. He would solve this problem elegantly and cleanly.

He needed a plan.

The daffodils had already opened by the end of February that year. Yellow was Antonio's favourite colour and when he rode in the fields his eyes were always attracted to everything that looked like gold. He bent down to pick one up.

'I'd be honoured if milady would accept it,' – he said offering it to her.

Agnese stopped and looked at the flower carefully then her attention turned to the knight and once again she could not escape his penetrating gaze. She took it and as she did so lightly touched his fingers.

'I think you are as much a gentleman as people say.'

She smiled at him and started walking slowly.

'I think it's a narcissus,' she said passing the flower under her nose.'

'Not like me then.'

'I wouldn't be so sure about that!'

'I'm pleased to see you're in good spirits today, milady.' Antonio knew that a young man of his rank was not permitted to speak to the Lady of Mantua in such a direct and personal way, but the words came out spontaneously breaking his code of conduct. In fact, she was a little surprised by the way he had addressed her. She paused for several seconds then decided she wanted to understand and learn more about this imposing presence.

'My nature generally allows me to see the positive side of life and things,' – she said continuing to walk and smell the daffodil.

'I have great admiration for you.'

This time Agnese stopped and stared at him assuming her haughtiness that was so hateful to many.

'I have a question for you, my brave knight.'

She had uttered 'my brave knight' with a hint of sarcasm that irritated Antonio, but he curbed his impulses pretending nothing was amiss.

'I'm just one of your simple servants, milady,' – he said with a firm tone. – 'Count on my honour, I beg you.'

'Counting on your honour, I want to ask you if your kindness towards me is within the instructions you received.'

Antonio frowned. Her doubt was legitimate but shocked him.

'Look at the sky,' – he said trying to look at the sun that was not yet strong. – 'There are no clouds. The sky is extraordinarily clear and the sun invites us to hug it... Around us, nature comforts us with its beauty. Green meadows, colourful flowers, little birds chirping happily... everything seems to be an immense stage. But we are not actors on it, milady. We are not playing any part.'

'Your words come from a gentle heart. But if this is a theatre, as in fact it is, what are we if not actors?'

'We are two souls who met by chance or maybe not by chance.'

'What do you mean? Your way of speaking confuses me... What can our souls have in common that we should meet?'

'I do not know. I cannot answer...But these few weeks at the palace I have felt something within myself that little by little has pushed me very close to you.'

The woman felt really confused. No other man had talked to her in such a way. He was still facing the sun and with the complicity of its rays she tried to see what there was deep in his eyes, beyond that brown colour with yellow and green narrow stripes. Who was this man? What was his role on the stage that he had described or what task had fate assigned to him that he should interfere in her life? Her mind was filled with images of that misty night and she observed both of them looking at each other in the doorway. Yes, something strange had started or happened then and there.

'I'm sure that you know everything that happens in the palace,' – she said. – 'It's difficult to safeguard privacy there...

But what do you know of my soul and of what is inside me?'

'What is inside you is reflected in your eyes which, despite your optimistic nature, is veiled by a deep melancholy... I know everything, or almost everything about you. I met your brothers many times when they were in Mantua.'

'Then you must have some news from them or about them... No! Don't say anything; I don't want to force you to lie or to be disloyal to your lord... You wouldn't see another day.'

'All that I know is that Carlo is in Verona...'

'Yes, I pray for him every day...'

'It will be difficult for his plans to succeed, milady.'

'They will succeed. It is not possible that God will allow the usurper to sit on our father's throne...My God! What am I doing? How can I confide my hopes in a stranger such as you are to me?'

'There must be a reason.'

'If there is a reason, it is beyond my rational understanding because I would never have imagined that I would be talking with you as we are today.'

'I like it.'

'You overstep the mark, my servant!'

'If being your servant is so pleasant, I wish to remain so forever.'

'Oh!...Words spoken in a moment of irrationality caused by the glow and warmth of this magnificent sun.'

'This glow blinds my eyes but enlightens my heart.'

'And what do these rays allow you to see in your heart that you did not see before?'

'Permit me to declare that I see you...'

'You are not cautious...You are risking your life...No other man's heart but my husband's has ever yearned for me...'

'It is not imprudence that makes me confess my feelings... Do not blush!... Or perhaps it is the rays of the sun that have kissed your cheeks turning their delicate complexion pink...'

'What is happening today?... The air is still, no clouds, all is calm... So, why this sudden hurricane from which I cannot find shelter?... Who are you to set ablaze this fire on my face that I myself do not know how much is due to this sun blessed by God?'

'This same hurricane strikes me too...'

'How can I believe your words?'

'If you do not believe my words, I will not ask you to... Just wait, and then listen to your heart.'

'And you, will you be listening to your heart when in front of your lord to whom you swore allegiance and loyalty? Or will your conscience whip your feelings and all your words suddenly vanish?...'

'If the words I have uttered today are a lie, may hell kidnap me and may I be chewed by the jaws of Lucifer!... Once in front of my lord, I will not forget my oath but I will look firmly in the eyes of a man who beats his wife.'

'*Messer* Francesco is sly and intelligent. You would come off worse.'

'Do you consider me so weak?'

'I do not know you whilst I know him. I know him very well.'

'When my lord entrusted me to look after you I felt an overwhelming happiness, I felt I could explode with pride. We had never talked to each other, I had only seen you from a distance and you seemed unapproachable. I did not even know if you knew who I was. Perhaps you had seen me at some tourney...although I doubt that you were ever interested in them. Happiness was my first sensation then. Yet, in the following days, having got to know you better, and being in close proximity to you, my enthusiasm cooled off somewhat. In fact, I did not feel I was the right person for this task because with all the rumours circulating I did not want to become embroiled in the family's personal matters. I was nervous, unsettled; I did not realise why before, but now I understand that I had already fallen in love with you…'

'Do not say any more, please…'

'I must, you must know, whatever you think and whatever happens…'

'This is too much, please, I'm not ready…'

'He does not love you.'

'But I am still his wife…'

'On paper.'

'Insolent!'

'It is the truth.'

'He didn't repudiate me.'

'He must have had his reasons.'

'He must have.'

'I love you.'

'Please, stop it!'

'I love you.'

'You're killing me…'

'With my love…yes, I am!'

'Please…please, please. I beg you. Your words are too big…'

'I have one question for you.'

'Don't scare me…Today I've got to know you better. Much better.'

'And you will know me even better.'

'If destiny wants.'

'Do you love him?'

Agnese turned her head hearing her daughter's voice.

'We have not been able to curb our tongues today…' she said. 'Your complexion, although dark, must be delicate too since your cheeks are red…They're coming… Elisabetta's eyes are on us. This woman is a common person and her tongue is sharp.'

'Almost everybody's tongue is a sharp knife in Mantua, milady...It's a small place, very different from Milan where you were brought up. People talk and often do not know what they are talking about...They just need to feed their imagination with gossip.'

'The imagination is empty when eyes do not see and ears do not hear... It is not only people who have eyes and ears... Now I beg you, keep some distance from me, my daughter must be tired and I can see that Elisabetta is out of breath.'

The walk in the country had been a turning point in this love story, in the sense that it had been a real hurricane, as Agnese had said. Since her brothers had left, she had been virtually alone. Her husband had created a vacuum around her. Despite his mistreatment of her, she had been able to survive only thanks to the existence of her daughter and to her strong personality. For a few days after the excursion, she lived in a state of confusion caused by an indisputable shock. She tried to see Antonio as little as possible because she needed to reflect and consider where they were both going. Francesco had been her only man and she had never even been tempted to think of others or to give in to their attention towards her. Now, everything seemed to have changed in such a short space of time. Life was decorated with new colours, her heartbeat was faster, 'he' was always in her mind, his words echoed and overlapped in her ears. In the palace she recognised his steps from a distance and whenever possible escaped before he saw her even though she wanted to be near him. The Captain had returned but she had seen him only once and noticed that he was not his usual brutal self. Strange. He had struck up a conversation with her saying that he had great plans for Mantua and intended to summon famous artists and architects to the palace on his return from France. Although the tension between him and his wife was high, he took her opinions into account on everything to do with culture and all forms of art. Then he asked her what she thought of the castle at *Canneto sull'Oglio*, but she looked absent minded, distant and as though she had not heard him. When he realised that she was uninterested, he said:

'Where are you today? Your eyes are brighter than usual and your face has a look of contentment...Either you have finally stopped mourning or you must have received good news from your brothers.'

'My brothers do not send messages on the wings of birds.'

'Perhaps snakes bring them.'

'If so, be careful, Captain, I tried to warn you against my cousin. The serpent is on the Visconti emblem...'

'And in their blood... Your pride makes you so blind that you cannot see the importance of this alliance!'

'He is a murderer and usurper.'

'There is no proof that he is the murderer of your father. Your sister is his wife... she is not as resentful as you even though she is the wife of the man that you call murderer and usurper.'

'My sister Caterina is innocent and naïve, like a child. I can only imagine how many lies she must have been told.'

'The ambassador was very angry at the scene you made, I'm sure that he told Gian Galeazzo about it. I'll be seeing him in a few days and I'll find out.'

He walked away without saying goodbye but did not seem to be in a bad mood. She wondered how long he would be absent for. 'The longer the better,' she thought. Without his presence she could relax and would find a way to contact Carlo. And not only this... Although she did not want to admit it, a pleasant torment made of images, words, palpitations and new emotions ran through her being making her days too short and too long, happy and painful. Every morning Antonio joined her to ask if she needed to be escorted anywhere. Beyond formal words and for convenience, they communicated their feelings with their eyes. She was never alone. Two dress assistants, babysitters, chaperones, servants...All these people started their invasion into her life in the morning not always doing anything useful. By an indecipherable mystery of human nature, people feel intrigued more by others' misfortunes than by their joy. One day, when we go to the world beyond, this mystery will also be explained. Maybe. After the public scene that Agnese had created at the Carnival party, she attracted much more attention and curiosity. Since she was not a woman to mince her words, many in her entourage feared her. In order to avoid her unpleasant reactions, they were careful not to engage in conversations that could offend her. 'A gang of hypocrites,' she had thought more and more in recent days. Strangely, though, those whom she called 'common people' admired her for her bravery and approved of her outbursts. After all, she was a foreigner and, as a lady from Milan, she would never have a true friendship in that small town surrounded by swamps that could boast nothing but its long history.

It was only in the second week of April, at Easter time, that the Lady needed Antonio to escort her to a public event to represent the Captain who was absent. It was the first time since the walk in the country that they had had the chance to be alone and to exchange a few words. A few banal words suited to the occasion that bore no resemblance to all the imaginary conversations of the past days and nights. After a tiring day, the coach entered the palace grounds in the evening while the shades of twilight became swallowed by the darkness of the approaching night. Besides the presence of a few guards and a varlet, everything was quiet. Antonio helped Agnese out of the coach and accompanied her towards the large staircase partly covered with a red carpet. A silent unequivocal understanding pushed them to climb the stairs together escaping the attention of the varlet. The torches on both sides lit up the portraits of the most famous personages in Mantua's history and their suspicious gazes which followed the couple's movements. Movements that became lighter with each step as though not wanting to attract the attention of the living or even of the objects around. In this lightness, perhaps caused by the effect of adrenaline, their minds seemed to lose contact with reality. The yearning that seized Antonio forced him to quash any form of hesitation and caution. The only thing which his mind dwelt on was the mystery of the unexpected power of this love, because it was love, definitely love. He had tried to fight and quench this fire but it was impossible. Even though there had been many girls who had momentarily fanned the flames of his passion, this time the strings of his heart played a different tune. Even the code of loyalty to his lord on which he had solidified his reputation and his honour was called into question. He wanted to better understand the man for whom he could sacrifice his life. Before meeting Agnese, he had been deaf to the gossip and rumours about the Gonzaga family. What the Captain was doing for Mantua gave him authority, which is the main pillar of power. As his wife had said, he was intelligent and rational. From his father he had learnt a lot especially regarding strategies for running and ruling the State. He had been able to progressively extend his territories handling the game of alliances diplomatically and shrewdly and thus enhanced his prestige. He had also won fame as patron of Mantua by making it a centre of high culture and with his proposals to implement large-scale constructions. All that had greatly impressed Antonio and his subjects. But there was the other side of the coin that he could not ignore since the woman he loved was the victim of a man who, in the name of power, was able to act unscrupulously. Not everyone in the court or amongst his subjects were in favour of his alliance with Gian Galeazzo. Even the knight's parents did not hide their doubts about it. On top of all that, the lord of Milan was believed to be the murderer of Agnese's father. So, what else was he capable of?...

On the walls of the wide corridor leading to her apartment there was a sequence of portraits. One showed Francesco flaunting all the symbols of his power. Walking past it, Agnese shivered momentarily and looked ahead. While flashes of searing doubt crossed Antonio's mind, hers became a whirlpool of a fragmented universe. Impalpable coloured bubbles rising to the sky, carrying the remembrance of innocence... *pluffpluffpluff*...She could not understand the exact meaning of the word *love* when she was a child. In her imagination it was something sweet and one day she asked her elder sister Taddea why people love pets in the same way as they love God, why children love their parents, why a man loves a woman, why everybody loves everybody... "Taddea, please, tell me, what is love? Why does everybody love? Is love like a big sweet cake that belongs to all of us?" Taddea was shocked by the observation of her little sister. How could she have such a beautiful vision of love? A big sweet cake... "Yes," she answered. "Love is like a big cake cut into a number of pieces. One piece is called friendship, one is called mercy and..." "What is the piece of cake called that brings children to parents? Where do parents go to get their babies? Is it true that they get them from the sky?" Very difficult questions for Taddea. She did not know how to answer except to say: "When parents wish to have a baby, they look up to the sky where the angels blow bubbles, bubbles, many coloured bubbles. In each bubble there's a baby."

The bubbles continued to mingle in the sky when the couple closed the door of Agnese's apartment. When Francesco touched her the first time she no longer saw the bubbles that Taddea had once described. She had other images in her mind all inspired by the *know how*... Although it had not been unpleasant, she did not remember it as a romantic moment. Now, she was there with another man, a stranger to her until sometime earlier, in the darkness of her private corner where the contours of objects could only be glimpsed thanks to a candle from which a shy little flame seemed to apologise for its presence and intrusion. In that vaguely golden dim light everything seemed to create an atmosphere conducive to a night of love. The velvet curtains ensured a protected intimacy, the dozens of ornaments of different forms and dimensions announced they would be discreet witnesses whilst the evergreens exhaled a delicate fragrance.

Francesco was not there.

He had left. Far away.

Did Francesco want this? Was this a part of his devilish plan?

Why, Francesco?

Oblivion enshrouded her whole conscience.

Hovering higher and higher.

Seduction had woven slowly but inexorably in the meanderings of her body and spirit unarming reason. She would wonder in the future how much her fragility had made her vulnerable to a lack of conscience at that time in her life. Her desire for Antonio was total; she needed him so much that she felt there was a hole in her stomach. A painful hole. But not tonight. No pain tonight. Only a deep immersion in the foam of pleasure where the fusion of souls and limbs defeats the restraints of her *ego* and *super ego,* both annihilated. She would neither regret nor deny the passion lavished in this love since their beings had become one. This feeling was completely different from the one that had tied her to Francesco. Although the marriage had been agreed by their families, they liked each other, which was not so common in arranged marriages. Yet, once wed, they were still at the age of innocence. Now this avalanche of emotions that chained her to Antonio was completely new to her.

'In many places in Italy it is said that love and sorrow cannot be hidden. They are depicted on one's face.'

The woman who said these words to the Captain's wife, one beautiful May morning, was Lady Beatrice while helping her to choose a dress for an important evening. It had happened that the two lovers, sunk in the unconsciousness of their passion, had become less and less cautious in keeping their relationship secret. Hearing these words Agnese betrayed an expression of surprise, not so much at what she had said but at her insolence in saying it. Yet Agnese did not react, pretending not to have understood the message. Lady Beatrice, though, was an experienced woman. She was loyal and affectionate to the whole family so her primary concern was to help her mistress. Therefore, after a few minutes she persisted:

'I beg you to forgive me, but I am warning you for your own good... There is gossip about you and Antonio, inside and outside the palace.'

This time her mistress appeared suddenly discomposed, like a child caught playing a prank. She understood that it would be counter-productive to deny it.

'Tell me everything, please,' Agnese said feeling tense and sitting in her armchair.

'There is not much to say, milady. There are rumours... only rumours. I hope. But in a small place rumours can be very loud and destructive, especially when the target is the Lady of Mantua.'

For the rest of the day Agnese did not utter a word and asked Lady Beatrice to leave her alone. No doubt the baby-sitter also knew as did the court ladies who attended the palace. When she saw Antonio at their next secret meeting, they discussed the situation but were unable to find a solution. Days passed apparently peacefully but that could not last since the two lovers continued to be indiscreet about their affair. Following another reprimand by Lady Beatrice, Agnese asked her to swear not to tell her husband about this gossip. Later she would ask the same of the babysitter. Francesco returned home after his long journey greatly enthusiastic about pressing ahead with the works in his town. Nobody knows if he had already heard about his wife's affair, it is very likely that his spies had already informed him, but what is certain, according to the records of the trial, is that one day, while Antonio and Agnese were out riding, Elisabetta, the babysitter, went to the Captain and informed him of the scandal. Thanks to his cold rationality, he was able to contain his furious reaction and, for the time being, decided not to intervene. Antonio, though, learning that his lord was now acquainted with the truth, suggested that Agnese leave the palace and that they escape somewhere together. However, she did not agree, maintaining that if she left in that way, it would be an admission of her guilt. The young knight's passion had literally clouded his ability to act rationally but, in time, this fire did not remain merely passion; it transformed into a true and strong love which made him realise that without her he could not survive. He needed to find a way to confront his rival head on. He began to foment a rebellion of the people against his lord with the help of Carlo and other enemies of the Gonzagas. The plan was to overthrow the Captain and turn Mantua into a republic. He worked meticulously for the realisation of his plan but spies and betrayers around him caused it to fail by reporting all the details of it to the lord. Antonio was imprisoned on the evening of January 27th, 1391. The same punishment was administered to Agnese with the concession that she was confined to her rooms.

The trial for adultery began on February 5th at ten o'clock in the morning with the questioning of the witnesses. Almost all of them had something to say on the dishonest and devious behaviour of the two lovers. Even Lady Beatrice and Elisabetta declared that their mistress had forced them to swear not to tell her husband the truth. Agnese did not want to be defended, and locked herself in a stubborn silence. Antonio tried to take all the blame with great courage and chivalry.

He was not believed.

Julie stopped talking and closed her eyes. I looked at the time. Six o'clock. It was getting dark. The narration had touched me. I could see the girl's intense participation in the story both as a witness and as an invisible protagonist. During the whole tale she was unaware of my presence, she looked at me but I don't think she had any visual perception of me.

- I know that you are tired, – she said after a long silence between us. – I need you to stay here for a few more hours... Please... I beg you.

She kept her eyes closed, her head slightly tilted to the right, her body relaxed in the armchair. Maybe she was in a state of semi-consciousness.

- I'll stay with you as long as you want, – I assured her. – Take your time.

'Here are all the ingredients of a good book or film,' I thought, trying to imagine the scenes and people described by Julie. But this possession or whatever else it could be, remained a great mystery. To believe or not to believe in the paranormal? In the world of theatre there are many people, not only actors, who believe in other dimensions of life, mostly related to the identification with the characters portrayed, as I have touched on previously. I am sure that my grandmother would have given me a thorough explanation of what it was that Julie was experiencing.

- Give me your hand. I beg you, give me your hand! – she implored. – In Mantua it's six hours later than here.

Without thinking I went over to her and sat on a low stool with a cushion on top. I took her left hand. It was the second time that we had touched each other, this time with more naturalness and familiarity. I wondered how my holding her hand could help her. A sense of protection? Warmth? A sharing of emotions?

- Now I'm with her. It's after midnight, – Julie continued. – She will be executed in a few hours. I am an external observer now, no longer inside her. She has lived the last few days in silence, perhaps in a sort of surreal dimension that only those condemned to death experience. She is not sitting in her armchair but on the bed, her eyes staring at nothingness, and her mind blank. No thoughts. No images. Nothing. It's a good thing that during the time preceding death our conscience is deprived of its vitality, otherwise its screams would echo in others' consciences like the swell of a tsunami. In fact, these screams would shake the apparent domination of the intellect displaying and drawing out from our abyss who we really are. Who you are. Who he is. Who she is... People would be scared of the truth and mankind would not be like it is now... Would it be better or not? I cannot divert my look from her, I feel very bad, I cannot express in words what is running through my body and my soul, I am present yet impotent in this role that she demands of me. I wonder now, looking back, who or what wanted this role assigned to me. Perhaps not her. Agnese, my dear Agnese, I have been chosen by the invisible powers that govern our lives to play this passive and incomprehensible part in the latter stage of your life, but for what purpose? Just to be a witness of your story? Or for some other reason? You are still so young; how different your short life has been from the lives of many other women your age! I admire you. I love you. In an epoch when women are considered as beasts or less, deprived of their most elementary dignities, you had the strength and courage to scream your scorn against power and injustice, to walk with your head held high among a crowd of envious hypocrites who tried to trample on you by any means. It is not possible that everything will come to an end before a new day brings light to the world. I am sure that this God and this Jesus, whether the same divinity or not that your husband heaps praise on by building churches, are with you at this moment, not impotent like me. They are preparing their welcome in the world where He, God, will reveal the truth to you, where He will prove to you that life spent on this earth, whether lasting a few days or one hundred years, is just a flash compared to what awaits us all. He will tell you that our short journey here, among suffering and injustice, is this way because sin makes us prisoners of its deceptive beauty and so it will be until the end of existence... Perhaps you will see Francesco heave a sigh of relief after your head is detached from your body, smiling and satisfied inside, with a message ready to be despatched to your cousin. You will see him celebrate with one or more of the many girls around here and make preparations for his next wedding.

It's four o'clock.

I hear noise outside.

The chief of the guards entrusted with the procedure of the execution opens the door and approaches Agnese ordering her to follow him. Automatically she obeys, stands up and follows the guards, two in front and two behind her through the corridors then down the stairs and into a narrow tunnel that leads into the yard where the execution will take place. Before entering the yard, Agnese will be blindfolded. Everything is ready. The executioner is waiting for her. A few metres to the right, the rope that will be used to put Antonio da Scandiano to death is ready. Antonio arrives a few minutes later. They are both blindfolded so do not see each other. They do not see with their eyes but with their souls yes, they are telling each other that in a few minutes they will be finally free to live their love forever.

Apart from the guards, the religious authority and the Captain's attorney nobody else is present at the executions.

The executioner of the two lovers, Giovanni Cavallo, first beheads Agnese with a firm and powerful blow of the axe, then immediately places the noose around Antonio's neck which, seconds later, ends his life.

Antonio and Agnese are buried together without any monument.

A few tears seeped from Julie's closed eyes... Then began to stream down her cheeks falling onto her shirt leaving large wet splodges. She started shivering. I called her. She didn't answer. Worried, I let go of her hand and with a tissue dried her cheeks. She was pale, her lips slightly livid. I cannot say whether she was conscious. I did not know what to do. My thoughts skipped to Della as always when I had problems or needed some help but once more something curbed my impulse. I called her once again touching her eyes and her forehead. Fortunately, she stirred then turned away as though wanting to hide her face. I realised that she was uncomfortable in that armchair so I decided to carry her to her bed. I did. Watching her lying on the bed and thinking of how worried I had been, I was overcome by a feeling that I had never experienced before. Like that of a father or an elder brother or perhaps it was a deeper affection that I did not yet recognise.

- Do you have any herbal teas? – I asked. – I think you could do with one.

- I have some lemon balm, – she whispered. – I feel so weak...

- Please, don't move. Stay here. I'll make it.

I went to the kitchen and found the lemon balm next to the kettle in a container labelled 'herbs'. After pouring some boiling water into a cup, I dropped the little bag of leaves in and added a small spoon of honey.

- Leave it to stand a few minutes, – I said placing the cup on the nightstand.

I remembered that my grandmother used to use herbs as a remedy for all kinds of ailments. I don't think that she ever bought medicines from a pharmacy.

- Mike, who or what are you to me? – the girl asked opening her eyes slightly.

The question embarrassed me a little. I was standing on one side of her bed and I could not take my eyes off her body.

- You should ask yourself this question, not me.

- Yes. You are always right... *Vous êtes monsieur le professeur!*...[53]

- Don't talk. You need to rest.

- There are no chairs in here... Please, stay a little longer with me; sit on the bed...here.

I did what she wanted.

- It was terrible, – she continued referring to her story. – I don't want to talk about it again for a long time.

- How do you feel? Do you feel freer?

- I don't know yet. Only time will tell.

- You're getting some colour back in your cheeks now.

- I feel better, thanks. Thank you, Mike. I wouldn't have been able to talk to anybody else as I have done with you.

I picked up the cup of warm lemon balm and helped her take a sip. She took my hand again and so we remained until she finished the drink. Then she turned on her right side and closed her eyes falling asleep immediately. I looked at her, this time as a father looks at his child. Lying there she looked very sweet. I reached for the wool blanket at the foot of the bed and covered her with it. Then, seeing a blank sheet of paper on the bookshelf, I took it and wrote a few lines telling her to call me the next day.

I left her flat around nine in the evening. It was not yet late, but I didn't want to do anything else except go home, so I went to my car and before ten I was in my apartment in Rue Laurier. I was so tired! And a bit hungry. Just a muffin with a hot cup of tea. In bed, I looked at the little calendar on

---

53  You are the professor.

my bedside table. Still February 6$^{th}$. But 7$^{th}$ in Italy. This is the date reported in Wikipedia on which the deaths of Agnese and Antonio took place. Hundreds and hundreds of years from the time this sad event happened, Julie had lived a replay of Agnese's agony on the same day and at the same time.

A coincidence?

Good night, my dear lovers, Agnese and Antonio.

★

*End of April in Verona.*
*House of Juliet. The yard.*

- Excuse me, *professoressa*, may I ask you in which year the story of Romeo and Juliet took place? – Ivan asked Ms Carla Sartori.
- It was set in 1303, when Verona was ruled by the Scaligeri family, rich merchants that dominated until 1387.

Julie turned pale. *Pluffpluffpluffpluff...* 'Yes, I've heard of this family,' she thought, 'they were enemies of Francesco.'

Ms Carla Sartori was the teacher at the University of Verona designated to lead and look after our group during our stay in the city. She came to meet us at the airport and took us to the hotel in the city centre. She was a very sociable woman with an extraordinary sense of humour that immediately created a relaxed and friendly atmosphere among us. Since we were suffering from jet lag, she suggested we settle in and rest for a few hours. We would reconvene for the *cena*[54] when she would explain the program for our week in Verona. In fact, at the *cena* she did present the program that the university had planned for us. The next day the group would be welcomed by the Director of the English Language Department then we would go on a short sightseeing trip. On the second day the students would perform the rehearsal in the morning while

---
54  Dinner.

the final show was scheduled for 6.00 p.m. The rest of the week included excursions to Lake Garda, Venice and Mantua, the place of the last act of Romeo and Juliet and where we would all visit *Palazzo Gonzaga*.

- I can't understand how Shakespeare could have known that this house belonged to the Capulets at the time of the tragedy. – Manuel butted in.

- The real name was Cappelletti... – she pointed out. – How did he know? Perhaps he had a second *dark lady*[55] in Verona who told him the secrets of the city...

Everybody laughed.

- I'm kidding of course! – she continued. – It wasn't strange at all in Shakespeare's time to find out almost anything about our countries... Please, don't leave this place without touching Juliet's right breast. It will bring you good luck and it will make it easier for you to win your beloved's heart.

Amidst so many other tourists in the small yard, my students had to line up to approach the statue and when it was Alfredo's turn to put his hand on the famous breast, he reeled off:

- I swear on my honour that after the performance, I, Romeo Montague, will kiss my Juliet on the balcony above us!

A noisy 'Wow!' exploded from the party attracting the attention of the other tourists.

Julie did not look very happy with Alfredo's initiative and tried to cover her embarrassed face with her hands.

- Don't worry, Julie! – Camila joked hugging her friend. – We will turn away during your love scene.

I had heard that spring is the best season to visit Italy. The climate is mild, the gardens and countryside are tinged with an extraordinary variety of colours and the trees and flowers exude pleasant smells that fill the air. Being there, one can

---

55 The teacher is referring to the mysterious person (probably a man) who gave inspiration to the Poet for his famous Sonnets.

better understand why this country is one of the world's major attractions. Apart from the fact, as Alfredo had said on several occasions, that it can be considered an immense museum from the top to the toe, the aspects that interest, seduce or appeal to people are many and diverse. A walk in the streets of any city, small or large, is like plunging into history, into a huge presentation of art, and the people's sociable and friendly way of doing things creates no barriers between locals and visitors. The architecture is magnificent, revealing the importance of aestheticism for Italians, and the borders between art and craftsmanship are hardly visible. Topping the list of irresistible seductions is, of course, food starting with unique ice-creams that people of all ages lick while strolling along at any time of the day. Italian food is very popular all over the world but in Italy the tastes and flavours are even more special.

We visited a few important places that day, but the most interesting for me was the Arena. I had seen it so many times on TV, but actually touching those eternal stones with my own hands and treading on the soil where slaves and wild beasts fought to their gruesome death stirred in me unexpected emotions. In the afternoon I had the opportunity to have a long conversation with my Italian colleague which confirmed to me their spontaneity and openness also towards people they meet for the first time.

Now that my students and I were at the end of our trip, looking at them all together, having fun or engaged in conversation my heart was gripped by the melancholy which characterises the eve of separations. This was not the first time that it had happened. I would not see many of them again and all the stories I had listened to and the situations we had been through together would stay with me for the rest of my life. And what would I be to them? The teacher associated with Romeo and Juliet, with the trip to Verona, the teacher who, with his friendly chats, broke down the barriers of age and status.

Regarding the main protagonist of these pages, Julie, I keep the experience that she shared with me not like a secret but like a taboo. A taboo because in my experience it is very difficult for friends, colleagues or anyone else to understand the consequences when you confide in them a story involving the paranormal. It becomes almost impossible when a student is involved. A few days after Julie's long account, I tried to confide in Della because I needed to hear her opinion, but I had to stop myself since she did not approve at all of my closeness to a student who – she said – would not have told me such things if she did not have strong feelings for me. This gave rise to a long discussion on the concept of infatuation about which our views diverged. I reminded her that we had talked on previous occasions about this issue, referring to cases both real and hypothetical. I was very upset when she said: "Your student doesn't need her teacher to confide such a ridiculous story in but a good psychologist or psychiatrist!" No comment.

The theatre was full. Many students were sitting on the floor or on uncomfortable stools brought in from the storeroom. The director of the department gave a short introduction then it was my turn to speak. It is always rather difficult to make a speech in front of a foreign audience, especially when so many eyes and ears are focused on you. I talked briefly about the pedagogical and methodological process that had inspired our academic project and I finished by expressing how privileged and proud we felt to perform Romeo and Juliet in their own city.

To be honest, while the play was in progress, I felt an uncontrollable wave of emotion thinking that I was there in Verona that beautiful spring evening, observing the reactions of people to the way that wonderful group of students was performing which, in terms of nationalities, race and culture, represented the whole world. None of them faltered, everything was perfect as I had demanded and as the circumstances also demanded. The lovers were brilliant, spontaneous, convincing. I hardly recognised them, astonished by the transformation they had made during the six months. Julie proved to identify very well with the character of Juliet capturing her psychology, expressing her emotions, showing a girl at a time when adolescence was not yet ready to have a realistic view of life, when the struggle between hesitations and enthusiasms makes the mind and the word linger on the veracity of feelings. The costume was splendid having the desired effect of accentuating the moderate prominence of her breasts thus closing the door on adolescence while her childlikeness was betrayed by her facial expressions.

The end of the play was greeted with thunderous applause and flowers for the female students. Then the actors mingled with the audience and hundreds of photos and videos were taken. A great feast followed that continued all night. In fact, after changing out of their costumes, the Canadians were invited by the students of Verona to have fun and celebrate in the city. I praised everyone, giving each of them a quick hug since the noise and confusion did not allow us to talk. I kept Julie in my arms longer showing her all my gratitude. I simply told her that I had no words right now and that we would talk as soon as we had the chance to be alone. Carla and my other colleagues wanted me to spend time with them at a restaurant in Piazza delle Erbe where we had a fantastic time. I think I drank too much wine switching from Lambrusco to Sangiovese and others. The thing is that as I was tipsy, I can't remember how and when I got back to the hotel.

Carla had to change the schedule for the next day because nobody got up before noon. The students said they were still tired and had no energy to get up early. They preferred to spend the rest of the day visiting other places in town or simply walking and relaxing enjoying a big ice-cream. A few had already arranged to meet up again with the Italian students they had met the previous night. I confess that I was very relieved not to have to go on an excursion because the drink from the night before had left me feeling a little worse for wear. But not so much that I would have to turn down an espresso in a bar opposite the hotel.

- Mike!

It was Julie calling me from the window of her room as I was about to enter the bar.

- I can't see the balcony, Juliet! – I joked. – Come and have a coffee here!

- Ok!... Cappuccino, please.

I have never understood why in many Italian bars there are no seats to quietly sip your coffee or cappuccino. The rooms, especially in the old streets, are small; people stand together in a little space waiting for the barista who races round serving coffee in small cups.

- I've changed my mind, – I said when Julie entered. – I feel suffocated in here. If you don't mind, we could have our coffee in some place where we can sit and talk without so many people around. It's impossible in here.

- Ok, let's do that... There are plenty of nice places in Piazza Bra.

We walked slowly towards the square enjoying the warm air, the characteristic little shops, the façades of the ancient buildings and houses. Julie seemed relaxed with a brighter look in her eyes. A new light.

- I wanted to ask you how you feel here, Julie, but I haven't had the chance to talk to you.

- I feel as if I've come back home... I must have the same genes as these people.

- I can tell; you look a different Julie here. Smiling and cheerful all the time... Good. I'm happy for you...

- At the moment I'm living in limbo... I need to

understand... I need a sense of direction. In the coming days there'll be a turning point, I'm sure.

Piazza Bra was not very crowded at that time of the day apart from a few tourists. Alfredo had explained to me that lunchtime in Italy is perhaps the most important time of the day. Italians call it *ora di pranzo*, which translates in English as lunchtime, but *pranzo* for Italians has a different significance. First, since the Italian breakfast is much lighter compared to breakfast in other countries, sometimes consisting only of a small cup of coffee or cappuccino, their traditional *pranzo* consists of several courses. The whole family gathers together because working hours are also different than in other places. In fact, children usually have a break from school between one and two p.m. and come home and offices also close for two or three hours. The *pranzo* time is also an occasion to talk about and discuss many issues. It is usually followed by a one-hour *siesta* when people relax in different ways. The strange thing is that during this break from one to four p.m., all activities stop, shops and stores close, restaurants included. Famous tourist places like Verona are exceptions, although some places do still close.

At last we were sitting outside a bar protected by a large green awning that kept the strong midday sun from burning our skin. We ordered an espresso, a cappuccino and two so-called *cornettos*.[56]

- Let me finally congratulate you, – I said inhaling the aroma of the espresso. – You were great. Thank you.

- It's me who should thank you. This experience has enriched all of us in many ways. Alfredo has prepared a speech for you... It's supposed to be a surprise, I shouldn't have told you... You will see...

- I won't let on that I know, don't worry... You know that I can keep secrets.

---

56  Sweet Italian bun.

- Yes, I was not wrong to trust you.
- What's your relationship with Agnese now?
- It seems a contradiction but I miss her a bit... I'm not possessed by her any longer but the thought of her is still a daily presence in my mind. Now that I am so near Mantua my heart keeps pounding thinking that in a few days I will actually enter the palace, this time as myself, in my own body. I don't know how I will feel in the yard where her execution took place... Perhaps I'll be shocked... I'll faint. Or I'll run away...
- I will be with you, if you want. I won't let you go in alone...

Julie's expression had completely changed in those few minutes. Her smile had disappeared and her eyes glazed over; she was again in the past. For a moment I looked back to when she had been in a trance-like state in front of me in her flat. She must have read my mind.

- I am not the same as that day, – she wanted to reassure me and herself too. – I have never thanked you for what you did for me... I expected to see you on the Saturday...You left me a note asking me to call you the next day, do you remember?
- Yes.
- I wanted to but I couldn't. I wrestled with myself all day about whether I should call you or not. I had a long sleep. I had been through an incredibly stressful time but fortunately, confessing it all to you helped and got rid of the tension. I dreamt of you but when I woke up I couldn't remember much of the dream. I was surprised to see the blanket over me and imagined you, the night before, covering me up, looking at my face as I slept, caught by pity and compassion for this weird student... Then I remembered the dream: we were in a desert, me and you, I wanted to stay there but you wanted to run away. And when you left I called you screaming out your name, desperately begging you to come back, not to

leave me alone. But you didn't... During our conversation I told you that I had started to wonder what or who you were to me... I continued to ask myself this question later, I was afraid of your presence inside me although I also liked it but I didn't understand exactly what it was that I felt for you, whether it was friendship, admiration, love or something else.

She had not drunk the cappuccino yet, but I had drunk mine and also eaten the wonderful *cornetto*.

- Have your cappuccino and *cornetto* first, - I suggested to her. - They'll be getting cold and then won't taste so good.

She started with the *cornetto* and for a while didn't speak. She seemed focused on something and I began to feel the same anxiety that had distressed me in my office and at her home. I thought of Della; I would not have liked her to hear what Julie had just said. And Della's words echoed in my ears: "Your student doesn't need her teacher to confide such a ridiculous story in but a good psychologist or psychiatrist." Was she right?... No, she wasn't. Della saw a danger in all the women I knew, which I couldn't bear or understand since she never missed an opportunity to tell me that she was my best friend. However, based on what she had just said, I sensed that Julie was going to say something important.

- I waited for your call, - I broke the silence. - I was worried and was tempted to give you a ring, but then I decided that a few days' break would give us both a chance to reflect.

- A few days yes, but not almost three months. I hoped we would talk somewhere, in your office or in a coffee bar after lessons, but you avoided me.

- I'm sorry for the misunderstanding. I didn't avoid you.

I lied. I felt bad. It's true. I avoided her because I was afraid of how close we were getting. And not only that. Her story disturbed me in some way; it was too big and complicated for me to comprehend. The whole day spent together like that, at times holding hands...

- You avoided me.
- Forgive me if I hurt you, I'm not a coward.

I was a coward.

- Mike, please, I'm not making accusations. How could I? I owe you a mountain of gratitude... I just wanted to talk to you because I needed to. Then I gave up, I felt guilty for having involved you in my mess... I understood why you did what you did, you were right, I want to apologise...
- To apologise for what? Julie, please, don't say that.
- Mike, have you ever thought of me as insane?... A girl with mental problems?
- Julie...
- If you have, tell me. I won't be offended, you won't hurt me... You wouldn't be the first to think that.
- Very intelligent people always seem a little bizarre to others... Diversity is accepted with difficulty, with great difficulty. That's why you need to be strong. If others detect any weakness in you then that could mean trouble... This is the country of Latins, of Romans. Do you know what they used to say? *Homo homini lupus,* which means 'man is wolf to man'... Unfortunately this is true...
- But you also said something else in the classroom.
- Remind me what it was.
- You said that only love can save us from the cruelty of others, it's our armour...
- From OUR cruelty!
- You knew my weakness; you could have torn me to pieces.
- Don't exaggerate, I'm not a hungry wolf.
- Did you change your mind?
- Why?
- In my flat you said you were a dangerous wolf.

- Did I?

- I understand: you're not dangerous when you don't like your prey.

- If the prey is a witch...

- Hahaha! Witches are not edible. Right!

I laughed.

- What kind of game is this? – I asked trying to ease the tension that had started to rise with that strange dialogue.

Observing the Arena on the other side of the square I wondered how advanced the technology of those ancient people must have been. Such a construction exposed to every kind of weather phenomenon was still standing perfectly after two thousand years. In North America we should learn more in school about ancient civilizations. I was lucky because I studied the history of theatre that was full of references to the Greeks and Romans.

Since it was the *ora di pranzo*, the air was filled with smells of Italian cooking. In the restaurant next to us we could see dishes with *lasagne*, grilled aubergines, spaghetti with clams and lots more.

- Fantastic food! – I commented. – It's different from *cuisine québecoise*.

Finally, Julie's good mood returned and she laughed.

- My mother spent some time in Italy, – she remarked. – She learnt a lot. She often cooks Italian meals.

- I want to try the *pizza*. The students say that it tastes different here.

- It's true; we ate some last night.

Just at that moment we were distracted by a boy playing the *mandolino*[57] and singing a famous Neapolitan song. It was pleasant to listen to. After the song we remained in silence for a long while. I hoped that she had let go of her resentment towards me. I felt guilty for causing her turmoil but I didn't understand what else I could do since she had asked for my help.

---

57  Mandolin.

- I want to enjoy a walk round the city today, – I said calling the waiter over. – And what about you, what are you going to do?

Julie hesitated. Then she plucked up the courage.

- If my company doesn't bother you, we could enjoy a walk together.

I remained a bit puzzled but I couldn't disappoint her. I paid the bill and we started our walk stopping here and there on streets we had already strolled along, then I suggested we eat an ice-cream sitting on the stone steps in Piazzetta Capretto. It was nice. We felt relaxed, the silence was not embarrassing, it was better to talk to each other with our mind than with words. After another walk of about twenty minutes, we reached Regaste San Zeno and then the Scaligero di Castelvecchio Bridge where the river Adige has a picturesque bay. We continued as far as Lungadige di San Giorgio and there we took a path that brought us to the riverbank. We had walked a lot and seen many things. We needed a rest and this place was perfect for it. We sat on the first bench we saw. Water was flowing gently in front of us and from time to time a few drops splashed on our faces. The sun slowly began to fall and the sky became tinged with sweet shades of colour. My head was completely empty; I could not formulate any thought. The only thing that I wondered looking at Julie, who stood up and walked towards the water, was who or what this young lady meant to me, the same thing that she wondered about me. After staring into the water for several minutes, she turned and stood in front of me.

- Thank you for this wonderful present, – she said, her eyes penetrating mine. – I had lost hope of being able to spend any more time with you.

- I cannot understand why you never knocked at my door or wrote or called.

- I don't understand it myself. These past months

I wondered if you ever thought of me and if so, what you thought. Your coldness and your indifference were unbearable.

- I hurt you. I'm sorry. Once again I ask you to forgive me.

- And once again I tell you that there's nothing to forgive. It's my problem, not yours.

- Do you consider me so callous that I could be indifferent to your pain?

- Indifferent no, perhaps it's too strong a word, but timorous, yes this is the right word. You asked me before what kind of game this is... It's not me who is playing a game, Mike.

- What do you mean?

- You cannot imagine how much I have learnt from Juliet and from the whole play. And this is another thing for which I thank you. I wouldn't be what I am today if I hadn't met you.

- And this play wouldn't have had as much success if I hadn't met you.

- We were meant to meet. You know that.

- Energies.

- I didn't miss one word of your lessons, you know.

- Yes, I know. You didn't miss one word.

- Energies, fate... Now I know you much better. Forgive me for daring to speak to you in such a direct and impudent manner sometimes. This is what scares you: fate.

- Julie, please...

- *Je t'aime.*[58]

What I didn't want to hear ran through my whole body shaking every little part of me as though I had been hit by lightning. Words, from the depths of her heart that she had restrained herself from saying for weeks or months, came out with the simplicity and clarity that only deep suffering can decide. She approached me and put her fingers on my lips.

- Don't say anything – she whispered. – Words are not necessary, they often ruin things. Let me live my dream for the

---

58  I love you.

next two days. In Mantua my life will change again.

What did she mean? She sat next to me. Our bodies were close, they touched each other. Her warmth invaded and wrapped round my person confusing me. She closed her eyes. We remained silent and motionless caught in an unspeakable daze. I was unable to think. Only when the air got cooler and the sun disappeared did Julie speak saying that she was hungry and that a pizza would be good. I welcomed her invitation because I was hungry too, so we walked back allowing our hands their own will, letting them search for each other, holding and letting go, whatever they pleased. We sat outside the first pizzeria we saw and at last I had the chance to taste a wonderful *Margherita*. Italians prefer to drink beer with pizza, but for two Canadians accustomed to their beers, a good bottle of Chianti was more tempting. Julie was happy, she joked all the time, a side of her that I didn't know very well and that I liked very much. She was telling me about the misunderstandings that happen especially in conversations when French people go to Québec. I don't want to say anything else about that day apart from the fact that I remember it as one of the most memorable of my life.

The next day we went to Venice. A wonderful and unique city. I promised myself that I would return there but not just for one day, for at least one week. Julie and I didn't talk to each other in Venice; I spent most of the time in the company of Carla and an English colleague who taught in one of the many language schools in Verona. He told me that we, native English speakers, could consider ourselves the luckiest teachers in the world since English teachers would always be needed. Which was true. I couldn't say much because apart from the six months I had spent at a Polish university, I hadn't taught in any other country. But in Italy, why not!

In the evening we had dinner all together, the atmosphere was brilliant. At a certain point Alfredo got up and requested that everybody be silent because he wanted to say a few words and make a toast.

- Our trip is almost over. And our project is finished. We do not know if any of us will ever have a similar experience again. The fact is that I am sure that what we have experienced these past six months will remain with us for the rest of our lives. I remember that when we started we were hesitant, sceptical and shy. Apart from a few of us, we didn't know each other; we came from different countries with cultural backgrounds very different from our own. Mike was not only a teacher to us; he was a charismatic Maestro to whom, day by day, we entrusted ourselves to bind a common lot. He understood our personalities, our psychologies, he dug down inside each of us pulling out the best of us, perhaps even things that we didn't know about ourselves. He helped us meet and get to know each other enabling our initial superficial contacts to become firm and cemented friendships that will last forever. Thanks to this experience we have made incredible progress in the language, and the play has been a wonderful opportunity to explore cultural fields, such as poetry, literature and history that we had little idea about before… Thank you, Mike!

No comment.

No words when you have a lump in your throat.

Entering Mantua from the bridge that divides *Lago Superiore* from *Lago Inferiore*, the view is so impressive, I'd say fantastic. Castel San Giorgio, visible from kilometres away, gives the visitor a clear idea of what kind of city he is going to see. Like Verona it plunges you into the past. And there is also Piazza Sordello with the Ducal Palace built between the 14$^{th}$ and 18$^{th}$ century mainly by the Gonzaga family. The buildings are connected by corridors and galleries and are enriched by inner courts and wide gardens. The entrance of the palace is from Piazza Sordello, onto which the most ancient buildings, the *Palazzo del Capitano* and the *Magna Domus* open. It was here that Agnese was welcomed by Francesco.

At the entrance I saw Julie who was hanging back a little from the rest of the group. I went up to her, she was pale, nervous, and looked like she could hardly stand.

- Stay close to me, please, – she begged me. – I don't know if I can keep up with everyone.

- Sure. I won't leave you alone.

- Mike, Agnese is waiting for me. I need to go into the yard where the execution took place. I have to.

- I will go with you.

- We must be alone. Only me and you.

I looked around and saw Carla approaching us.

- What's wrong? – she asked. – Are you all right, Julie?

- I don't feel very well actually, – Julie answered, – but I'll try to go in.

- Mike, if you need any help, I'm here, ok?

- Thanks, Carla. I hope she'll feel better soon.

While Carla caught up with the rest of the group we remained a little behind.

- The square, the façade with its porch and the cathedral bell tower are the same – Julie said almost talking to herself. – Very little has changed.

We had a long walk around inside. Julie said that some smells were the same but remembered very little of what she saw. It was the same in the other part of the palace too. The visit lasted almost two hours, after which we gathered in Piazza Sordello where Carla explained to us where we would go next. Julie said she didn't feel well enough to go. I told Carla to stay with the students; she would be more useful to them.

- Just in case we don't meet before, – Carla said, – the bus leaves at three p.m. from Piazza Sordello. The city centre is small, so I'm sure you'll find us easily. We'll stay in that area.

- Thank you, Carla. You are very kind.

Julie and I. We were alone. We turned to the façade of the palace and Julie stared at the main entrance.

- It's there, – she said.

- How do you feel?

- I don't know. I'd like to bring some flowers, at least one rose... I can't see a florist's round here.

- Let's go in now and we'll get some flowers after.

- 'After' doesn't exist.

- What do you mean? How can 'after' not exist?

- I'll tell you later.

Strange. Really strange. What else was I to expect from her? At the entrance to the courtyard, now called Piazza Pallone, I saw two statues in front of me. Julie didn't take any notice of them and, sure of where to go, turned left. In front of us, three metres from the ground, fixed to the wall, a commemorative plaque marking that there, in February 1391, Agnese Visconti, married to Francesco Gonzaga, Captain of the People, was beheaded at the age of 23. Julie bent over suddenly as if someone had punched her in the stomach. I supported her as she started to cry. A few tourists were looking at us, so, still supporting her, I took her to the farthest bench in the yard where there were fewer people.

- It's there, – she said calming down and holding onto my arm. – It's there. I remember it very well... That morning at dawn. Take me away from this place, Mike. I don't want to see it again for the rest of my life. Poor Agnese, what a horrible destiny was designed for you! Why?... And you, Antonio, the people of this town should erect a monument to you, for your generosity, for your courage, for your beauty.

She glanced at her watch.

- There's not much time, – she said.

- For what?... There is time, calm down and get your strength back.

- Mike!

- Yes?

- I have to tell you something, something important.

*...And there is also Piazza Sordello with the Ducal Palace built between the XIV and XVIII century.*

She brought her hand to her face and remained in that position for a few minutes, contemplating how she would tell me.

- I love you, – she said as though talking to herself.

Again! Again that short sentence whipped my conscience.

- Don't ask me why or how this passion started, – she continued. – It's a mystery, you know, I don't have to tell you that. I struggled with myself, I kept repeating to myself that it was only a stupid infatuation and that one day I'd wake up without you in my mind. Nothing...

- You hated me then!

- I have hated you too... but now I regret that. Now I understand that in your position you had to appear hard, like a stone, to me. I didn't understand you, forgive me. A mist blinded the eyes of my reason and I couldn't see... or, I didn't want to see... because suffering for love is painful but beautiful at the same time.

I asked myself what I had done to trigger this earthquake in her heart. A crush. A strong infatuation. It happens. But she was convinced that it was love.

Silence.

Fortunately, the corner where the execution took place was on the opposite side from where we were sitting and a fence created a barrier in between.

- Mike, what would your grandmother suggest that you do in this situation?

Incredible creature! How she could think of my grandmother? Wonderful Julie. I smiled first and then I burst out laughing.

- I'm sorry, – I said. – I can't think of my grandmother sitting in this cursed yard in Mantua.

- Yes, it does sound ridiculous.

- If I told you what she would think... she, a Native American, who could read the moon and the stars, who interpreted the chirping of the birds at dawn...If I told you what she would think ...you would be happy...she would think I was stupid for holding back and... I'm not going to say any more for now.

She laughed too.

- Mike, in a few minutes I have to go.
- Where? I'll go with you.
- Let me explain something to you.
- My God!... What's going on? What else have you got to tell me?
- Do you remember that old book on Mantua that I showed you?... Do you remember?
- Yes, I do.
- There was an address on it.
- Yes, there was, I remember.
- The address belonged to the family who had given me the book in my uncle's restaurant. One day I wrote to them and they replied to me. We exchanged several letters from which I learnt that the woman was from a very ancient family from Mantua. Their roots probably went back to the time this tragedy happened. One of her ancestors, she disclosed, was very close to Francesco and Agnese. I told her that from the day she left I started to experience symptoms of possession and she said that perhaps it had happened through her. She had thought about writing to me in the months that followed, she had thought of me a lot, but she didn't contact me. Last month I informed them that I was coming to Mantua and that I wanted to meet them. Their son, Giacomo, who is around my age, is now waiting for me in a place not far from here. Until yesterday I wanted you to meet him and his parents. This morning I changed my mind... Don't say anything, please...I'm sure I've disappointed you. I've already called my parents to inform them that I won't be going back to Canada. Not yet. I need to spend some time far away. I need

to understand who I am and what happened to me these last few years: Agnese, you, a lot of other things too. I've written a letter to Camila. She'll find it on her bed when she goes back to the hotel... Mike, you must understand me, I know that you will, I don't have any other choice... Now I'm going to get up and walk away. Please, wait here a few minutes then go and find your students... You and I will be going in different directions. Don't make me say any more.

Julie got up as if in a trance, she took a few steps then stopped. I think she wanted to turn back. She didn't, and after a few seconds she mingled in amongst the crowds of tourists and disappeared. Where was she? Where had she gone? Mike got up worried and frantic...

- Julie! – he screamed. – Juliet... my Juliet, who has kidnapped you?

A group of tourists turned to look at that strange, delirious man and somebody whispered that he was probably insane...

Insane... mad. He was. Lost.

*

The following months were awful for Mike. Misfortunes and bad things go hand in hand. He lost a lot of money in stocks and what was worse, doctors found a cancerous lump in his armpit. It started with a small, almost invisible red point on his skin. Luckily it was caught in time, but for months he was very ill. Months of suffering; a lot of pain, but it was a chance to see life in a different way. He had been at death's door and when his health started to recover he believed that it happened by a miracle because never in his life had he thought of God as he did when he felt so ill. 'You see, my God,' he used to say, 'I'm a coward, I'm a coward also with You... I look for You only when I need you.' One day he entered a church, perhaps by chance or called by a mysterious voice. He lit a candle and would also have liked to light a candle for Della. It was difficult to understand if she believed or not, sometimes she just liked to sit inside a church. She said that God is the same God for everybody. She was very close to Mike during his illness. She went to see him and help him every day; she cooked for him, took him to the hospital when necessary, she also helped him to wash, to comb his hair and to shave. 'Della, I love you, I will never be able to repay you.' 'What? Did I hear that right? Did you say that you love me?' 'Yes, I do!' 'Hahahahahaha! I'm not one of your daydreaming students watching you act during your lessons. You are not a good actor with me, darling, I know you too well... I'm too old for you to love me.' 'What do you mean? I love you as a person...' 'Ah, yes, I know that. But you men, apart from very few, are all the same; the older you are, the younger you want your women.'

'You still love her,' said Della one day while Mike, deep in thought, was looking out of the window. 'Did you ever see her again?' she insisted on trying to break his silence. 'Yes, I saw her... A few days ago. I was driving along King Edward Avenue, where she lived or still lives, just as she was going through the garden gate. She was not alone; at her side there was a young man, presumably Giacomo, they were holding hands and seemed happy. Instinctively, I slowed down and she turned. She must have recognised the car. In the rear-view mirror I saw her stop; she looked puzzled, confused, then she turned to the guy and hugged him strongly as though cancelling me from her life once and for all.' 'How did you feel?' 'Della, let's close this chapter, please. You say you know me, but you don't know me at all.' 'What don't I know? Give me an example?' 'A wise teacher never falls in love with students.' 'I consider you a wise teacher!' 'Let me finish. I was convinced that she was infatuated with me. It was just a crush. I was not wrong. As for me, I loved, yes. But it was Juliet I loved, not Julie.'